THE YEAR OF FOG

On a beach in San Francisco, Abby Mason looks away from her six-year-old step-daughter for a moment. By the time she looks back, Emma has disappeared . . . Devastated by guilt, Abby refuses to believe that Emma is dead. But as the days drag into weeks and the police lose interest, Emma's father wants to start moving on with his life. Unable to forgive Abby, he withdraws from their relationship. It is left to Abby to keep hoping and to follow the evidence no matter where it might lead . . .

MICHELLE RICHMOND

THE YEAR OF FOG

Complete and Unabridged

CHARNWOOD
Leicester

First published in Great Britain in 2009 by
Ebury Press
an imprint of
A Random House Group Company, London

First Charnwood Edition
published 2011
by arrangement with
The Random House Group Limited, London

The moral right of the author has been asserted

This novel is a work of fiction. Names, and characters
are the product of the author's imagination and any
resemblance to actual persons living or dead,
is entirely coincidental.

British Library CIP Data

Richmond, Michelle, *1970 –*
 The year of fog.
 1. Missing children- -California- -San Francisco- -
 Fiction. 2. Loss (Psychology)- -Fiction. 3. Psychological
 fiction. 4. Large type books.
 I. Title
 813.6–dc22

 ISBN 978–1–4448–0726–4

Published by
F. A. Thorpe (Publishing)
Anstey, Leicestershire

Set by Words & Graphics Ltd.
Anstey, Leicestershire
Printed and bound in Great Britain by
T. J. International Ltd., Padstow, Cornwall

This book is printed on acid-free paper

For Bonnie and John

'Viewfinder cameras have a simple plastic or glass viewer and no adjustable focusing system. The viewer is located just above or to the side of the lens, and indicates approximately what the final photograph will look like (though some parallax problems — the difference between what the eye sees through the viewer and what is actually recorded through the lens — are apparent in the processed negative or print).'

— Henry Horenstein,
Black and White Photography: A Basic Manual

'The light of memory, or rather the light that memory lends to things, is the palest light of all . . . '

— Eugene Ionesco,
Present Past, Past Present

1

Here is the truth, this is what I know: we were walking on Ocean Beach, hand in hand. It was a summer morning, cold, July in San Francisco. The fog lay white and dense over the sand and ocean — an enveloping mist so thick I could see only a few feet in front of me.

Emma was searching for sand dollars. Sometimes they wash up by the dozens, whole and dazzling white, but that day the beach was littered with broken halves and quarters. Emma was disappointed. She is a child who prefers things in a state of perfection: sand dollars must be complete, schoolbooks must be pristine, her father's hair must be neatly trimmed, falling just above his collar.

I was thinking of her father's hair, the soft dark fringe where it touches his neck, when Emma tugged at my hand. 'Hurry,' she said.

'What's the rush?'

'The waves might wash them away.'

Despite our bad luck so far, Emma believed that on the beach ahead lay a treasure of perfect sand dollars.

'Want to go to Louis's Diner instead?' I said. 'I'm hungry.'

'I'm not.'

She tried to extract her fingers and pull away. I often thought, though I never said it, that her father spoiled her. I understood why: she was a child without a mother, and he was trying to compensate.

'Let me go,' she said, twisting her hand in my own, surprisingly strong.

I leaned down and looked into her face. Her green eyes stared back at me, resolute. I knew I was the adult. I was bigger, stronger, more clever. But I also knew that in a test of will, Emma would outlast me every time. 'Will you stay close by?'

'Yes.' She smiled, knowing she had won.

'Find me a pretty sand dollar.'

'I'll find you the biggest,' she said, stretching her arms wide.

She skipped ahead, that small, six-year-old mystery, that brilliant feminine replica of her father. She was humming some song that had been on the radio minutes earlier. Watching her, I felt a surge of joy and fear. In three months, I would marry her father. We hadn't yet explained to her that I would be moving in permanently. That I would make her breakfast, take her to school, and attend her ballet recitals, the way her mother used to do. No, the way her mother should have done.

'You're good for Emma,' Jake liked to say. 'You'll be a much better mother than my ex-wife ever was.'

And I thought, every time, how do you know? What makes you so sure? I watched Emma with her yellow bucket, her blue cloth shoes, her black ponytail whipping in the wind as she raced away from me, and wondered, how can I do it? How can I become a mother to this girl?

I lifted the Holga to my eye, aware as the shutter clicked — once, softly, like a toy — that Emma would be reduced to a blurry 6×6 in black and white. She was moving too fast, the light was insufficient. I turned the winding knob, clicked, advanced again. By the time I pressed the shutter release a final time, she was nearly gone.

2

Here then is the error, my moment of greatest failure. If everyone has a decision she would give anything to retract, this is mine: a shape in the sand caught my eye. At first it looked like something discarded — a child's shirt, perhaps, or a tiny blanket. By instinct I brought the camera to my eye, because this is what I do — I take pictures for a living, I record the things I see. As I moved closer, the furry head came into focus, the arched back, black spots on white fur. The small form was dusted with sand, its head pointing in my direction, its flippers resting delicately at its sides.

I knelt beside the seal pup, reaching out to touch it, but something stopped me. The wet black eyes, open and staring, did not blink. Spiky whiskers fanned out from the face, and three long lashes above each eye moved with the breeze. Then I saw the gash along its belly, mostly hidden by sand, and felt some maternal urge bumping around inside me. How long did I spend with the seal pup — thirty seconds? A minute? More?

A tiny sand crab scuttled over the sand by my toe. The sight of it reminded me of those miniature creatures that littered the beach at Gulf Shores when I was a child. My sister Annabel would capture them in mason jars and marvel at their pink underbellies as they tried to climb out, legs ticking against the glass. This crab kicked up a pocket of sand, then disappeared; at most, another ten seconds passed.

I glanced eastward toward the park, where the fog abruptly ended, butting up against startling blue. As a transplant to this city from the bright and sultry South, I had come to love the fog, its dramatic presence, the way it deadens sound. The way it simply stops, rather than fading, opaque whiteness suddenly giving way to clarity. Crossing from fog into sunlight, one has the feeling of having emerged. Traveling in the other direction is like sinking into a mysterious, fairy-tale abyss.

Just beyond the beach, along the Great Highway, a hearse led a line of cars south toward Pacifica. I remembered the last funeral I attended, a healthy guy in his late twenties who broke his neck in a rock-climbing accident; he was a friend of a friend, not someone I knew well, but because I'd talked with him at a dinner party two weeks before the accident, it seemed appropriate to go to the funeral. This recollection took another five seconds.

I looked ahead, where Emma should be, but did not see her. I began walking. Everything was saturated a cool white, and distance was impossible to measure. I clutched the plastic Holga, imagining the great images I'd get, the deep black of Emma's hair against the cold white beach.

I couldn't help thinking of the dead seal pup, how I would explain it to Emma. I believed this was something mothers instinctively knew how to do. This would be a test, the first of many; at that moment I was not thinking entirely of

5

Emma. I walked faster, anxious to know if she had seen the seal; it was a good thing for her to see that day, alone on the beach with me. I wanted her to be frightened by the dead seal pup so I could step delicately into the role of stepmother.

I don't know exactly when I realized something was wrong. I kept walking and did not see her. I pushed my hands in front of me, aware even as I did so of the absurdity of the gesture, as if a pair of hands could part the fog.

'Emma!' I called.

The panic did not strike immediately. No, that would take several seconds, a full minute almost. At first it was only a gradual slipping, a sense of vertigo, like the feeling I used to get as a child when I would stand knee-deep in the warm water of the Gulf of Mexico, close my eyes against the white-hot Alabama sun, and let the waves erode the platform under my feet. First the sand beneath the arches would go, then the toes, and finally I would lose my balance and tumble forward into the surf, mouth filling with seawater, eyes snapping open to meet the bright spinning world.

'Emma!'

I yelled louder, feeling the shifting, unreliable sand beneath my feet. I ran forward, then back, retracing my steps. She's hiding, I thought. She must be hiding. A few yards from the dead seal pup stood a concrete drainage wall covered with graffiti. I ran toward the wall. In my mind I pictured her crouched there, giggling, the pail propped on her knees. This vision was so clear, had such the ring of truth, I almost believed I

6

had seen it. But when I reached the wall, she wasn't there. I leaned against it, felt my insides convulse, and vomited into the sand.

From where I stood, I could make out the shape of the public restrooms down the beach. Racing toward them, I felt a sense of dread. I knew, already, that the search had somehow shifted. I crossed the highway and checked the women's room, which was dark and empty. Then I circled around to the men's side. The windows were made of frosted glass, dim light spilling onto the tile floor. I plunged my hand into the trash bin, looking for her clothes, her shoes. I got down on hands and knees and looked behind the urinals, holding my breath against the stench. Nothing.

As I crossed back to the beach, I was shaking. My fingers felt numb, my throat dry. I climbed to the top of a sand dune and turned in circles, seeing nothing but the impenetrable white fog, hearing nothing but the soft hum of cars along the Great Highway. For a moment I stood still. 'Think,' I said out loud. 'Don't panic.'

Up ahead, more fog, a half mile or so of beach, then the hill leading to the Cliff House, the Camera Obscura, the ruins of the Sutro Baths, Louis's Diner. To the right, there was the long sidewalk, the highway, and beyond it, Golden Gate Park. Behind me, miles of beach. To my left, the Pacific Ocean, gray and frothing. I stood at the center of a fog-bound maze with invisible walls and infinite possibilities. I thought: a child disappears on a beach. Where does that child go?

3

I will return again and again to that moment. I will keep a notebook in which I record the details. There will be poorly done sketches, graphs of time and motion, page after page on which I attempt to recover the past. I will pretend that memory is reliable, that it does not erode as quickly and completely as the brittle lines of an Etch-a-Sketch. I will tell myself that, buried somewhere in the intricate maze of my mind, there is a detail, a clue, some tiny lost thing that will lead me to Emma.

Later, they will want to know the exact moment I noticed she was missing. They will want to know whether I saw anyone unusual on the beach, whether I heard anything in the moments before or after she disappeared. They — the police, the reporters, her father — will ask the same questions again and again, staring into my eyes with desperation, as if by repetition they might make me remember, as if by force of will they can conjure clues where there are none.

This is what I tell them, this is what I know: I was walking on the beach with Emma. It was cold and very foggy. She let go of my hand. I stopped to photograph a seal pup, then glanced up toward the Great Highway. When I looked back, she was gone.

The only person to whom I will tell the entire story is my sister, Annabel. Only my sister will know I wasted ten seconds on a sand crab, five on a funeral procession. Only my sister will know I wanted Emma to see the dead seal, that in the moment before she disappeared, I was scheming to make her love me. For others, I will choose my words carefully, separating the important details from misleading trivialities. For them, I will present this version of the truth: there is a girl, her name is Emma, she is walking on the beach. I look away, seconds pass. When I look back she is gone.

This single moment unfolds like a flower in a series of time-lapse photographs, like an intricate maze. I stand at the labyrinth's center, unable to see which paths lead to dead ends, which one to the missing child. I know I must trust memory to lead me. I know I have one chance to get it right.

The first story I tell, the first clue I reveal, will determine the direction of the search. The wrong detail, the wrong clue, will inevitably lead to confusion, while the right clue leads to a beautiful child. Should I tell the police about the postman in the parking lot, the motorcycle, the man in the orange Chevelle, the yellow van? Or is it the seal that matters, the hearse, the retaining wall, the wave? How does one distinguish between the relevant and the extraneous? One slip in the narrative, one mistake in the selection of details, and everything disintegrates.

4

Pi times radius squared equals the area of a circle. Time is a continuum, stretching forward and back infinitely. I learned these things in school.

In a ninth-grade classroom at Murphy High School, Dr. Thomas Swayze, an exhilarating and shady character who was rumored to have received his doctorate through the mail, drew a giant circle on the chalkboard. On the outer rim of the circle and on a straight line drawn from the midpoint to the circle's edge, he scribbled numbers and formulas. His biceps flexed, straining the white sleeve of his T-shirt. 'Radius, diameter, circumference,' he said, his FM radio voice inciting in me sweaty adolescent desires. He turned to face the classroom and rolled the gleaming white cone of chalk from palm to palm, looking straight at me.

The sun glared through a long row of windows, turning the copper hair of the girl in front of me to flame; she smelled like Juicy Fruit gum. My hand lay on the desktop in a pool of burning light; all around my thumbnail were flecks of blood where I had chewed the skin to shreds. In my head, a steady, maddening hum. Dr. Swayze turned toward the blackboard. Some hidden object formed a faded and perfect circle on the back pocket of his blue jeans.

'And the greatest of these is area,' he said. My

knees slid apart, and I could feel little pools of sweat gathering on the plastic seat beneath my thighs.

Years before, Mrs. Monk, my third-grade teacher, had moved the hands on a giant cardboard clock and extolled the virtues of time. Seconds were grains of sand, she said. Minutes were pebbles. Hours were the bricks of which past, present, and future are made. She talked of days and years, decades, centuries. She talked of the millennium, when we would all be grown. She opened her big arms wide and whispered the word *eon*. In our portable classroom, the air conditioner sputtering mildly against Mobile's April heat, Mrs. Monk, teacher of the year for 1977, preached and glowed and sweated.

I sat at my wooden desk, looking up at that huge circle with its eternally trapped hands, and cried. She came over to me and laid warm, damp fingers on my neck. 'Abby, what's wrong?' she asked. I leaned into her ample, motherly waist, buried my face in deep folds of polyester, and confessed, 'I don't understand time.' It wasn't the clock itself that confounded me, the half-past and quarter-till, the five-of and ten-after, but rather the essential nature of time. I did not have the words to explain this to Mrs. Monk.

What disturbed me most were the lost stretches between bedtime and waking, those dark hours when my mind went on fantastic and terrible journeys. I knew time was a place where one could be lost, a place where bliss or horror might go on and on, though when I woke, my mother would look the same, my sister Annabel

11

would not have aged, and my father would get up and put on his suit and go to work as if nothing had changed. I believed I lived in a different world than they, that my family slept while I traveled. I felt invested with responsibility, as if I had been chosen to shoulder a burden for my entire family.

Mrs. Monk's voice stayed with me, and long after I had learned to tell time I was still disturbed by the clock's steady, unstoppable rhythm. Sitting in Dr. Swayze's class, looking at the dull chrome clock on the wall above the blackboard, I wished there were some way to make it stop, to make the days last longer.

'How do we measure the area of a circle?' Dr. Swayze asked.

I imagine that the circle begins as a cosmic pinpoint, small as the body of a child. The child is stooped on the beach, reaching for a sand dollar. A tall figure appears in the fog. A hand clamps over the child's mouth, a strong arm lifts her up. With each step the stranger takes, the circle widens. With each second, the area of possibility grows.

Where is the child? The answer lies within a maddening equation: pi times radius squared.

5

The room is small, with hard plastic chairs and a concrete floor. In the corner there's an odd touch, placed here perhaps by a secretary or thoughtful wife — a mosaic end table and pretty lamp. The bulb clicks and hums as a moth flutters beneath the shade. A large metal clock ticks off the seconds. Jake is in another room, behind a closed door, strapped to some contraption. The polygrapher is asking him questions, monitoring his heart rate, watching for signs of a hidden motive, a carefully concealed lie.

'We must first eliminate the family,' Detective Sherburne said last night. 'Nine times out of ten, it's the mother, or father, or both.' He watched my eyes when he said this, waiting for me to flinch; I didn't.

'I'm not the mother,' I said. 'Not even the stepmother. Not yet. The mother picked up and left three years ago. Are you looking for her?'

'We're considering all possibilities.'

The clock is ticking, the circle is widening, and I am waiting my turn.

Cops stand around the station, singly or in pairs. They sip coffee from Styrofoam cups, shift from one foot to the other, talk quietly, making private jokes. One stands with a hand on his gun, the palm closed gently over the metal, as if the gun itself is an extension of his own body.

13

Yesterday, Jake raced home from Eureka, where he was visiting a friend for the weekend. We spent the night in the station filling out forms, answering questions, going over every detail. Now it's eight a.m. Twenty-two hours have passed. While I sit here, waiting, who is searching?

It's no secret that the longer a child is missing, the more difficult it is to find her. Danger grows by the second. Time is the kidnapper's greatest friend, the family's most formidable enemy. With each passing minute, the kidnapper moves farther away in some indiscernible direction, and the area that must be searched, the diameter of possibility, grows.

Yesterday, Sherburne arrived at the Beach Chalet within ten minutes of the first squad car and immediately took charge. Now, he works at his desk, clad in a pale blue shirt and odd, iridescent tie, surely a gift that he feels obliged to wear. I imagine him at home, getting ready for work amid the domestic chaos. I imagine a happy wife, a couple of very clean children. There's something comforting about his presence. He reminds me of Frank Sinatra, with his broad forehead and immaculate haircut, his sloping blue eyes. He moves with a kind of old-fashioned grace.

I catch his eye. He holds up a hand with fingers spread and mouths the words 'Five minutes.' He reaches for his coffee, lifts it to his mouth, sips, and sets it down again. Six more seconds have passed. Say Emma is in a car, going 60 miles per hour. In 6 seconds a car moving at 60 miles per hour can travel 170-something yards. Square that and multiply it by pi. In the time it took him to take that sip of coffee, the search area broadened by more than 870,000 square feet. If each sip is another 870,000 square feet and if there are 100 sips in a cup, I wonder how large the circle will be when he is finished, and how many cups he would have to drink to expand this circle around the globe.

I consider all the possibilities of human bodies in motion. Did the kidnapper take Emma by the hand? Did he pick her up? If the latter, then what is the length of his stride? How many feet can he cover in a minute? And how far did he go on foot? How many yards was it to his vehicle? Did she struggle, and, if so, would this have slowed him down? Does he try to appease her when she's hungry?

I imagine a van stopped at a diner on some dusty highway. Inside the diner sit a shadowy figure and a girl. They are eating breakfast. Perhaps he wants to make her trust him, so the girl is having chocolate chip pancakes with an unhealthy dose of syrup, maybe even chocolate milk. Would Emma know to eat slowly in order to stall their departure? Take your time, I think, willing the message telepathically through the void. Chew each bite carefully. A song comes to me from summer camp in the Carolinas when I was an unhappy member of Girls in Action: 'Give each bite fifty chews and follow with a sip of juice . . . ' During those minutes in the diner, they are not moving in any direction; the clock is still, the circle remains static.

This is not the only possibility. The police are already leaning toward a theory of drowning.

Yesterday, not long after the police arrived, the Coast Guard boat appeared. I stood on the beach answering questions, watching the boat plow through the freezing water. Overhead, an orange chopper came swooping in from the north. Its nose tipped toward the ocean, and the loud thwack-thwack of the blades reminded me of movies about Vietnam. Hours later, as evening pressed in, the Coast Guard boat disappeared. The ocean was blue-black beneath a darker sky, and the wind had picked up, pushing the fog eastward. As the sand cut into my face and neck, I worried about Emma in her sweatshirt, not warm enough for this kind of wind. I hoped she had worn socks, but I couldn't remember.

At some point Jake arrived. I don't remember how it happened — only that for the longest time he wasn't there, and then, suddenly, he was. Cruiser lights flashed red and blue over the dark beach. There was the strong creosote smell of a bonfire down-wind. A few surfers were coming in, their bodies slick and seal-like in black wet suits. The police questioned them one by one.

Eventually, someone from the Coast Guard approached us. His uniform looked neatly pressed despite the fact he'd been working all day. 'There's not much we can do in the dark,' he said. 'We'll start again early in the morning.'

'If she's out there,' Jake asked, 'what are your chances of finding her?'

The Coast Guard man looked down, dug the toe of his shoe into the sand. 'Hard to tell, depends on the tides. Sometimes, after a drowning, the body will wash up on shore, sometimes not.'

'Emma's terrified of water,' I said, looking to Jake for confirmation. 'She wouldn't have gone near it.'

Sherburne turned to me. The pages of his yellow legal pad flapped in the wind.

I explained how I'd recently taken Emma to the birthday party of a bossy girl named Melissa. Screaming children played Marco Polo in a yellow-tiled pool in Millbrae, while Emma sat cross-legged on a lounge chair, terrorizing a ladybug that had fallen into her root beer float. 'She refused to go in the pool,' I said. I could see Emma in her blue bathing suit, sitting there, clear as a snapshot. Every now and then she'd squint, glance up at the glittering pool, and move her foot by a fraction, as if she might get up her nerve and go in, but she never did. In the car on the way home, when I asked if she'd had fun, she propped her skinny feet on the dashboard and said, 'I don't care for that Melissa.'

Sherburne looked at me in a pitying way, as if to say this was no kind of proof. But from the way he lowered his head and put a hand on Jake's shoulder, I could tell he wanted to believe me.

'She's a really smart kid,' I said, desperate to make him understand. 'If I thought for a second she'd get anywhere near the water, I wouldn't have let go of her hand.'

Jake turned away from me then, toward the ocean, and I realized that some tiny part of him was actually considering it, that somewhere in his deeply rational mind this idea was taking hold as a minute but distinct possibility: Emma might have drowned.

'I've got two kids,' Sherburne said. 'I'm going to do everything I can.'

Now, Jake emerges through a door, head bowed. I touch his shoulder as we cross paths. He jerks as if he has been stung, then looks at me, his eyes red and swollen. With obvious effort he moves his hand in my direction, clasps my fingers, and lets go.

'How could you?' he said, moments after hearing the news. 'God, Abby, how could you?' It was on the phone, long-distance to Eureka; his voice was shaky, he was crying. Now, I can see in his face that it's an effort for him not to say it again — to repeat it over and over, an angry refrain. And I'm thinking, *How could I?* The guilt is a physical sensation, a constant, sickening pain.

The polygrapher stands in the doorway, hands on his hips, smiling as casually as a friendly neighborhood salesman. 'Norm Dubus,' he says, shaking my hand. 'Ready?'

The room is blank and white and very warm. A space heater beneath the window buzzes, its coils glowing red. A smell of sweat and burned coffee. Norm shuts the door behind us and motions for me to sit down. He loops cords around my chest, tells me to sit up straight, and adjusts the height of the chair so my feet are flat on the floor.

'Relax. I'm going to ask you a few questions.'

18

On the table in front of him is a legal pad, and beside it a gold machine with a needle. He flips a switch and the machine begins to hum. The needle starts moving, scratching four flat blue lines across the paper. The questions, at first, are mundane:

Is your name Abigail Mason?

Were you born in Alabama?

Did you attend the University of Tennessee?

Is your current place of residence 420 Arkansas, Unit 3, San Francisco, California?

He records answers on his pad, checks the needle mark, makes notations. After a while, the tone of the questions changes.

Have you and Jake been arguing lately?

Do you have children?

Do you want children?

Did you ever fight with Emma?

Norm's hair is glossy black, except for a couple of gray strands above the ears. He has purplish spots around his hairline, and he smells like green apples. He must have just dyed his hair in the last day or two, possibly even that morning.

Half an hour has passed since the polygraph began.

Have you ever punished Emma?

Do you know where Emma is?

Did you have anything to do with her disappearance?

Did you lose your temper?

Did you drown her?

Did you kill Emma?

As the session comes to a close, I fall apart.

Norm offers me a tissue and leans over to detach the monitors from my pulse points. The sweet apple scent of his shampoo grows stronger. 'Emma loves applesauce,' I find myself saying. He lifts an eyebrow, smiles in a distracted way, and an absurd jingle rolls through my head, the sort of phonic litany one memorizes in kindergarten. *A is for apple, A is for Adam, A is for Abraham.*

'We're done here,' Norm says. 'You may go.' Then, more gently, 'It's routine. Just something we have to do.'

'I know,' I say.

A is for Anywhere.

Outside the police station, a reporter for Channel 7 is waiting with her cameraman. Jake looks directly into the camera and speaks into the woman's outstretched microphone. 'If you have Emma, please let her go. Just leave her in a public place. Walk away. No one has to know who you are.'

The reporter waves the microphone in my face. Her makeup has a shiny plastic look, and her lip liner extends slightly beyond the natural edges of her lips. 'What is your relationship to the child?'

'I'm her father's fiancée.'

The woman presses herself between me and Jake. 'Is the wedding still on?'

'I just want to find my daughter,' he says.

She barrages Jake with more questions, never pausing long enough to get a complete answer. 'How do you feel? Where is Emma's mother? Do you know who might have done this?' I know she's looking for the perfect sound bite — an outpouring of grief, a statement implicating the mother, the mention of a creepy neighbor or crazy uncle — anything to make her story more interesting.

Jake fields her questions calmly, professionally. Not once does he show impatience or break down into tears. He's made for such moments of crisis, this sturdy Californian who is always in command. His great-great-great-grandfather was a 49er of the gold-panning kind; his father-was a 49er as well, a football hero whose name still gets mentioned in the sports page, a bigger-than-life talent who died in his early forties, wasted by alcohol. Jake played football in high school and was pretty good, but he happily gave up the sport when his father died. Still, there is something of the football player's swagger in him, a good-natured confidence that never fails to win people over.

Watching him, I know that he will play well on TV. The public will admire his air of gentle sobriety, his thick, wavy hair that is always slightly out of control, the full lower lip he bites when contemplating a question, the subtle glasses that make him look like a quiet intellectual. They will like the dimpled boyish-ness of his smile, the way he glances down at his feet when anyone pays him a compliment. I think of the television audience, watching us and judging, the way I have done in better times.

We drive to Jake's house at Thirtieth and Lawton. There, another reporter is waiting. Jake pauses to make a statement pleading for Emma's safe return. Once inside, we close the curtains and stand in the dark living room, not speaking and not touching, just standing, arms at our sides, face to face. Emma's things are scattered around the room: on the coffee table, a magic wand fashioned from tinfoil; in a basket by the stairs, a pot holder she was making for her teacher; beneath the couch, the red ballet slippers she liked to wear around the house.

I lean into his chest and put my arms around him. We've always fit best this way, standing up, my head reaching just to his sternum, his arms wrapped around me in a way that makes me feel protected. But he doesn't embrace me this time. Instead, he pats me on the shoulder — once, twice, three times — like an acquaintance at a funeral.

'I'm so sorry,' I say.

He lets his hand drop to his side. 'I know, it's not your — '

But he can't say it's not my fault, can't say he doesn't blame me, because it is, and he does.

He reaches behind his back to unclasp my hands, then goes upstairs, into Emma's bedroom, and shuts the door behind him. Bedsprings creak, and his sobs carry down through the floorboards. I think of Emma's bed, the yellow comforter with white flowers, the small pillows she likes to hide things under: crayons, doll clothes, crisp dollar bills. Minutes pass before I hear movement upstairs, a door opening, heavy feet shuffling across the floor, another door closing, then the swish of water into the bathroom sink.

Leslie Gray on Channel 7 reports the story in this way: 'A six-year-old San Francisco girl, the granddaughter of legendary 49er Jim Balfour, disappeared yesterday at Ocean Beach. Although the girl's father and his fiancée have not been ruled out as suspects, sources say they both took a polygraph and passed. Authorities are attempting to locate the girl's estranged mother. Police fear the girl may have drowned.'

A photograph of Emma appears on screen, last year's school portrait. Her bangs are cut unevenly, and she's wearing a blue barrette. She's missing a tooth, front and center. I remember the day this photograph was taken. I helped her pick out the barrette, and she persuaded me to style her bangs with a curling iron. I placed my hand between the curling iron and her forehead to keep from burning her, the way my mother used to do, and as she chattered on about a boy named Sam who'd poisoned the class canary, I realized she was beginning to like me.

Leslie Gray frowns in a practiced way, forming a series of creases in her peach-colored makeup. 'Anyone who may have seen the girl should call this hotline.' A number flashes on screen. I pick up the phone and dial. The girl who answers is probably no more than seventeen.

'Missing children hotline,' she says cheerfully. 'How may I assist you?'

I want to tell her to please find Emma. I want to tell her that Emma loves potato chips with salt and vinegar, that she's been taking cello lessons. I want to tell her that Emma made a perfect

23

score on her last spelling test, and that I've been teaching her how to use a camera. Instead, my throat freezes and I say nothing.

'Hello?' she says. 'Hello?' Her voice changes from perky to annoyed. 'Hello,' and the line goes dead.

6

For work, I have always used my Leica R8. It's easy to manipulate, allowing maximum control over my images. But in the past few months, I began feeling that my photographs lacked something — some quality of depth I couldn't quite define. I wanted to try a camera without gadgets, without special lenses and precision focus, which is why I chose the Holga for that day at Ocean Beach. With no focusing mechanism and only two f-stops, the Holga is the simplest kind of viewfinder camera.

It is the day after Emma's disappearance, the middle of the night. Jake is out searching. Today, a few dozen volunteers fanned out across Golden Gate Park, with the intent of covering all 1,017 acres — the dense woods and enormous soccer fields, botanical gardens, lakes and playgrounds and equestrian rings. A woman named Bud with the Park Police led the search on horseback. I recognized her from a tour Emma and Jake and I took of the Presidio stables in the spring. On that day, which seems like a lifetime ago, Officer Bud showed Emma how to feed the horses carrots from the palm of her hand. There were several other children on the tour, and I was embarrassed when Emma, overcome with excitement, stealthily skipped to the front of the line. I didn't remember ever having been that bold as a child, and I

25

wondered, with a mix of amusement and unease, what forms Emma's precociousness would take as she grew older.

For me, tonight, the search leads back to my apartment, to the darkroom with its chilled air and chemical smell. I take yesterday's film out of the Holga, remove the film from the cassette, and wind it carefully around the reel. It's something I've done thousands of times, yet my fingers shake. I drop the reel into the processing canister, put the cap on, and turn on the overhead light. I check the temperature of the developing fluid, pour the chemicals in, and gently rock the canister back and forth. Then I do the same with the stop fluid and the fixer, timing each action precisely, aware that I'm holding the most important film I have ever shot. Finally, I take the top off of the canister, run water over the reel, unroll the film, and hang the strips to dry.

It's three in the morning when I cut the negatives into strips of three, slide them one by one into the enlarger, move the arm until the image is in focus, then lay the photo paper on the counter and expose the film, four seconds per print. Then the basins: developer, stopper, fix. Finally, the water bath.

Each photo captures the moment with some degree of accuracy, and yet I am struck by the inadequacies, the story the pictures fail to tell. One is a close-up, her face just inches from the camera, a big grin, a spot of flour on her face from our pancake-making adventure earlier that morning. In the second, she is a few feet away, bending to examine a sand dollar, caught in profile, her hair hanging down and concealing her face. The third is shot from behind. The photo shows a small, blurred figure in the left-hand side of the frame. If you were to come upon this photo in a gallery, or on someone's living room wall, you might find it mysterious, pleasing: a child's black hair, white fog, a vast expanse of beach.

Yet something essential is missing from the photos. What is missing is the truth, what is missing is the answer. Again and again, I scan them with a magnifying glass, looking for a dark figure lurking in the shadows. Within the grain, I search for some kind of clue, some hidden meaning or simple, obvious thing that has slipped my mind. I search until my vision goes blurry, unwilling to believe that there is simply nothing there. It's seven a.m. when I leave the darkroom, sick with disappointment.

To any problem there is a solution: it's something my mother told me as a child, and I've lived my life believing it. But now that old aphorism falls flat — just an optimistic deception with no practical application. The one thing I know is this: there is a girl, her name is Emma, we were walking on the beach. She was there, and then she wasn't. There is no way to retrieve that moment, no way to rewrite the script; I looked away. It cannot be undone.

7

The phone rings and rings. I see myself as if from a distance: the receiver clutched in my fingers, the emerald engagement ring on the hand that holds it. Everything feels impossible, like some terrible scene from someone else's life.

Finally, a man with a high, strained voice comes on the other end. 'Nine-one-one,' he says. 'Do you have an emergency?'

'I lost a little girl,' I say, my voice trembling.

'When did you realize she was missing?'

'Thirty-five minutes ago.' I'm staring at my watch, unbelieving. Thirty-five minutes. What can happen to a child in thirty-five minutes?

'Where did you last see her?' the man asks.

'Ocean Beach. I went back to the parking lot to look for her, but she wasn't there.'

'The important thing is to remain calm,' he says.

But I know he is wrong; to be calm implies some sort of rest, sitting back and waiting.

'Where are you now?'

'The Beach Chalet.'

'Speak up,' he says. 'I can barely hear you.'

'The Beach Chalet.' The volume of my voice startles me. People in the restaurant turn and stare: a man in an apron rolling silverware into napkins, a heavily tattooed couple sharing an omelet by the window, a group of German

28

students contemplating the menu. The restaurant's hostess, a prematurely maternal woman with a thick Russian accent, stands in front of me, wringing her hands.

'Is the little girl your daughter?' the voice asks.

'No, my fiancé's daughter.'

'How old is she?'

'Six and a half.' The volume of my voice rises again. 'Please send someone. When are you going to send someone?'

'You need to stay calm, ma'am. I'm dispatching a patrol car.'

'How long will it take?'

'Five minutes. Stay right where you are. The officer will meet you there.'

He sounds so sure of himself, not the least bit nervous. I feel vaguely comforted by the tidiness of protocol, imagining the dispatch going out over the airwaves to be picked up by a coterie of well-trained officers. Within seconds they'll be racing toward Ocean Beach, sirens wailing, and within minutes, surely, Emma will be found.

'I get you some coffee,' the Russian woman says. She disappears into the kitchen.

The silverware man comes over and puts a hand on my shoulder. 'What's her name?'

'Emma. Emma Balfour.'

He unties his apron and tosses it on the counter. 'I'll check the park.'

I fight off a mental image of Emma with some stranger behind the trees on a rocky path. I check my watch. Thirty-nine minutes. She could be anywhere by now.

The tattooed couple wolfs down the last bites

of their omelet. 'What can we do?' the girl asks, pulling on her jacket.

'I don't know,' I say. 'I can't think.'

'We could go back to the parking lot,' the boyfriend says. 'We could take down license plates.' He seems eager, almost excited, as if he's caught up in some movie, the role of his life.

'Here, take this.' I hand him my Holga. 'There are only five shots left.'

'We'll bring it back when we're done,' the girl says. She slaps a twenty on the counter, and they head out the door. The German teenagers keep glancing up from their menus and whispering, as if this is somehow part of the entertainment, a play staged just for them.

The Russian woman returns with a thick mug of coffee, a little pitcher of cream, two sugar packets, and a spoon. 'Your daughter,' she says, 'we will find her.'

I pick up the phone again and dial Jake's cell, almost hoping that he won't answer. I imagine calling him a little while later, after I've found her. Part of me thinks that, in a few minutes, all of this will be over, and life will return to normal. Emma is simply playing hide-and-seek, or she ran off to find a bathroom, or she got lost in the fog and it took a while for her to get back to the parking lot. She's probably standing by the car right now; she must be. I should have stayed there and waited for her.

Jake's phone rings twice, three times. I know that in the moment I tell him, the nightmare will become real. On the fifth ring, he picks up.

'Abby?'

I hear voices in the background, sports announcers, the ambient noise of a crowd. I don't know how to begin.

'You there?' he says.

'I have to tell you something.'

A wild cheer goes up from the crowd, and Jake lets out a whoop. 'Delgado just hit a home run!'

'Jake, you have to come home,' I say. Even as I say it, I'm calculating the time it will take him to drive the 270 miles if he leaves right now, if he goes over the speed limit and doesn't have to stop for gas, if there isn't much traffic.

'What?'

'You have to come home. It's Emma.'

'I can hardly hear you.'

'Emma,' I say.

The tone of his voice changes. 'Is something wrong?'

'She's gone,' I say.

'What?'

'Emma. She's gone.'

His voice strikes a high, unfamiliar note. 'What do you mean?'

'We were on the beach. We were walking.'

How to finish the conversation? Nothing about the moment seems real. I know there must be some appropriate words to utter, but I have no idea what they might be. This is a glitch in time, a mistake, a joke. At any moment Emma will walk through the door.

'What do you mean?' he says again.

'There was this dead seal, a pup. I looked away for a few seconds, I swear it was only a few seconds. Then I looked up and she wasn't there.'

31

'But . . . where is she now?'

Where is she? A valid question. The obvious question. How to answer?

'Lost,' I say. As if she simply strayed, the way children do. As if she is standing patiently at some fixed point, waiting for me. 'The police are on their way.'

On the other end, several seconds of silence. A stranger's voice says, 'Hey, man, you okay?' I will later learn that this is the voice of the hot dog vendor. Jake's legs have given out. One moment he's standing, mind on the game, holding up two fingers to indicate that he wants two hot dogs. Then he's sitting on the ground — no, not sitting but kneeling, knees to the cement.

'This isn't possible,' Jake says. 'Abby, how could you?'

In the background there is the smack of a baseball bat, the roar of the crowd.

★   ★   ★

I met Jake a year ago at the high school where he teaches. I was doing a slide presentation on the landscape photography of the Southwest for a group of juniors and seniors. Before I cut the lights, I saw a man sitting alone in the back row, looking a bit out of place. He had wavy black hair, glasses with thin silver frames, and he wore a blue button-down. When the lights came back on, he gave me a thumbs-up.

I opened the floor for comments. There were none. The art history teacher, an anorexic brunette with very short bangs, asked a couple of predictable questions to make up for her students' lack of interest. When the bell rang, the students rushed the aisles, jostling each other and shouting. The sudden activity stirred up unpleasant odors of adolescence — cheap perfume, hair spray, sweat, and pent-up lust. When the din cleared, the guy from the back row was standing in front of the platform. 'You were pretty good up there,' he said.

'You're just being nice.'

'Really, they're a tough crowd. You held your own.' He reached out to shake my hand. 'Name's Jake.'

'Should you be wandering around without a hall pass?'

'Last period was my lunch break, and this is my prep time. I couldn't bear the thought of sitting in the teachers' lounge.'

Just then the lights went off, plunging us into darkness. 'Budget cuts,' Jake explained. 'All the lights are on automatic timers.' The auditorium was empty save for the two of us. We both reached for the shut-off switch to the slide projector at the same time, and when our hands touched, there was a quick fuzz of static electricity.

'Sparks,' he said.

I smiled.

We pushed through the crowded hallway, a chaos of backpacks and cell phones and iPods, a hothouse of colliding pheromones. The place felt unpredictable, unsafe, as if at any moment a gun might be drawn or a knife fight might break out. A skinny kid in a sagging sweater gave Jake a high five, and a girl in a vinyl miniskirt blew him a kiss. Several students shouted his name. I wondered how he'd managed to earn their trust. I'd never liked teenagers, even when I was one myself. I assumed the feeling was mutual; surely they could see right through me, could sense my dislike and smell my fear.

'What subject do you teach?' I asked, swiveling to avoid a television being wheeled through the hallway by an obese, balding boy.

'Philosophy.'

'Do you like it?'

'To be honest, I only get one section of philosophy per year. The rest is soccer and American History.'

'A Renaissance man.'

'More like a hired gun,' he said. 'Who roped you into this?'

'During a moment of weakness I volunteered for Artists in the Schools. This isn't exactly what I had in mind; I had visions of cute little third-graders in jumpsuits and pigtails.'

'What kind of photography are you into?'

'Whatever pays the bills. Mainly corporate events and weddings, with a sideline in photo restoration.'

'My mom was a photographer,' Jake said. 'Trains, landscapes, abandoned streets. It was just a hobby, but she was pretty good. I've often wished that she'd passed that talent on to me.'

We emerged from the damp, fluorescent interior into sunlight. From the parking lot I could see the ocean in the distance, and the fog line circling the city, a bright white necklace around a patch of brilliant blue. Jake loaded the slide projector into the trunk of my car, shook my hand, and said, 'I guess this is where we part.' He seemed to be waiting for me to disagree, but it had been so long since I'd approached a guy for a date, I couldn't remember how it was done.

'Thanks for the help,' I said, silently willing him to ask for my number. Instead, he gave an awkward salute and started to walk away.

I was turning the key in the ignition when he reappeared at my open window. He placed his hands on the windowsill and leaned toward me. 'Hey, busy tomorrow night?'

'Actually, I have two tickets to the Giants game.'

Jake was surprised. 'Really?'

'Meet me by the statue at six-thirty.'

'I'm there,' he said.

I waved goodbye in my best I-do-this-all-the-time fashion. Driving home, I couldn't stop thinking about his hands on the windowsill and the endearing way his right foot turned slightly inward when he walked.

When I arrived at the Willie Mays statue the next night, Jake was already there. Over a dinner of hot dogs and garlic fries, he asked dozens of questions, somehow charming me into revealing a comprehensive list of my past employment, the lengths of my former relationships, the contents of my CD collection, even the name of a champagne-colored cocker spaniel I had when I was seven. Neither one of us paid much attention to the game.

As the eighth inning came to a close, I dusted crumbs off my lap and said, 'I feel like I've been through a job interview.'

He shrugged. 'I just ask the important questions.'

'Am I hired?'

'Depends. Do you want the job?'

'I don't know much about the company.'

By then, the Giants were up by eight. 'Did you drive?' Jake asked.

'I took Muni.'

'Good, I'll drive you home.'

Later, we stood outside my apartment for a long time, making small talk, neither of us knowing quite how to end the date. After a few minutes he put his hands in his pockets, looked at the ground, and said, 'How do you feel about kids?'

I laughed. 'Aren't you getting ahead of yourself? You haven't even kissed me yet.'

He put his hands on my waist, pulled me in, and unsteadied me with a long, slow kiss that left me wanting more. 'There,' he said. 'Now that we've crossed that hurdle.'

'You sound like Alvy in *Annie Hall*,' I said, 'that scene where they're walking home from their first date and he kisses her just to get it over with, so it won't be awkward later.'

'That's my favorite Woody Allen film,' he said. 'No, second favorite, after *Crimes and Misdemeanors*.'

We just looked at each other for a few seconds, smiling awkwardly, and I had that surprised, happy feeling you get when you realize you've connected with someone.

'Seriously, though,' he said. 'What about kids?'

'I can honestly say you're the first man who's ever asked me that on a first date.'

'I like to get things out in the open.'

'Sure, I want to have one someday. But I don't hear my clock ticking, if that's what you mean.'

He kissed me again, longer this time, one hand pressing into the small of my back while the other cupped my elbow in a sweet and familiar way. It had been a year since I'd broken up with my previous boyfriend. The relationship had ended badly, with late-night phone calls that went on for months. As Jake kissed me, I felt some wall inside me crumbling.

He took my hair in his hands and flipped it over my shoulder. 'Say you were to meet an intelligent, funny, handsome guy.'

'Know any?'

'Say this guy had a daughter. Could you still fall for him?'

I searched his face for some sign of a joke, but there was none. 'You're serious.'

'She's five years old. Her name is Emma.'

I remember clearly the image that flashed through my mind just then. It was a silly image of Jake and me and a little girl. We were in a park, and I was pushing the child on a swing. Her hair flew out behind her as she rose higher and higher. I found something pleasing and surprisingly comfortable in this idea of a ready-made family. Then I realized the picture was incomplete. 'Her mother?' I asked.

'Lisbeth took off a couple of years ago. She

met some guy in a band, got caught up in a weird scene. Then one day I came home from work and she was gone. That was probably the worst day of my life. By then, things were pretty bad between us, but I still loved her. Or maybe I just thought I could rescue her, help her go back to being the person she was when we met.'

'Where is she now?' I asked.

'I don't know.' Jake paused. 'I didn't hear from her for several months after she left, then there was a rash of phone calls asking for money. About six months ago, she called in the middle of the night all weepy and apologetic. She claimed she was clean, the guy was out of the picture, she missed me, she wanted to try again. The sad thing was that she never once asked about Emma. I think Lisbeth always thought of motherhood as a burden, something that held her back.'

'What did you do?'

'I told her to stay away, that we were doing just fine without her. By then I'd told Emma that her mother wasn't coming back. Maybe I hadn't completely gotten over Lisbeth at that point — I'm not sure you ever entirely get over someone you really love — but I knew she wasn't good for Emma, and I didn't want her in our lives.'

He smiled then, a shy smile that stood in contrast to the side of him I'd seen that night. 'You know, I actually haven't dated much since she left. Have I scared you off?'

As we stood there, his hands on my shoulders, the chocolate-and-coffee taste of his kiss lingering in my mouth, I realized this was not the casual date I set out on a few hours earlier. I touched the faint scar on his chin. 'How did you get this?'

'Mike Potter. I was nine. Vicious playground battle.'

I stood on my tiptoes and kissed the scar, then took a deep breath. I'd never before dated a man with a child. I wasn't sure what the rules were. 'When can I meet her?'

'Soon.'

Two weeks later, on a warm Saturday, there were burritos at Pancho Villa, followed by a kids' movie at the Balboa. Emma sat between us, a giant bucket of popcorn on her lap. Several times I reached into the bucket and my hand collided with Emma's, or Jake's. Each time he touched me, I felt a warm sensation spread through my bones, some hard thing inside me breaking apart. At one point, Emma leaned forward in her seat and Jake reached over, put his hand on the back of my neck, and pulled me to him. We kissed fast and hard, like teenagers whose parents were just around the corner.

In the weeks to follow, it became a routine, those Saturday movies with Emma sitting between us, the fast kisses that overwhelmed me. Jake would drape his arm over the back of Emma's seat, place his hand on my neck, and leave it there for the entire movie. By the time the credits began to roll, my neck would be hot, my vision blurred, my body weak with longing. Jake would press his thumb into the groove above my top vertebra, or slide his hand beneath my collar, or trace patterns on my skin with his finger, and I would lose track of the movie's plot, forget the characters' names, miss key conversations that revealed important backstories. It would be hours before I could have him, hours before we'd be back at his place, Emma asleep in her room, Jake and I undressing quietly, climbing into bed and making love under layers of blankets while, outside, the foghorn moaned in its lonely, animal way.

Months later, after the Saturday movies had dwindled to once every three or four weeks, and nighttime had become a comfortable sleep with a familiar body rather than an occasion for passionate lovemaking, I once woke in the middle of the night to find Jake awake, lying on his side, watching me.

'Can't sleep?' I said.

'I'm observing you.'

'Why?'

'I'm waiting for you to talk in your sleep and reveal your deepest, darkest secrets.'

'You already know them.'

I was lying on my stomach, my head turned toward him. He reached over and touched my neck. 'I've memorized the skin on the back of your neck,' he said. 'You could blindfold me and line up a hundred necks, and I'd know when I got to yours.'

I moved closer and kissed him. We made love in the slow, easy way I had always imagined married people do. We were both tired and at some point, before we finished, we fell asleep, with me lying on top of him, my head resting on his chest. Some time later, I was awakened by floorboards creaking. I looked up to see Emma in the hallway. The bathroom light was on, and she was standing in a pool of pale light, staring at the floor, not moving. I put on my robe and went to her, took her hand, and led her back to bed.

She looked confused. 'You were sleepwalking,' I said, tucking her in.

'I was?'

'Yes. Go back to sleep.'

'Stay with me?' she asked.

'Of course.' I sat on the edge of her bed until she fell asleep. In some way, I already wished she was mine.

8

The police are interested in facts: the movement of the tide, the angle of the sun, the direction of the wind, exact times and locations. From these facts they construct scenarios, from these scenarios they extract a series of possibilities, and the possibilities themselves are arranged in a distinct hierarchy of probability. Each search takes its focus from a clear set of general rules which must be applied with precision to the specific case. Leads must be considered, then discarded or followed to their logical end. The orderliness of the search is paramount.

'The key to any mystery,' one energetic young policeman tells me, 'lies in deconstruction. The sum must be dismantled to uncover its individual parts. The parts, therefore, are more meaningful than the sum.' Of course, I know this to be false. The sum itself is all-encompassing. The sum is Emma, and she is gone.

There isn't a minute in the day that I don't go there in my mind, to that place on the beach, that fog-bound maze, the very moment when I realized she was missing. With each return to this moment there is a deeper clarity, a slowing and stoppage of time, a new detail presenting itself as if in bas-relief against the flat gray surface of memory: a brown paper bag whirling upward in the wind, three plastic straws lying side by side in the sand, a bottle cap, upturned, with the words

Sorry, Try Again. It is in this slow-motion presentation, this continual reconstruction, that I hope to find the clue that will lead me to her. But I cannot help but wonder whether the details that emerge each time I journey into my subconscious are the stuff of buried memory, or of imagination. The task is in separating fact from desire.

I want her to come back, and in this wanting, substance is created from nothingness. I remember how I stepped behind the cement wall, certain that I would find her there. I wanted it so badly that I constructed an image, and the image shuddered with life: Emma, crouched and waiting behind the wall, holding the yellow bucket between her knees. When I rounded the wall and behind it there was no Emma, I felt reality like a whiplash across my face, and with reality, a terror so intense it bent me over, my insides heaving.

I gazed up toward the cement steps leading to the sidewalk, the parking lot, and beyond it the Great Highway. She wouldn't have gone that direction. She'd been begging me to take her to the beach all week; the sand was what interested her, not the city beyond it. That left three directions — north, south, and west. A multidirectional task butted against the linear restrictions of movement. A human body can move in only one direction at any given time, and the eyes' capacity for detecting motion is limited to 180 degrees, while the most important tasks require a spreading out, a 360-degree vision.

Had I remembered at that crucial moment the orange Chevelle, the man sitting in the front seat alone, partially hidden by his newspaper, perhaps I would have chosen differently; he seemed oblivious to us but in hindsight he could have been watching, waiting for the moment to strike. Or maybe the yellow van held the answer, the handsome surfer standing by the driver's door, waxing his board, the woman behind the parted curtains, waving to Emma. Had I thought of them, I might have raced back toward the parking lot immediately, it might have been my first choice. Had I arrived at the parking lot quickly enough, I might have found the surfer lifting Emma into the van. Or what of the postman, perched on the retaining wall, eating his sandwich? I could have forced my way into the mail truck, sent packages flying as I searched for her in the small dark space.

Instead, I searched the restrooms, then headed north toward Seal Rocks. Sometimes Emma and I would stand on the beach beneath the Cliff House and listen to the seals; she liked their high-pitched barking, the way they craned their necks and lolled over each other like lazy sunbathers. But I got to the end of the beach and she wasn't there. That's when I remembered the first lesson of being lost, the one thing children are always taught to do: stay in one place until someone finds you. Only then did I think of the parking lot, my car, Emma's highly logical nature. She is not the kind of child to panic. Of course, I thought, she would have gone back to the car to wait for me. I ran.

I'm not sure how many minutes passed before I climbed the embankment toward the parking lot, a new hope surging up in me. Of course Emma would be there, standing by the car, a little upset with me for having lost sight of her. Maybe she'd be crying, or, more likely, pouting. Or maybe she'd be sitting on the hood, sifting through her bucket of sand dollars. She would be there, I was certain. This girl whom I had come to love would not be lost. Tragedy, in its full and life-altering form, happened to other people. Girls like Emma did not disappear. They didn't drown or fall victim to kidnappers. My panic was unfounded. And later, I thought, when the danger had passed, I would tell the story to Jake. We would sit around the table, a threesome, a family, and Jake and I would look at one another without speaking, filled with wonder, feeling grateful, never acknowledging aloud just how close we had come to the unspeakable.

It only took seconds to locate my car, a heart-wrenching instant to see that she wasn't there, another to realize I'd left my cell phone at home. That's when I headed toward the nearest building, the Beach Chalet, furious with myself for not making the call from the Cliff House.

Now I know that a few crucial moments could have changed everything. But those decisions are lost to me forever. The simple fact is that I did everything wrong.

'What were you thinking?' Jake says late on the third night, lying in bed, unable to sleep, no parts of our bodies touching. 'It's Ocean Beach, it's a monster.'

'It was just a few seconds,' I say.

'But Ocean Beach isn't like the beaches where you grew up. You have to respect it. Haven't you felt the riptide? Haven't you seen the signs?'

Of course I have. Wooden signs posted every mile or so, with dramatic warnings. *Intermittent Waves of Unusual Size and Force. People swimming and wading here have been swept to their deaths.*

'I know she's still alive,' I say. 'I know she didn't drown.'

He turns away. 'We don't know anything.'

★ ★ ★

At four in the morning, I wake to find the bed beside me empty, the downstairs lights ablaze. Jake is in the kitchen, standing at the counter, staring at a pot of coffee. It occurs to me that nights will always be the most difficult. We can fill our days with activity, with searching and phone calls and the organization of volunteers, but at some point we have to go home. Every night until Emma returns will find us like this, trapped and helpless, waiting for morning to come.

'How early is too early to start calling people?' he asks.

It is raining. Down the street, a traffic light flashes red. Each flash lingers for a second on the wet asphalt, making the world seem sad, restless, insomniac. A large man in a black T-shirt and jeans stands in front of the Laundromat across the street, alone.

'Mary!' the man shouts. His head is tilted down slightly, as if this woman to whom he is speaking is standing by his side.

From the kitchen comes a sliding sound, a soft thud, and I turn to see Jake sitting on the floor, hugging his knees, shoulders shaking. He lets out a long moan, a helpless sound dragged up from the gut. I go into the kitchen, kneel on the floor, and put my arms around him. I ache to give him something, but I can't fathom anything that would make up for the horror I've caused.

'Where could she be?' he says.

Where? The sheer number of possibilities hits me with a paralytic weight. It's impossible to know where to begin. I see, as if through the lens of a movie camera, a circle on the beach. A woman stoops to have a conversation with a child. They part and the lens pulls away, taking in a spot of something white and dead on the beach. The clock ticks. As the lens rises higher and higher, the circle expands to include the entirety of the beach, the ruins of the Sutro Baths, the Great Highway, the broken windmills, the furry bison grazing in the park, the Golden Gate Bridge, sailboats strewn like white buttons across the blue fabric of the bay, rows of brittle houses dotting the hills of Daly City, the vast graveyards of Colma, the long bleakness of Pacifica. The lens continues to rise, the search area grows with frightening speed.

'Her friend Sven was having a birthday party tonight,' Jake says. 'They were supposed to go to Sea Bowl.'

'We'll take her when she comes home,' I say.

47

'The odds — ' Jake begins, but is unable to finish his sentence. He's referring, I know, to the statistics Sherburne gave us yesterday: 60,000 non-family child abductions occur each year. 115 of these are long-term kidnappings by strangers, the kind that make the news. Of the 115 victims, half are sexually assaulted, forty percent are murdered, and four percent are never found. But fifty-six percent — 64 children — are found. In my mind there is no question: Emma is one of the 64. She simply has to be.

9

After sundown on the fourth day, I park my car at Fort Point at the base of the Golden Gate Bridge, about five miles north of where Emma disappeared. I walk along the waterfront, looking for clues on the narrow, rocky beach. I'm not sure exactly what I'm looking for — an article of her clothing, her yellow barrette, some unlikely message scratched in her childish hand?

The last time I was here was with Emma and Jake, about three months ago. I have a picture of her standing at the foot of the bridge, gazing up at the enormous arcade that was rushed to completion on the eve of the Civil War. At six years old, Emma was already shaping up to be a student of history, full of questions about the soldiers who once occupied the brick fort — where they slept and what they ate and whether or not their parents got to come live in the fort with them.

I stop at the Warming Hut to give flyers to the clerk. A little farther on, I walk out onto a floating pier. A man stands at the edge, perfectly still, fishing line slack in the water. Beside him is a cooler, empty except for a single fish lying in a bed of ice. The fish lifts and lowers its head, and a shudder wracks its silvery body. 'This is my little girl,' I say, holding the flyer up. 'She's missing.' The man is watching my lips, not my eyes, and I realize that he's deaf. He shakes his head and turns back toward the water. In a moment of disconnect, a second outside of time, I wish Emma was here with me, because she's been learning sign language in school. As quickly as the thought comes to me, I'm aware of its absurdity. In the weeks following my mother's death, I found myself reaching for the phone to call her before remembering that she was gone. It's like this with Emma — each time I turn around, I expect to see her there.

Around midnight I end up at the Palace of Fine Arts. The ducks in the pond are silent. Wind blows through the columns, bitterly cold. In the moonlight, the carvings of weeping women atop the columns seem lifelike, as if their tears are made of something more than stone. Tucked away among the urns and statues are homeless people in tattered sleeping bags. I approach them one by one, handing out dollar bills with the flyers, hopeful that one of them might know something.

A few hours later I walk into my apartment in Potrero Hill without turning on the lights, feel my way up the stairs, kick off my shoes, and stumble into bed. It seems I've just closed my eyes when the phone rings. It's my sister Annabel, long-distance from Wilmington, North Carolina.

'What time is it?' I ask, reaching for my glasses.

'Seven a.m. in your part of the world. How are you holding up?'

'Not so well.'

'I wish I could come to San Francisco,' she

says, and I know she means it. She would give anything to be here, helping with the search. Once an avid traveler, she hasn't left Wilmington since her youngest child, Ruby, was diagnosed with a severe form of autism last year. Ruby is five years old, a sweet but distant child who communicates with an elaborate system of hand signals. Ruby can hardly stand to be touched, and her sensitivity to sound is so exaggerated that the phones and doorbells in Annabel's home don't ring, they blink.

'What can I do?' Annabel says. 'Do you need money?'

'I have a little in the bank.'

'How much is a little?'

'Not much. I've canceled all my jobs for the next month.'

'What's your rent?'

'Holding steady at twelve hundred, thanks to rent control.'

'Look,' she says, 'I'm going to transfer twelve hundred into your checking account on the first of every month until this whole thing is over with.'

'Every month?' I ask, my heart sinking. 'It's terrible enough to imagine another week without knowing where Emma is. I can't even fathom the idea of this stretching on for months.'

'I hope you find her tomorrow, but this gives you one less thing to worry about.'

'I can't take your money, Annabel.'

'No argument. Rick just made partner. Case closed.'

'Thank you. I'll pay you back.'

'Abby,' she says, 'are you okay?'

'Everything was coming together,' I say. 'Everything seemed so perfect.'

I tell Annabel how I went over to Jake's early Friday to help Emma see him off. He was spending the weekend in Eureka with Sean Doherty, a roommate from college who had recently divorced. Sean was in the throes of depression, and Jake went to his rescue, leaving Emma in my care. This would be our first weekend alone together, a kind of test. When Jake returned, he would tell Emma about our plan to marry.

That morning, Emma and I had French toast and hot chocolate at Tennessee Grill. After breakfast we made a rag doll from a kit, with patchwork knees and blue buttons for eyes, thick black yarn for hair. In the afternoon, we saw an animated movie about a sickly girl of indiscriminate nationality who befriends a horse and saves her village from destruction. Emma had too many Swedish Fish, and on the way home from the theater she got a stomachache and began to cry. Learn to say no, I thought, as I reached over and rubbed her back.

At my place, I gave her a glass of water, and she curled up next to me on the sofa while I read to her from *Old Hasdrubal and the Pirates*. She fell asleep with her head on my shoulder. I sat for some time reading silently, lost in the comfort of my favorite book from childhood, loving the weight of Emma's head against my shoulder. When I picked her up and carried her upstairs to bed, she opened her eyes drowsily, just long enough to say good night.

I changed into my pajamas and crawled in bed beside her. Watching her sleep, I felt content. Perhaps motherhood was something I could do — or if not motherhood, then this other thing, stepmother, this role that was somewhere between motherhood and friendship. Emma was a willful, sometimes wild child, just as I had been, but in sleep she was deceptively calm. I thought of my own mother, who had me at the age of twenty-two, and I pictured her standing in the doorway of my bedroom in her short cotton bathrobe, her red hair pulled back in a ponytail, as I'd seen her do every night of my childhood. I wondered if she too had felt, as I did now, suddenly mature, suddenly at home in the world, possessed of great responsibility.

'It was the first time in so many years I felt a connection with Mom,' I tell Annabel. 'I felt like I was finally beginning to understand her. I wished she was alive so I could share it with her.'

No matter what successes I met in my career, what interesting turns my life took, I knew my mother had always considered me ill-accomplished, not quite grown. Without a husband and a child, to her I was simply a girl adrift.

'Did I ever tell you what she said to me toward the end?' I ask Annabel. 'When I was back home taking care of her, she made me promise to find a good man, somebody who wanted children. And I did the dumbest thing. I made the promise, but I kept my fingers crossed behind my back, because, back then, I didn't really see children in my future. Not that I was opposed to having them; it just wasn't a priority. What kind of person lies to her mother on her deathbed?'

'I'm sure you're not the first,' Annabel says. 'Anyway, she probably knew you were faking it.'

'But the weird thing was, I actually lived up to the promise. I found Jake, fell in love with him, fell in love with Emma. Sometimes I get this uncanny feeling that Mom was orchestrating the whole thing from outer space, like some big cosmic joke.'

'I wouldn't put it past her.'

I tell Annabel about how Emma and I got up early on Saturday to make pancakes. 'I earned points for letting her crack the eggs and stir the batter. I actually thought of it that way, you know? I felt like, with Emma, I'd started with all these marks against me: I wasn't her mother. Jake was spending time with me, when she was used to having him all to herself. I didn't have the faintest clue how to make a little kid happy. And each thing I did correctly was a point in the positive column. I figured the more points I got, the more she'd like me.'

'She does like you, Abby.'

'No, that's not even it. I wanted to make her love me. I felt like every minute we spent together was some kind of test.'

Finally, for the first time, I tell Annabel the whole story, not leaving a single thing out: how I felt a slight tinge of happiness when I saw the dead seal pup. What a great picture it would be. What a fine opportunity to comfort Emma and teach her some sort of important lesson about

54

the transience of life. I even tell her how I smiled at one of the guys in the parking lot — a surfer, waxing his board beside a yellow van. How my smile was maybe a tad too friendly, how I wondered, just for a second, what it would be like to kiss him.

'It's not a crime to think about kissing someone,' Annabel says.

'I know. My point is, maybe I wasn't all there. I should have been concentrating on Emma. Maybe if I'd been more focused, this never would have happened.'

'You can't put yourself through this,' Annabel says.

I think of the sympathetic young policeman who tried to console me that first night at the station. 'It could happen to anyone,' he said. This, I know, isn't true. It couldn't have happened to Annabel. It couldn't have happened to Jake. It would not have happened to either one of them, because they would not have looked away.

10

My neighbor Nell Novotnoy believes that books can save us.

She lives next door in the loft of her dead son, Stephen. Six years ago, when he died at thirty-five, he left her the loft, which he had paid off during the gravy years of the dot-com boom. Now, Nell's wrecked face gazes out from big banners attached to lampposts all over the city. She is a spokesperson for the AIDS Walk campaign, the Quilt of Hope, and the Mothers for AIDS Research Foundation.

She's also a librarian and has worked at the Mechanics Institute Library on Post Street for thirty years. Every Monday, she stops by with a book she has chosen specifically for me. Thanks to Nell, I've been introduced to John Fante and Josef Skvorecky, Halldor Laxness and Lars Gustafsson, the diaries of Robert Musil and the essays of Edmund Wilson. Name almost any author, and she can name a title. Mention any year, and she can identify the winners of the major literary prizes.

Six days after Emma's disappearance, I knock on Nell's door. Her apartment is warm and smells unmistakably of her home-made macaroni and cheese. For the past week she's been leaving casseroles and cakes at my door, offering to do my laundry, help in any way she can. Now, she ushers me to her kitchen table, pours me a cup of coffee.

'Talk,' Nell says, pushing a thick lock of black hair away from her face. 'I'm a good listener.'

'I keep trying to figure out if there's something I missed that day,' I say. 'Something I saw or heard but can't remember. Something that seemed insignificant at the time but could lead me in the right direction. I feel like I've got this key that will unlock the mystery, but it's buried underneath tons of rubbish, and I have no idea how to find it.'

'Do you know what Saint Augustine said? 'Great is this power of memory, exceedingly great . . . a large and boundless inner hall.' '

She gets up to take the macaroni out of the oven, fills two bowls, and hands me a fork. 'Eat.'

I know in my mind it's delicious — the same macaroni and cheese I would have dropped everything for just a week ago — but now it seems to have no taste, and I struggle to get it down.

'You've lost weight,' Nell says, spooning more macaroni into my already full bowl. 'I know food's the last thing on your mind, but you can't run on empty.'

She finishes her own bowl, then goes to her bookshelves. 'Memory is a science,' she says, rummaging through the titles. 'Gobs of stuff have been written about it.'

Within minutes the kitchen table is piled high with books and file folders. There are books about how the brain stores information, photocopied articles on memory retrieval, writings on the art of mnemonics by Aristotle,

Raymond Lull, and Robert Fludd.

'You've just got all this stuff lying around?'

Nell shrugs. 'Once a librarian, always a librarian.' She flips through the books, marking a few pages with Post-it notes, showing me diagrams of the brain — the elegantly curved hippocampus, the almond-shaped amygdala, the mysterious temporal lobe. 'It's in here,' she says, tapping my head. 'This is where you'll find the answer. It's well documented that traumatic or emotionally trying events wreak havoc with memory, so that information stored in the brain becomes very difficult to access. But the information is still there. You just have to figure out how to get to it.'

Late that night, sitting alone at my place with a pencil and notebook by my side, I delve into Nell's books. In a recently published volume called *Strange Memory*, by a renowned professor of psychology named Stephen Perry, I come upon the story of Sherevsky, the man who could not forget. Perry references the classic work *The Mind of a Mnemonist*, wherein the Russian neuropsychologist Alexander Luria refers to his patient Sherevsky simply as S. It strikes me as odd that a man with so many memories would be reduced to a single letter.

What did S. remember? Every word of every conversation, stretching back into childhood. Every meal he had eaten, every sound he had heard, every feature of every face he encountered. While amnesiacs have no ability to remember, S. suffered the impossibility of forgetting. Any page of text, any conversation, was a minefield; a single word would cause an avalanche of memories that made it impossible to complete his train of thought.

Imagine a street in any city, on any given day. Now, imagine that a walk down this street leads to thousands of permanent memories. For you, there is no such thing as the short term, no such thing as the forgettable. You will remember every storefront, every person standing behind the glass, each individual stance. Say this street is home to a bookshop. Walking past the shop, you glance in and see a few titles on display. Forever after, you will remember not only the titles, but also the covers of the books, the order in which they are arranged, the woman standing in line to make a purchase, the tilt of her head as she turns and sees you. You will remember the color of her lipstick, red, the shape of her leg, slim and long, lifted slightly, the black leather sandal sliding off her heel. You will remember, too, the man behind the cash register, his haircut, the gold watch he wears. You hurry on ahead, aware, as you do so, that in the previous seconds you have supplied your memory with thousands of impressions you will have to carry with you until you die. Walking, contemplating this truth, you stub your toe. You look down and see the culprit — a raised spot in the sidewalk. This, too, will be your memory: the imperfection in the sidewalk, the painful sensation in the toe, the image of your own shoe in motion. And you will not be able to forget the fact that, on that

59

particular day of that particular year, in that exact location, you were contemplating your own curse, your lifetime of remembering.

What is a search if not a dual exercise in hope and helplessness? It is hope that makes the search possible, helplessness that makes it simultaneously absurd. I want to believe that, buried deep within the gray matter, inside the complex folds of cerebral cortex and corpus callosum, hippocampus and amygdala, there exists a single detail, a minute piece of knowledge, a precise and crucial memory, that is sufficient to save a missing child.

Like Funes, the memory-laden hero of Borges's famous story, the one thing S. desired most was simply to forget. What I want, above all, is to remember, to see with absolute clarity the events of that day on Ocean Beach. I would gladly trade a lifetime of memories — birthdays and Christmas mornings, first dates and splendid vacations, wonderful books and beautiful faces — for the one memory that matters, the one that would lead me to Emma.

11

The command post is housed in the Castro, in an empty shop space that was donated by a good Samaritan. Passersby are greeted by Emma's eyes, staring out from dozens of flyers papering the windows. Volunteers sit at long tables, stuffing envelopes and answering phones. Everyone is wearing the same uniform: a white T-shirt with Emma's face on the front, and under the picture, the words *Have You Seen Emma?* On the back, in large black letters, an 800 number, and beneath that, *www.findemma.com.*

Most of the volunteers are Jake's students, but there are others: teachers, friends, a few people I know from the photography world, strangers who responded to our postings on craigslist.

One week has passed since Emma disappeared. While I've been out frantically searching the streets, running one direction and then another, Jake has been organizing the troops. His approach has been methodical, rational, planned — as is his approach to everything.

A grid map of the Bay Area, dotted with multicolored pushpins, covers most of one wall. Phones ring, voices rise and fall. A pimply kid with perfectly combed hair is giving instructions to a group of teenagers.

'Post these flyers anywhere you can in the shaded area,' he says. 'Coffee shops, bookstores, supermarkets, you name it.' He passes around a shoebox filled with buttons bearing Emma's photo. 'Wear these. Take a few extra to pass out. We want her face to be on everybody's mind.'

The group disperses, and the kid comes over and shakes my hand.

'Abby Mason,' I say.

'I know,' he says. 'I'm Brian.' He has the overconfident yet somewhat charming demeanor of a class president or chairman of the Young Democrats. 'Do you want a canvassing zone, or are you here to see Mr. Balfour?'

'Both.'

Brian gives me a stack of flyers and a map. 'Our Colma person didn't show up. Had a track meet. You can fill in.' He produces a photocopied map, blocking out a tiny portion with an orange highlighter. Each square inch of the map represents ten square miles. I imagine my square as a vast maze filled with shops, apartments, houses. Ditches, Dumpsters, cars, bushes.

Jake spots me and comes over.

'Anything?' I ask.

'Not since we last talked.'

That was half an hour ago. We've been living on our cell phones. A constant back and forth, exchanging information, encouragement. There have been dozens of leads, but the cops don't know which ones to follow. Some guy in Pescadero thought he saw her in a Chinese restaurant at the same time she was spotted by a jogger in Oakland, a 7-Eleven clerk near Yosemite, and a postal worker in San Diego. Jake's ex-wife, Lisbeth, still hasn't been located.

'I hope they're together,' Jake told me when

62

this whole thing began. 'I never thought I'd say that, but, God, I hope they are. At least — '

He didn't finish his sentence, but I knew what he was thinking. If his ex-wife was behind it, at least Emma would still be alive.

I'm remembering what Sherburne has said more than once, in regard to Lisbeth: 'It's not so easy to find someone who really doesn't want to be found.'

Emma's-face stares back at me from Jake's T-shirt. To me she looks like Emma, with her low, long-winded laugh, Emma who can go from happy to moody in five seconds flat, Emma who loves peanut butter and honey sandwiches on toasted sourdough bread; but to strangers she must look like any number of black-haired, green-eyed, dimpled girls. Do the phone calls draw us closer, or do they lead us farther away? Emma could be in Pescadero or Oakland or Yosemite, or she could be twenty yards from here, locked in someone's apartment, drugged and dizzy. The flyers say 'Black hair. Green eyes. 4'0". Last seen wearing a red sweatshirt, blue pants, and blue Paul Frank sneakers with EMMA stitched onto the toe.' But the kidnapper could have easily cut and dyed her hair, changed her clothes. She could be with her mother, frightened but relatively safe, or she could be with some psychopath.

Jake surveys the room, then sits down on a desk and presses the palms of his hands to his eyes. He must wish he'd never met me. I want to wrap my arms around him and tell him that I'm sorry, that I know we're going to find her, but there are too many people, too much noise. As the hours drag on, as the search area grows, so does the distance between us.

When we first met, we were both astonished by the number of things we had in common. It went far deeper than a mutual affinity for the Giants and our ability to quote Woody Allen films. We each lost a mother to cancer. We each had a father who dropped off the map, albeit for different reasons: Jake lost his to alcohol, while I lost mine to his new wife and young family, his overwhelming desire, following the ugly divorce from my mother, to start over again.

On our fourth date — a visit to a William Eggleston exhibit at SF MOMA followed by dinner at the Last Supper Club — Jake and I talked in depth about our families. 'When you're an adult, you're supposed to just accept that your parents are gone,' he said, 'but it was never easy for me to do that. Being a grown-up doesn't exempt you from feeling like an orphan. I think that's one reason I was so devastated when Lisbeth left. I decided a long time ago that family was going to be my first priority, and when she left I felt like a failure. There Emma was, three years old without a mother, and I couldn't help feeling that it was my fault.'

Looking back, I think that night was the first time I allowed myself to consider the word *love*, the first time I accepted how deep my feelings for Jake were. After that, everything moved so quickly, and suddenly we were talking about marriage, and it seemed like the most natural step in the world.

In the weeks before all of this happened, the wedding was foremost in my mind. Now, of course, it no longer matters. Yesterday, the subject came up for the first time, and Jake and I agreed that the wedding should be postponed. The word neither of us spoke aloud was *indefinitely*. All of our hope is concentrated on some unfixed point in the future, the precise dot on some invisible timeline when Emma is found. In the moments after she disappeared, I was certain that point would come within minutes. As the day stretched on, I amended my hope to allow for hours. By the next morning, I had prepared myself for days of desperate searching, days of unknowing. And now, as those days proceed with no sign of her, no clue, we are left with the unfathomable possibility that this horror may go on for weeks.

As I leave the command post, a stack of flyers tucked into my bag, a song comes on the radio, some catchy number I can't get out of my head, a Wilco tune that's been everywhere the past couple of weeks. Even though I've been humming the melody, I never before noticed the lyrics.

'Every song is a comeback,' the voice sings. And then the chorus repeats over and over, so catchy and so depressing, 'Every moment's a little bit later.' I look at my watch and do the calculations, pi times radius squared, a series of numbers ticking off in my head.

★ ★ ★

I haven't set foot in Colma in years, for good reason. It's nothing but endless second-rate shopping centers and chain restaurants, four-lane roads and no sidewalks. I post flyers at Burger King and Cost Plus, Pier 1 and Home Depot, Payless Shoes, Marshalls, and BevMo. The clerks, for the most part, are friendly and concerned. At Nordstrom Rack, a pregnant woman asks for extra and promises to put them up in Westlake. 'Those poor parents,' she says, running a hand over her enormous stomach. 'I can't imagine.'

Around midnight, after talking to hundreds of shoppers, showing Emma's picture to anyone who will look, I come to Target. It's the only place in Colma that's open this late. The store is alarmingly bright. At the door, a greeter pushes a basket my way, and in exchange I give her a flyer. She takes a pair of glasses out of her pocket, pushes them up her nose, and says, 'Cute kid. Breaks your heart. It's been, what, a week? She's probably in a ditch somewhere.'

I wander the wide aisles, giving flyers to a dozen late-night shoppers. At some point, I find myself standing face-to-face with Dream Time Barbie, who is dressed in a flannel nightgown and fuzzy slippers, a clear plastic bag slung over her arm. The bag contains a comb, shampoo bottle, and tiny eye mask. I put Dream Time Barbie in my basket. Suddenly, all the plastic and garish colors that would have seemed crass to me just last week look wildly appealing. I add a red Nerf ball, a clear jump rope filled with purple glitter, the board game Operation, and a

66

battery-operated dog that barks, rolls over, and fetches. Even the gender-specific toys I've always hated are suddenly enticing: the Easy-Bake Oven, Barbie's Malibu Mansion, a microphone and speaker set featuring the Spice Girls.

I'm carrying my loot to the checkout when a television in the electronics department catches my eye. Emma's picture appears in a small box to the right of Leslie Gray. 'Martin Ruiz, a former English teacher at the school where Jake Balfour teaches, has been brought in for questioning. Ruiz was admitted to the psychiatric ward of Kaiser Permanente last February and later released.'

I know Ruiz, who attempted suicide following an ugly divorce — thus the bout in the psych ward. Jake invited him over for dinner a couple of times. Ruiz struck me as a deeply depressed man attempting to hide his sadness with jokes and a bit too much alcohol. I immediately liked him, as did Emma, for whom he built an impressive house of cards on the living room floor after dessert. I'm sure he's got nothing to do with this — nothing about him struck me as strange or untrustworthy — but then I realize I can be sure of nothing. I was certain Emma would be safe with me, certain that when Jake came back from his trip we could be a happy family. Everything I've known, all the basic rules, have been rendered meaningless.

A boy of about sixteen is standing in the headphones aisle, watching the televisions, dressed in Target red. His name tag says Pete. 'Need help finding anything?' he asks.

'No, thank you.'

Pete looks at the television. 'My mom can't get enough of this story. She thinks the dad's involved, says it's just a little too convenient that he was out of town the day the kid disappeared. My money's on the crazy English teacher. What about you?'

The store starts to swirl, and I lean against the counter.

'You okay?' Pete says, reaching over to steady me.

I leave the basket and make my way toward the exit. 'Hey,' Pete says, following. 'Hey, you want this stuff?'

The parking lot is nearly empty. Neon signs cast eerie shapes on the glistening asphalt. A woman walks toward the door, pushing a row of shopping carts. There must be twenty or more, a long red snake, rattling as it goes. A car full of kids speeds through the lot and swerves just in time to avoid the carts. The woman shakes her head and curses, the driver shouts something obscene in response, and a snippet of music wafts from the car windows. It's that Wilco song again.

12

Several years ago, I visited New York City with a girlfriend to celebrate her thirtieth birthday. A guy I knew from college, someone I once loved intensely, was living there. We hadn't spoken in many years, though I had thought about him often. I didn't have his address, and his phone number was unlisted. That didn't stop me from looking for him everywhere I went: Dean & Deluca, a ballet at Lincoln Center, the Shakespeare Garden, the C train traveling uptown.

Twice, from a distance, I believed I saw him, but when I got up close, it turned out to be someone else. I began to wonder if I would even recognize him these ten years later. What if he had gained weight, or cut his hair short, or developed a fondness for business attire? Was I fooling myself to think I would know him from his face alone, the arch of his eyebrows, a certain gesture? Was I looking for him, or for the person he was ten years before? I began to wonder whether I had already been near him unaware, whether I had sat next to him at a restaurant or brushed arms with him on the street.

Emma, now, is everywhere. Every time I round a bend, every time I open the front door of my apartment, every time I go to the bank. I haunt the parks and playgrounds, restaurants, cinemas. I visit the grimy motels of the Tenderloin, the four-star hotels at Union Square, the chaotic shops of Chinatown, the trendy cafés of North Beach. No female child of Emma's approximate height is exempt from my curiosity and my hope. I wander up and down the hills of Noe Valley, peering into faces of children on their bikes. I go to health clinics the city over, searching the glum faces in the too-bright waiting rooms. I hike the hills of Oakland.

On the morning of the tenth day, I drive out to Point Reyes, climb to the top of the lighthouse, and scan the surrounding beach and ocean with binoculars. On the way down, I watch for a small foot or hand sticking out of a nook in the tower. On day eleven, I comb the Laundromats and burger joints of the Richmond, the crammed residential streets of the Sunset. That night, I spend ten hours straight riding Muni from one point to another, crisscrossing the city like a madwoman, quarters jingling in my purse. On the twelfth day, I do BART. On the thirteenth, Caltrain.

On day fourteen, I take the cable car out to Fisherman's Wharf, push my way past tourists buying postcards and saltwater taffy. I order crab and sit at a sidewalk café, watching the crowd. The faces of strangers take on murderous features. I spot a man coming out of a souvenir shop. He's in his fifties, pale, wearing jeans and a tasteful sweater. Under one arm, he holds a package wrapped in delicate white paper. Even as I follow him, I know this doesn't make sense. I know the chances of this man being the kidnapper are about twenty billion to one. I know I'm behaving irrationally, and yet I can't stop myself. I walk close behind, but not close enough to attract his attention. I follow him to Ghirardelli Square, into a café where he orders a cup of coffee and a piece of lemon cake. Then down to Pier 39, where he settles on a bench to read the *Chronicle*. Finally a Sausalito ferry arrives and the passengers disembark. An attractive Italian woman in an unusual red hat pushes toward him through the crowd. After they hug, he hands her the gift. I walk away, feeling lost and utterly foolish.

On day fifteen, I wander the Embarcadero, up Stockton, left on Montgomery, and climb the narrow stairway past quaint apartments with slanted doors, up to the top of Telegraph Hill, where Coit Tower stands in the center of Pioneer Park. Inside the tower, I circle the lowest level, with its larger-than-life murals, soft shapes, and brilliant colors — women picking calla lilies, broad-shouldered men drinking pints of ale at polished bars. I take the winding stairway to the top and look out at the streets sloping down to the bay, the Golden Gate Bridge, the island of Alcatraz. From here, the water looks calm and pleasant, perfectly safe.

Outside at the refreshment cart, I order a Coke and hot dog. I pay the vendor and hand him a flyer. 'I lost my little girl.'

He moves a pair of glasses from the top of his head to his face, holds the picture up close. 'I saw her on TV,' he says. 'I feel for you. I do.' He gestures toward the stack of flyers in my hand. 'You got some extras there? I'll be happy to pass them out. I sell lots of hot dogs, talk to lots of people.'

On day sixteen, I rent a bike near the Presidio and ride it out to China Beach, Fort Point, over the Golden Gate Bridge, and into the towering Headlands. I take a room for the night at a youth hostel perched over the roaring Pacific and poke around the empty hallways. Over a breakfast of eggs and toasted sourdough bread, I show Emma's picture to a dozen backpackers. They listen sympathetically to my story, say they'll keep an eye out, then return to animated conversations about scoring cheap hash in Phuket and getting dysentery in Bombay.

Day seventeen, near Alamo Square, I slink around dark bars that reek of pot. I visit tattoo parlors and head shops before heading toward the Upper Haight, where I post Emma's picture at pricey boutiques, show it to a group of tourists standing outside the Grateful Dead house on Ashbury. I wander the vast aisles of Amoeba Records, where Jake and I used to come to unwind, and pass out flyers to the hipsters waiting in line. In Cole Valley, I question florists and waitresses, work the back patio at Reverie, and talk to the clerk at Cole Hardware who's been selling me a tiny Christmas tree each year for the past decade. Everywhere I go, I pass out my phone number indiscriminately, urging strangers to call me if they see anything. Everyone has the same thing to offer: sympathy, but no answers.

On day eighteen, I pace the quiet alleys of Chinatown, looking like a stranger in a sea of

Chinese faces. Old men in no hurry, with hands clasped behind their backs, stop and stare. On Waverly Street, the clatter of dice drifts from behind the closed doors of gambling houses. I become a tourist in my own city, an observer of neighborhoods, a watcher of faces, a spy. San Francisco, which has always seemed so small, now feels impossibly large, a vast topography of irrelevant things, all working in tandem to obscure the truth. I have no idea what I'm looking for, no inkling of where I should look, what street, on what day, and at what time. Emma is everywhere, and she is nowhere.

Jake, meanwhile, is pulling farther and farther away. Most nights I sleep at his place. He insists that I stay there while he goes out in his car, searching. 'Someone needs to be here, just in case,' he says. In case what? It is as if some part of him believes that Emma will just walk up to the door.

When he returns from these nighttime searches, his clothes are dirty, his hair a mess, his eyeglasses smudged. His transformation has been so rapid, so complete, that if you were to put two photos side by side — one of him three weeks ago and another of him today — they would look like photos of two different people. I know he is trying not to hate me, trying not to blame me. But sometimes I'll catch him staring at me — across the table in the morning when we're drinking our coffee and planning the day's search, or at night as he's coming out of the bathroom, his body still steaming from the shower — and what I read in his face is nothing like the look of a man who has found the woman he wants to marry. It is a look of confusion, anger. I know he would easily trade all our months together, all our plans, for just one more second with Emma. I am startled to realize that I would do the same.

13

An orange Chevelle. New paint, old tires. Windows halfway down. The Virgin Mary dangling from the rearview mirror. In the driver's seat, a man. Gray hair. Blue shirt, five o'clock shadow, reading the paper. I saw the headline as we passed: *Relations with China Strained*.

'Look,' Emma said. She pointed to an army of ants carting a tiny, dead sand crab across the pavement. She crouched over the procession, mesmerized. 'Where are they taking him?'

'Home.'

'Oh,' she said. 'They're going to look after him.'

'That's right,' I said. I was marveling at her endearing innocence when she did something unexpected: she took her red plastic shovel and brought it down hard against the crab, crushing the shell. The ants stopped moving.

She looked up at me, gleeful. 'I killed them!'

'You did.'

But then the shell began moving again. This time, she lifted her foot and stomped both crab and ants to oblivion. 'There,' she said, swinging her yellow bucket. We continued across the parking lot toward the beach. I glanced over at the man in the orange Chevelle. He was still reading his paper, drinking his coffee. There was a hula girl ornament on the dashboard, which he kept tipping back and forth with his finger as he read.

Each day, I seem to remember a bit more of the man's face, another small detail about his car: a scratch on the hood, a yellow stripe down the side. But the clearer the details become, the more I doubt my own memory. Memory, it seems, should become more impressionistic as time passes, the lines going soft, the colors muted, one shape blending into another. Instead, what begins as impressionism moves steadily toward close-up photography, until one is left, ultimately, with alarming specificity. How many of these specifics are true, and what have I simply conjured?

During my freshman year at the University of Tennessee, I took a required course in collegiate study methods. The first half of the class was devoted to memory. I have forgotten most of it, but one thing that sticks with me is the relationship between physical space and memory. A student who sits in the same desk every day will retain information better than a student who moves around. If one is at a loss as to the specific order of some event, it generally helps to return to the place where the event occurred. By viewing the layout of the place and the various details of setting, one's temporal memory may be jogged. And if you lose something, you should retrace your steps, back to the last place you remember having possession of the lost object.

It is with these things in mind that I make a daily pilgrimage to Ocean Beach. Emma went missing at 10:37. I return each day from 10:00

to 11:10, to allow for about a half-hour window in each direction. It's not only my own memory I hope to recover as I retrace our steps, day after day. I'm looking for the orange Chevelle, the yellow van, the motorcycle, the postal truck, anyone who might have seen Emma on that day. I'm looking for clues.

I find a lot of things along the cold gray stretch of sand, but never what I'm really looking for. At the intersection of Sloat Boulevard and the Great Highway, among the bits of concrete and stone that make up the jumbled seawall, I come across an uneven slab of stone bearing a faded inscription. I can just make out the words *in memory* and *died 187* . . . the last number has been rubbed away.

I'm reminded of a bit of history Jake shared with me early in our courtship. In the 1800s, Ocean Beach was the outer edge of a vast sweep of sand dunes stretching several miles inland. The area, known as the Outside Lands, belonged to Mexico. It wasn't until 1848 that the U.S. government annexed the Outside Lands; almost twenty more years passed before it was made part of the city. Still, to San Franciscans, the remote beach, with its dense fog and uninhabitable sand dunes, seemed like another country. For the rest of the century, the Outside Lands were home to saloons and cemeteries.

After a 1901 law prohibited burials within city limits, the cemeteries fell into ruin. By 1950, all had been closed, and most of the bodies had been moved south to Colma. The City Cemetery, a grave for paupers and minorities, was razed in 1909. After removing the unclaimed gravestones, the city put them to practical use. At Buena Vista Park, one often comes across strange words and dates inscribed in the stone gutters. Old photographs of Ocean Beach show sandy hillsides covered with discarded headstones — a makeshift seawall.

In 1912, construction of Lincoln Park Golf Course began atop the old City Cemetery. A few times, Jake and I played golf there. We took Emma with us — she loved the long walk over green hills, the amazing views. From the 17th fairway we could see Golden Gate Bridge and the mouth of the bay. I often wondered if the golfers were aware of what lay beneath their feet. In 1993, during a renovation project, 300 corpses were unearthed. Among the buried belongings were dentures, rosaries, and Levi's. The discovery led city officials to look into what had happened to the 11,000 bodies interred at the City Cemetery. They could not be accounted for in Colma. They could not be accounted for anywhere. They appear to have simply been left behind.

14

The Holga lens is exactly opposite of what a true optical quality lens should be. It is constructed of cheap plastic, and often has inherent distortions. The result is an unpredictable, soft focus which imparts its own sense of mood and atmosphere.

— Lomographic Society International

I cannot remember now if Emma was running or skipping. I try to re-create that moment in my mind, the moment she turned away from me. Was she laughing? And why didn't I ask her to slow down? I knew she was going too fast, at too great a distance from me. I knew the image would be blurred. And yet I snapped the picture thoughtlessly, as if it were just any snapshot, expendable. How could I have known it would be one of my last pictures of her?

Now, no matter how many times I print the third photo on the roll from Ocean Beach, no matter how much I experiment with focus and exposure time, burning and dodging to adjust light and contrast, the print always comes out gray and grainy, always vague. In the foreground, the seal pup: white fur dusted with sand, black spots, the C of the spine. In the distance, Emma. The black-and-white film and the softening effect of the foggy light lend the images a mysterious quality, dreamlike.

Each photo is a single moment, seemingly complete, but what is missing is the context: the absence of breath, the utter stillness, the fact of the seal pup's death. What is missing is the kidnapping, which played out beyond my field of vision.

In the days after Emma's disappearance, as my mind wandered to a million terrible places, I imagined her trapped in the wet depth of a wave, tumbling in the dark, breathing salt water into her lungs. I imagined the awful panic she would have felt as the water pulled her under. But I know this isn't what happened. Jake and I had taken Emma to the beach dozens of times before that day. Never once had she gone near the water, not so much as to put a toe in. What Jake says about Ocean Beach is true — the waves are wild and unpredictable — but still, in order to have drowned, Emma would have had to wander very close. It simply isn't something she would have done.

15

It's day twenty, eleven p.m., and I'm on the phone with Annabel again.

'Where are you?' she asks.

'The casting pools.'

'What?'

'In Golden Gate Park.'

'Are you out of your mind?' she says. 'It's not safe.'

'I have mace.'

'But why are you there?'

'The police say they've covered every inch of the park, but that's not possible. It's too big.'

Emma, Jake, and I came here together once, on a Saturday, for a fly-fishing lesson. It's part of what makes Jake such a good father — his insistence that Emma constantly experience new things. That day the three huge cement pools were glassy, lit by sun streaming through the conifers. Tonight they are shrouded in mist. I remember how Emma held my hand tightly that day, standing several feet from the pools, and asked, 'Is it deep?'

My voice sounds strange in the quiet of this place. I don't tell Annabel about the large trapdoor at the west end of the pond, how I tried the heavy cover and was surprised to find it unlocked, how I lifted it, aimed my flashlight into the darkness, and cautiously made my way down the damp steps. I don't tell her that as I lay awake last night, I thought of the ponds, and the trapdoor, and I imagined Emma crouched down below, shivering in the dark, captive to some maniac.

I called her name as I made my way down the steps. My own voice echoed back. I reached bottom, found nothing.

Now I hold in my hand a tiny wooden fly, painted an iridescent purple, with white feathers and strangely luminescent fur. Feeling its faint weight in my palm, I peer into the darkness of the ponds. Would it be possible to conceal a body there?

'I want you to walk back to your car right this minute,' Annabel says. 'I'm not letting you off the phone until I know you're safe.'

I walk past the stone lodge, through the paths of lavender and rosemary. In the distance, the copper dome of the new de Young Museum rises above the tree line, glittering strangely in the moonlight. I get in my car and pull the door shut.

'Is it locked?' Annabel asks.

'You sound like Mom.'

She sighs. 'God, you scare me sometimes.'

I start the car and head toward home. I used to love driving through the park at night. In the dark, it seemed less like an urban oasis than some jungle at the edge of the world. Now, it just looks dangerous, like some hideout for misfits and murderers.

'Hey,' Annabel says, 'I've been wondering. Do you remember Sarah Callahan?'

'Of course. I'd completely forgotten. Then,

82

when all of this happened, she immediately came to mind.'

'I think about her all the time,' Annabel says. 'Did I ever mention she used to let me cheat off her paper during math tests? She only did it because she wanted so desperately to be friends. Just a couple of weeks before she disappeared, she invited me to go to a movie to celebrate her birthday. I made up some excuse to get out of it.'

Although I had rarely spoken to Sarah, I remembered her face. We went to a small private girls' school where everyone knew everyone else. Cliques were clearly defined, and one stuck to one's own group religiously. What set Sarah apart was that she had no group. As far as I know, she had no one.

'She used to bring this red Tupperware lunch box to school,' Annabel says. 'It had smaller pieces of Tupperware inside it. Every day she'd spread the little boxes out on the ground — her sandwich, her chips, her cookies — and take a bite from each item, one after the other, until everything was gone. She wouldn't have anything to drink until she'd eaten every last crumb.'

One Tuesday toward the beginning of the spring semester, the headmaster came into our classroom and asked if anyone had seen or talked to Sarah on the previous day. No one answered. 'Think,' the headmaster said. Still, no answer. 'Okay,' he said somberly. 'Carry on.'

That afternoon, he went to every classroom and asked the same question, receiving the same blank response. By the end of the day, news had circulated that Mr. and Mrs. Callahan had last seen Sarah early Monday morning, when they both left for work. On Monday night, the Callahans came home late from a dinner party, and Sarah wasn't there.

The bus driver reported that Sarah hadn't been at the bus stop on Monday morning. On Tuesday afternoon, two policemen showed up at school, along with Sarah's parents, and came around asking questions. I don't remember much about Sarah's parents, only that her father seemed distracted and her mother was wearing a thick blue scarf, even though it was hot out. All the girls had different theories. Maybe Sarah had been kidnapped by a serial killer. Maybe she had run off with an older guy, someone in his twenties, who was her lover. Maybe she was on a bus bound for New York City, where she would fall into a life of prostitution or become a Broadway star. Maybe her parents knew something they weren't saying.

In the days following her disappearance, Sarah enjoyed a new-found celebrity. A few weeks later, though, the novelty had worn off. The teachers stopped mentioning her, and the students, over time, pretty much forgot. In April, her body was discovered in a stand of oak trees at Blakeley State Park. The cord that had been used to strangle her was still looped around her throat, and she was naked below the waist. The man who killed her, having left behind telling clues, was quickly arrested. When she was found, not a single teacher at the school said anything about it; perhaps they thought it was better to let her death pass unmentioned. It was as if she had never existed.

'I've always wondered if there was something I could have done for her,' Annabel says now. 'I remember this policeman on TV a couple of days after she disappeared. He said that with every passing day, the chance of finding her alive dropped drastically. By the time a month had passed, it was as if the police had given up. But when they arrested the guy who did it, he revealed he had kept her alive for seven weeks. We all should have been out there looking.'

Had Sarah been popular, it's likely the school would have banded together to find her. We would have met at the Delchamps parking lot, with several concerned parents acting as chaperones, and we would have roamed the city in groups, handing out flyers, knocking on doors. We would have held candlelight vigils. We would have cried for her. Instead, Sarah passed quickly from our collective memory, into an even deeper obscurity than when she was among us.

'Why are you telling me this?' I ask.

'Because you can't make the same mistake we made with Sarah.'

'The police keep pushing their theory that she drowned. Even Jake is beginning to give it some credence.'

'You have to trust your instinct, to hell with what everyone says.'

There's a child's voice in the room on the other end of the line. 'Alex honey,' Annabel says, 'what are you doing up?'

'Must be late there,' I say.

'Say good night to Aunt Abby.'

Alex's sleepy voice comes on the line. 'Night, Abby.'

'Good night.'

Then, as if he's just remembered something, he says, 'When can I meet Emma?'

'Soon,' I say, swallowing hard.

Annabel comes back on the line.

'You haven't told them?' I say.

'I keep thinking I won't have to,' she says. 'I keep thinking that if I just wait long enough, all of this will be over.'

'Me too.'

'I'll call you tomorrow,' she says.

16

On the afternoon of the twenty-third day, I walk into Jake's house unannounced. The house is strangely quiet, except for a teakettle whistling on the stove. I go into the kitchen and turn off the burner.

'Jake?'

No answer.

I walk upstairs. I'm standing in the hallway when I hear a voice, just barely, not a voice in conversation but rather a faint, monotonous chant. I look through the open door into the dimness of Jake's bedroom. He is kneeling by the bed, his back to me, his elbows moving slightly. The floor creaks under my feet and he turns, startled. His face is wet. He is holding a rosary.

'Oh,' I say 'Excuse me.'

He nods and holds my eyes for a moment, then turns his head and resumes his incantation. I shut the door and stand in the hallway, my back to the wall, startled by the formality of the moment. As long as I've known Jake, he has not been a religious man. He grew up Catholic but abandoned the church in his teens when he took a serious interest in philosophy.

I think of the Southern Baptist churches of my childhood, the low drone of the preacher's voice during the invitation. 'Jesus is calling. What are you waiting for?' he would say, while behind him the choir in their long white robes swayed slightly, singing 'Come as You Are.' I smelled the oversweet scent of my mother's perfume, felt the slight pressure of her hand on my back. I was certain the preacher was looking straight at me while he stood on the steps in front of the pulpit, waiting.

I knew exactly what my mother wanted: for me to step away from the pew and walk the long aisle down to the front of the church. She wanted me to take the pastor's hand, to weep as he put his arm around me and led me to salvation. If I could do that, if I could stand before the congregation and make my profession of faith, she would love me completely. But as much as I desired to hear God's call, I couldn't. So I stood there, week after week, year after year, hearing the soft voices of the choir, smelling my mother's perfume, feeling her hand in the small of my back; yet I did not go. I waited for the Holy Spirit to whisper in my ear, but the longer I went without hearing it, the more certain I became that I never would.

Now, standing outside Jake's bedroom while he prays and weeps at the foot of the bed where we have made love so often, I feel that old familiar longing, a desire to be touched in some deep place by the mysterious hand of God. No, it is not God I desire so much as the communion faith might bring me — communion not with a higher power, but with the man I love.

Throughout childhood, my inability to hear God's voice made me separate from my parents; it set between us some high wall that was impossible to scale. Even Annabel had a moment

88

in her youth, before rebelliousness set in, when she walked to the front of the church, held the preacher's hand, wept and prayed, and was declared saved. No matter what rifts grew between her and my parents — and there were many — I knew they would always think of her as the daughter who had been saved, the daughter for whom there was hope, while I would forever be some alien creature they could not understand.

The next day, Jake persuades me to go to mass. It's is the last place I want to be, but I don't have the right to refuse him anything now.

In a cavernous church a few blocks from Ocean Beach, we kneel and stand, kneel and stand, while a man in long strange garb speaks softly. During Communion, Jake touches my elbow, urging me to go. I follow him into the aisle and wait my turn in line. Jake kneels before the priest, makes the sign of the cross, and takes the wafer onto his tongue. The church is cold, the organ is loud. I look at Jake, the pale skin of his bent neck, the sweet dark fringe of hair, and realize I no longer know him.

In turn I kneel, make the cross self-consciously, open my mouth to a stranger's hand, and taste the salt of the man's finger. The wafer is dry and bland, the carpet rough beneath my knees. Looking up into the expressionless eyes of the priest, I feel as if I am committing some grave offense. I follow Jake to another priest, who wipes the rim of a heavy silver cup and holds it to my lips. The organ drones on.

Afterward, in the car, Jake says, 'I feel it all coming back.'

'It?'

'Faith.'

'Are you sure you're not just reaching for something that will make things easier?'

'Maybe. But that doesn't mean it isn't real.'

We come to a red light. A woman crosses in front of us, three children following at her heels. One of the children, a little girl, looks up at us and grins. For a moment, the pale hair turns black, the face becomes familiar, and I am smiling not at a stranger's child but at Emma. In a fraction of a second, the illusion ends.

'You must have felt something,' Jake says, looking at me hopefully.

'No.'

'It doesn't happen overnight. Come to mass again next week.'

'It's a waste of time.'

'It's only an hour.'

The light changes, we creep forward. I open the glove compartment, close it, just for something to do. 'I can't pretend to believe in something that means nothing to me.'

Jake puts the blinker on and turns left onto Lawton. 'We can't get through this alone.'

'We're not alone,' I say. 'We have each other. What happened to your healthy agnosticism? What happened to philosophy?'

He sighs. 'I admit it's a little weird. Don't think I haven't had huge doubts. But I have to figure out a way for this to make sense.'

'Maybe there isn't a way to make sense of it.

The fact is, there are horrible people in the world, one of them has Emma, and it's up to us to find her.'

He pulls into the driveway. The garage door opens, then rattles shut behind us. As we sit in the darkness of the garage, Jake puts his hands in his lap and stares at the ceiling. 'She's very small. One wave could have done it. That would explain why you didn't see anyone on the beach, why you didn't hear anything.'

'There are other explanations.'

'But the police think — '

'I don't care what the police think.' I fight to control my voice. 'She's not their daughter.'

'She's not your daughter either.' He opens the car door, gets out, and goes into the house.

I sit for half an hour, maybe more, smelling the spent oil, the musty scent of newspapers stacked in the recycling bin. In my head, seconds are ticking by, the circle of possibility is widening, as some imagined car takes her farther and farther away from us.

Later, in bed, Jake's fidgeting wakes me. When I put my arm around him, I realize he's drenched in sweat. I pull the sheet down, baring his shoulders. He wakes up.

'You're soaked,' I say.

He blinks and runs his hands through his hair. For a moment he looks at me, I swear, as if he doesn't know me. 'I can't get comfortable,' he says. 'I'm going to sleep downstairs.'

'If anyone's sleeping on the sofa, it's me.'

'No, no. I will. Just for tonight. Go back to sleep.'

He hugs his pillow to his chest, takes a blanket from the closet, and goes downstairs. I can hear him turning on the lamp, settling on the sofa. Then the muted sounds of the television.

When I go downstairs at six in the morning, he's already gone. I know he's wandering the streets as he does every morning. Glancing in the windows of houses and apartments and parked cars, searching. Soon, I will go off in another direction and do the same.

17

Near the end of my first semester at the University of Tennessee, my mother told me a story. We were in the Chevy Impala, pulling a U-Haul packed with books, clothes, everything I had so hopefully carried with me into my new life at the university. My mother had arrived at my apartment the day before and announced she was taking me out of school until the following fall. There was a huge blowup, I refused to go, but she reminded me that I had no money and no job, no way to pay the rent.

What happened was this: she had come across a stash of photographs my boyfriend Ramon had taken of me the previous year. When the photographs were taken, I was sixteen, Ramon was twenty-seven, and the photos were a bold testament to the things we did together. After a long talk with the youth minister at their church, my parents concluded that I suffered from an abnormal sex drive. 'We've enrolled you in a group,' she said that day when she showed up at my apartment.

'What kind of group?'

'A therapy group for sex addicts.'

'Sex addicts?' I asked, incredulous.

'Your father and I saw the photos, Abby. Those things just aren't normal.'

'How could you look at those? They were private.'

I was furious. I didn't want any part of the life she was taking me back to. By that time, Ramon was already gone — killed in a motorcycle accident just a few months before. I could not stand the thought of my parents picking through the remnants of our life together, examining them like some kind of sordid evidence.

We were on the road by noon the next day. We drove in and out of a storm for several hours, one of those erratic thunderstorms so common in the Deep South. One minute we'd be slogging through a downpour, the windshield wipers on full blast, the road in front of us blurred and dangerous, and the next minute we would emerge into sunlight, onto dry road surrounded by endless miles of green. She kept talking, while I stared out at the vast emptiness rolling by and pretended not to hear.

Near Linden, Alabama, the rain came down so hard our windshield wipers were useless, so my mother inched off the highway and pulled into the parking lot of Stuckey's. Inside, we bought two coffees and my mother's all-time favorite snack, the Stuckey's pecan log. There was no one else in the place except the woman behind the counter and a rough-looking truck driver with three gold crosses in each ear. My mother took the side of the booth facing the trucker, so he couldn't get a look at me.

The coffee was burnt and there was no cream, just little packets of nondairy creamer so old it had solidified. As we sat there, damp and exhausted, waiting for the storm to clear, I tried to plan a route of escape. When I left for school

94

in August, I had felt that good things were finally happening. Then, when Ramon died in September, it seemed as though every link to my previous life, with the exception of Annabel, had been severed. Sitting in Stuckey's with my mother, I had the despairing sense of traveling backward in time.

'Do you remember when we went to Gatlinburg?' my mother said, peeling the wrapper off her pecan log.

'No, when was that?'

'You were ten.'

I had been to Gatlinburg once with Girls in Action, but I didn't remember going with the family. My mother was smiling, though, and the memory seemed to soften her, so I didn't admit that I had no recollection.

'We had the best time,' she said. 'We drove through the night, with you girls sleeping in the backseat, and we got to Gatlinburg early in the morning, remember? Our hotel was beside the Little Pigeon River. We took a chairlift to the top of the mountain and had our photo taken at one of those old-fashioned portrait studios. Then we skied down and had hot chocolate in an old caboose that had been converted into a restaurant. The waiter gave you and Annabel free slices of apple cake.'

It sounded so sweet and homey. Gradually, the memory returned to me. As the rain beat down outside and the trucker hummed softly to himself, I traded reminiscences with my mother. It was the first civil conversation we'd had in months. 'The water was freezing,' I said, remembering how I had waded in the Little Pigeon River, where the broad stones were topped with snow.

'Remember taking the luge ride with your father?' she asked.

Of course. I sat in the front of the sled with his arms wrapped around me, and we sped down the mountain, wind rushing past. 'And I got an Indian girl doll at a souvenir shop,' I said, remembering stiff braids, a tiny beaded head-dress, eyes that blinked, and the smell of plastic.

The rain stopped. My mom popped the last bit of pecan log into her mouth, and we went out to the car. 'I'll drive,' I said. To my shock she let me, and I thought things might be different between us now. I thought that, a day or two after we got home, I could convince her to forget the nonsense about the sex addiction classes and let me go back to school. But as we pulled onto the freeway, she clutched the dashboard and sucked her breath through her teeth and said, 'Watch where you're going.' The spell was broken.

We didn't speak for the rest of the ride, and she didn't forget her reasons for bringing me home. As it turned out, I would spend the next several months sitting in a cramped room with a creepy Christian counselor named Sam Bungo and a dozen sex addicts. In my mother's defense, she could not have foreseen that my sexual education would begin in earnest in Sam Bungo's class, that the students would get together on weekends in parked cars and dingy motel rooms. In truth, my sex drive up to that point had been average, nothing special. Then, suddenly, I was spending time with these people who had sex on the brain round the clock. I was like a weekend poker player forced to hang out at a highstakes table in Vegas.

A few years after that conversation at Stuckey's, Annabel used her spring break vacation to visit me in San Francisco. One afternoon, I mentioned the trip to Gatlinburg.

'Where was I?' Annabel asked.

'What do you mean? You were there.'

'I've never been to Gatlinburg.'

'That's impossible. We wouldn't have taken a family vacation without you.'

'I'm calling Mom,' she said. 'I swear you're making this up.'

She dialed Mom's number and put her on speakerphone. Annabel didn't let on to the fact that she was with me.

'Where was I when you took the trip to Gatlinburg?' Annabel asked.

'What trip?'

'Abby says that when she was ten, we all went on vacation. But I'm sure I've never been there.'

There was a long pause. Then my mother said, 'Oh, that. She brought that up? Listen, honey, how's school?'

'School's fine. You're changing the subject.'

'That was years ago. I don't remember.'

'Mom. Why didn't I go?'

I could hear my mother eating on the other end of the line. It sounded like popcorn. She had always been bone thin, but every time I talked to her on the phone, she was eating. We didn't know then that the cancer had already taken root, a little cluster of angry cells multiplying beneath the skin.

Mom took a drink of something and chewed on the ice. 'Can you keep a secret?'

Annabel looked at me and grinned. I turned up the volume on the speakerphone. 'Sure.'

'We never went to Gatlinburg.'

'But Abby said — '

'I know. Swear you won't tell her, but I made it up.'

'Why the hell would you do that?' Annabel asked.

'You may not remember this, but your sister was a very difficult teenager. She thought I was Mommie Dearest or something. I wanted her to have at least one good memory of childhood.'

'So you lied?'

'You make it sound so sinister. I just wanted her to have something happy to look back on, especially after the mess with that child molester, Raul.'

That's when I chimed in. 'It's Ramon, and he wasn't a child molester. He was my boyfriend.'

'What are you doing there?' Mom said. 'You tricked me.'

'It doesn't make sense,' I argued. 'I remember the caboose restaurant and the Little Pigeon River and the chairlift.'

'You must be thinking of your Girls in Action trip.' It was just like her to be so nonchalant after getting caught red-handed in a lie.

'That's impossible. I couldn't have remembered everything wrong.'

'Well, we never went, and that's the truth. But you have to admit it was a good story.'

Later, I took Annabel for drinks at Sadie's. She was perfectly at ease, ordering a vodka martini with a twist like a seasoned barfly and making eyes with some guy in leather pants. 'It's pretty funny when you think about it,' she said. 'I wonder what else she told us that wasn't true.'

That night, I couldn't sleep. Annabel had gone to a party with the guy in leather pants, and I was alone in my studio in the Mission, the noise of motorcycles and rap music throbbing beneath my window. I lay awake staring at the ceiling for a long time, recalling other moments that were part of my version of my life, things I remembered with great clarity: riding a green bicycle through a new subdivision where all the homes were unoccupied, picking pecans with Annabel on our grandparents' land in rural Alabama, steering the boat while my father coached me on a family outing to Petit Bois Island. I wondered how much of it was true. I knew I should take my mother's deception in stride, should just let it be a funny story I'd tell to prove how off-kilter my family was, but instead, I felt tricked. I couldn't trust my mother; worse, I couldn't trust my own memory.

Maybe that's one reason I'm drawn to the medium of photography. Unless a photo has been doctored, if something appears in a photo, it was really there. It's a version of history you can trust, even if it's just history as seen through one person's eyes. Despite the inevitable element of distortion, despite the difference between what the eye sees and what the camera records, a photograph is still evidence, a historical record, a frozen moment whose physical veracity is more accurate than memory.

Even photographs, however, are prone to human error. Again and again, I look at the photographs from that day on Ocean Beach. The last few frames, taken by the young couple in the parking lot about forty-five minutes after Emma disappeared, reveal nothing. When I handed them the camera, I failed to tell them about one of the Holga's quirky features. Whereas most cameras are designed to prevent multiple exposures, the Holga allows you to click the shutter release button as many times as you want without advancing the film. The van does not appear in the photographs, nor does the orange Chevelle, the postal truck, the motorcycle. Instead there are the foggy outlines of cars and blurred faces of strangers, layered one atop the other. In every picture, there is also a finger in the frame, a strand of someone's hair.

18

Here is one piece of the truth, one thing I know: there was a yellow Volkswagen van, gone to rust in places. In the windows hung gauzy blue curtains, pulled to one side. A woman was looking through the window, her face deeply tanned, her blonde hair cut short. She waved at Emma. Emma waved back. Something in the woman's gesture — a tilt of her head, the lifting of her chin as she smiled — struck me as familiar. I felt I had seen her somewhere before.

We were in the parking lot above the beach. It was cold. Waves thundered onto shore. The beach was nearly empty — just a few joggers, people with dogs, the resident homeless, and a couple of tourists in bright orange sweatshirts boasting *I Survived Alcatraz*. Emma was holding my hand and I was feeling extraordinarily well, as if life had, at the age of thirty-two, finally begun. I loved this cold, this salty smell, the foggy gray of a summer morning. I loved this child.

The driver's side door of the van was open. A man was standing there, wearing a navy blue wet suit peeled down to the waist. On his hairless chest was a tattoo of a breaking wave; the wave curled over his right nipple. He was waxing a longboard, which was propped against the van beside him. The board was a faded shade of red with some sort of symbol at the center. The surfer's biceps flexed as he moved the wax in slow circles over the board. He was maddeningly good-looking, even though he clearly could use a bath. His tan was deep and golden, his blond hair badly in need of combing.

'Hello, ladies,' he said. When he smiled, three dimples showed — one on each cheek, one below his left eye.

'Hi,' I said.

He winked at Emma, and she looked to me for direction; she knew, after all, not to be friendly with strange men. I squeezed her hand.

'Hey,' she said to him, flashing that Emma smile, the right side of her mouth raised slightly higher than the left. And then we were out of the parking lot and on the beach. This entire exchange took twenty seconds at the most.

I told these things to Detective Sherburne at the police station the night of Emma's disappearance. I left out the fact that, as Emma and I were walking down the steps to the beach, I imagined how the surfer's hair would smell up close, like salt and sun.

Sherburne nodded, arms folded across his narrow chest. Occasionally he unfolded his arms and scratched something on a yellow pad.

'Difficult to find a vehicle with no license plate,' he said.

'It was yellow. Rusty. Blue curtains in the windows. There was something odd about this couple, I can't put my finger on it. And when I got back to the parking lot after Emma went missing, the van was gone.'

'The Chevelle?'

'Gone. And the postal worker who'd been sitting there, he was gone, too. So was the motorcycle.'

Repeating it for the umpteenth time, I began to question my own narrative — the sequence of events, the minute details. What if, through repetition, my story had been slightly altered, the order changing, one detail replaced by another? Would this be reason enough for the police to discount it entirely? I'd seen this happen before. The parents say one thing one day, something slightly different another, and suddenly the investigation grinds to a halt. All energy is focused on the family, while other leads go untended. I knew the search for Emma would depend on memory, an imprecise art. Her life depended on my getting every detail right, every time.

Sherburne nodded to a photo of Emma that was tacked to a bulletin board. 'Listen, she's a cute kid. People are friendly to cute kids. That doesn't mean they're kidnappers.'

The board covered half of one wall and featured hundreds of faces of children captured in some casual moment — school photos, picnics, playgrounds. The far right side of the board was reserved for the newer cases, those children who had disappeared within the last six months. Each photo had a date scrawled beneath it in thick black ink. Emma's picture was at the top of this section. I was startled to realize that in this sea of faces, hers did not stand out; on the board she looked like just another victim, another missing child.

The far left was reserved for successes — each picture had the word FOUND stamped across it in red block letters. There were also thankful notes from parents, newspaper clippings with headlines like *San Rafael Girl Found*. But most of the faces took up the big middle space — all of the children who had disappeared in California in the last five years whose cases had not been solved. Some of the photos were accompanied by age progression sketches — the hair slightly longer or shorter, the temples broader, the lips thinner. In these sketches, the eyes all had a haunted, waiting look. I wondered where the pictures went after five years had passed. I imagined a huge filing cabinet in some basement room, thousands of photos fading in manila folders, never to be viewed again.

19

Day twenty-six. The meeting is held in a classroom at City College of San Francisco. I arrive twenty minutes early. To kill time, I walk the loop road that circles the campus. The college is sadly urban — a jumble of angular buildings with too few windows, arranged with no apparent concern for aesthetics. On the front lawn, a cement statue of some Catholic saint extends its hands in blessing to Phelan Avenue.

At seven forty-five p.m., I stand at the entrance to Cloud Hall, willing myself to go in. The air inside is damp and stale. The floors are unadorned cement, the walls institutional green. I climb the stairs to the third floor and locate room 316, where a man is arranging desks in a circle. He smiles and extends his hand. 'David.'

'Abby.'

'How long has it been?'

'Three weeks, five days. You?'

'Seven years.'

I do the math. In seven years, Emma will be thirteen, a teenager. She'll be old enough to get her period, meet boys, go to movies with friends. I can't imagine seven years of absence. I can't imagine how this man manages to go on.

'Girl or boy?' he asks.

'A little girl. She's six. What about you?'

'Jonathan would be twelve. What's your little girl's name?'

'Emma.'

He nods. 'Of course. I thought you looked familiar. I've been following the story.'

I should tell David that I'm not just here for moral support, to bare my soul and cry on somebody's shoulder. What I'm hoping to find is of a more practical nature. I want someone who's been there to tell me how to continue the search. I want to know what mistakes to avoid, what these people would have done differently.

David goes over to a table in the corner, scoops coffee from a can into a cone filter. He hands me the coffeepot. 'Mind filling this up at the water fountain?'

My steps echo in the long hallway. It's Wednesday evening and the classrooms are mostly empty. The walls are covered with announcements for English tutors and tae kwon do classes. The water fountain is at the far end of the hall; a piece of chewing gum is stuck to the rim. I'm reminded of an afternoon at the zoo almost a year ago, Jake and Emma and I walking the path beside the tiger cage. The tiger was sunning on a rock. He looked at us and blinked. 'I'm thirsty,' Emma said. There was a water fountain a few feet ahead. 'Race you to it,' I said. I let her beat me, then lifted her so she could drink. She was wearing a sleeveless top, and the skin under her arms was soft and damp.

I had only met Jake a couple of weeks before, and things were moving so quickly. Holding Emma up to the fountain, I understood that if I was going to fall in love with Jake, I must also fall

106

in love with her. Jake didn't come unencumbered; he was a package deal. I marveled at the ease with which she had trusted me, how she held out her arms and waited for me to lift her. I was amazed by the unexpected completeness of this child — how she craned her pale neck to drink from the small trickle of water, how she kicked her legs in the air when she was finished to let me know it was time to put her down. I had never really thought of children as people, just as mysterious and needy creatures on their way to something greater. But standing there, holding Emma, I saw a girl who was already forming her own personality, her own ways of looking at and being in the world. I set her down. She ran back to her father. He lifted her in his arms and swung her in a circle. She let out a howl of laughter. Something kicked in my gut — fear, excitement, joy. *My God*, I thought, *I'm falling for them.*

Back in the classroom, I pour water into the coffeemaker and flip the switch. The water begins to gurgle. 'How do you manage?' I ask. 'How do you keep looking?'

'I don't. Not anymore. We found Jonathan back in October. He was identified through dental records. Buried on a garlic farm in Gilroy.'

'I'm so sorry.'

'I keep coming to these meetings because I need to be around people who know what it's like. When your child is taken, it feels like you're living in a foreign country where you don't speak the language. You open your mouth to say something, and you get the impression that no one understands. The people you knew before — parents of your children's friends, especially — avoid you. You're a walking reminder of their worst fear. It seems that everyone you meet can tell that you're not like them.'

'Maybe we have a certain look,' I say. 'Maybe we give off some scent of tragedy.'

'Cream, sugar?' David asks.

'No thanks.'

He hands me a cup of black coffee, then sits down in a wooden desk. I sit across from him in the circle. It feels like high school again — desks too small, the room permanently out of date, the smell of old erasers.

'Funny,' I say. 'I've taken coffee with cream and sugar all my life. When Emma disappeared, I started taking it black.'

'That's normal. After Jonathan's kidnapping, I couldn't remember to wear a tie to work. My socks never matched. I forgot to trim my fingernails and water the plants and put gas in the car. All the details of daily life become irrelevant.'

He sips his coffee. I look at the clock. It's five minutes before the meeting is scheduled to begin. How far can she go in five minutes?

'Your wife. Does she ever come to the meetings?'

'We split up two years after Jonathan disappeared.' David spreads his hands out on the desk, stares at them, and folds them into fists. 'Everyone in this group is either divorced or separated. Jane and I were the perfect couple, or so we thought. After Jonathan was gone, there was too much pain. We were a constant reminder to each other of what we'd lost. And there's always the blame.'

'How did it happen?' I ask, finding myself drawn to his story the way others must be drawn to Emma's.

'Jane was in Minnesota visiting her mother, and I'd taken Jonathan to the Russian River for Father's Day weekend. We were on a canoe trip with several other fathers and their sons. While I was setting up our tent, I gave Jonathan permission to go look for frogs with a couple of older boys. The kids weren't gone more than ten, twelve minutes. I was putting in the last stake when the two other boys came running out of the woods, panicked. The moment I saw them, I knew something terrible had happened. They'd been approached by a man with a gun. The man, for some reason, chose my boy.'

'I remember hearing about it. The manhunt went on for weeks.'

'Media frenzy. It's creepy, the way people get into the story, but you put up with the pushy reporters and the curiosity because you think it might help. With all those people tuning in to your story on the five o'clock news, you think your child will be found.'

My heart sinks, remembering the droves of volunteers who combed the woods with flashlights and walkie-talkies. *America's Most Wanted* covered the story, as did CNN. There were posters and flyers and candlelight vigils. Even with all that, they couldn't find his son.

'Jane never forgave me for letting him out of my sight. If she had, it wouldn't have mattered, because I never forgave myself. Every morning when I wake up, the first thought that comes to my mind is that goddamn tent. If I'd just told Jonathan to wait until I was finished . . . '

'There was this seal pup,' I say. 'It was dead. I obsess about it every minute of every day. What if the seal hadn't been there? What if I hadn't had my camera? I looked away from Emma for forty seconds, maybe a minute.'

'We're all cursed with that — thinking about the seconds.'

'And then there was this funeral procession on the Great Highway,' I say. 'I had no business stopping to look, but I couldn't help myself. I've always felt the same way about funeral processions that I feel about terrible car accidents — it's depressing, it's morbid, and even though you know the people involved deserve some privacy, it's impossible not to look.'

David nods, taking it in.

'I'm not her mother,' I explain.

'Yes.'

'I'm engaged to Emma's father.'

'I know.'

I wonder if this makes me less in his eyes. No matter how much guilt I feel, no matter how much grief, I can't really understand the suffering of a parent who has lost a child.

'Your fiancé didn't want to come?' he asks.

'He's busy. Command post.'

'And?' David says, as if he can read my mind.

'He thinks the support group is a waste of time. I think he's beginning to consider me a waste of time, too. We used to be so good together, but of course things are different now. And I don't blame him. I just keep thinking that, when we find her, everything can go back to normal.'

'You know the statistics,' David says softly, reaching for my hand. His hand is cool, slightly damp. 'You have to be prepared for the worst.' As he closes his hand over mine, I suddenly regret telling him so much.

A woman appears in the doorway, and David pulls his hand away. The woman's shirt and pants are crumpled, her eyes tired. There's something wrong with her hair — thin in some places, thick in others, a bald spot above one ear.

'Sharon,' David says, standing up. He goes to the door and puts an arm around her shoulder, leads her to the desk. She looks at me blankly.

'Hello,' she says.

'Hi.'

I recognize her. Her story was huge for a few weeks a while back before fading into obscurity. I'm ashamed to realize I had forgotten about the high school cheerleader who vanished from a movie theater one Saturday afternoon, leaving behind no clues.

She tugs at her hair. Several strands come out in her fingers, but she doesn't seem to notice. 'Fourteen months, three weeks, two days,' she says without any prompting. 'Her name is Tanya. She'll be fifteen tomorrow.'

111

20

Among the reading material from Nell is a book entitled *Lost Time: The Problem of Forgetting*. The book contains a quote from Aristotle's essay 'On Memory and Reminiscence': 'It often happens that, though a person cannot recollect at the moment, yet by seeking he can do so, and discovers what he seeks.'

Twenty-eight days after Emma's disappearance, I call Nell at the library and ask for a copy of the Aristotle essay. She brings it to me that night. The search, Aristotle proposes, is best executed in a sequential fashion. 'One must get hold of a starting point,' he writes. A person 'discovers what he seeks' by attempting to recollect an event from beginning to end, 'by setting up many movements, until he finally excites one of a kind which will have for its sequel the fact that he wishes to recollect.'

What I must determine, then, is the 'starting point,' the thing that will lead to 'the fact' or clue — that which I need to recollect. But this method supposes that the seeker has some idea as to the nature of the fact she's seeking, and this is where my search comes to a standstill. I don't know whether I should be attempting to remember the features of a stranger's face, the license plate on someone's car, the sound of a voice in the distance, or something else entirely. The only thing I'm certain of is that I lost Emma and I must find her. The only outcome that is acceptable is this: Emma, home, safe. But everything leading up to that desired outcome, the specific steps I should take to get there, remain a mystery to me.

It occurs to me that my starting point may be wrong. All these weeks, I've focused on those terrible moments at the beach. But maybe the story begins before that, maybe there's something I've been missing because I've been trapped in too small a pocket of time. Perhaps the clue lies somewhere in the days and weeks prior to her actual disappearance. I take out the black notebook in which I've been recording every memory, every detail. The pages are clogged with drawings, graphs, names or identifying characteristics of everyone I have contact with on a regular basis, including the clerk at Trader Joe's, the UPS guy, the woman who walks her Great Dane by Jake's house every morning.

I turn to a clean page and try again to retrace my steps, one by one, beginning with the day before she disappeared. Every store I visited, every person I spoke to, every lunch, every dinner, every client. Sometime in the middle of the night, I wake with the notebook on my lap, both my legs tucked underneath me. When I try to move them, it feels like thousands of tiny pins piercing my skin. I reread the notes — five days' worth of dull minutiae — searching in the mundane details for some element of truth. Nothing.

The next evening, I go over to Jake's house to

stuff envelopes. We sit at the dining room table, not speaking. We've been sending flyers to radio and television stations across the country, police departments, sheriffs, universities. Today, we're working on hospitals. Our time together now is always spent this way — silently, engaged in some rote work, keeping our hands busy. When Jake speaks to me, it is only to say that the reward money has increased or there's been another report of a possible sighting. The reports always lead to dead ends, as do our conversations.

'We should go out,' I say. I'm thinking that if we could get away just for an hour or two, if we could spend just a tiny fragment of time together in some place other than the command post or in this weary house, we might find a way to reconnect, and in doing so we might figure out how to help each other through this.

'What?'

'Just me and you. To dinner. One of our old spots. Park Chow maybe, or Liberty Café.'

'And do what?' he says, looking at me as though I've lost my mind.

'Eat something that doesn't come out of the microwave. Have a drink, relax, talk to each other. We haven't stopped for a moment since — ' I don't know how to finish this sentence. The word *kidnapped* is too terrible, but somehow, *disappeared* sounds even worse.

'I'm not ready to go out. Not yet.' He peels the sticky strip off the lip of an envelope, seals it, lays the letter in the wire basket.

'At the support group, they say you have to

114

keep up some semblance of normality in your life.'

'Normality?' Jake says, his voice cracking. He picks up the wire basket and dumps the sealed envelopes on the table between us. 'Every one of these will be opened by an employee at a hospital, who's going to compare Emma's picture with the unidentified corpses they have in the morgue. And we're supposed to act normal?'

I gather the envelopes and put them back in the basket.

He shakes his head. 'I just feel like everything's unraveling.'

'I'm sorry. I know.'

We return to the silent work of stuffing envelopes. My mind, meanwhile, is somewhere else. I begin where I left off the previous night: five days before Emma's disappearance. I go through my activities one by one — the places Emma and I went together, the people we talked to. Five days, six, seven.

Eight days before it happened: a meeting with a client at my studio. A bridal shoot at the Presidio. Then Emma's cello recital and ice cream at Polly Ann's, where you can either pick your flavor or take your chances by spinning the wheel. Emma, always adventurous, chose to spin, and ended up with Bubblegum Banana. I went with Rocky Road. Emma didn't like hers and, in typical Emma fashion, insisted that we trade. We had some time to kill before Jake was due home. Where did we go?

'Of course,' I say.

Jake looks up, startled. 'What?' There's no mistaking the look in his eyes: hope.

'Eight days before it happened, I had Emma for a day, remember? You had a meeting at school. Emma and I went to the tourist information center across the street from Ocean Beach so she could look at the murals.'

'The place beneath the Beach Chalet?'

'Yes. I guess I forgot about it because we went there so often, it was no big deal at the time. There was hardly anyone there. Just me and Emma, the kid behind the information desk, and this blonde woman. Thirty-five, forty years old — she looked like she'd had a hard life, smoked a million cigarettes. She was talking to the kid, and she told him she was on vacation with her husband. The only reason I noticed her was that she was talking in an unnaturally loud voice. She was wearing these satin sweatpants that made a swishing sound every time she moved.

'The kid asked her how long they were staying in San Francisco, and she said she didn't know. It was a road trip, they were just taking things as they came.'

'What does any of this have to do with Emma?' Jake asks.

'She kept tapping her fingers on the desk, shifting her eyes around the room. Once, her eyes focused on Emma for a few seconds, but she never looked at me. That was it. Then she turned and walked out of the building.'

'I don't understand,' Jake says.

'The woman in the yellow van at Ocean Beach, the one who waved at Emma? I think she

116

was the same woman I saw at the Beach Chalet.'

'Are you sure?'

'I really think so. I mean, I never looked her in the eyes, but there was a very strong resemblance.'

Jake is up from the table immediately, taking the phone from its cradle on the kitchen wall. 'I'm calling Detective Sherburne.'

'Are you positive?' Sherburne asks me a minute later. He's at home, and the TV is going in the background.

'Yes.'

'It's been a month. It's a strange thing to remember this late in the game.'

'I really think it was her.'

'I don't want to be the naysayer, Abby, but one thing I've learned in this job, the later someone remembers something after an event, the less likely it is to be accurate.'

'I'm not making this up.'

'That's not what I meant. I just think your mind might be playing tricks on you. We can make ourselves believe pretty much anything, you know, when we need to.'

'You don't understand. I can see her clear as day in my mind. Anyway, it's the best thing we've got, isn't it? Let me come in for a forensic sketch. I can describe both of them — the woman and the surfer from the van.'

'We don't usually call in a forensic artist unless we have a pretty strong lead.'

I imagine some big ledger hidden away at the police station, where dollars and cents are subtracted each time money is spent. Maybe there's no room in the budget for a forensic artist in a case like this. Maybe they're trying to save their funds for surer bets.

'Do you have a better idea?' I ask.

There's a long pause on the other end. I can hear Sherburne's wife in the background, talking. Maybe she pities me, maybe she just wants Sherburne to get off the phone, but I'm pretty sure I hear her tell him to humor me.

'Okay. I'll schedule a meeting for you with our forensic artist, but I don't want you getting your hopes up.'

'Thank you.'

Before I even hang up the phone, I've already started doubting my own story, looking for holes in my memory. There must be dozens of scraggly blonde women of indiscriminate age who pass through Ocean Beach every day, not to mention hundreds of transient surfer guys. What if Sherburne is correct, and my imagination is just filling in the blanks where actual memory left off?

'God, I hope this turns out to be something,' Jake says, putting his arms around me.

It feels good to have him hold me this way; it's been so long since he did this, so long since he has looked at me with anything resembling tenderness. I wrap my arms around his waist and hold on, breathing in his smell — a mix of fabric starch and something else that is solely him, that sweet, distinctive smell that I used to breathe every night as we fell asleep, my face pressed to the warm skin of his back.

21

Day thirty-three. Her name is Amanda Darnell, and she tells me to relax. She offers me coffee and doughnuts. The doughnuts are still warm, and the sweet smell that fills the room reminds me of Saturday mornings in Alabama when I was a kid, when my mother would take me and Annabel to the Krispy Kreme on Government Boulevard to watch rows of doughnuts, dripping glaze, glide over the big silver rollers.

'They just opened a Krispy Kreme near my house in Daly City,' Amanda says. 'I've gained five pounds in two months. Now they're putting in an In-N-Out Burger, Lord help me.' She's dressed in jeans and a red turtleneck, with feather earrings dangling to her shoulders. She begins by asking me what I do, where I grew up, whether or not I like to cook.

'I'm nothing special in the kitchen,' I confess, 'but I do make these drop biscuits with gravy that would drive you out of your mind. The trick is the crumbled bacon. You mix the bacon right in with the dough.'

'I could go for that right now.'

We're sitting side by side in comfortable chairs, and her sketchbook is on the table in front of her, opened to a clean white page. She has a plastic case full of chalk, pencils, and erasers. This room in the police station is a warm green color, filled with leafy plants in ceramic pots, but no pictures on the walls.

'Do you cook?' I ask.

'I make a decent chicken pot pie.'

It feels good to be talking about something as mundane as cooking, good to be treated like a regular person, not a victim or a criminal. Still, there's no denying what I'm here for. I find myself looking at her hands, the long pink nails and turquoise rings.

'So,' I say, trying to sound casual, 'how does this work?'

'We're going to play Mr. Potato Head.' She lays a slim book on the table between us. 'The FBI Facial Identification Catalog,' she explains. The book contains hundreds of photos of chins and cheekbones and eyes, noses and ears and heads. 'We'll do the woman first, then we'll move on to the guy. Let's start with the head shape. If anything looks similar, point it out.'

I flip through a few pages, past square jaws and short foreheads, egg shapes and circles and ovals.

'There,' I say, pointing to a woman with a narrow face and high forehead.

Amanda starts to draw. 'Talk to me. You're the boss here. Tell me when something looks off.' We move from the head shape to the eyes, deep-set with slightly down-turned corners. 'Like this?' she says.

'That's the right shape, but they were farther apart.'

From there we go to the cheekbones, not prominent, and the nose — narrow, with a slightly rounded tip. She draws quickly, glancing

120

up every few seconds to see my reaction. She draws and erases, softens lines by smudging them with her thumb, leans forward to blow eraser bits from the page. A face begins to emerge, recognizable, and my memory becomes clearer as Amanda draws. Little things that have nothing to do with the woman's face return to me: an empty red stroller parked beside the information booth at the Beach Chalet, a take-out box sitting on the information desk, an overturned tree in the scale model of Golden Gate Park.

When we come to the ears, though, I'm at a loss. I can't remember if they were small or big, protruding or flat, and whether or not she was wearing earrings.

'That's normal,' Amanda says. 'Most people have trouble with the ears.'

The hair is easy: blonde, straight, coarse. Amanda adds shading to the face, then says, 'Show me anything that doesn't look right. Take your time.'

Two hours into the process, we have a completed sketch. 'That's her,' I say, stunned by the accuracy of the picture. 'You're really good. Did you study art in college?'

'I took some drawing classes in school, but my major was psychology. It's not about art so much as it is about listening, asking the right questions. You're not working with your imagination, you're working with someone else's memory.'

She takes a different book out of her bag and lays it on the table — the same type of catalog, but this one is filled with men's faces. An hour and a half later, we have a second sketch. That day at the beach, the man in the yellow van looked so normal, indistinct from dozens of other surfers. Is it the effect of the sketch or is it these long weeks of angry, fearful waiting that make the same face seem less friendly, somehow untrustworthy? The features that appealed to me — his lazy eye and windblown hair, his high cheekbones and full mouth — now seem somehow suspect. Looking at his face, the day comes rushing back: the cold sand, the white fog, the hope I felt walking hand in hand with Emma. And then the panic, the sense of the world turning inside out.

'What happens now?' I ask.

'I'll give these to Detective Sherburne, and he'll make copies for his FBI liaison, who will distribute them to FBI offices all over the country. You'll get copies, too, of course.'

That night at my place, unable to sleep, I take a snapshot of Emma from the photo album, sit down on the sofa, and attempt to draw her. I start with the shape of the face — wide and rounded — then move on to the big eyes with their long dark lashes, the upturned nose, the small mouth. I'm working on one of her errant eyebrows when I stop cold, unable to complete another stroke. At two a.m. I take four sleeping pills. When I wake the next morning on the sofa, my legs are cramped, and my head feels swollen and heavy. The sketch lies in my lap, the poorly drawn features so blurred it's impossible to tell whether the sketch is of a boy or of a girl. It looks nothing at all like Emma. I wonder how long it would take for my memory of her face to fade, how long before I could look at a badly done sketch and not see the inaccuracies.

22

'Tell me something I don't know,' I once said to Jake. We had been dating for three months. I was in love, but hadn't yet told him. We were having dinner at Foreign Cinema, sitting outside under the big white canopy, a heat lamp humming over our table. We had started the evening with oysters on the half shell, and were well into a bottle of chardonnay. *Last Tango in Paris* was playing on the rear wall of the restaurant, a young, confident Marlon Brando dancing in a crowded bar. Emma was at home with the babysitter.

'Long before the Giants, there were the San Francisco Seals,' Jake said. 'For a single season in 1914, they played at Ewing Field, west of Masonic. The place was so foggy that, during one game, a mascot had to be sent to the outfield to tell Elmer Zachar, a player for the Oakland Commuters, that the inning was over.'

'Interesting,' I said. 'But I meant something about yourself.'

'That's more difficult.'

'Think.'

'Okay, I was the runner-up in the National Rubik's Cube Championship, 1984.'

'You're kidding.'

'Nope.'

'Why haven't you mentioned this before?'

'What did you expect? Hi, my name is Jake,

and twenty years ago I was good with a Rubik's Cube?'

'If I were you, I'd slip it into conversation every time I got the chance.'

'The cube just requires patience, and a system. Do you know how many possible combinations it has?' Jake wrote a number on his napkin: 43,252,003,274,489,856,000. The digits got smaller at the edge of the napkin where he was running out of space.

'How do you even say that number?'

'Beats me.'

'Then how do you remember it?'

'I don't remember it as a whole. I remember it by numerical units, each of which has some meaningful association. For example, 43 is the age my father was when he died, 252 is the number of career home runs for Bobby Murcer, and so on.'

'I've never solved a Rubik's Cube. Ever.'

'If I locked you in a room with just a Rubik's Cube and food and water, you couldn't help but solve it eventually. It's simply a matter of mathematic probabilities.'

'The year you were runner-up, how long did it take you?'

'Twenty-six point nine seconds. The world record now is 13.22 seconds. Finnish kid named Anssi Vanhala.' He speared a piece of squid and offered it across the table.

'If you're so good with math, figure this one out. How many minutes do you think it will take for us to pay the bill and get back to your place?'

'This is only a rough estimate, but I'd say

about thirty-four. Plus five to pay the babysitter and get her out the door.' He raised his hand to signal the waiter.

The more I got to know Jake, the more sense it made that he'd been so good at the Rubik's Cube. He approaches everything in his life as a task that will ultimately be completed, as long as he follows through. Everything is methodical and driven by logic. Maybe his belief that the right amount of persistence and planning will allow him to solve any problem accounts for his confidence. This time, though, his plan is falling apart. Five weeks, twenty thousand flyers, a couple dozen radio interviews, 247 volunteers, two 'person of interest' sketches — and still, we are no closer to Emma. Lisbeth has yet to be found, and Jake has all but lost hope that Emma might be with her.

Last night, I went to Jake's house with my bag packed to stay over. I had just been to Channel 4 with the sketches of the couple from the van, but the producer for the six o'clock news said the program was full. It was my third attempt to get them to run the sketches, to no avail. Though she didn't say it, I think the producer believes that Emma is old news.

'What's that?' Jake said, eyeing the bag.

'I haven't spent the night in a while. I thought — '

'Tonight's not a good time.'

'There's not going to be a good time.' I took off my coat and laid it across a chair. 'I don't want to lose you, too,' I said. As soon as the words were out of my mouth, I knew they were the wrong words. I suddenly felt ashamed of the bag, ashamed I'd thought that I could make him forget, for a few minutes at least, how I'd wrecked his life.

'I'm going out,' he said.

'Where?'

'I don't know.'

'Come over to my place later?'

He didn't say anything, just pulled on a jacket and opened the door.

'Talk to me. I need to know what you're feeling.'

He was standing in the open door, one foot inside the house, one foot on the porch. 'I'm feeling like my life is over,' he said, his back to me. 'I'm feeling like I've done everything I know to do, and none of it has worked. I'm feeling like, whatever my baby is going through — if she's even still alive — I can't do a goddamn thing to help her.'

He turned to face me. 'When all of this first started, I couldn't get one thought out of my head — the thought that when I found who did this, I was going to kill him. I vowed to make him pay. The rage helped keep me going. But now it's been more than a month, and I don't have any energy left for rage. I never should have left that weekend, and I never should have given you permission to take her to Ocean Beach. It was a goddamn stupid thing to do, for what? So I could go let some old buddy who'd gotten a divorce cry on my shoulder? And I keep making these crazy speculations, going back further and further in time, thinking of ways it could have been avoided. There was a moment when I even blamed the whole thing on Sean, because he cheated on his wife, which led to her leaving him, which led to my being gone that day. But I'm the one who introduced them in the first place, twenty years ago. It's this endless cycle of thinking what I could have done differently, and it all comes down to one thing: I should never have left town.'

'You couldn't have known. No one could anticipate something like this.'

He moved so that his face was in the lamplight, and I realized he had a tan. A very dark tan, the kind construction workers get. I could see the line at the neck of his shirt where the tan ended, giving way to his natural skin color, which was pallid in comparison. There was a split second of disconnect when I couldn't figure it out, this healthy brown tan that somehow made him look younger, despite the strain and lack of sleep. Then I realized it was because he'd been spending so much time outside, wandering up and down the streets for hours at a shot, searching.

'No,' he said, 'but I should have been there. So tell me what I'm supposed to do. Do I kill myself? Or do I keep living like this for the next fifty years, hating myself, envying every parent I see on the street with their kids? Do you know what goes through my mind when I see girls Emma's age? I think, *I wish it had been her instead of Emma.* I hate myself so much for thinking it, it makes me physically ill, but I can't help it. I wish it was any other kid.'

I flinched as his voice rose, felt something deep in my gut tightening. The Jake I used to know would have never talked this way. But the Jake I used to know was gone, and this terrible transformation was my fault.

'You look horrified,' he said, 'and you should. The kids at school, friends' kids whom I've watched grow up. I go to church and pray, and even while I'm praying my mind is engaged in these calculations, wishing it was any other kid, any ten or twenty kids, instead of Emma. What kind of person does that make me?'

He looked at me for a few seconds, then turned and left, slamming the door behind him. The house was quiet and cold; a faint odor of garbage emanated from the kitchen. I pulled the curtain aside and watched him drive away. I waited until his car had rounded the corner, then went up to Emma's room. She and I used to play this game where we'd sit in her walk-in closet and pretend it was a spaceship. Together, we came up with an elaborate set of rules for the ship: as soon as we closed the door behind us, time came to a standstill; we ceased to age, and we no longer needed food, water, or air. By closing our eyes, we were able to see into the future. In this way we solved mysteries and grew famous throughout the world. I went into the closet, shut the door, and tried our old trick. I closed my eyes and concentrated, imagining myself into a future when Emma would sit there with me. In this future she is the same age as she was on the day she disappeared. In this future she has not changed, nor has Jake. In this future things are just fine, and we are a normal family, leading ordinary lives.

23

Day forty-two. It's late at night and I'm online, answering e-mails at findemma.com, when someone knocks on the door. For a moment, I allow myself to indulge in the fantasy that it might be Jake, coming to spend the night. But when I look through the peephole, it's just Nell.

I open the door. She's in her bathrobe, her hair wet. She smells like mint. 'I know it's late,' she says. 'But I thought you might be interested in this article I just found on forensic hypnosis. Did you know that memories retrieved through hypnosis have in some cases been allowed in court?'

'Decaf?' I say.

She nods. 'Thanks.'

While I'm pouring the coffee — hers black, mine with a touch of Bailey's, a habit I've picked up in the last few weeks — she opens a file folder and pulls out a photocopied article with accompanying photographs. The male face in the first photo is familiar, but I can't place it. Below it is the face of a young girl. She's smiling, looking slightly to the right of the camera. Her hair is styled the same way I wore mine as a little girl in the late seventies — thick, layered bangs swept back from the face.

'Ted Bundy,' Nell says. 'His conviction in the Kimberly Leach kidnap and murder' — she taps the girl's picture with her fingernail — 'was largely dependent on testimony provided by the only eyewitness, a man named Clarence Anderson. Anderson came forward five months after the abduction, but he couldn't remember anything of note. The assistant DA requested that Anderson be put under hypnosis. Afterward, he identified both Bundy and the little girl. He even described their clothing. His testimony was the missing piece that made all the circumstantial evidence come together.'

From the file folder, she produces a business card. 'No pressure,' she says, 'but this gentleman is a friend of a friend. His office is in North Beach.'

The card is white, with a name, James Rudolph, printed in red block letters. Beneath the name is a single italicized word, *hypnotherapist*, followed by a phone number and e-mail address.

'I'm pretty much willing to try anything at this point,' I say.

'Why don't you call him right now?'

I pick up the phone. 'If you told me a couple of months ago that I'd be calling a hypnotist, I never would have believed you.' I dial the number, and a woman answers on the first ring. 'Hello?'

'Oh,' I say, 'maybe I have the wrong number.'

'You looking for Jimmy?' she asks in a thick Boston accent.

'Pardon?'

'Rudolph, Jimmy Rudolph.'

'Yes.'

'One minute.'

There's some shuffling on the other end, and a man's voice comes on the line. 'Yes?'

'I was calling about the hypnosis.'

'Sure,' he says. 'Sorry about the confusion. I'm out of the office today, had my calls forwarded. When are you looking to come in?'

'When are you available?'

'How does tomorrow sound?' he says. 'One o'clock sharp?'

'Okay.'

'Wear something comfortable.' The line goes dead.

'Well?' Nell asks.

'I'm not so sure.'

She shrugs. 'It's worth a try, anyway. It's well known that trauma can impede memories of a given event. Hypnosis is supposed to allow you to bypass your psychological defenses and tap into repressed material.'

She flips through the folder and produces a full-color photocopy of a painting by John William Waterhouse. Two men recline side by side, nearly identical save for their coloring. One is red-haired, pale, brightly lit, slumbering against the other man's shoulder. The second is dark-haired, olive-skinned, shadowed, draped in a funereal cloth. One is accompanied by flutes, the other by a lyre.

'Hypnos,' she explains, 'the Greek god of sleep, shown here with his brother Thanatos, god of death.'

Nell has plenty more to say on the subject of hypnotism — case histories and court precedents, odd ephemera, the two major theories of

133

hypnosis currently in vogue. 'Retrieval holds that all of a person's experiences are stored in a sort of memory bank, and hypnosis helps you access them. Construction, on the other hand, posits that the past is continually remade in the interest of the present, and memories are constructed based on a number of factors.'

I marvel once again at Nell's capacity for learning, her ability to absorb and process a vast amount of information about any given subject on any given day. I cannot help but wonder if her passion for information has something to do with her son's death, if the constant consumption of facts is her attempt to fill a never-diminishing void. I imagine her grief as a black hole, never satisfied, that sucks up knowledge with alarming speed. It is the same ever-expanding black hole that has taken hold of my mind and heart in these long weeks of Emma's absence. While Nell feeds hers with learning, I feed mine with this endless search.

The next afternoon, when I get home, she greets me at the door. 'Well?' she asks.

'The guy was a quack. He had me sit in this armchair that looked like it had been rescued from the Salvation Army. The office reeked of cigar smoke. The session was about as relaxing as a trip to Home Depot. After we'd finished, he tried to sell me on some hypnosis seminar he's conducting next month in Tahoe.'

'That's unfortunate,' she says. 'It seemed like a promising path to try.'

I don't tell Jake about the hypnosis. Alternative psychology doesn't fit into his worldview, and I

134

imagine he'd see the whole thing as an absurd charade, a pointless grasping at straws. But the fact is I'll grasp at anything now, take part in any charade that offers even the most infinitesimal promise. There is no other choice.

24

Once, when we were children, Annabel and I saved our allowance for a month, then sent it to the Everlasting Toy Corporation. We had seen an ad in the back of *Highlights* for miniature sea horses, just $4.95 plus shipping and handling. For several weeks that summer, we sat on the front porch with Kool-Aid and a deck of Uno cards, waiting for the UPS truck to arrive.

But the sea horses did not come via UPS. They came, unceremoniously, in the mail, in a padded manila envelope. When we opened the package, I was disappointed to find that it did not say *sea horses*, but *sea monkeys*, and these monkeys weren't even alive; they were just pale nuggets in a cellophane bag. The aquarium itself was a flimsy plastic number, ten inches tall and six inches wide. The kit came with a little packet of multicolored pebbles, which we scattered in the bottom of the aquarium. Annabel and I still had hope. We dropped the monkeys in and waited for something to happen.

Finally, a couple of hours later, one of the nuggets expanded, then began to wiggle and swim. We did not even bother to name it, for it was clear that this was not a sea horse, it was not even a sea monkey, it was just some kind of mutant shrimp. Within a week, all our shrimp were dead. Our mother dumped the grimy water into the toilet and said, 'Well, girls, so much for Everlasting Toys.'

It wasn't until several years later, on a trip to Marine World with Ramon, that I saw actual sea horses. ' 'Hippocampus,' ' he read, running his finger along the label. ' 'From the Greek words for horse, *hippos*, and sea monster, *campus*.' ' We watched two of them changing colors and performing an elaborate dance. The sign explained that most species of sea horses are monogamous. Each day during pregnancy, the male and female exchange a dance of greeting. After the dance, they separate for the rest of the day.

'Sexy,' Ramon said. The fish transformed before our eyes, their vibrant colors shifting as they moved side to side in graceful pirouettes.

The placard revealed that it is the male sea horse, not the female, who endures pregnancy, fertilizing the eggs in a brood pouch on his abdomen and carrying them to term. Ramon turned me around to face him and playfully pinned my body to the glass. 'I'd do that for you,' he said, 'if you'd marry me.'

'Ask me again in ten years.'

'By then, it will be too late.' He let me go. I could tell he was upset. He wanted the relationship to move faster, to go places I knew it never would. I knew he was too old for me, and that there were things I wanted to do with my life that didn't involve him. I could not have imagined how little time we really had together. I could not have known that, in less than a year, he would be dead.

I'm flipping through one of Nell's books on memory when a drawing catches my eye — a sea horse, in bright blues and greens. The chapter heading is 'The Role of the Hippocampus.' The hippocampus is a curved portion of the brain located in the medial temporal lobe, just above the ear. It got its name because early anatomists believed the structure resembled a sea horse. Although the function of the hippocampus remains, in large part, a mystery, neuroscientists do know that it is crucial for learning new facts, remembering recent events, and transferring new information into long-term memory. If the hippocampus is damaged, old memories remain intact, but no new ones are formed.

I feel as if some invisible line demarcates the space in my mind, creating an unbridgeable division in time: before Emma disappeared, and after. In one portion of my brain there exists an entire lifetime of memories, a complex network of emotional and intellectual information — sensory impressions and remembered voices and mini-movies of important and mundane events — all the stuff of which my personal history is made. Emma is there, and Jake, and Ramon, Annabel, my mother, my childhood. All I must do to relive a happy moment with someone I love is to conjure one among billions of memories embedded there. And yet, I cannot help but wonder why my memory performed so poorly on the day Emma disappeared. What synaptic impulse chose the details to be saved and the ones to be thrown away?

25

Jake and I drive out to the Sutro Baths on a cold morning at the end of August. There are only a few tourists milling about. The place smells faintly of fish, and of the cypress trees lining the adjacent cliffs. Neither of us has mentioned what brought us here. Neither of us dares give voice to our fears as we peer over the edge of the parking lot into the gray ruins, shrouded in mist.

A search team covered this entire area within forty-eight hours of Emma's disappearance and found 'nothing. I've already been out here a couple of times myself. We keep retracing our steps, searching the same places again and again.

The old Sutro Baths sit near the end of the peninsula. The baths, which opened in 1896, were destroyed by fire seventy years later. A green-tinted building with a two-acre glass roof once housed 517 private dressing rooms, six tanks containing almost two million gallons of salt water, and an amphitheater and promenade that could seat more than seven thousand. Now, only the cement footings remain. There's an end-of-the-world feel to the place, as if the apocalypse descended on this small portion of cliff and beach, leaving the rest of the city untouched.

When the tide comes in, the current pulls everything past the baths and into the bay. Things get stuck in the ruins and stay for days before being dragged back out to sea. Looking down into the catacombs, watching the ocean tumble over the shattered seawall, one has the feeling of having stepped into another, darker century. The large circular structure, which once served as a holding tank for seawater being pumped into the baths, is now filled with stagnant rainwater and a thin green layer of slime.

'My dad used to swim here when he was a kid,' Jake says. 'I have a photograph of him standing on a diving board in one of those rented, black wool bathing suits that visitors were required to wear.'

I peer through the binoculars into the cold Pacific. A barge moves through the choppy waves toward the bay. Freight boxes stacked three deep bear giant Chinese characters. I move the binoculars by a fraction and am staring suddenly not into the vastness of the ocean, but into a single catacomb. Things are floating there: a Coca-Cola can, its label faded to pink; some tattered item of clothing; a paperback book, waterlogged. One by one I search the compartments, terrified by what I might see. Those who commit the most horrific acts must find somewhere to conceal the evidence; every few weeks there's another report of a body found in a ravine, a Dumpster, an abandoned building. I do not want to think about the myriad places where a child's body might be hidden, but it's impossible not to think of it, impossible not to envision the most terrible possibilities.

Jake's back is turned to me. Though he

doesn't say it, I know he is praying. Since that day when I went to mass with him, he hasn't pressured me to go again, but I know he's been attending every week, occasionally meeting with a priest. It angers me that he'll pour his grief out to a stranger when he confides so little in me, when he considers the support group to be a waste of time. I was surprised this morning when he called and asked if I would go with him to the Sutro Baths. I was grateful to him for reaching out to me, for trying, in his way, to reconnect.

I scan the ruins one last time. 'Nothing,' I say, relief welling up in my chest.

Jake's whole body relaxes, like a kite string going slack.

We walk the steep path down past the baths. At the end is a dark tunnel cut into the rock. Inside, the temperature drops sharply. There is an echo, a constant drip-drip of water falling from the cave walls and splashing into the shallow pools beneath. A cone of light shines through from the other side. Jake does something he has not done in weeks: he takes my hand. We emerge at the other end of the tunnel. The rocks beneath our feet are slick, and water swirls among them. In the distance, the Marin Headlands roll out toward the sea, their sharp edges softened by fog.

'Do you remember when we brought Emma there?' he asks.

'Yes.'

'She was in heaven when we explored the old fort,' he says, jingling his keys in his pocket. 'Remember how she insisted on going back to the car and getting all her dolls so you could take a picture of them sitting on top of the cannon?'

His voice catches and he puts his arms around my shoulders, holding on. Maybe, if Emma had died, if we had seen it happen and attended the funeral, we could bear to relive the memories. Maybe we could repeat little things she said, recount our outings together in great detail. Maybe, if she were dead, we would discover some language with which to talk about her. But not knowing where she is, not knowing if she is suffering, if she is alone, if she is terrified, makes it impossible. With each pleasant memory that our words conjure, there are other, darker images lurking in the background.

The wind whips Jake's hair around his face, drops of seawater cling to his wool sweater, and we stand silently for a while, shivering, staring out at the freezing water.

From here we can see the antlike figures of surfers bobbing on the waves, waiting. I remember reading somewhere that a swell can travel for thousands of miles across the ocean before it reaches shore. Surfers look so relaxed astride their boards, but the truth is their bodies must be intimately attuned not only to the surface of the water, but also to what's going on underneath. By some magical trick or instinct or vision, they must be alert at the exact instant when the well-traveled swell drags the ocean bottom in a certain way and forms a wave. It seems like some divine accident, that the wave and the surfer should meet at all.

26

The Holga was invented in Hong Kong in 1982. Its name comes from the term *ho gwong*, which means 'very bright.' The camera is made almost entirely of plastic, and its parts do not fit together perfectly. The result is that light leaks through the seams, causing streaks and flashes of over-exposure on the images. Viewing a Holga image is always somewhat disorienting, like stepping into someone else's dream.

The fourth photo on the reel is a double exposure, consisting of two disparate images, layered one on top of the other: Emma walking away from me, and the dead seal, shot from a distance of several yards. The effect is that Emma seems to be floating inches above the seal. Between her small feet and the seal, there is a strip of bright light.

I think about how this image might appear to someone who came across it years later, unlabeled. Unaware of the double exposure, the viewer might accept as fact that these two figures — the child and the seal — existed in that position, in that moment, simultaneously. Perhaps they would imagine that she was leaping over the seal, which would explain the narrow space between her feet and the seal's curved body. They would not suspect that at this moment the child is seconds away from meeting her abductor.

When we view a snapshot — out of context, out of time — we automatically create a story to go with it, a way to make sense of the subject. We are voyeurs, entering into a one-sided relationship with the person in the photo. We see; they are seen. Viewers, as a rule, have the upper hand.

27

September 22. Two months to the day since Emma disappeared.

Thanks to an old acquaintance from college who works at NBC, Jake has landed a spot on the *Today* show with Katie Couric. He took the red-eye to New York last night. On TV, he looks slightly different, although I'm not sure why. As he tells Katie the details of Emma's disappearance and describes identifying characteristics — the small scar on her left forearm, the mole just to the right of her nose — I realize he's wearing makeup. A little foundation, a little concealer beneath the eyes. Yet another transformation, as he becomes, by degrees, less and less recognizable.

NBC runs a home video in which Emma skates down the sidewalk on Rollerblades, waving as she nears the camera. After the clip, Katie Couric's eyes water and she goes to commercial.

'We're looking for Emma's mother,' Jake says at one point. He looks directly into the camera. 'Lisbeth, if you're watching this, I need to talk to you.' There's a strange intimacy in the way he speaks, despite the fact that his plea is being broadcast to an audience of millions. I'm thinking, as he says it, that he's the one grasping at straws. If Lisbeth wanted to be found, surely she would have stepped forward by now. A photograph flashes on the screen. It's a close-up of her face, the same photo Jake gave to Sherburne at the beginning of the investigation. 'One of only a few I kept,' he told me. 'I would have gotten rid of all of them, but I figured one day Emma might want to know what her mother looked like.'

In the picture, Lisbeth has long dark hair, and her face is thin. She's smiling, but it isn't a very convincing smile. The photo has been cropped for television. I remember the original and am aware of what has been left out of the frame — Emma as an infant, lying in a stroller beside her mother. When I first saw the picture, I was struck by the fact that Lisbeth was not looking at Emma or touching her. The picture had been taken outside on a foggy day, and a slim line of white light separated mother from daughter.

I never told Jake that I sympathized with the woman in the photograph. She has dark bags under her eyes, milk stains where her full breasts press against her T-shirt. It's clear from her eyes and her stance that she's still suffering from the twenty-three-hour labor and the emergency C-section, a kind of physical pain I can't begin to imagine.

At noon, Jake calls me from LaGuardia to tell me he's catching the next flight out. 'Maybe this is the break we needed,' he says, his tone guardedly optimistic.

Over the course of the day, leads come in by the hundreds, and hits soar on www.findemma-.com. The following day, over pizza at the Sausage Factory, next door to the command post, Jake talks about all the things we're going to do together when Emma comes home: we'll visit Disneyland, we'll take a cruise to Alaska. I don't remind him that, just days ago, he was convinced that Emma had drowned. He used to be the most even-tempered person I knew, never given to mood swings or drastic shifts in opinion. Now, his perspective changes from one day to the next, and I never know in what state I'm going to find him.

He drops his fork on the floor twice during the meal. Normally a fastidious eater, he keeps getting crumbs all over his shirt. 'You okay?' I ask.

'I haven't slept. In a while. A week, maybe. Last weekend I cleaned out the garage. Can you believe it? The garage, as if it matters! But I'd let everything go for so long, and I've searched every nook and cranny of the city so many times, talked to everyone I can find to talk to. I couldn't sleep, and I found myself walking toward Emma's room, but I just couldn't go in there again. I had to find something to occupy all those hours in the middle of the night. So I cleaned out the garage.'

I know what he means about filling the hours. David from Parents of Missing Children has persuaded me to start working again. 'You don't have to go full throttle,' he said. 'Just a gig here and there, to get your feet wet until you're ready to wade back in.' He says it's the first stage to putting my life back together.

'How can I reconstruct my life when a vital piece is missing?' I asked.

147

'If you can't do it for yourself, do it for Jake,' he said. 'Work will make you calmer. Believe me, after Jonathan was gone, work was the only thing that saved me.'

It occurred to me that maybe he was right. And even if he wasn't, I'd already accepted too much money from Annabel. So last week I reluctantly returned a phone call from a potential client. I decided to start with something easy, safe — not a wedding or a child's birthday party, just a restaurant opening.

After lunch, I visit my favorite photo store, Adolph Gasser. The store looks exactly the same — a jumble of lighting gear in the back, expensive equipment locked away in glass cabinets, some books and digital printing stations in the middle of the store. The only difference is a picture of Emma in the window. The flyer is still taped to telephone poles and shopwindows all over the city, and I imagine that people walking by no longer see it; to them, it is simply a picture of that girl who went missing a couple of months ago — a sad story, but in no way a part of their lives.

Marly is at the high wooden counter, just as she was the day before Emma disappeared. She's twenty-nine, gigantic, heavily tattooed, a grad student at California College of the Arts. In the six years I've been coming here, a seemingly endless succession of photographers-in-training have worked behind the counter.

I find film, batteries, and photo paper, take them to the counter, and hand Marly my Visa card.

'We've missed you around here,' she says, busying herself with the card. 'I'm so sorry about Emma.'

'Thank you.'

She drops my purchases into a paper bag. The bag feels foreign in my hands, like a prop from a play that has finished its run.

On my way back to Muni, I pass a row of televisions in the window of an electronics store, all tuned to the same channel. Emma's face flashes across the screens. Emma's black hair, Emma's dimpled smile, Emma's crooked bangs, in multiple. A sheriff appears, standing at a lectern before a big microphone, a crowd of press and onlookers gathered around him. My throat tightens. Worst-case scenarios flash through my mind: they've found Emma, and she's dead.

A bus screeches to a halt on the street behind me. The crowd surges past. Someone's arm brushes against my back. A girl and her mother stop at the window. The girl is about fourteen, wearing tight jeans and a midriff-baring shirt. 'Any news on the missing girl?' she asks.

'I don't know.'

'A shame,' the mother says. 'Hundreds of kids dying in the Middle East every day, but they focus on this one kid. Because she's white, cute, and American.' She shakes her head and takes her daughter by the arm. They saunter off, shopping bags swinging from their hands.

I go into the store and turn up the sound on one of the televisions. The sheriff is in Morro Bay, about four hours south of here. Behind him stands a row of men in suits and police

149

uniforms, each one straining to stay within the frame of the camera. A red-faced man with a few strands of hair brushed over his bald head steps forward, ostensibly to adjust the microphone, but it's clear he just wants to get closer to the camera.

'We have new information in the Emma Balfour case,' the sheriff announces. My first response is shock, followed by that old familiar panic — heart racing, a kind of tingling heaviness in my skull — then a cautious sense of hope, all of this in the span of a second, while I wait to hear what the sheriff has to say. 'At noon today, a woman came into the station claiming to be Lisbeth Balfour, the mother of the missing girl. We have confirmation that she is indeed who she says she is. She's going to talk to you for a few minutes, following which I'll answer any further questions.'

It takes a few seconds for the information to register. I experience a brief moment of elation, quickly followed by doubt. Why now? I wonder. Why, after all this time, has Lisbeth chosen this moment to present herself?

The sheriff clears his throat again and retreats. The men in suits step aside to allow a woman through. She's not what I imagined. She looks very little like the photograph that was taken almost seven years ago. Judging from Jake's descriptions of her, I expected the sunken eyes of a heroin addict, slurred speech, ratty hair, bruises left by her latest poor choice in boyfriends. But she is nothing of the sort. She's medium height, slightly chubby. Her dark hair is tastefully styled, and she's wearing a subtle navy dress.

'My name is Lisbeth Dalton,' the woman says slowly. 'That's L-I-S-B-E-T-H.'

She pauses, smiles. She's wearing red lipstick, pearl drop earrings, a strand of beads that matches neither the dress nor the earrings. She's attractive in a suburban housewife sort of way, with a small, straight nose — Emma's nose — and a tan. I try to picture Jake with her, but it's impossible. What did he see in her? What could they possibly have had in common?

'I'm Emma's mother,' she says. 'I just found out about this terrible tragedy yesterday when I heard about my husband — pardon me, my ex-husband — being on the *Today* show.'

I know she's lying. There's no way she could have been living in Morro Bay all this time and not heard about Emma. It was all over the news.

Lisbeth reaches up and touches one earring. I suddenly realize that I have an identical pair — Jake gave them to me on the six-month anniversary of our first date. It was a sweet gesture, but I rarely wear them; it's the kind of jewelry my mother used to wear, an emblem of feminine respectability. It occurs to me that Lisbeth's earrings were probably a gift from Jake, too, and I find myself feeling foolish, wondering what other gifts he may have duplicated.

Lisbeth smiles, activating her dimples; the resemblance between her and Emma is unmistakable. 'I just wanted to stand up here today and say to the kidnapper, whoever you are, please give her back. And, Emma, if you can hear me, I love you, sweetie. I'm praying for you. We all want you to come home.'

This from the woman who took a monthlong vacation to Cancun, alone, five months after Emma was born. The woman who walked out on Jake and Emma three years ago and has rarely bothered to phone.

'Were you in contact with your daughter?' a reporter asks.

'Yes,' she lies.

'If you could talk to Jake's fiancée, Abigail Mason, what would you say?'

She touches her earring again, looks straight into the camera. 'It breaks my heart what happened. It tears me apart. But I want that woman to know I forgive her.'

'Given the circumstances, do you wish Emma had been in your custody?' another reporter asks.

'Of course, but you can't second-guess. What's happened has happened. Now we just have to take it from here. We just have to find my baby.'

What comes across as Lisbeth speaks into the microphone is not despair or desperation. Every word, every gesture, seems premeditated.

'If she is found,' another reporter says, 'will you seek custody?'

'That's a strong possibility. I am her mother, after all. Her father and I had our differences in the past, but it's time to put all of that aside and find our little girl.'

Our little girl? I feel a rush of anger, fueled by a possessive streak I didn't know I had.

I call Jake on my cell phone, but he doesn't

answer. I push through the crowd in Union Square, so angry I have trouble focusing on the mundane business of getting home.

I try again to reach Jake at the command post. It's Brian who answers. In the background, the television is going and phones are ringing, and there are voices and more voices colliding against each other.

'Did you see the press conference?' I ask when Jake comes on the phone.

'Yes. I'm stunned.'

'What do you think she's after?'

'Hard to tell. Sherburne's bringing her in for questioning this afternoon. She already agreed to a polygraph.' His voice is hoarse, weary. 'I just kept hoping — '

'I know.'

All this time, Jake has been holding on to some vague hope that Emma might be with her mother, and I allowed myself to entertain this notion as well. At least that would mean she's relatively safe. At least it would mean she's alive. But if Lisbeth were involved, surely she wouldn't be holding a press conference.

This new development feels like a major defeat. Another dead end. Another false hope. The search area widens once again.

'I'm going to come right over,' I say.

'I'm heading over to KQED right now to do a follow-up to the Couric interview. Meet me at my place afterward.'

The line goes dead. Most of our conversations these days go something like this. We never say enough to each other.

I arrive at Jake's place at seven o'clock. I wasn't counting on the car parked in his driveway, a red Cabriolet. I try the front door but it's locked, and, somehow, I don't feel that I should use my key. So I knock. No answer. I ring the doorbell. Jake opens the door, and I know something's off when he doesn't go in for the customary peck on the lips. Despite everything else, this has remained a habit, one thing I can count on: that he will always greet me with a light kiss.

'You've got company?'

He nods and steps aside to let me in. 'Lisbeth's here.'

I don't have time to prepare myself, time to hide my shock. She's sitting on the sofa in the living room, a cup of coffee balanced on her knee. 'Hi,' she says, smiling.

'Abby,' I say.

'Oh.' Lisbeth looks me up and down. 'The fiancée.'

I want to ask her how she could have the nerve to come here and sit on Jake's couch as if she belongs, as if the past three years never happened. Instead, I blurt, 'I saw you on TV.'

'Did you? I was so nervous. I'm no good in front of cameras.'

Jake motions to the armchair by the window. 'Have a seat.' Cordial, as if I'm just some neighbor dropping by 'Coffee?'

'Sure.'

'I'll make a fresh pot.' He disappears into the kitchen.

154

Lisbeth is wearing the same navy blue dress she wore at the press conference, but she has undone the top two buttons.

'What are you doing here?' I ask. It seems, at the moment, like the only logical thing to say to this woman who has simply appeared from out of the blue.

She sips her coffee. 'Pardon?'

'What do you want from him?'

'I don't know what you're getting at.'

'You walked out on him. Worse, you walked out on Emma. Hardly a word from you since you cleared out. Then you cozy up to the cameras like the heartbroken mother.'

She sets her mug on the end table and crosses her legs. Her dress slides up her calf, revealing a large oval birthmark just below her knee. 'You think I have no feelings? You think I don't love that little girl?'

Her eyes are deep green, pretty — Emma's eyes. She leans forward, rolls up her sleeves and stretches out her arms, palms up. Her skin is wrecked, a road map of needle marks and wasted veins. Instinctively I look away.

'No mother who gave a damn would stick around in that condition,' she says, rolling her sleeves down. 'If you'd ever been addicted, you'd know. You can't raise a kid like that.'

Part of me wants to believe her, but this impulse only lasts a moment. Why can't I feel the same sympathy for her that I feel every time I see a junkie panhandling in the Tenderloin? Why do I feel this hardness, this anger, when I look at her? I struggle to keep my voice calm. 'You never even called to see how she was. Not so much as a birthday card.'

'My life was shit,' she says. 'I had to get my act together first.'

'But you had to have known she was missing. How could you not have known?'

'I don't watch TV,' she says. 'I don't keep up with the news. A friend told me about the *Today* show bit.'

'Right.'

Jake returns from the kitchen and hands me a cup of coffee. In the old days, when we played off each other like a couple in a comedy routine, I would have made some crack about what a rotten host he was, leaving the two of us alone to fight it out. But there's nothing funny here, no way to save the party.

'Jake was just telling me where the investigation stands,' Lisbeth says coolly, as if our whole ugly exchange never happened.

He sits down on the sofa beside her. They look like a couple, sitting there, and a history unfolds before me, a family portrait I've never had to confront before. There are no pictures of Lisbeth in the house, no snapshots of Jake, Lisbeth, and Emma together. Jake rarely speaks of her. As long as I've known him, it has been just Jake and Emma, happy together, but not entirely whole. I always had the sense that something was missing from that small family, but it never struck me as a thing that had been there before. Instead, there was a space open and waiting, and I was the right one to fill it. I had relished the idea of entering their family, completing the picture.

Now, observing Jake and Lisbeth together, I recognize something natural in the pairing, something that makes sense. Even though they haven't seen each other in years, there's an ease between them — in the way he leans back into the sofa beside her, the way she reaches over to extract a bit of dress caught beneath his leg.

He closes his eyes. He looks so tired, sapped of strength. I want to go over there and hold him, put his head in my lap and stroke his hair, the way I used to do after he'd had a bad day at work. I want to reclaim that good thing we used to share. But Lisbeth reaches over and squeezes his hand. And I'm not imagining this: Jake squeezes back.

Later, after she's gone, I can't help asking what seems to me the most obvious question. 'So Lisbeth suddenly cares about Emma?'

I feel it again, that possessive streak running through me. I know Emma isn't my daughter, but the love I feel for her isn't small and tidy, it doesn't take into account the proper semantics of our relationship. There is nothing of *stepmother* or *stepdaughter* in this love, nothing so manageable that I can simply stash it away when her biological mother walks into the picture. When Jake and I decided to get married, he broached the subject of adoption. 'Not right away,' he said. 'It's just something we might want to think about in the future.' I was startled but then elated by the possibility, and I stood there in stunned silence, trying to burn the moment into my memory. Now, I don't know how to process this new information, the fact of Lisbeth's presence.

'She really is concerned,' Jake says. 'It's not an act.'

'Come on, Jake. Think about it. She had to have known about Emma from the beginning if she's been living in Morro Bay. So why did she wait until two months after the fact to make her appearance? It's obvious, isn't it? She showed up now because she didn't have a choice. Her picture was on national TV. She knew someone would recognize her. This sudden appearance isn't about Emma — it's about *her*, Lisbeth. You're the one who told me she never thinks about anyone other than herself.'

'I'm not condoning her actions, Abby. I've never pretended to understand why Lisbeth does the things she does. To be honest, I think she's on another planet. She — ' He doesn't finish his sentence, looks away.

'She what?'

'She actually had the audacity to ask if we had a chance.'

'What chance? What do you mean?'

'Me and her, if — when — Emma comes back. She wanted to know if we could give it another go, try to make a family.'

I'm trying not to succumb to this feeling of the ground sliding beneath my feet. It's a physical sensation, like the tremors after an earthquake, that sense of unsteadiness, that feeling of being entirely at the mercy of forces beyond my control. 'That's insane,' I say.

He bites his lower lip, a gesture that takes me

back to the first moment I met him, in the auditorium of his high school. 'It is.'

But I can tell there's a part of him, just the tiniest part, that doesn't think it's such a crazy idea. That's Jake's albatross: he's forgiving to a fault. He has even tried, I know he has tried, to forgive me.

28

The next day, on the way to the restaurant shoot, I'm worried I won't be able to pull it off. Especially now, with the image of Lisbeth fixed in my brain, her words running through my head on continuous loop — 'I am her mother, after all.'

When I arrive at the restaurant, it's already packed. I'm often astonished, on a job, how much of San Francisco seems to be made up of the young and beautiful, the rich and carefree, the perfectly coiffed and tastefully clad. When I moved here in the early nineties, the city was still a little dirty, a little ragged around the edges. It still had, in some ways, the feel of a Western outpost, where artists and writers rented shabby apartments, two to a bedroom, and got their social fix at dive bars in the Mission and the Lower Haight. To be honest, I liked it better the old way, before every bar had a wine list and every twenty-something had stock options.

As I work the crowd, I remember the grand ideas I started with. I planned to take raw, honest photos of illegal immigrants and the urban poor, aging sex workers, single mothers scraping by on minimum wage. After finishing my degree in documentary photography at the University of Tennessee, I moved to San Francisco and rented a studio apartment with bad plumbing and peeling paint in the heart of the Mission. I turned my bathroom into a darkroom, took a job waiting tables at a tapas bar, and spent my free time wandering the streets with my camera. I thought my photos would make a difference, would help people to see one another. Back then, if someone had told me I would end up photographing posh restaurants and corporate Christmas parties, I would have laughed. But it didn't take me long to realize that the kind of pictures I wanted to take didn't pay the bills.

The first few shots are almost impossible, but eventually, I get into a rhythm. I'm little more than a machine, identifying the appropriate scenes, framing the shots, checking the light, focusing, pressing the shutter release. Afterward, driving home through patches of fast-moving fog, I wonder if Emma could forgive me for this: for doing something as mundane as working, taking pictures at a party, when she's still out there, waiting.

29

Day seventy. Bright sun and wild, crashing waves. The highway has been closed for erosion control. Sand is spread across its four lanes, and the traffic lights are blinking red. Jake once told me that, when he was a kid, the Great Highway was a long stretch of smooth ocean road where teenagers would drag race. Now, with the sand moving in thin sheets across the pocked surface, it looks abandoned. A major American city on a Friday afternoon, and on its western edge lies this deserted road, this no-man's-land.

I pull up beside Sutro Heights Park and climb to the top of the parapet, which is all that remains of the grand old Sutro House. From here I have a perfect view of Ocean Beach. It's nothing like the day Emma disappeared. Then, the fog was white and clean-looking, so dense it was impossible to see. Today, I can see down the length of the beach, which stretches three miles south to Daly City. While most of the country is preparing for fall, San Francisco is heating up. This is our true summer, September to October. Telltale black spots bob up and down in the surf along the coast-line — wet suits. When I first moved to San Francisco, I met a man who surfed. Sometimes I'd tag along with him for the drive to Pacifica or Bolinas, where the waves are calmer and a beginner can try his luck; or we'd pick up sandwiches at Joe's Deli and take them down to Ocean Beach, where we'd sit on a blanket and watch more-intrepid surfers battling the wild breaks at Kelly's Cove. My friend could not conceal his awe.

'Unbelievable,' he'd say, watching some veteran gracefully catch an overhead wave. 'I'd give anything to be able to do that.' Anytime a surf flick was playing at the Red Vic, he'd make a point to get tickets to the first showing, and he had copies of *September Sessions* and *Step into Liquid* that had gone blurry and dim from being played so many times. About a year after I met him, he moved back to the East Coast, but not before his admiration for the surfing life rubbed off on me. I never got up the nerve to try the sport myself — something about the speed, and the sharks, and the freezing Pacific. I'd always thought the ocean in this part of the country seemed beautiful but terrifying.

On foot, I head down toward Louis's Diner and the Cliff House, and stand for a minute in front of the empty storefront where the Musée Mécanique used to be. The arcade housed elaborate coin-operated mechanical games dating back to the 1880s. I brought Emma here a few times. She loved the miniature carnival, with its rides that lit up and started moving when you dropped the nickels in. And the Mighty Wurlitzer, with its player piano and mandolin rail, bass drum, and flute pipes. But her favorite was Laughing Sal, a life-size redheaded woman ensconced in glass. Emma would put her quarters in the slot and watch open-mouthed as Sal rolled her eyes and nodded her head, passing her fingers over an

163

array of colorful cards, before a printed fortune was dispensed through a little slot. Emma kept the fortune cards on a bulletin board in her room. They're still there: *You will travel to far-off lands. A handsome stranger will bring surprising news.*

The smell of burgers wafts downhill from Louis's, and I realize I haven't eaten since yesterday. I walk the steep hill down to Kelly's Cove and head south, surprised once again by the day-to-day flux of this stretch of sand I've walked hundreds of times since Emma's disappearance. The beach today is littered with dead fish, a man's drenched sock, an empty toothpaste tube, clumps of seaweed, a broken tennis racket, and rotting driftwood. Every few hundred feet there's another abandoned fire pit, some of the embers still smoking. They're a nightly ritual here, the bonfires around which teenagers drink beer and surfer girls dance and homeless people heat their tins of food. While the Richmond district caters to Russians, the Mission to Mexicans, Pacific Heights to the obscenely wealthy, and Bernal Heights to the granola set, Ocean Beach defies the boundaries of San Francisco's neighborhoods. Everyone comes here, rubbing elbows in the wind and fog.

Today, there isn't a sand dollar to be found amid the natural and man-made detritus. Sticky black patches dot the sand, and the air smells of tar.

About half a mile down the beach I come upon two girls, sisters, about ten and eleven years old, gathering shells by the water's edge.

They're barefoot, laughing, jeans rolled above their ankles.

'Where are your parents?' I ask. 'You're not here alone, are you?'

The taller girl grabs her sister's hand. They stop laughing and walk away, eyeing me with mistrust. I look around but see no adults. Who would allow them to be out here alone?

At the intersection of Judah and the Great Highway, I cross the two-lane highway and go into the public restroom, the same restroom I searched that day in the frantic moments after I noticed Emma missing. A homeless woman is washing up at the sink. Spread on the floor beside her is a makeshift toilette — plastic comb, sliver of soap, new lipstick tube, and a small plastic container of blush. By force of habit, I pull a flyer out of my pocket.

'I'm looking for a little girl,' I say.

She takes a quick glance and hands the flyer back to me. 'No offense,' she says, 'but who isn't?'

I cross La Playa, navigate the circular bit of road where the electric buses of the N-Judah line curl together like a gigantic centipede, turning around for their return trips inland. The wind blowing off the ocean drives sand into the bare skin of my neck. I can hear the roar of the waves, smell the sweet saltiness of the ocean before a rain. Boxy houses in ruined pastels present their haggard faces to the wind. The outdoor tables at Java Beach are empty except for an elderly man with a thick gray beard reading a battered paperback copy of *The Charm School*. The right side of his face is marred by a dark growth the circumference of a silver dollar. Inside, I order an Americano from a towering guy named Darwin with a bald head and a yellow piece of yarn tied around his wrist. 'For my brother in Iraq,' he explained to me once. Darwin has taken my order so many times I suspect he lives at Java Beach.

'Any good news yet?' he asks, punching up my purchase.

I shake my head. 'I have more flyers,' I say, setting them on the counter. It's the ninth stack of flyers I've brought to Java Beach — one a week for the past two and a half months.

I follow Forty-eighth Avenue down the alphabetized streets — Kirkham, Lawton, Moraga, Noriega, Ortega, Pacheco, Quintara, Rivera, Santiago. I've always loved the streets of the Sunset district, the elegant procession of names that roll easily off the tongue. I turn left on Taraval and walk up the avenues toward Dean's Foggy Surf Shop, fingering the manila envelope tucked inside my jacket. I used to come here with my surfer friend what seems like ages ago — he came not to shop so much as to chat, run his hands over the custom boards, see the old-timers and listen to their stories about surfing in nothing but swimming trunks back in the fifties and sixties. There's something vaguely frightening about the young guys who are always lurking out front in blue jeans and flip-flops. They speak their own language, they don't meet your eyes, they look out of place on land. Even in this foggy outback they manage to stay sleek and sun-tanned, their hair saltwater stiff with a kind of Jon Bon Jovi flair. A quarter of them look like off-duty models, and 97 percent of them look like they have rowdy sex on a regular basis.

Inside, behind the counter, there's a petite girl with long brown hair pulled back in a ponytail. She's wearing a *Chicks Who Rip* T-shirt, the neck stretched wide. Her nose is pierced with a tiny blue stud. She puts her hands on her hips and smiles at me when I approach. 'Hey.'

I wonder how old she is. Eighteen? Nineteen? I've never been good with age, have always judged incorrectly, maybe basing it on size rather than years. This girl's punky and compact.

'Hi.'

I take the manila envelope out of my jacket, slide the two sketches out, and lay them side by side on the counter. 'I was wondering if you'd seen these folks.'

'Wow,' she says. 'Are you some kind of special agent?'

'Not exactly. Do they look familiar?'

She looks at the sketches for several seconds. 'No. Who are they?'

'The guy's a surfer, he was at Ocean Beach a little over two months ago. He's traveling with this woman. I was hoping maybe you could post these in the store, ask around.'

'I'll be happy to,' she says. She's not eighteen, I realize. She's more like twenty-three or twenty-four. When she smiles, she has the slightest beginning of crow's feet. She has a little mole on the tip of her ring finger, just above the nail.

'I'm Tina, by the way,' she says. 'But people just call me Goofy.'

I smile as if I understand, but she can tell I don't.

''Cause I surf goofy foot,' she says.

I nod, and she laughs. 'You don't have a clue, do you?' She holds her arms out like she's surfing and squares her legs, leading with the right. 'You know, right foot first, like Frieda Zamba, my idol.'

'Oh.'

Goofy is pretty in an unnerving way, with this one front tooth that's a little crooked, situated at a weird angle to the others.

'So what's all this detective shit?' she says.

'I'm looking for a little girl.'

I tell her about Emma. I tell her about the day at the beach, how I got distracted and looked away — not for long, but long enough.

'God,' Goofy says. 'That's awful.' She pauses, then says, 'I remember that day.'

'Pardon?'

'That day. I remember. I saw the news that night, and I remember thinking how weird it was, them saying that the little girl probably drowned.'

'Weird why?'

'Because the water was calm, just these little mushy waves. Barely an undertow. That never happens at Ocean Beach.'

'What does that mean?'

'Just that it seemed strange for a kid to drown on that day. That morning I went down to the beach with Tina D. from the shop,' Goofy says.

'We call her Tina D. on account of my name being Tina, too, even though I go by Goofy. Go figure. So Tina D. and me, we went out into the water for a while, and we just sat there on our boards waiting for a wave that never came. We must've sat there for a couple of hours. Summer's not prime surfing season around here. Occasionally, you know, you get out there and you know your chance of catching a wave is slim. The thing is, that happens all the time at places like Rockaway and Año Nuevo, but not so much at Ocean Beach. So we're just sitting there, not talking, letting the waves lift us up and down, up and down, and it's this strange, calm day, and I was thinking about the water at my apartment, which had just been cut off because I hadn't paid the bill, and I was about to ask Tina D. if I could come over later and take a shower.

'Then all of the sudden I heard sirens, and I looked back at the beach and saw cruiser lights spinning in the fog. It was weird. I figured maybe it was a drug bust or something, just some kids caught holding in the parking lot. But before long the Coast Guard boat showed up, and that's when Tina D. and me paddled back in. A cop asked us if we'd seen anything, and we told him we hadn't, and then he asked Tina D. out for a date, which was pretty tasteless, considering.' Goofy tugs her hair out of her ponytail, then pulls it back again and says, 'Of course, I'm no expert.'

'But you know the water.'

She looks down at my hands. I realize I've been picking at my cuticles, and now my thumb

169

is bleeding. She plucks a tissue out of a box behind the counter, reaches over, and presses it against my thumb. 'You're hurting yourself.'

'Nervous habit.'

'You're right,' she says. 'I know the water. And for what it's worth, I think it's not the most likely scenario. I mean, sure, Ocean Beach is always hairy, but usually when you hear about a drowning, there's been a wicked rip current. Usually, it makes sense. That day, I remember sitting on Tina D.'s couch and thinking it didn't.'

'That's the best news I've heard in so long,' I say. 'I've never believed that she drowned, but I can't seem to convince anyone that I'm right. Maybe this will help.'

'I hope you find her,' she says. She smiles, exposing that errant tooth. 'Hey, where are you headed now?'

'Toward the park.'

'I'll walk with you. My lunch break started five minutes ago, and I'm going to the Bashful Bull 2. You ever been there?'

'I don't think so.'

'Oh, you'd remember. Let me grab my jacket and I'll meet you outside.'

It feels good not to be alone, just to have someone next to me, walking. These days, I do everything alone, and I wonder whether I'm slowly losing the ability to have normal conversations. My tunnel vision has made me into the kind of person I hate to be around. 'How long have you been surfing?' I ask, and it feels good to ask it, to engage in a give-and-take with someone like Goofy, who doesn't judge me at all, who doesn't look at me and automatically see someone who made a fatal, unforgivable error.

'Since I was eight,' she says. 'My dad taught me, before he ran off.' She looks me up and down. 'You should let me teach you. I bet you could learn. You've got a good surfer's body — strong legs, small on top. But you better not wait too long. There's a statute of limitations on this offer. I'm going to college.'

'When?'

'Oh, I'm not, like, enrolled or anything. But it has to be soon.' She moves with a little dance in her step, like there's some tune playing in her head that only she can hear. 'I woke up a few weeks ago and realized I'm pushing twenty-five.'

'What do you want to study?'

'Marine biology. I'd like to go to the University of Hawaii. I figure I can put myself through school teaching tourists how to surf.' Then we reach Noriega, and she's patting me on the shoulder, saying, 'This is my stop. Want to join me for lunch?'

'Thanks, but I've got some stuff to do. You'll call me if you hear anything?'

'Sure. And you'll have to drop by again. Next time, come before noon. The Bashful Bull 2 has a breakfast special. Eggs, bacon, hash browns, and coffee for three-fifty.'

'It's a deal.'

In the park, I follow the winding path past the lake where Emma and I used to feed the ducks, past the casting pools and the bison corral and the golf course, past a second lake where the

171

mossy trees are draped with mosquito traps tracking West Nile virus. By the time I emerge on Fulton, the sky has gone dark. The young driver of a black Mercedes catches my eye before gunning through the yellow light. Across the road, an elderly man is leaning on a stick, watching the light as it changes from red to green to red again. I head left on Balboa, toward the beach. For years I've been meaning to bring my camera out here and photograph the odd businesses that make their home in the Richmond: the Archery Store, Scissor Man, the typewriter and vacuum cleaner repair shop, Hockey Haven, Gus's Bait & Tackle. Out here, it's like a different city, no hip nightclubs or bookstores, no clothing boutiques or trendy restaurants.

It's after seven when I reach my car. There's hardly anyone on the road fronting the park, just a young couple making out in a Honda Accord and a guy alone in a Jeep Cherokee eating a sandwich and listening to Johnny Cash. It's that Kris Kristofferson song — 'on the sleepin' city sidewalks, Sunday mornin' coming down.'

Driving home, I call Jake and tell him what Goofy said about the rip current.

'You don't know Ocean Beach,' he says. 'That's what I keep trying to make you understand. Even on its mildest day, Ocean Beach is a monster. When my dad was playing for the 49ers, one of the defensive linemen waded out a little too far and got pulled out to sea. I'm talking about a huge, strong guy. The only reason he survived was that he managed to swim for three miles with the current before a fishing boat picked him up.'

'Can't you see this is good news?' I ask.

'I'm just trying to be realistic.'

I call Detective Sherburne, and his reaction is even less enthusiastic than Jake's. 'Let's not jump to conclusions,' he says. 'We know about the wave conditions that day. We covered that base with the Coast Guard at the very beginning.'

'Why didn't you tell me?'

'Because it's a red herring, Abby. You've got to look at the facts. We still don't have a single solid piece of evidence to suggest a kidnapping.'

He's so convinced of Emma's drowning, so certain his theory is correct. Add to that the fact that Lisbeth passed the polygraph, and everything about her story checked out. 'Most kidnappings are by family members, and a huge percentage are noncustodial mothers,' he reminded me after the results of the polygraph came in. 'Lisbeth was our best hope.'

Sherburne would never admit it — neither would Jake — but I know that both of them are close to giving up.

30

Nell stops by with a new stack of books a few days later. She stands in the doorway, glancing over my shoulder, and I know she's looking at the cello on its stand in the center of the room, the rich mahogany I've polished to a reddish gleam.

'Emma only had four lessons,' I say.

'Oh, hon,' Nell says, looking me up and down. She must be wondering about my blue sequined gown, my upswept hair, my costume jewelry. It's ten o'clock on a Monday night; she must think I'm losing my mind. And maybe she's right. I rarely sleep. I eat just enough to keep going. I spend hours alone, day and night, week after week, walking the streets like a vagrant, riding Muni, accosting strangers with my stacks of flyers. Often, I find myself talking aloud to no one, running through the possibilities.

Before all this happened, I thought I was well prepared for traumatic situations. I believed I had some source of inner strength, some deep well of sanity from which to draw. If things got bad in my personal life, I always had my work to turn to. But I can't concentrate on work. Although I've finally lined up a few jobs, my business is falling apart, and Annabel is still paying the rent.

'Emma was planning to do a concert for me that weekend,' I say. 'She insisted on packing her black velvet Christmas dress and patent leather shoes, and she wanted me to wear this old dress — it's from Mardi Gras in Mobile ages ago.'

Nell steps inside my door, lays the books on a table, and reaches out her arms in such a big and motherly way that I lean into her and fall apart.

'You're going to make it,' she says, stroking my back. Then she rearranges the straps of my ridiculous dress, as if I have some business wearing it. 'That's a real pretty fit.' She taps a pink fingernail on the stack of books. 'Read these, hon. You never know what might surface.'

'Thanks, Nell.'

'You just come knock on my door, anytime, day or night, you hear?'

'I'll do that.'

Then she's gone, and I'm alone with the overwhelming space of my loft, which once seemed airy and open and now just feels cavernous and drafty. And there, in the center of it, awash in lamplight and swirling dust motes, Emma's cello. The absence of sound, those cracked, sweet notes that Emma coaxed so earnestly from the instrument, which hid her almost entirely from view when she sat behind it. Of all the instruments she could have chosen, she wanted the cello.

Last spring, Jake and I took her to a San Francisco Symphony concert at Stern Grove. We sat on a big yellow sheet in the grass, and she sipped Coke and munched on pretzel sticks for a solid hour while the symphony played. After-ward, as we were walking to the car, she asked, 'What's the really big guitar called?'

'You mean the cello?'

'The one you play with a stick.'

'Yep, that's the cello.'

'I want to play that.'

The next week Jake found a small version of the instrument, one-fourth the size of a regular cello, at the music store on Haight, and signed Emma up for lessons in Noe Valley. He brought the cello home and laid the case on her bed — a surprise. When she walked in and saw it, she got so excited she wet her pants.

'That's the great thing about kids,' he said, relating the story to me over the phone. 'I mean, when was the last time you were so excited about something you actually wet your pants?'

That's one of the things that drew me to Jake — the sheer delight he took in fatherhood. His ability to see the world through Emma's eyes made him seem almost innocent in a way that few men do. When I told Annabel about how good he was with Emma, she said, 'Hold on to him. A happy kid is like a big stamp of approval across a guy's forehead.'

I was so flattered by the fact that he was willing to share her with me; it made his love seem bigger somehow, his commitment greater. He once told me that, after Lisbeth left, he worried he'd never find someone who was right for both him and Emma. 'And then you came along,' he said. 'I fell in love with you for a dozen reasons, and only one of them is that you're so good with Emma.'

'What are the other eleven?' I asked.

'Number one is that trick you do with your

tongue,' he teased. 'Number two would have to be your biscuits and gravy. As for the other nine, I'll just keep you guessing.'

What I miss most, more than Jake's hands and his chest and the taste of him, more than his generosity to waitresses and his rule of never sitting down on Muni if it meant someone else had to stand, more than his passion for the Giants and key lime pie, is the fun we had together. The way he'd come up to me in the bedroom, lift me off my feet, throw me on the bed, and tell dumb jokes until I was laughing so hard my stomach hurt. His dead-on impersonations of Dwight Yoakam and Richard Nixon. Now, all that is gone, and I hate knowing that I'm responsible for this change.

It's close to midnight, and I'm still wearing my sequined gown. I've been thumbing through Emma's *My First Cello* book. The book has scales, line drawings of children holding cellos, diagrams that tell you where to place your fingers. I have my dress hiked above my knees, the cello pressed between my thighs, and I'm trying to find C major. There's a bottle of Maker's Mark on the coffee table. I opened the bottle after Nell left, and I'm halfway down the label. My fingers won't work on the strings. I don't know how to hold the bow. I try to make music, but all I can muster are painful sounds like a squawking seal, a dying whale. The phone rings.

'Abby?' Jake says.

'Hi.'

'You sound strange. Have you been drinking?'

'No.' My answer is too emphatic, like a cartoon drunk with a bubble over her head, a NO in capital letters.

'You're drunk.'

'I just had a little.'

I'm embarrassed for him to hear me this way. I know this is no way to cope, that this is yet another test I'm failing.

'You've got to stop this,' he says. 'It isn't helping.'

'It helps a little.'

Long pause. This is not a comfortable silence, not like the ones we used to have, when we could let a minute or two pass between us on the phone without a word, and I was comforted just to know he was there, on the other end of the line. 'I'm sorry,' I say after a while, knowing that the words are inadequate, that this is more proof that I am not the woman he thought I was when he asked me to marry him. What does it matter that I could stage private cello concerts and make sock monkeys if I could lose Emma after a few minutes on the beach? Motherhood requires so much more than devotion, much more than simply love.

31

N. was the man who could not remember.

In December of 1960, while living in an Air Force dormitory, his roommate, practicing with a miniature fencing foil, accidentally stabbed N. through the right nostril; the tip of the foil lodged in the left side of his brain. What N. would recall in years to come were the details of his life before the accident. For example, he remembered a road trip across the U.S. in an old Cadillac, a trip he took two years before the accident occurred. But he would never again enjoy watching a movie, because halfway through he wouldn't be able to remember the opening scenes.

Imagine, in that amnesiac state, trying to do something as simple as preparing a meal. Because your short-term memory is intact up to a few minutes, you're able to put a pot of water on the stove, wash the tomatoes, dice a clove of garlic, set the table. But by the time the water begins to boil you won't remember what you had planned to make, or who you were making it for. Only by the details — the untouched dishes, the empty feeling in your stomach — will you know that you haven't already eaten. Only when the doorbell rings and you open it to find your sister standing before you will you know that she is your dinner guest. You are like a computer with a full hard drive; anything typed onto the screen will be lost the moment the file is closed, because there is no way to store the file, no way to save it for future reference. Fundamentally, you are a person with a past but no present. You will never form another emotional attachment, because you cannot remember what you like about any new person you meet. A few minutes after the best orgasm of your life, you won't even know you had one.

You exist, each moment, as if waking from a dream, with no awareness of where you are or how you got there, no knowledge of what, or who, might be waiting for you in the next room. Each thing you perceive has no more significance than a random snapshot in a stranger's photo album. A life without memory is a life without meaning.

32

David from Parents of Missing Children has been calling me. Once a day, twice, sometimes more. His phone calls are life preservers, holding my head above water. He doesn't offer me God or praise the healing powers of meditation. He understands that getting up and showering, pouring cereal for breakfast — the most mundane things — cease to be routine, the smallest tasks require impossible concentration. One's clothes must be washed, one's hair must be brushed, one's dishes must be done. The tank must be filled with gas, the bills paid, the trash taken out, the mail brought in.

Some days, even dressing is an effort: the buttons, the zippers, the shoelaces. To force the round disk through the hole, to fit the tiny metal stay into the zipper pull, to form the loop and fasten it tightly. It's impossible to do these mindless things; some mornings I end up sitting on the edge of the bed, staring down at my open blouse, unable to navigate the row of glaring buttons.

When I feel I can't make it through the day, it's not Jake I call, but David.

'What's wrong?' he says.

'I don't know what to do, where to start.'

'Go in the kitchen,' he instructs. 'Run water into the coffeepot. Take the coffee out of the fridge. Measure three scoops into the filter.'

While the coffee is brewing, he tells me to get a pencil and a notepad, make a list. He begins with the simple things — pay the gas bill, take out the recycling — then moves on to more difficult items, such as calling Detective Sherburne, making my daily trek to the beach, stuffing envelopes, visiting the command post, raising money to add to the growing reward — $300,000 and counting. Task by task, he revives me, until I'm ready to hang up the phone and get on with my day alone.

'But the uselessness,' I say one night. 'How do you handle that?'

It's past midnight, day eighty-four. Down on the street a police cruiser's lights are flashing. Someone's car alarm is going off. I never sleep at Jake's house these days. Our bodies no longer seem to fit together.

'Think back,' he says. 'Before this happened, what did you do when you felt things falling apart? How did you wind down?'

'I'd go into the darkroom and work.'

'Do that.'

'How can I waste time in the darkroom when Emma's still out there?'

'Force yourself. You're going to have to do it at some point.'

The darkroom. That small space where I once spent hours every day, losing myself the way some people lose themselves in books or movies. That room where I could be alone, nothing but me and the red glow of the light, the slick feel of the paper when it comes out of the fluid. The solid mass of the enlarger, the heft of the arm as

182

it locks into place. The methodical precision of fastening the negative to the tray. I've barely entered the darkroom since that one time in July, the second night after she disappeared, when I developed the roll of film from the Holga. The clients for the shoot at the restaurant wanted only color photos, so I took the film to a processor rather than doing it myself.

'Now?' I say.

'Yes, now.'

I hang up the phone, climb the stairs to the darkroom, and shut the door. I take the apron off its hook, slip it over my head, and tie the strings around my waist. For several minutes I just stand, not knowing what to do. Finally, the old familiar rhythms take over. First I prepare the chemicals, the basin of cool water. Then I take down some negatives that I left drying a few days before she disappeared, cut the negatives into strips, place them on the light board, and make my selections. One by one, I expose the negatives to the light, then guide the photo paper through the chemicals. At the end of an hour, the water bath is full of prints, floating one on top of the other.

The photos are from a wedding I shot months ago. These are the prints I didn't make for the happy couple's memory album, the ones the clients wouldn't want to see. Over the years I've been collecting these candid wedding shots, hoping to bring them together one day in some sort of meaningful sequence. I imagine a solo show that tells the grim truth about weddings, the kind of show that would make the viewers laugh uncomfortably.

This roll is from late in the evening, when everyone was already two sheets to the wind. The bride's dress is askew, the groom's paper party hat wilting. Around ten o'clock, the mother of the bride told me to go home. 'I'd rather not have this part of the night captured for posterity,' she said, fingering the pearls around her neck.

'Nonsense,' the drunken bride said to me. 'You're staying.'

So I did. There's the bride with her mouth open wide, her carefully constructed hairdo toppled, making a toast to her husband. And there's the maid of honor, a teenager in a miniskirt, dancing inappropriately with the father of the groom. Somebody's great-aunt with a martini in hand, demonstrating saucy maneuvers for the honeymoon.

The photos have a grainy, documentary quality. It's my thing, it's what people hire me for. Couples come to me when they want the candid shots, not the carefully posed groupings of the wedding party on the lawn and the polite still life of the wedding cake.

I suspect these people don't know just what they're getting into, and for this reason I rarely show my clients all the contact sheets. Would the groom, for example, want to see his father's meaty hand groping the maid of honor while they danced? Wouldn't the bride prefer to forget shouting at the florist? Weddings bring out the worst in people. Perhaps the air of new and hopeful love inspires cynicism and drives law-abiding citizens to debauchery. Maybe drunkenness and general bad behavior are everyone's way of thumbing their nose at the idea of a perfect future, their way of saying 'till death do us part' is really just so much fluff.

You'd think attending so many weddings as the impartial observer would have turned me off to having my own. The fact is, it only made me want it more. A wedding is still, despite its flaws, a demonstration of optimism, one couple's brazen pronouncement that they're going to make it. Underlying every wedding is the bold assumption that the divorce statistics don't count, that this couple will beat the odds.

The date for our wedding came and went. It was to have happened last Saturday, at a small chapel in Yosemite. The reception was to be held at the Wawona, a rustic hotel on the edge of the park. When Jake and I saw each other at the command post that day, neither one of us brought it up. The wedding now seems like a moot point, a frivolity that doesn't make sense in the context of our radically changed lives.

The last shot on this roll is of the bride and groom standing on the street, waiting for the valet to bring their car around. His tie hangs loosely around his neck, and she's holding her shoes in one hand. She's standing in front of him, and he's got both arms around her waist. Her mascara is smeared, her lipstick gone, and the padding of her bra peeks up from the low neckline of her dress. His head is bent and he's whispering something in her ear. The expression on her face is impossible to read.

One by one, I hang the prints up to dry. It

185

feels good to be back in this room beneath the red glow of the lamp. The chemical smell returns me to the deep dark of that tiny darkroom in Alabama, returns me, unexpectedly, to Ramon. The bulb cast a strange red glow over his hands as he shepherded the photographs through the bins. In one hand he held the tongs, swishing the glossy paper back and forth in the developing fluid. The other hand was cupped between my legs, and he was telling me to come.

Come where? I thought. He said it again, more urgently. I wasn't sure what he meant; I had some idea, but *come* seemed like such a strange word, so out of touch with what we were doing. I wanted him to define it for me, but it seemed like a bad time to ask, and I didn't want him to know how inexperienced I was.

I was sixteen years old. He was twenty-seven. I dug my finger-nails into the soft leather of his belt. On the photo paper, shapes began to emerge: the silhouette of my sleeping face, the curve of my naked calf, the bell-shaped slope of a lampshade. He pushed his finger inside me, whispering into my ear, and I thought of the secluded beach near the Fairhope pier where he took me for the very first time. *Took.* At sixteen, I knew what that word meant. I knew Ramon had no business dating a girl my age.

The fluid sloshed over the paper and the image became clearer — the striped print of the man's shirt that just reached the tops of my thighs, the small star dangling from my charm bracelet, a big hand intersecting the frame of the photo and resting on my ankle.

He lifted the photo from the developing fluid and slid it into the stop solution. Then he went down on his knees in front of me, held my denim skirt around my waist, and slid his tongue inside. I did not think that I loved him, or even that I would know him for very long. I considered him an instructor of sorts — more interesting and adept than boys my own age, who lacked skill and grace. Despite my youth and inexperience, I could still discern from some inflection in his voice when he said my name, and the way his body shifted and his stance softened when I walked into a room, that for him things were not so simple or so temporary.

We met in February of my eleventh-grade year. Eighteen months later I left Mobile for college in Knoxville, Tennessee. I refused to let him follow me. He called me every night for three weeks, begging me to reconsider. In mid-September, I got a phone call from Annabel. When I picked up the phone, she wasn't her usual nonchalant self. The sarcasm was gone from her voice, and I knew something was wrong. 'It's Ramon,' she said.

'What?'

'There was an accident.'

I was standing in the kitchen of my apartment in Sunsphere Suites. I leaned against the counter. I had just made a fresh pot of coffee, and the smell was suddenly too strong.

'And?'

'On his motorcycle. He didn't — '

She couldn't say it, but I knew what she meant. What she meant was he didn't make it.

What she meant was, he was gone. It turned out he had been drinking. He had called me early that morning, and I had let the machine pick up. 'I know you're there,' his message said. 'You've got to talk to me.'

Maybe it was partly in homage to Ramon that I became a photographer. I had planned to be a journalist, write for newspapers, take pictures only as a hobby. But a couple of semesters later, I declared my major as photography.

Later, I was saddened to realize that I didn't have a single photograph of Ramon. He was always behind the camera, a perpetual watcher — always seeing, never seen. I tried to imagine that he maintained his vision after death, that he would always be an astute eye, hovering, taking things in. But even with my Southern Baptist background, I could not bring myself to believe that any part of him survived after his body's physical death. I knew, deep down, that he was simply gone.

33

At four-thirty in the afternoon on the twenty-eighth of October, Detective Sherburne pays a house call. When I open the door, he thrusts a white cake box into my hand. He must notice the alarm on my face, because he says quickly, 'Nothing's happened. I was just in the neighborhood, so I thought I'd drop by and see how you are.'

'I'm good,' I lie.

'It's chocolate,' he says, pointing to the box. 'Arizmendi Bakery, my favorite. I went in to buy some cookies and I saw the cake. It seemed to be calling your name.'

'Thank you. I never say no to chocolate.' The words sound blank, ridiculous. Everything sounds ridiculous. Every ordinary thing has ceased to make sense. It has been three months and six days. Three months and six days without a sign of her.

'I just made coffee,' I say. 'Cream and sugar?'

'Please.'

'Have a seat.'

He looks out of place here, in his dark suit and bright tie, his perfectly combed hair, his air of reliability. 'Nice place,' he says, sitting on the edge of the sofa, elbows on his knees.

'I used to keep it cleaner. Before — '

I bring him a cup of coffee and sit across from

him in the small leather chair that Emma used to love. She would curl up here with a cup of hot chocolate, a blanket over her lap, and watch Disney movies. There's a mark on the left arm where she cut into the leather with a pair of scissors several months ago. She'd asked to watch some PG-13 cheerleading movie, and I had refused. When I came out of the kitchen a few minutes later, I saw an inch-long line where the stuffing showed through. I confronted her and she denied having done it, despite the fact that the scissors were on the table in front of her. Because I didn't know what else to do, I pretended to believe her. I remember thinking at that moment that I wasn't cut out for discipline.

'I just wanted to tell you how sorry I am,' Sherburne says, staring into his coffee. 'I keep thinking there might have been something we could have done differently, I don't know what.'

'You've done everything you can.'

He leans back and looks me in the eyes. 'I don't know how to say this, Abby.'

'Go ahead.'

'Three months. You need to prepare yourself. You need to think about the fact that she might not be coming back. It's a terrible thing to have to say, but when this much time passes — '

He nervously sips his coffee, and I think of his children at home, doing the things children do — watching cartoons, doing homework, sneaking sweets from the kitchen before dinner.

'She's not dead, I know it. How can we find

her if you don't believe there's a reason to look for her?'

'That's not what I said. I just want you to be prepared.'

I lean forward in my chair. 'If it was one of yours, would you be prepared?'

He shifts his leg, looks away.

'Would you?'

'I don't want to fight with you.'

'This isn't a fight. I just want you to know that nothing you say will convince me to stop looking.'

Sherburne stands up. 'I understand, I do.' I wonder how many times he has done this, how many times he has shown up at someone's door to deliver the news that they have to give up hope. Where is he going now? I imagine him stopping at some other house, delivering a somber speech to the family of some other victim.

I follow him to the door. 'I don't want you to think I'm not grateful. You've been wonderful to us through all of this. But you can't give up on Emma yet. You just can't.'

He puts his hands in his pockets and looks at the ground. 'I've talked to Jake. I know that you're not sleeping. I can look at you and tell you're not eating. Life goes on, it has to. You can't keep searching at this frantic pace forever. At some point you have to get back to the routines of your life. If you don't, then you'll be lost, too.'

He pats me on the shoulder and closes the door behind him. I can hear the echo of his shoes on the stairs. And I'm thinking that he's wrong. Despite all his experience, he's simply incorrect. Life does not go on. Everything stops, and there's no way to make it start again.

34

The next morning, I drive to Stonestown Mall. This isn't the first time I've searched Stonestown, and it may not be the last. I can't bring myself to do nothing, can't bring myself to believe, as Sherburne does, that it's time to give up.

In the food court, among the tables, I search for a child of Emma's approximate height and weight; she could be blonde, I remind myself, she could be wearing boys' clothing, she could be barely recognizable. I search every shop, checking behind racks, in dressing rooms.

In the restrooms, I go from stall to stall, opening doors. Then I stand by the sink and wait for the occupied stalls to empty. There is the odor of diapers and Lysol. Pearly pink soap drips from dispensers lined up like IV bags along the wall. Muzak emanates from invisible speakers. Behind each closed door, hope. So my search for Emma has been reduced to a bathroom version of *Let's Make a Deal*: choose door A and you get the girl, choose door B and you go home empty-handed. With each flush of the toilet, each rattling of a lock, I hold my breath and wait for the door to swing open, for Emma to emerge. She will walk out into the bright light of the restroom, approach the sink to wash her hands; then, looking up, she will see me. For a moment, confusion, and then my presence will register.

She will run into my arms. I will whisk her out of the bathroom and into the bright chaos of the mall. Hand in hand, we will make our escape. I will kidnap her from the kidnapper.

One by one the stalls empty out, until I'm standing alone in the restroom, staring into a row of open doors, nine identical toilets, thin white paper spilling from silver rollers onto the floor.

On 280, driving south toward Tanforan, I'm thinking about what separates the logical from the irrational, the sane from those who are mentally lost. A logical person bases her hopes and actions upon facts, statistics, well-reasoned probabilities. For the irrational mind, mere possibility is sufficient. I tell myself that I cannot be losing my mind, because a person who is truly insane is unaware of her downward spiral. I tell myself that as long as I can question my own logic, as long as I can pinpoint the ticks in my mental process, I'm still in control.

Tanforan takes two hours. Then I do Stanford Mall, Hillsdale, and Serramonte.

It's nearly midnight when I get home. I call Jake and ask him if I can spend the night, even though I know what his answer will be. 'You shouldn't be alone so much,' I say, feeling somewhat dishonest. I'm the one who doesn't want to be alone, I'm the one who can't face my empty loft.

'I'm sorry,' he says. 'Not tonight.'

Unable to sleep, I settle in front of the television. USA is showing *Total Recall*, in

194

which Arnold Schwarzenegger plays a construction worker haunted by dreams of Mars, a planet to which he has never traveled. The premise of the movie is that Schwarzenegger, unbeknownst to himself, was once a secret agent on Mars. Thus his dreams are not mere dreams at all, but actual memories. I tune in just as a psychic mutant, drenched in phlegm, asks Schwarzenegger what he wants.

'The same as you,' the hero says. 'To remember.'

'But why?' the mutant asks.

'To be myself again.'

35

I've taken another job, this time in Marin. It's a garden party for a couple's fiftieth wedding anniversary. The couple has five grown children, all of whom are in attendance, accompanied by children of their own. Everything is perfect: the calla lilies flanking the patio, the silent caterers dressed in black and white, the violinists wandering among the guests, playing something forgettable but soothing. I'm the odd one out with my clumsy camera bag and comfortable shoes, my messy hair. I barely make it through the cake cutting, then duck into the house and find an upstairs bathroom, where I try to compose myself. My hands are shaking, and I can't get my mind to focus. From the bathroom window I can see the crowd below, milling about the garden in the fading sunlight. The children have organized a game of hide-and-seek. I open the bathroom window and begin to press the shutter release, knowing, even as I struggle to keep my hands still, that these are the pictures the clients will love: the barefoot girl peeking from behind the tree while her brother creeps up behind her; the tiny boy concealing himself behind a rosebush; the little girl who is 'it,' in wrecked linen dress and scuffed shoes, standing in the center of the garden, hands on her hips, scouting out the possibilities.

In a couple of weeks, I know, the clients will

196

come over and select their favorite shots. The photos will go on the mantel, will be distributed to friends, copied, and sent out as Christmas cards. And the clients will be content in the belief that their anniversary has been saved for posterity, that this moment will last forever; the security of my profession rests on this false notion.

A painting can last for centuries, even millennia. The Sistine Chapel, the *Mona Lisa*, and the Mayan cave drawings are proof of this. But a photograph is, by its nature, a transient work of art. The moment a photograph is transferred to paper, the slow process of erasure begins. The purpose of photography is to stop time, but time inevitably erodes. Not only are photos easily damaged by heat, humidity, and handling; every photograph is light-sensitive, its delicate chemical balance constantly altered by exposure to light.

Color photos printed on Kodak paper, which are advertised to 'last a lifetime,' actually begin to fade in a decade. Even the most resilient prints, grayscale images processed on archival quality paper, don't survive much longer than one hundred years.

Photographs represent our endless battle against time, our determination to preserve a moment: the sweet baby girl before she becomes a difficult teenager; the handsome young man before his body is won over by baldness and fat; the honeymoon trip to Hawaii, before the happy couple become two strangers, living angrily under the same roof. I have a hunch that our obsession with photography arises from an unspoken pessimism: it is in our nature to believe that the good things will not last.

We put such faith in this flimsy mnemonic device, a moment written in light. But photos provide a false sense of security. Like our own flawed memory, they are guaranteed to fade. Over time, the contrasts within a photo diminish, the contours soften, the details blur. We take photographs in order to remember, but it is in the nature of a photograph to forget.

36

Ocean Beach, day 105, 10:43 in the morning. A postman is sitting on a concrete wall, looking at the sea, eating a sausage biscuit. On the wall beside him, a McDonald's cup. Perhaps it is the way he flicks the crumbs off his lap with two fingers — delicately, precisely — or perhaps it is the tilt of his body as he stares out to sea. Maybe it is the way one ankle is crossed over the other, each sock a slightly different shade of white. His feet don't touch the ground. I can't pinpoint the exact mannerism, but something about him is familiar. Like the driver of the postal truck I saw in the parking lot the day Emma disappeared, he is Chinese American. Could it be the same man?

I sit in my car for some time, watching him, debating. After so many days of visiting the beach, I am as nervous about being right as I am about being disappointed. After half an hour he folds the napkin into little squares, puts it inside the cup, gets down from the wall, and deposits the trash into a wastebasket. Then he gets into his postal cart and sits listening to music on his iPod.

I approach his cart, smile up at him.

'May I help you?' he asks, removing his earphones.

'Have you heard about her?' I say, handing him the flyer bearing Emma's picture.

'This is the little girl who disappeared around here a while back.'

'I was wondering if you saw anything that day.'

'Pardon?'

'You were here on July 22nd, the day she disappeared. I remember seeing your truck in the parking lot.'

'Sorry, it wasn't me. I just started this route in September.'

'Do you know who had it before you?'

'Fellow named Smith, real nice guy, family man. In the hospital now. Lung cancer.'

'What about them?' I ask, handing him the sketches of the couple from the yellow van. 'Do they look familiar?'

He looks at the sketches for several seconds, scratches his head, then hands them back. 'Wish I could help you, miss, but I've never seen them before.'

I wait another half hour in my car, watching, then drive home. It has begun to rain. On the sidewalk in front of my building, someone has drawn a hopscotch grid in blue chalk; only a vague outline of the grid remains. A soggy beanbag lies on the topmost square.

In the evening, I call Detective Sherburne. His wife answers, and I don't even have to identify myself. 'Abby Mason's on the phone,' she says.

'Evening,' he says a few seconds later.

'Sorry to bother you at home again. Just wondering if there's any news.'

'Sorry,' he says. 'Nothing.' A child is fussing in the background.

'How's the little one?' I ask.

'Two hands full, but he's more than worth it.'

'Dinner's ready,' his wife calls. 'Have you finished setting the table?'

'Almost,' he says. Then, to me, 'How are you holding up?'

'So-so.'

There's a pause, and I can hear commotion on his end — silverware, plates, children running. 'Listen, Abby, you know I'll call if we come up with anything.'

'Okay. Sorry to bother you.'

I hang up, feeling foolish, thinking of the family picture again: Sherburne, his wife, their little daughter, and the toddler, sitting down to dinner. The simplest tableau, repeated in thousands of homes across the city. To think that we might have formed a similar picture — Jake and Emma and me — if only I hadn't looked away. In some parallel version of events, some alternate universe in which a few seconds months ago played out in an entirely different way, none of this is happening. In that alternate world, we are simply a family, sitting down to dinner. Emma is safe, and Jake and I are married, and tomorrow we will get up and have breakfast together before I take her to school.

I call Jake. The phone rings four times, the machine picks up, his voice crackles like a bad record. 'I'm home for the night,' I say. 'Call me.'

I put a miniature frozen pizza in the oven, then pick at it in front of the television, just to hear the comfort of voices in my empty loft. One of my favorite movies, *Wall Street*, is playing on

201

A&E. Charlie Sheen, unkempt and crazed-looking in crumpled suit and loosened tie, argues with Michael Douglas in Central Park. The camera circles above them, swooping in and out, bird-like, as the corrupted boy and the corrupting man enact a verbal sparring match in the shadows of midtown Manhattan. Meanwhile, I'm planning dialogues in my mind, rehearsing the things I'll say to Emma when she is returned to us. First I'll tell her I love her, then ask her forgiveness, and finally tell her there's nothing I want more than to be her mother.

In the dark, with the credits rolling and cars' headlights shining on the wet pavement beneath my window, I almost believe my own story. I almost believe a day will come when Detective Sherburne will appear at my door, hand in hand with Emma. 'She's home,' he'll say, and Emma will step across the threshold, into my waiting arms.

37

'The frontal lobes are right here,' Nell explains, locating a spot on my forehead with her fingertips. 'The frontal lobes control the executive functions of the mind — self-monitoring, our awareness of our own behavior.'

Nell still knocks on my door once or twice a week, bearing a homemade dinner. Under her watchful eye, I force myself to eat while she talks about some interesting tidbit she's uncovered in her research. Tonight, the menu is comfort food — lima beans, mashed potatoes, and meat loaf.

'There's this tiny blood vessel in the brain called the anterior communicating artery,' she continues. 'When this blood vessel erupts, it cuts off the normal flow of oxygenated blood to the frontal lobes. The result is something called confabulation.'

I stir the beans in with the potatoes, hoping she won't notice I'm not eating.

'I read about one patient, J.D., who didn't leave the hospital for several months. When his doctor asked what he had done the previous weekend, J.D. told a story about going to the movies with his girlfriend, Anna, and mowing his lawn. The memory was incredibly vivid — down to the title of the movie, the street where the theater was located, even the dress his girlfriend was wearing. He did indeed have a girlfriend named Anna who had visited him at the hospital, but of course he couldn't have gone to the movies or mowed his lawn, because he'd been in the hospital the whole time.'

'So he was lying?'

'Not lying. J.D. thought he was reporting the events of the weekend accurately. Basically, confabulation is the unintentional creation of false memories. A common misconception is that memory is like some sort of computer that stores and retrieves information. The truth is, memory is an act of reconstruction. Every time we remember an event, we piece together rough drafts of the event based on our lifetime of experiences. A person with normal functioning in the frontal lobes would know that he hadn't left the hospital, and that therefore he couldn't have gone to the movies. But someone who confabulates doesn't have any mechanism by which to filter out the fictions.'

'Don't we all do that to some extent?'

'Of course. Mark Twain put it this way: 'It is not so astonishing, the number of things that I can remember, as the number of things I can remember that are not so.' '

That night, after Nell leaves, I think about how I supplied details to my mother's fake story about the trip to Gatlinburg. How I wanted so badly to believe in this image of family harmony that I created a memory of a luge ride with my father and an evening spent watching television in the motel room with Annabel while my parents were out at dinner.

When I asked Annabel about the scene in the motel room, she conferred. We had, indeed, stayed up late one night watching *Eight Is Enough* on a tiny TV in a room with vibrating beds. But this had been in Chicago, not Gatlinburg, and we weren't there on vacation. We were there to attend the funeral of one of my father's friends from college. According to Annabel, my mother later confessed that the reason my entire family made the trip was that she believed my father was having an affair, and she didn't want to let him go to Chicago alone for fear of what might happen.

Memory is not unlike a photograph with multiple exposures. One event is layered on top of another, so that it is impossible to distinguish between the details of the two. The older we get, the more multiple-exposure memories we have. Temporal relationships become elastic. As the years progress and we experience more and more, the mini-narratives that make up our lives are distorted, corrupted, so that every one of us is left with a false history, a self-created fiction about the lives we have led.

38

Here is the truth, this is what I know: I was walking on the beach, holding Emma's hand. I looked away, at a dead seal. Seconds passed. Three months, twenty-eight days, twelve and a half hours passed.

Another night, the two of us alone in Jake's house, the spot on the floor in front of the television where Emma used to sit conspicuously bare. It's eleven o'clock, and we've been stuffing envelopes for hours. We take a half-hour break to watch *The Office*, eating dinner in front of the television: takeout from Pasquale's on Sloat. It's the one holdover from before Emma's disappearance, the one thing we still do together that smacks of normalcy. For that half hour each night, we can almost pretend things are the way they used to be.

'How are your classes?' I ask, trying to make conversation. Jake just shrugs his shoulders and says, 'Nothing new.' At the beginning of October, he returned to work part-time, in order, he said, to hold on to his health insurance, but I suspect it is also a way of holding on to his sanity.

When the show is over I get up to leave, following the pattern that has become the norm. No overnights for us anymore, no casual settling into bed after the TV goes dark. I grab my purse and keys from the end table, and when I bend to kiss Jake goodbye he clutches my hand. 'Don't go.'

'What?'

I have to do a double take to make sure I heard him right. He's pulling me down on the sofa beside him. 'Stay.'

I sit down. He takes both of my hands in his and stares down at my lap. I can tell there's something he wants to say. My purse strap is still around my shoulder, and I don't know how to extract myself from it gracefully. I am poised for flight. I try to make eye contact with him, but he keeps his head bowed. I notice a smattering of gray hairs among the black.

Jake grips my hand harder, and I can tell from a slight movement of his head, an uncharacteristic lifting and lowering of the shoulders, that he is crying.

'What is it?'

'Today at school.'

I rub his back, feeling like some kind of impostor. It's startling how quickly intimacy can fade, how little time it takes for two people to become strangers again. 'What happened?'

'It was fifth period. I was giving a lecture on Charlemagne. The kids were so polite. No one was cutting up or passing notes or even talking. And I realized that they pitied me. Every one of them sitting in their seats feeling sorry for the teacher who lost his daughter.'

'Give them time. They're just nervous, they don't know what to say.'

'There was a knock on the door. It was Silas Smith, I had him last year in American History.

Smart kid, very quiet, wears these leather belts with odd buckles he makes in iron shop. 'There's a call for you at the office,' he said. I asked who it was, but he said he didn't know. He said it in a real apologetic way, and I knew it couldn't be good. So I gave the kids a free-writing topic, and I went to the office. When I got there, June Fontayne was waiting for me.'

'Who?'

'June Fontayne. She's the new guidance counselor. Ex-hippie sort. A real quack. Long flowing skirt and all sorts of bangles and beaded necklaces. She's got crystals all over her desk and a dream-catcher hanging over her door, a little Buddha shrine on the shelf where her books should be. I know there's bad news coming, and I don't want to hear whatever it is she has to say. She tells me the police were on the phone, but when she found out who it was she decided to take the call herself. She thought it would be better for me to hear it from her. Like she has any right to be the messenger.'

Oh God, I think. Hear what?

'The police found the body of a young girl and they wanted me to try to make an identification.'

'No.'

Jake's watch peeks from beneath the cuff of his shirtsleeve. The second hand moves with painful precision. Time expands. A few seconds never felt so long. I remember the way Annabel and I used to count for hide-and-seek, one-*Mississippi*, two-*Mississippi*, three-*Mississippi*.

'June offered to drive me, but I needed to go

alone. I took Portola, even though 280 would have been faster. I think I was hoping that maybe the coroner's office would be closing by the time I got there.'

Jake gets up and paces the room, back and forth, hands in his pockets. I just want him to get to the end of the story, just want him to tell me it wasn't her.

'I drove as slowly as I could but I got there. Of course I got there, of course it was open. And I'm sitting there in the parking lot of the coroner's office thinking that I can't possibly do this. I can't possibly walk into that building and look at the body of a girl who may be Emma. But I went. I shut my brain down and I just went. What choice did I have, really? On the outside it's just a plain white building, pleasant even, with bougainvillaea climbing the walls and nice benches positioned in the entryway, but on the inside it looks like a hospital, all white and sterile. It smelled even worse than it looked. A mixture of ammonia and some cloyingly sweet human smell — not like body odor but something else, something worse. It only occurred to me later, as I was driving home, that what I'd been smelling was death, death really does have a smell.'

Jake keeps pacing the room, and he has begun to sweat. 'It's boiling,' he says, 'are you hot?' Without waiting for an answer, he goes over to the window and opens it. He leans out and breathes the night air. A faint scent of ocean drifts in, mixed with diesel fuel. A car passes slowly on the street and Jake is briefly illuminated, his body

209

casting shadows over the sofa, wall, and rug.

He looks at me. 'How do you think they'd act at a coroner's office?'

'What do you mean?'

'You'd think they'd be sympathetic, right? You'd think they'd understand the delicacy of the situation.' He laughs — a weird, unsettling laugh. 'But it's not like that at all. They're just doing their job. They might as well be working at the mall. It's like they're completely immune to the whole thing.'

He comes over and sits down again. 'So I went up to the desk and I gave the girl my name. She said, 'You here to identify a body?' Just like that. She leaned into a little microphone and called for Mr. Brewer. A few seconds later a big white door opened and a man came through. He was in his fifties, wearing a white lab coat, and he smiled and shook my hand. Roger, he said his name was, then he motioned for me to follow him.

'We walked through an endless maze of hallways, and he told me it was his first week on the job. Then he started talking about that show *The Love Squad*, about how the night before this beautiful young woman from Manhattan had been paired up with a nightclub owner from Miami. Roger asked me if I'd seen it, and before I could answer he started apologizing profusely. Said he talks when he's nervous.

'To be honest, I was grateful for the chatter,' Jake continues. 'I don't think I could have taken silence. He didn't give one of those speeches the way they do in movies. He didn't tell me to brace myself. He just walked, and talked, and at the

210

end of one of the hallways he opened a door, and then we were in a small, bright room with three metal tables lined up in the middle. The tables were scratched and shiny; they reminded me of the cafeteria at school. But they were bare, no one on them, just tables. I was so relieved. I thought maybe the whole thing had been a mistake, maybe someone else had already come and identified the body, some other father had made the awful pilgrimage and had found his daughter there, the body had already been removed, the table washed, and now that father was driving home. I felt sorry for the guy, but I was glad it wasn't me. I was turning to walk out the door when Roger said, 'In here.'

'That's when he opened the refrigerator. That's what it was, an enormous steel refrigerator fitted with drawers. He pulled out one of the drawers, and I didn't have time to think about it, didn't have time to cover my eyes or ask questions or give myself a pep talk. He just slid it out and there was this body, this mutilated young girl. No sheet, no clothes, just the body, cold white skin and her little hands and these small, bluish feet.'

Jake is sobbing. He's not the crying type, he's only done it a couple of times since Emma disappeared, and the fact that he's crying now terrifies me.

'I looked at her hair,' he says. 'That's the first thing I saw, the hair. She was blonde, this poor little girl was blonde.'

My heart settles back into place. Time resumes its natural movement, and he puts his arms around me and holds on so tight it feels as if my ribs might break. I find myself crying, too, with the relief of it, and also the guilt, knowing what Jake has had to go through because of me, knowing all the pain I've brought down on him, all the grief and horror I've dumped on his previously happy life.

After a couple of minutes he lets go. He sits up straight, wipes his eyes, and puts his hands on his knees. 'After that I was able to look at her face. Her eyes were closed. She had the tiniest ears, and little pinpricks where her earrings had been. She must have been about Emma's age. There were bruises around her neck, like she'd been strangled, and scratches all over her body. Roger must have thought I'd made a positive identification, because he put his hand on my back and stared down at the floor, and I could tell he was trying to think of something to say. When I told him it wasn't her, he seemed very relieved.'

Jake reaches over, puts his hand on the back of my neck, pulls me toward him, and kisses me. It's an aggressive, hungry kiss. There is nothing apologetic in this kiss, nothing reserved; he kisses me as though he must have me, as though letting go of me at this moment is not an option. And something in me stirs, too, a desire I haven't felt in months, haven't wanted to feel because it didn't seem fair to Emma. He slides his hand up my shirt, and minutes later we're in the bedroom, unclothed and desperate, awkward as high school kids. 'Wait,' I say, rolling off him.

'What?'

'Let's go slowly.'

We lie there for some time, just touching, talking quietly. I run my fingers over his body, feeling the tiny hard knob lodged beneath the skin at the top of his right thigh — that small anomaly I've come to love. He touches the wide scar below my belly button, a remnant from a skating accident when I was ten. In this way we reacquaint ourselves. And as he moves into me, I am reminded of our first time, at a bed-and-breakfast in Bodega Bay, while the ocean roared just outside our window and a group of teenagers played a loud game of hacky sack. Afterward, we sat on the balcony in complimentary bathrobes, drinking fizzy water, making plans. Watching the teenagers, I had a pleasant sensation of the future, when we would bring Emma to places like this and she would meet kids her age, and we would watch her closely, but not too closely. I vowed that she would have a happy childhood, an even happier adolescence. I thought of my parents' miscalculations in child rearing and swore not to make them myself. A bean-bag sailed over the balcony rail. One of the hacky sack players waved up to us, a bright-eyed girl in a green bathing suit. 'Good throw!' she said, after Jake tossed the beanbag into her waiting hands.

Around two in the morning we disentangle, each of us retreating, as we have always done, to our separate sides of the bed. Jake snores softly, and I lie awake thinking of the blonde girl, the steel refrigerator in which she lies, waiting to be identified. I think of her tiny ears, the bruises around her neck. She is embedded in my brain, an image I can't shake, a horror that won't let me sleep. At three a.m. I get out of bed and walk across the hall to Emma's bedroom. The door is shut. I turn the knob. The floor is uneven, the room at a slight tilt after seventy years of frequent tremors. I've felt them many times, the house rattling and jerking slightly, but always standing, always remaining intact. When the latch is loosened, the door slowly swings open. I sit on Emma's bed. In this room there is a still faint smell of her, that sweetish, muddy odor that she always carried with her into the house after she spent the afternoon playing outside, mingled with the milk-salty smell of Elmer's glue and the musty scent of construction paper.

Time passes. I look up to see Jake standing in the doorway, hands at his sides, tears in his eyes, watching me.

39

I wake at five in the morning, make coffee, sit in the kitchen, and try to read yesterday's paper. The small words blur. The headlines run together, forming nonsensical sentences. The phone is on the table, inches from my hand. I consider calling Jake. In the distance, a fire truck's sirens wail.

It is the seventeenth of November. Day 118.

Today, Emma turns seven.

Around noon, I call Jake. His machine picks up, the same out-going message that was there before Emma disappeared. An hour later, I call again. No answer. Driving up Eighteenth Street through Eureka Valley, I try to plan our conversation, try to think of all the things that should be said.

His car is in the driveway. Next to it, Lisbeth's Cabriolet.

I park across the street and sit for several minutes, willing him to see me, willing him to come to the door and invite me inside. A very long half hour passes before the door opens and Lisbeth walks out, gets in her car, drives away. As soon as she's gone, I go to the door and stand there for a couple of minutes, trying to work up the nerve to knock. Down the street, a motorcycle guns its engine. A man and two children pass on the sidewalk. The man is carrying a shopping bag, the children hold ice

215

cream cones, and they chatter loudly about a pet rabbit they have at school.

I ring the doorbell and nothing happens. I ring it again, wait for a couple of minutes, then slide my key into the lock. Inside, the curtains are drawn and no lights are on. It takes a moment for my eyes to adjust to the darkness. Jake is sitting on the sofa in the living room, elbows on his knees, head in his hands. The floor around him is crowded with gifts wrapped in bright paper with elaborate bows. Tape and scissors rest on the mantel.

'Jake?'

He doesn't look up.

'I saw Lisbeth leaving,' I say.

Still no response. I can't help wondering why she came, what she wants from him. I can't bring myself to trust her, can't bring myself to believe that she has Emma's best interests in mind.

I thread my way through the presents and sit on the sofa beside him. I want to touch him but don't know how. I just sit and wait for him to talk to me, trying not to look at the vast array of packages. Sometime later I hear steps outside, a tapping sound, the hushed scrape of paper against metal, a soft thud as the mail hits the floor. Inside, everything is still. We sit this way for a very long time. At some point I sense a leaving of light, the cool approach of night.

Driving home, the red of the traffic lights appears lurid, the noise of car radios strikes me as somehow obscene. As always, I drive slowly, keep the windows down, scanning the streets. With each intersection, each doorway, each glittering shopwindow, I am struck anew by the fact of her absence, that permanent, insurmountable thing. I find myself winding through the Mission, then doubling back on Guerrero. Then I'm in Dolores Park, walking. There are two kinds of people who hang out in Dolores Park this late — those selling drugs and those buying them. As I walk through the park, voices softly call out the evening's wares — weed, coke, meth. I shake my head, thrust flyers into strangers' hands.

'What the fuck is this?' someone says, grabbing my arm when I hand him the flyer. He's wearing a pink wool cap, and the cap strikes me as oddly childlike. Then I realize he is a child, sinewy and pale, no more than fifteen.

I breathe deeply, try not to show my fear, and repeat my mantra, the phrase that has become as second nature to me as breathing: 'I lost my little girl.'

'You're in the wrong place,' the kid says, giving my arm a painful squeeze before letting go. Minutes later I'm in my car, hands shaking on the wheel. Jake doesn't know that I do this. He doesn't know about my trips to Ocean Beach and Golden Gate Park and the Tenderloin at night, doesn't know about all the ill-advised places I go at ill-advised times. He has his own way of searching — the command post, the radio, the organized lists and charts — and I have mine.

Back home, I call Annabel. 'She turns seven today,' I say.

'I know. I called several times. Alex wanted to

send her a present. I don't think he really understands.'

Annabel is eating something. She's like our mother that way — an enormous appetite and a blessed metabolism.

'Did I ever tell you that Mrs. Callahan sent me a card when I graduated from college?' she says after a little while. 'It was weird, just this ordinary graduation card, and a gift certificate to the Gap. But there was a letter stuffed in the envelope, written on notebook paper. It was all wrinkled, like it had been wadded up and then straightened out again. It was this long, rambling letter about how she and Mr. Callahan had split up a few years before, and he was living in Dallas, and she was the director of a children's choir at some church in Satsuma, Alabama.'

'I've been thinking about what you said, how the guy kept Sarah alive for seven weeks. Where did he keep her?'

'In his house, just a couple of miles from where her parents lived. He even took her to the mall three weeks into the kidnapping to buy a new dress. He had her wear a wig and lots of makeup so no one would recognize her.'

I think of Sarah standing in the mall, the kidnapper's big hand crushing her fingers. 'Why didn't she run?'

'He had her convinced that if she tried to escape, he'd kill her parents.'

'I realized a few days ago that, whoever did this, I want them to die. A long, slow death.'

'Abby, that doesn't sound like you. I can't believe I'm hearing this from the woman who

218

staged the huge death penalty protest in college.'
'I don't feel like me. I don't think I'll ever feel like me again.' I pause. 'I've been making lists.'
'What kind of lists?' Annabel asks.
'Of kids who've disappeared. There are thousands, stretching back decades.'
'Why are you doing this to yourself, Abby?'
'It's as if they all just vanished into the fog.'

I think of a family trip we made to San Francisco when we were teenagers. It was July, and like so many tourists do, we had packed for summer in California. In shorts and light sweaters, Annabel and I set out to walk across the Golden Gate Bridge. Within seconds we were shivering. The bridge that day was shrouded in fog so dense we didn't even see the famous orange towers. The great white mass moved over the bay, obscuring the city skyline. Annabel and I posed for pictures. Many years later, when we went home to divide our mother's things, we found a shoe box marked 'San Francisco scrapbook.' Our mother never got around to making the scrapbook, but she had kept ferry ticket stubs, a key chain for Alcatraz, and the photographs. In the pictures, it is impossible to tell where we are, or even who we are. All that is visible are our ghostlike silhouettes, floating in a bright white haze.

40

Day 138. Three a.m., insomnia, a bottle of Johnnie Walker Blue at my elbow — a gift last year from a grateful client. Outside, a storm, wind rattling the window-panes. Inside, the computer screen glows a milky white. For hours I've been scouring chat rooms, telling Emma's story, leaving the web address like a calling card: www.findemma.com. Hits soar on Emma's site, the electronic guest book bulges with messages, sympathy abounds, but no one has a clue. There is perhaps no greater proof of the despairing loneliness of the world than a latenight romp through cyberspace.

Sasha67 writes, *She looks just like my niece who died of leukemia six years ago.*

Snowboard4ever says, *It's 4:00 a.m. in Missoula. Call me.* He leaves his phone number and, inexplicably, his date of birth; he's young, probably a college student.

Bored2tears says it's snowing in Vancouver, then posts a list of all the girls who've left him over the past fifteen years, along with a detailed account of their reasons.

It is a wonder that the vast circuitry of the Internet remains intact minute by minute, hour by hour, as the sins and the sadness of millions of Web surfers crash down upon it like some monstrous wave. There is something comforting in the fact that the technology of the Web is immune to human grief, that the wires and chips process all these desperate confessions like so many numbers. Death and destruction, broken hearts and angry threats, missing girls and panicked mothers — it all amounts to just so much data that can be sent and stored and forgotten.

An instant message to my private e-mail address — the one I also use for work — pops up on screen. *Howdy. Just got back from Finland. When can I come get the pictures? — Nick Eliot.*

I had completely forgotten him, Nick Eliot with his spiky hair and impressive family history of longevity, Nick Eliot whose great-grandmother Eliza recently turned ninety-nine. He grew up in Oxford, England, but had been living in the Bay Area for several years. The week before Emma's disappearance, he came to my place with a small stack of photos that he wanted to have restored. 'I found you through your website,' he said, placing the envelope carefully in my hand. 'I liked your picture. You have a trustworthy face.' He allowed his fingers to linger a second or two more than necessary.

I'll admit I felt something, some quick electricity that traveled from his fingers through the envelope to my palm. He had a familiar smell, like pound cake. He was wearing a dark blue suit with a French blue shirt underneath. I thought of Jake and pulled my hand away.

'Let's see what we have here,' I said, opening the envelope.

There was Eliza at seventeen in a broad-rimmed hat and puffy sleeves, waving from the window of a train. And Eliza with squinting eyes and buckled shoes, sitting on the steps of a court-house with her new husband. Eliza a few years later, one hand resting on top of a small child's head, the other on her bulging stomach. In each photo, Nick's great-grandmother was faded, her skin ghostly pale, as if she'd been too long in the dark.

'Think you can fix them?' he asked.

'I'll see what I can do.'

He handed me his business card; the vague job title *Consultant* was printed in tiny, neat letters beneath his name. As he was leaving, he turned around, scratched his head, grinned in a slightly embarrassed way, and said, 'I don't usually do this, but when I come back to get the pictures, could I take you out to dinner?'

I held up my left hand and twiddled my engagement ring. Even as I did it, I couldn't help but wonder what it would be like to sit across a table from Nick, discussing travel and books, learning about his tastes, his family history. It was the first time since meeting Jake that I'd been confronted with someone who made me consider what I was giving up — the heady thrill of experiencing a first kiss with someone new, the kinetic moment of connection, the freedom to act upon this connection, to follow it through to some possibly surprising end. I loved Jake, I loved Emma, I was so happy to be on the cusp of this new life with them; yet I could not help but think about everything I'd be trading in the moment I walked down the aisle.

'Oh,' he said, smiling. 'Never mind, then. Congratulations.'

Two days before Emma disappeared, I called Nick to tell him that the photos were ready, but I never heard back from him. A few days ago, he left a message on my answering machine saying he'd gotten caught up in business, but I haven't called him back.

Now, I type, *The photos turned out well*, and press Return, imagining him across town in some posh condo, sitting in front of the computer in flannel pajamas and leather slippers.

When can I come get them? Tomorrow?

When? A simple question, but fraught with impossibility. At eight o'clock tomorrow morning, I have a fund-raising breakfast with the Mothers for Safe Neighborhoods Committee in Marin, where a couple dozen well-meaning and well-to-do mothers will offer their sympathy over fresh fruit and paper-thin crepes. From ten to eleven, my daily vigil at Ocean Beach. Next stop is the command post, where Brian will mark my canvassing zone with a pink highlighter on a photocopied map of the Bay Area and hand me a stack of flyers that he has meticulously designed. Each day the flyer is slightly different, with some catchy new font or elaborate border, the position of Emma's face on the page slightly changed. The volunteers have dwindled from 257 to 19, but Brian is still there three days a week after school.

In the afternoon, I'll return to Ocean Beach. This is always the most difficult part of the day

— those long hours of inactivity that bring me no closer to Emma, those long hours when I wander up and down the cold beach, past the joggers and the dog walkers, the hand-holding couples, the meager bonfires built by the homeless. Past the surfers who congregate in the gray water, waiting for the next wave.

Late at night I'll go to Jake's house, where I'll prepare a simple dinner while he works the phone, calling newspapers and radio stations, trying to get Emma's name back in the news. Media interest has dwindled to almost nothing now that more than four months have passed. Other children have disappeared from other states in the meantime. There have been highway shootings in Montana, a bomb in a high school in New York, a pregnant woman murdered in Monterey, an earthquake near Eureka. Getting attention for Emma's case becomes more difficult by the day.

Jake and I barely speak now when I visit, but neither of us seems to know how else to spend our evenings. Other than that one night after Jake visited the coroner's office, we have not made love since Emma disappeared.

We used to do the dishes together, and then I'd follow Jake upstairs, careful not to wake Emma. We would talk while we undressed and slid under the covers. Sometimes we would make love, but more often we'd just lie there, talking, until one of us fell asleep. It felt as if the rhythm of our marriage had already been established, as if we had already mapped out the way we would live together. I imagined that our nights, year by year, would progress much in this same manner. The thought both comforted and frightened me.

Words appear in my instant message box. *You still there?*

Sorry, I was just checking my schedule. Tomorrow's not good.

My fingers are poised on the edge of the keys and I'm trying to figure out what to write, trying to think of some scheme by which to dissuade him without telling him that my life is upside down, that I'm in no state to socialize or even to carry out the most mundane tasks, that Emma is gone and I am lost and I would prefer to just drop the photos in the mail, when another message pops up: *How about now?*

It's the middle of the night.

Technically, he responds, *it's morning. You're up. I'm up. I just flew eighteen hours from Helsinki, and I've got a meeting in seven hours, and if I go to bed now I'll never wake up in time.* I imagine him smiling as he writes this. Maybe he even surprises himself with his boldness, or maybe this is simply his natural mode of operation, the persuasive tactics of a man accustomed to getting what he wants.

It's storming.

I'll risk it.

How can I say no? Annabel can't pay my rent forever. Nick is a client, and right now I need clients. He will arrive with a checkbook and pen, I will give him the photos — a simple transaction, an exchange of money for services rendered.

I'll make some coffee, I type.

See you in twenty.

I change out of my pajamas into jeans and a sweater. I put coffee on, brush my teeth, hide the dirty clothes in the closet. I wipe the bathroom sink down with a sponge — how long has it been since I've done that? I'm changing sweaters — from the red one that makes me look ghostly to a blue one that, I hope, vaguely compliments my pallor — when the buzzer rings.

As Nick's footsteps sound on the stairs, I apply a subtle layer of lipstick, feeling guilty as I do so. Here is the dilemma, here is what I know. At 3:45 in the morning, all bets are off. At 3:45 in the middle of a storm, when the streets are empty and the shops are closed and the whole city is sleeping, it's easy to forget one's commitments, a relief to forget one's troubles. Particularly when you've gone months without real sleep and you're three glasses into a bottle of Scotch, and the man at your door is smiling, stepping forward, kissing you lightly on the cheek as if he's come for a date instead of for business, and his hair is damp from the rain, and his umbrella stands dripping at his side, and he's wearing a crumpled but very expensive suit and no tie, and he still, despite eighteen hours on a plane from Finland, smells faintly of pound cake. He's holding something, a small red bag trimmed with gold ribbon, and he's saying, 'I got you this. It's not much, just something I picked up across the pond.'

The red bag contains kitchen utensils, a rubber scraper, and a whisk.

'Odd choice, I know,' Nick says as I unwrap

226

the tissue paper. 'Do you cook? I don't even know if you cook.'

'They're lovely. Thank you.'

'In Helsinki,' he explains, 'everything's stylish, even the kitchen utensils.' It's true. The scraper and whisk have green rubber handles and sleek aluminum trim, like something you'd see in a magazine photo of a celebrity kitchen. 'You must think I'm weird,' he says.

'Not weird. Thoughtful.'

'Then I should really get points for this.' He opens his blazer and pulls out another bag. Inside, a hat of thick blue wool, with earflaps and a red yarn ball on top. 'They're all the rage among the Finns. I saw it and thought of you.'

I laugh, a genuine laugh, something I haven't had the pleasure of in quite some time. 'Thanks. You're soaked. Let's get you out of that jacket. I just made a fresh pot of coffee.'

That's how Nick ends up sitting in my kitchen, his light gray pants spattered with dots of darker gray from the rain. As I'm taking down the coffee cups, he sees the bottle of Johnnie Walker Blue on the counter and says, 'To tell the truth, I could use some of that.'

'Good. I hate drinking alone. How do you take it?'

'Neat, please.'

Something about the way he says 'neat,' with an odd little accent I can't locate — not British, but not American either — makes me like him even more.

I pour some for both of us, then sit across the small table from him. He smiles and lifts his glass. 'To ill-advised late-night rendezvous,' he says.

'Cheers. But it's just business, right? Nothing ill advised about that.'

He nods. 'Sure, just business.'

The Scotch is warm in my mouth and throat. Each sip leaves me feeling slightly more tingly, the tips of my fingers pleasantly numb. For a minute or more, neither of us says anything, and I know I have to tell him about Emma, know he's probably not familiar with the story since he's been out of the country. I'm trying to formulate the words, trying to figure out how to explain what has happened, when Nick reaches over and moves a strand of hair out of my face. It's the most obvious move, and yet it leaves me speechless, this moment of tenderness that has nothing to do with pity.

'You'll think I'm crazy,' he says, 'but I've been thinking about you.'

'You have?'

'Sorry, I shouldn't be saying this. I barely know you, and there's your fiancé, of course.'

This is when I should tell him about Emma, before he goes any further, but it's good to hear what he's saying, I want to hear it, want to feel this moment of normalcy.

'You remind me of this girl I knew in high school. Her name was Simone. Same eyes, and something you do with your mouth when you smile.'

'This Simone,' I say, feeling guilty, but wanting so much to have this conversation with a kind, attractive man, this man who, unlike Jake, has no reason at all to hate me. 'Where is she now?'

'Who knows? We had three dates, I fell helplessly in love, and then her family packed up and moved to Utah.'

'Twenty bucks says she's living in a big house in Salt Lake City with a whole passel of children.'

'Probably.'

'Do you have siblings?'

'One brother, two sisters. What about you?'

'There are only two of us. My sister's two years younger.'

'Where is she?'

'North Carolina.'

Nick tilts his glass to drink off the last drop of Scotch, then sets it down and runs his fingers along the rim. His nails are perfectly manicured, slightly rounded, and bearing a wholesome shine. He's the type of guy who would seem utterly at ease in a fancy salon, reading the *Wall Street Journal* while a young woman in red lipstick fondles his hand, filing and buffing.

'So this is a live-work loft?' he says, glancing around.

'Yep. I got lucky and locked it in back before the dot-com boom. Rent control. The dark-room's upstairs.'

'Could I see it?'

'Sure.'

At the top of the stairs, I'm overtaken by vertigo. 'You okay?' Nick asks, reaching forward to steady me.

'It's the Scotch. Is the floor moving or is it just me?'

'Maybe you should sit down.'

The bed is at the top of the staircase, and beyond it the door leading into the darkroom. We're standing at the foot of the bed. My back is to the mattress and Nick is facing me, holding me by the shoulders, but keeping a polite and brotherly distance. Bed or darkroom? Bed or darkroom? Instead of choosing, it simply happens; my body seems to fall of its own accord onto the bed. Nick just stands there, hands at his sides.

'Can I get you anything? Aspirin?'

'No thanks. Just a minute. I'll be fine.'

He looks around, presumably for somewhere to sit, but there are no chairs. 'Here,' I say, patting the bed beside me. 'Have a seat.'

The mattress sinks slightly with his weight. The clock reads 4:25. It is that precise time in the middle of the night when no one in her right mind is awake. At 3:15, the most energetic partygoers are just getting home. By 5:00, the most diligent workers are reaching over and turning off their alarm clocks. But at 4:25, just about everyone is in bed. Surely this is the witching hour, when strange and unpredictable things happen. Surely things that happen at this hour can be forgiven, or at the very least forgotten.

I don't move away when Nick's hand brushes my thigh, or when he leans over to kiss me. His kiss is soft, lingering, not too insistent. Maybe this is what I need. Maybe this is the thing that will help me snap out of the strange, stunned state I've been in since Emma disappeared. Is it

230

possible that sex with this man could break the cycle of my paralysis? Could making love to him wake me up, help me retrieve the lost threads of my sanity? Could one simple act rearrange my memory, set things straight?

As he's kissing me, three words thump around in my head: *Situation, Participation, Extrication.* Three words straight from the mouth of Sam Bungo, who led the sex addiction sessions my parents forced me to attend when I was seventeen. Sam was no psychiatrist; he wasn't even a certified therapist. He was just a Christian counselor with a lowercase *c*, but he was the best my parents could afford. He'd once been a youth minister at a small Baptist church in Montgomery, but had left the church under mysterious circumstances. By the time I met him, he'd been leading the sex addiction classes for three years, and he had the answer to temptation down to a formula. He made us chant those words several times every session.

Situation, Sam said, opened the door to evil. The first defense against sex was to avoid compromising situations, those circumstances in which you would be most vulnerable.

Participation, he advised, was the enemy. Christians must hold themselves apart from sinners, and in doing so they would be protected from sin. 'You should not be unequally yoked,' he said.

Finally, there was Extrication. Say you took a wrong turn and found yourself in a Situation, and it was clear that you were headed straight for Participation. Your only option then was

Extrication: snap your bra, zip up your pants, and get out of there as fast as you can. 'Don't look back,' Sam used to say. 'It's no accident that Lot's wife turned into a pillar of salt.'

Sam wasn't smart, but maybe, it occurs to me now, he was right. Maybe his slogan was divine inspiration masking as idiocy. I broke the first rule, Situation, by letting Nick come over. Kissing him would certainly be considered Participation. But it isn't too late for Extrication.

'We shouldn't,' I say.

'Right, sorry.' He leans back on his elbows, sighs, gives me a sad little smile. 'What's his name? The fiancé?'

'Jake.'

'Nice guy?'

'Very.'

I get up and open the door to the darkroom, flipping on the overhead light. 'Come in here,' I say. He follows me, perhaps thinking that I've had a change of heart and am planning to continue the romantic interlude among the chemicals and drying trays. One glance around the room, though, and his face changes.

'What's this?' he says, taking in the photos of Emma, dozens of them, papering the walls. Emma at the zoo, Emma at the beach, Emma in Jake's backyard on the Slip 'N' Slide. Emma standing in front of her school, holding hands with Ingmar, a boy she loved briefly in kindergarten. Emma and Jake standing in the sunlight at Tsunami Town in Crescent City.

I tell him the story of Emma. I tell him how I lost her. I tell him I might very well be losing my mind, and he reaches forward and takes me in his arms. There's nothing sexual in his touch this time, no hint of desire; he's just doing the only thing he can think of to do. He ends up putting me to bed in my clothes. 'If you don't mind, I'm going to just go downstairs and plug my laptop in for a bit and try to prepare for my meeting,' he says.

'Stay as long as you like.' Part of me hopes he'll climb in my bed an hour from now and put his hands all over me. The more rational part hopes he'll leave before I have a chance to do something stupid. I fall asleep to the sound of his fingers clicking over the keyboard of his laptop.

In the morning when I wake, I can hear him moving around in the kitchen. I quickly change into fresh clothes, brush my teeth, rinse my face, and go downstairs. He's sitting at the table fully dressed, hair combed, sipping coffee. I pour some for myself and join him. 'The two-day beard suits you,' I say.

'Thank you.' There's an awkward pause, both of us staring into our cups. 'Sorry about that thing last night,' he says.

'You have nothing to apologize for.' I slide the envelope containing his great-grandmother's photos across the table. 'Here's what you came for.'

He lays his manicured fingers on top of the envelope. 'Kind of you to pretend this is the only reason I showed up at your door in the middle of the night.'

'Kind of you to be such a gentleman. I'm

afraid my willpower might not have held up under pressure.'

'I wish I'd known you under different circumstances,' he says. He goes to the sink and washes his cup, sets it on the dish rack, dries his hands, and pulls a checkbook out of his coat pocket. 'What's the damage?'

'Two hundred seventeen.'

'A bargain,' he says, jotting the numbers on a check with his Mont Blanc pen.

'I gave you the sleepover discount. Aren't you going to look at the pictures?'

'I trust you,' he says, handing me the check.

And then he's gone, and I'm alone, and the sun through the big loft windows is too bright, too intense, like the sun on the beach in Alabama in the summer, when every body, every object, bore a hazy gold outline, and it was impossible to see anything with definition or depth, because the light made everything waver; it made everything untrue.

41

No kidding,' Jake said the first time I told him about Sam Bungo's sex addiction classes.

It was a warm day, Emma was at zoo camp, and Jake and I were at Java Beach. He dipped an almond biscotti into his coffee and said, 'I know you've got quite a sex drive, but I never figured you for an addict.' A guy at the neighboring table glanced up from his *Bay Guardian*, gave me a quick once-over.

'I wasn't. My parents got this idea in their heads, and there was no convincing them otherwise.'

'I guess we've known each other long enough now that I can ask this question,' he said. He was wearing a Giants hat and a fitted black T. He looked good, really good, and I wanted to go to bed with him. We hadn't done that yet. We'd come very close, and we both knew it would happen soon, but we were waiting for the right moment.

'What question?'

'The old how-many-partners-have-you-had question.'

'Let's not,' I said.

'What's the harm?'

'Okay. You first.'

The table was littered with crumbs, his and mine. Jake used a plastic knife to scrape the crumbs into a little pile. 'There was Betsy

Paducah when I was fifteen — her father owned horses in West Virginia, and she was in San Francisco for a summer arts program. Then there was Amanda Chung when I was seventeen, Deb Hipps during my freshman year of college. Janey, forget the last name, the same year, then a serious girlfriend from sophomore year to graduation, Elaine Wayne.' He kept going for a couple of minutes, finishing off the list with Rebecca Walker from a few months before.

'Where did you meet Rebecca?'

'At the high school.'

'Was it a relationship or just a fling?'

'Three months, if you call that a relationship. She's the only woman I've dated since the divorce. Being a single parent doesn't leave much time for socializing.' He clinked my coffee mug with his own, a toast. 'Until you, of course.'

'Who broke up with whom?'

'At the time, I thought it was mutual, but Rebecca kept leaving bitter notes in my box at school for several weeks afterward, so I guess I probably came out as the bad guy.'

'Does she still teach there?'

He nodded. 'English lit, conversational French.'

I imagined Jake sitting across the table from Rebecca Walker in the faculty lounge, trying to concentrate on his sandwich — turkey-bacon-Swiss — while she slid a loafer-clad foot toward him under the table, whispering saucy French words.

'Twelve,' I said. 'A very reasonable number.'

'You counted?'

'I thought that was the point.'

'Your turn. First to last.'

So I began with Ramon. Ramon who taught me about oral sex and f-stops, simultaneous orgasm and film speed. Ramon who took photographs of me, hundreds of them, which my parents got hold of after he died in the motorcycle accident. 'He had a sister who found the photos and my address after he died,' I explained. 'She took it upon herself to mail them to my parents.'

'Quite an age difference,' Jake said.

'I know, but it wasn't like it sounds. He was ready to marry me.'

I told Jake how, on the phone from Mobile to Knoxville during the last month of his life, Ramon had said, 'I can't live without you.' And I had said, 'Sure you can. I'm in college, I can't do this right now.' The last conversation I ever had with him.

'What kind of photographs?' Jake asked.

'You can guess.'

'Creepy.'

'It wasn't like that. I mean, sure, he was too old for me, but he really was a nice guy.'

'If Emma ever got involved with a guy like that,' Jake said, 'I'd have to chase him down with a shotgun.'

I didn't tell Jake how Ramon used to pose me. How he'd undress me, item by item, in his downtown apartment, bright light flooding through the high windows. How I'd stand naked in the center of the room and after a while the warm floorboards would seem to shift beneath me, and I'd feel dizzy, unbalanced, while

237

Ramon's camera clicked. There were the close-ups — an elbow, a knee, the white skin of the inner thigh, the arch of the foot, my ears with their twin ruby teardrops, a gift from him. Much later, my mother laid those photographs out on the glass coffee table and said, 'And what, pray tell, is this?'

I'd never seen her so angry. She was crying. She really thought I'd gone to the devil. My father couldn't look at me. He sat in the rocking chair in the corner of the room and stared at the piano, for lack of somewhere else to rest his gaze. The piano had been polished to a yellowish shine. On top of it there was a statuette of a bluebird with a tiny gold crank that made it sing, a row of Russian nesting dolls, and photographs of me and Annabel from when we were much younger, wearing matching gingham outfits my mother had made. And on the coffee table those other photos, my body laid bare, my pleasure so obvious and humiliating.

'It isn't natural,' my father said.

'Sex is a sacred act between a man and a woman whom God has brought together in marriage,' my mother said, as if quoting from a religious textbook.

My father nodded, rocked back and forth, didn't look at me. It was the same chair he had used to rock me to sleep in when I was small.

'When you do that with someone, you give them your soul,' my mother said. 'Forever after, that disgusting man will own a little piece of you.'

I was thinking about the motorcycle, wondering how much Ramon had felt as he slid over the wet road, if there was a lot of pain or just a sudden blankness. At the funeral in September, he had an open casket. I stood there with his sister, whom I'd just met. She looked like him, with olive skin and green eyes, messy eighties hair. 'Too much blush,' she said, taking a Kleenex out of her purse to wipe his cheeks. The tissue turned pink. I couldn't help thinking how unhappy he'd be about wearing makeup.

While my parents lectured, the TV was on low, tuned to CNN, Christiane Amanpour reporting on the situation in Syria. I wanted to be like Christiane, on the other side of the world, doing something that mattered.

I didn't tell Jake how the guilt washed over me like a wave, how I felt somehow responsible for what had happened to Ramon. Instead I said, 'They took me out of school for a whole semester. I had to go to group therapy three times a week with this weird dude named Sam Bungo, who was very fond of slogans.'

'Pretty rough for a seventeen-year-old kid,' he said, and I was grateful to him for not saying anything bad about Ramon. Grateful that he didn't make me finish the game, that after he'd tallied his partners I didn't have to tally mine.

Jake looked so wholesome sitting there in his baseball cap, so willing to trust me. 'So,' I said, 'do you find my past a bit too checkered? It's not too late to back out.'

'That stuff makes you more interesting. Besides, maybe it will turn out your parents were right and you really are a sex addict, lucky me. Whatever happened to Sam Bungo?'

'Odd story. I met his sister by coincidence about ten years ago. This FBI agent named Sandy Bungo visited my political science class at the University of Tennessee. It's an unusual last name, and there was definitely a resemblance, so I went up to her after class and asked if she was related to a guy named Sam Bungo. She asked how I knew him, and without thinking I blurted, 'I used to take these classes he taught.' She got this funny look on her face and said, 'Yikes.' I asked how Sam was doing. Turns out he was serving fifty-six months for some crime she didn't care to identify. I just stood there looking kind of stunned, then I asked her to tell him hello for me.'

That was the first and last time Jake and I talked about Ramon, or about anyone we used to date. Even the subject of Lisbeth rarely came up. One thing I liked about Jake was that he was content to leave the past in the past; with him, everything felt like forward motion.

42

The last Sunday in November, I spot the orange Chevelle at Ocean Beach. The car is there when I arrive at ten o'clock for my daily vigil. It's an unusually sunny day, and the fog has already burned off. A sailboat moves slowly across the horizon.

I jot down the license plate, then pull in beside the Chevelle, leaving two parking spaces between us. My hands shake, my heartbeat speeds up, my whole body tenses. The driver is the same man I saw that day, with graying hair and the beginning of a beard. He's reading a newspaper and drinking coffee. His face is a bit heavier than I remember, and there is no yellow stripe on the side of the car — but other than that, the details add up. A hula girl on the dashboard, the Virgin Mary hanging from the rearview mirror.

I call Detective Sherburne. His voice mail picks up. 'He's here,' I say. 'At the beach. The guy in the orange Chevelle.' I recite the license plate number, then call Sherburne's pager and his home number as well. No answer.

For half an hour I watch the man. He doesn't skim the paper but really reads it, spending a long time on each spread. At last he gets out of his car, goes over to the retaining wall, and stands there looking out at the ocean. I grab my coffee cup, wander over to the wastebasket, and drop it in, lingering just a couple of feet from the man. He's wearing a pair of very nice shoes, too nice for the beach.

'Pretty day,' he says.

'We've been due for one.'

'This is my first year in San Francisco,' he says. 'Not exactly what I had in mind when I decided to move to California. During the summer, it got so cold I nearly packed my bags and went home.'

'Where's home?'

'Nevada. You?'

'Alabama.'

'I used to have one of those,' he says, nodding toward a boy walking a dog down the beach.

'A kid?' I say, startled.

'No, a dog. Chocolate lab.'

'Oh.'

'Frank. Dumbest, sweetest dog I've ever known.'

'Where is he now?'

'Wish I knew.'

The guy has an air of loneliness about him, like he's been by himself for a long time. I'm trying to think of the right question, the proper approach. 'What brought you to San Francisco?'

'That story could take a while.'

'I'm in no hurry.'

He crosses his arms over his chest. 'Tell you what. I'll give you the ten-minute version over a cup of coffee at Louis's.'

I tell myself to be calm, sound natural. 'It's a deal.'

We lock our cars, then walk the paved path up toward the diner. We sit at a table by the window with a view out to the ocean. A young couple is picking their way over the concrete ruins of the Sutro Baths.

'I never got your name,' he says, stirring cream into his coffee.

'Dana.' The lie rolls easily off my tongue. 'Yours?'

'Carl Renfroe.'

Down below, the young couple finds a pocket of space hidden from the surrounding paths. Down there, with the sea battering the ruins it's easy to think you're alone. I'm trying to think of some way to extract information from Carl without alerting him to my motives, when the girl lifts her skirt, squats, and pees.

'Ringside seats,' Carl says.

The girl is oblivious, taking her time. The boy lifts his hand to his eyes and looks in the direction of the restaurant. He says something to the girl, who quickly pulls up her underwear, flattens her skirt over her thighs, and stands up.

'We get this once a week or so,' our waitress says. 'People got no clue we're up here.'

A family walks in and sits in the booth behind Carl, talking quietly. The parents don't look old enough to have such a big family — a teenage son, a toddler, and a baby with an oddly shaped head. The father sinks into the seat, white baseball cap pulled low on his forehead, and tells his kids to settle down. 'They can hear you all the way back in Iowa,' he says to his wife, who's marveling at the prices on the menu.

'You were going to tell me how you ended up here,' I say to Carl.

'My wife died two years ago. Bus accident in Guatemala.'

'I'm sorry.'

'She was only forty-three. Down there working on a documentary. A few months later, my son left for college.' He opens a packet of Sweet 'n' Low and pours it into his coffee. 'There was nothing to keep me in Nevada.'

I briefly consider the possibility that he knows exactly who I am. Maybe he remembers my face clearly from that day at the beach. Maybe he's returning to the scene of the crime. But all of this, I know, is false. Another dead end, another possibility to be crossed off the dwindling list. This man is not a kidnapper, child molester, or murderer. I'm not sure how I know this, I just do. Some people you can live with for years and never understand their true nature; others are easy reads, like a book with all the important passages underlined.

Our food arrives. Carl sprinkles salt and pepper on his omelet. 'Alabama. You're a long way from home. But I guess San Francisco's an easy place to love.'

'Used to be.'

'Sounds like a mystery.'

'I'm looking for someone.'

'Yeah?'

'A little girl. She disappeared from this beach in July.'

His face changes — recognition, pity. 'I heard about that, big news for a few weeks.' He frowns. 'Emily was her name?'

'Emma. *Is* her name.'

'I'm sorry. It must be horrible. I can't imagine.'

'You were here.'

'Pardon?'

'On the day she disappeared. You were here, in the parking lot. I remember your car. Your headlights were on. I considered telling you to turn them off, but then I didn't. You looked absorbed in your paper.'

He puts his coffee down, stares at me, suddenly understanding. 'You thought — '

I shift in my seat. 'You were alone. We walked right past you.'

'You've been waiting for me to come back?'

'Yes.'

'And?'

'It's not you. But I had to be sure.'

'For what it's worth, I'd be doing the same thing.'

'Do you remember anything?' I ask. 'Did you see anything — anyone — suspicious?'

'I can't remember. It's been a bad year, it all runs together.'

'Think. Anything. It was Saturday, July 22nd. Ten-thirty in the morning. A cold day, really foggy.'

He concentrates, shakes his head. 'I'm sorry.'

'Please.' My voice is too loud, too desperate. The dad from Iowa is staring. His teenage son is buttering the toddler's toast, while the mother stuffs packets of sugar and nondairy creamer into her purse. I lower my voice. 'Something. You must remember something.'

'It was months ago. I've had a lot on my mind.'

Instead of using the paved path back to the parking lot, we take off our shoes and walk on the beach. The water swirls around our ankles, ice cold. On Seal Rocks, the seals are barking. 'I have this place in Stockton,' Carl says. 'A one-bedroom with a view of the bay. The first night I was there, I heard this racket coming from the pier, couldn't for the life of me figure out what it was. Sounded like a pack of dogs. Finally figured out it was the seals. Couldn't sleep for weeks, thought I'd made a mistake coming here. But after a while I stopped noticing it. Now, when I go visit my son at school, I can't get a wink of sleep; the silence drives me nuts.'

'I guess you can get used to anything over time,' I say.

A Russian woman is sitting on a blanket by the water, talking on her cell phone. She watches as her husband dips a naked, laughing baby in and out of the water.

'Do you still see Emma's face?' Carl asks. 'Is it clear?'

'Yes.'

'My wife's is getting blurry. When I close my eyes, I can visualize her hairstyle, the color of her eyes, her earrings. But I can't remember the actual shape of her face. Then I rush to the dresser and pick up her photograph, and it all comes back to me — but a day later, she starts to fade again. And her voice, I can't hear it at all anymore.'

'Maybe forgetting is a subconscious act of self-preservation,' I say. 'Maybe, over time, if we can't see or hear them clearly, their absence is less painful.'

'There's a line from a Tom Petty song,' Carl says, kicking a broken sand dollar into the surf. He clears his throat, sings, 'I remember the good times were just a little bit more in focus.'

I recognize the song, 'Here Comes My Girl.' Though I remember only the lyrics and not the tune itself, I'm still aware, somehow, that he's slightly off-key.

43

Nell's books are piled high on my bedside table. At night, unable to sleep, I pore through them, making notes, searching for a way to jog my memory.

In 477 B.C., the Greek poet Simonides fathered the art of memory. Simonides discovered his calling by chance when he was invited to a banquet by a wealthy nobleman named Scopas. At the banquet, Simonides recited a long lyric poem, part of which celebrated Scopas, and part of which was devoted to the gods Castor and Pollux. The nobleman, angered at having to share glory with the gods, refused to pay Simonides his full fee.

Later, the poet was summoned out of the banquet by two young men. Simonides would eventually learn that the young men were Castor and Pollux themselves, who called him away in order to save his life. While Simonides was outside, the roof of the banquet hall collapsed. The carnage was so great that the relatives of Scopas and his guests could not identify the corpses for burial. Simonides, however, was able to identify the bodies by recalling where each guest had been sitting at the table. It was from this incident that Simonides formulated the method of loci.

The method is simple: imagine some real or imaginary place — a house or a church, for example, complete with furniture and multiple rooms — and mentally place the things you want to remember in a sequential order within this environment. Then walk through the assigned space, picking up items as you go.

During the Renaissance, Giulio Camillo of Bologna took the process one step further by building a wooden memory theater as a gift for the king of France. The theater contained markings, little boxes, ornaments, and figurines. Camillo believed that, by walking through this theater and attaching images and words to the physical things ensconced there, a man could remember anything he desired. According to Camillo, anyone who spent two hours in his memory theater would emerge with the ability to discuss any topic with the expertise of Cicero.

S., the man who could not forget, had never heard of Simonides or the method of loci. Yet, given a list of things or passages to remember by his doctor, S. would take a mental walk down Gorky Street in Moscow. In his mind, as he walked, he would place words and images at specific points along the street: in store windows, at monuments, in front of gates. Recalling the memorized passages was simply a matter of imagining the mental walk, picking up sentences at each location. Unfortunately for S., the one thing he wanted to remember was simply how to forget.

One night, after reading the passage about Camillo's memory theater, I have a dream in which I approach, at night, a vast building in an empty field. The building is white and windowless, with a large, arched doorway at its center. Upon entering, I find myself in a complex maze of rooms, each crowded with ornamental items: vases and ceramic figures, heavy draperies, boxes of varying sizes made of wood and silver and jade.

I walk slowly through the rooms, picking up jars and turning them over. Objects fall into my hands: pebbles and plastic beads, letters of the alphabet, crumpled pieces of blank paper, paper clips and pushpins, broken seashells and scraps of wood. There is a golden frog that leaps away the moment I touch it, and a piece of hard red candy, half eaten. I open the boxes, searching, but find only useless things. All of the objects are small enough to fit into my hand, but not one of them has anything to do with Emma, not one of them is the clue I'm looking for. I wander through every room, exhausting every possibility.

When I emerge from the building, it is no longer night. The exterior is lit by a blinding sun, and it is no longer a field but a square, crowded with commerce and people — bicycles and vendors and newspaper stands and children playing jump rope, men in suits and women in summer dresses. Pushing through the crowds, I know there is somewhere I need to be, but I cannot remember the place or the reason, or who might be waiting there for me.

44

Day 147.

'How would you describe your relationship with Emma?' asks Deborah Haze. Deborah is the host of a local morning talk show. Her eyebrows are arched in high, inverted Vs, like a child's drawing of a bird. Deborah is known for her tall lace collars reminiscent of period movies, the dark foundation she wears beneath rust-colored blush. Her stiff blonde hair adds a good three inches to the top of her head. I'm trying hard not to stare.

During the weeks leading up to Christmas, Deborah is doing a retrospective of all the stories that captured the public's heart this year. Emma's story is number four in the series. I've never liked Deborah Haze, but I'll do anything to get Emma's face back on television.

'Would you say you were more of a mother to Emma,' Deborah asks, 'or a friend?'

'I guess I tried to be a little bit of both.'

The show is being taped in a big warehouse, way in the back, on a small platform that everyone keeps referring to as 'the living room.' On TV, the sofas look plush and inviting, but in fact they're very uncomfortable, with hidden springs poking up in awkward places.

'So you're both her mother and her friend,' Deborah says, nodding and pressing her lips tightly together as if I've just said something

251

revelatory. 'How do you find a balance?'

The lights are hot on my face, the tiny microphone tugs at my lapel. Deborah leans forward, waiting for her answer. I remind myself that every time I speak into a microphone or look into a camera, my motives are judged, and interest in Emma's case rises or falls depending on how sympathetic I appear. I imagine a little graph that records public sympathy, the line dipping or rising each time I speak.

'Well, it's not like you step in and *poof*, one day you're the mother,' I say. 'It takes time to develop a relationship, to find the right balance.'

'Did you ever think you might not be prepared? Did you ever worry you couldn't replace her mother?'

'Of course I was nervous. I don't know anyone who's completely prepared for children. But I wasn't trying to replace her mother. I was going to be her stepmother; there's a distinction.'

What that distinction is, I haven't figured out. Had things gone on as planned, would Emma have one day come to accept me as her mother, or would I have always been slightly on the outside, one step removed from family? A couple of weeks after the engagement, while we were cooking dinner together, Jake asked, 'What do you want to be called?' I was standing with my back to him, sautéing mushrooms and garlic on the stove.

'Mommy?' he said. 'Or Mom?'

I turned to face him. It was Jake's job to make the salad, and he was holding the whisk he'd been using to stir the dressing. I licked the whisk. It was a tart, creamy dressing, with just the right amount of sweetness. 'Come on,' I said, avoiding the question. 'What's the secret ingredient?'

'No can do. It's a Balfour family secret.' He wiped a spot of dressing off my chin. 'Or would you prefer something more Southern? I can see you as a Mama.'

The garlic simmered on the stove, the butter sizzling. Emma had always called me by my first name; I didn't tell Jake that I could not imagine answering to anything else. 'Can I ask you a question?' I said.

'Anything.'

'If it weren't for Emma, would you have proposed to me?'

He stood back. 'What?'

'Would you want to marry me even if you didn't have a child who needs a mother?' I glanced away, embarrassed by my question.

'Look at me,' Jake said, placing his hands firmly on my shoulders. 'When you're not with me, I think about you. When we're in bed together, I feel like I'm nineteen years old again. When I read something interesting, you're the first person I want to tell, and when I buy a great new album, you're the first person I want to play it for. I love who you are with Emma, but I also just love *you*. Get it?'

I nodded, smiled. 'Got it.'

Deborah leans back in her chair, sips from a red coffee mug, sets the mug down — lining it up exactly with a cup-shaped mark on the polished table. I imagine the notes scribbled on her script: *meaningful pause here.* 'If I may ask, how has this affected you and Jake? I understand you canceled the wedding?'

The interview has gotten off track. Deborah is speaking in non sequiturs, trying to catch me in a trap. I wonder what it would do for the TV station's ratings if I were to to confess that Jake and I talk less and less, that his affection for me has turned to resentment. If I felt it might help find Emma, I'd gladly allow myself to cry. Instead I hold back the tears, try to evade the question. This isn't about me and Jake. It's about Emma.

'Not canceled, just postponed. We'll think about the wedding after we've found her.'

'You still believe that's possible?'

'I do.'

Deborah taps her peach fingernails on her notepad and shifts gears. 'How did you and Emma get along?'

'Wonderfully. She's a sweet kid.'

'You liked each other?'

'Very much.'

Deborah blinks at me, her eyelashes spiderlike under the thick black mascara.

'Like any child,' I say, 'she had her moments of rebellion.' I hear myself talking, saying too much, trying to fill the blank air. 'Of course there were times when she tried to push my buttons, but that's to be expected.'

'I see,' Deborah says. I imagine the line on the public sympathy chart taking a steady dive. Deborah tips her head to one side and smiles. On her teeth, a slick film of Vaseline. 'So you take it day by day?' She asks this of everyone she interviews. It's her wrap-up question, her trademark. It usually has nothing at all to do with the conversation at hand.

'Yes.'

'I suppose that's all any of us can do. Thank you so much for being with us.'

'Thank you.'

Deborah turns to the camera. 'Later in the program, we'll look at this story from a different perspective.'

She smiles for two more seconds. A guy who's been standing below the platform with a clipboard in his hand says, 'That's a wrap,' and Deborah's smile fades instantly. She removes the microphone from her collar and stands up.

'What did you mean by a different perspective?' I ask.

'I always like to get more than one side of any story.'

She reaches out to shake my hand; she could crack pecans with that grip. 'Good luck,' she says, scurrying off the set. A skinny kid in a flannel lumberjack shirt trails after her, carrying a cell phone and a Tully's coffee cup.

A guy comes over to unhook the microphone from my lapel. His hand brushes my breast. 'Sorry,' he says, but I can tell he isn't.

In the lobby on my way out, I spot Deborah's next guest, clad in a black sweater, black pants, and pearls. It's Lisbeth. She's lost weight, had her hair highlighted.

'Hello,' she says, beaming a recently bleached smile my way.

I try not to let the shock register on my face. I don't like the person I'm becoming, don't like the fact that, by the simple fact of her presence, Lisbeth can make me feel so angry, even jealous. When Jake and I first met, he made it clear that he was relieved to have Lisbeth out of his life. He once told me that he had grown to love me more than he ever loved her. I believed him; I still do.

But there is one thing over which I have no control. Despite her flaws, despite everything she did to hurt him, Lisbeth must represent for Jake something I never will: a connection with Emma. It was Lisbeth who carried Emma in her womb, Lisbeth who brought that beautiful girl into the world. Surely, in some part of his mind, Jake must see Lisbeth as the one who gave Emma to him. And he must see me as the one who took her away.

45

The week before Christmas, Annabel calls to tell me there's someone she wants me to meet. 'Her name is Dr. Shannon. She's a therapist.'

The lights on my Christmas tree are blinking. On the floor is a set of ornaments I bought from Emma during her school fundraiser last year: a wooden reindeer with twigs for antlers, a tiny metal caboose painted blue, an angel with glittering gold wings. I had this vision of how Christmas would be — me and Jake and Emma decorating the tree together, with Booker T playing in the background and orange peels simmering on the stove. Jake in a Santa suit on Christmas Eve, making lots of noise as he puts the gifts under the tree.

'Are you listening?' Annabel says.

'I just don't think therapy is going to help.'

'Dr. Shannon isn't a psychiatrist. She specializes in hypnosis.'

The miniature angel has golden hair and a porcelain face with tiny features painted on. Bright red lips, a dot of a nose. She's missing one eye.

'I already tried that, remember?'

'I know,' Annabel says, 'but this one comes highly recommended. She has a Ph.D. in molecular biology from Stanford and has published important research on hypnosis. Her practice is in Palo Alto, and she's done work for the CEOs of several Fortune 500 companies, not to mention that senator in Delaware whose intern was murdered a couple of years ago.'

'What makes you think she'd be willing to meet with me?'

'Rick just did a good turn in court for one of her biggest clients. She owes him a favor. She's agreed to one meeting, but she can't see you until the end of January. She's expecting a call from you.'

'Really?'

'Really,' Annabel says. 'Think of it as a Christmas present.' She clears her throat, pauses. 'That's not the only reason I called. I don't know how to say this.' Another pause, longer than the first.

'What's wrong?'

'Nothing's wrong. It's just — '

'Just what?'

'There's a letter,' she says, using our father's phrase. 'You know, in the mailbox.'

I swallow hard, trying to think of the right words. 'That's wonderful. How long have you known?'

'I'm almost eight weeks along.'

'When are you due?'

'July 17.'

'Why didn't you tell me as soon as you knew?'

'Rick and I agreed to wait a couple of months before we let the cat out of the bag.'

'Congratulations. It's terrific news.'

Mentally, I'm doing the math. She must have conceived about three months after Emma disappeared. Is it possible that she and Rick

258

decided to have another child in part *because* of what happened to Emma? I remember a conversation we had when she was pregnant with Ruby, her second. 'I can't imagine having just one,' she had said. I was sitting in a hard chair in a doctor's office, and she was lying on the table. On the screen, a tiny white thing pulsed in its dark, mysterious sack. I stared at the large head, the small curled body, that living thing growing within my sister's womb, and wondered if I would ever have the courage to bring a baby into the world. 'What if something happened to your child?' she had said. 'How could you go on if you didn't have another one to take care of?'

'Did you plan it?' I ask now.

'Hardly.'

'How does Rick feel about it?'

'A little nervous, but happy.'

I try to think of the appropriate questions, all the normal responses. I should ask if they're going to find out the sex of the child, if they'll add another bedroom to their house. I should ask if Rick plans to take paternity leave, and how Annabel will handle Ruby once the baby is born. Instead, I'm sobbing into my coffee.

'Abby? You okay?'

'Sorry, it's just — '

'Listen,' she says. 'I went online. In 1999, a little boy was snatched from a park in Nashville. He was discovered six months later in an apartment just two blocks from his home. In 2001, a fifteen-year-old girl was kidnapped in Houston and taken across the border to Mexico. They just found her last year. She'd been living with her kidnapper in Tijuana. Detroit, 2003. A nine-year-old girl opened the door of a car going fifty miles per hour and jumped out. She landed in a grassy ditch and was rescued by a jogger. The kidnapper was arrested an hour later, and the girl was given the key to the city.'

'What are you saying?'

'That there's still hope. Miracles happen. They're rare, but they do happen.'

I insert Emma's face into each of these scenarios: Emma jumping out of a speeding car; Emma walking across the border; Emma stepping out the front door of some house, unharmed.

'Give her my love,' a voice in the background says. It's Rick. I imagine Annabel sitting on the bed, legs stretched out, a pillow behind her back, and Rick there beside her, his hand on her belly.

'Right back at him,' I say.

She makes a kissing sound into the phone. 'I gotta go. The bathroom calls.'

'Annabel?'

'Hmmm?'

'I'm really happy for you.'

'I know.'

After we hang up, I drink a bit of Scotch, trying to work up the nerve to call Jake. When I finally get him on the line, he sounds sleepy, or maybe just depressed. 'Hey,' I say. 'I'm having trouble with this tree. It's lonely work. Want to come over?'

'I don't think I'm up for it tonight.'

'I'll make eggnog.'

'Rain check?'

A woman's voice in the background says, 'I'll let myself out.'

'Lisbeth is here,' Jake says, before I can even ask.

'What?'

On his end, a door closes. I imagine him walking over to the window and peering out, making sure she gets in her car safely, the way he used to do with me.

'She stopped by,' he says. 'It's not like I called and invited her over.'

'This reappearing act doesn't bother you?'

'Of course it does.'

'You don't act like it.'

'That's not fair,' he says.

'How can you let her back into your life while you push me away?' I hate the desperation that creeps into my voice, but I can't stop it. Losing Emma was the most devastating blow. To lose Jake too is a possibility I can't fathom.

'I'm just trying to get through this,' Jake says. 'I don't know how to explain it, but with Lisbeth, I'm able to remember things.'

'What things?'

'Little things that wouldn't matter to anyone else,' he says. 'Like when Emma was born, the woman we shared the hospital room with watched *The Price Is Right* all night long, turned up really high, and she kept arguing with the nurses because they wanted her to breast-feed her newborn, but the woman wanted to use a bottle. And I just remember sitting there staring at Emma, this tiny little baby with a full head of dark hair, amazed that she could sleep through

261

the commotion. I remember being totally astonished by this calm, beautiful baby — I just couldn't believe she was mine.'

What can I say to that? No matter how much I love Emma, there are some things I simply wasn't there for, some things Lisbeth and Jake will always share.

'You remember her performance on *Bay Area Morning*,' I say quietly.

'Yes.'

'She actually said she *missed* Emma. After everything she's done.'

'I think she may have meant it. I'm not forgiving her. I'm just saying it's complicated.' He sighs, the kind of sigh that means we've been over this before, let it rest. The thing is, we haven't been over this, not really.

'She's Emma's mother,' he says finally. 'There's no getting around that.'

The word *mother* falls like a dead weight on my ears. He's right, of course. I remember my own parents, how they suffered through twenty-five years of a rotten marriage for one simple reason: they had two children.

I can hear my mother's voice, nearly five years ago now, a few weeks before she died. 'The best thing I did with my life was having children,' she said. And I remember thinking I didn't want to say that on my deathbed. I didn't want motherhood to be the thing that defined me, that made my life worthwhile. I needed something else, too: I wanted my *work* to make a difference. I had tried to express this to my mother in the past, and she had always looked at me with pity, as if I was sadly misguided, as if I was missing some crucial moral center.

When I was ten and Annabel was eight, my mother bought us a book about reproduction. She sat us down on the couch one Sunday after church and proceeded to explain what happens when two people who are joined in holy matrimony pray to God and ask him for a baby. She recited some very vague information involving a bedroom and God's divine will, then opened the book and showed us the pictures. There was a line drawing of a pregnant woman in profile: long hair, slender legs, upright breasts, a slightly curved belly. Low inside the belly, a sack, and within the sack a little curlicue of a thing, so small that when my mother pointed to the picture, the curlicue was entirely hidden by her fingernail.

'That's the baby?' Annabel said, moving my mother's hand away.

'Yes.'

'It looks like a sea horse,' I said. I was already feeling disappointed about this whole baby thing. I remembered the mail-order sea horses from Everlasting Toys, how they'd turned out to be nothing special.

'That's just the very beginning,' my mother said, flipping the page. The next picture showed a slightly bigger belly, and this time, inside the sack, there was a little alien-looking thing with a big head and fishlike limbs. The final drawing was of a swaddled newborn. She closed the book and patted our heads. 'One day you'll both have babies of your own.'

'I want to have seven,' Annabel said.

'How many do you want?' my mother asked, tilting my chin up and smiling down at me. I remember feeling privileged, because she wasn't often affectionate like this. But I also felt sad, as though she and Annabel shared something I didn't. Babies were sweet and soft, I liked them, but I couldn't imagine having some strange thing growing inside me, just like I couldn't imagine doing what apparently came first — the vague, disturbing act she referred to as holy matrimony. I tried to think of the correct answer to her question, something that wouldn't disappoint her.

'Maybe three?' I said, looking up into her soft eyes. She was wearing tiny gold earrings, and her breath smelled too strongly of coffee. I wondered if she could tell I was lying.

46

'Truce,' Jake says. It's Christmas Eve, and he has shown up at my door bearing tickets to the San Francisco Gay Men's Chorus performance at the Castro Theatre. 'Will you be my date?'

'Of course,' I say. 'Just give me a few minutes to get dressed.'

It's what we did last year, what Jake has done every year for the last decade. I know he's trying hard to act normal, trying to act like there is cause for celebration, like Christmas means something to him still. But we're not good at pretending, and we leave during the intermission. Last year before the show, we took Emma to Cable Car Joe's for her favorite meal: a hamburger, onion rings, and a milk shake. We ate there so often that Joe knew Emma by name, and before we left he gave her a gift — a five-inch-tall teddy bear wearing a T-shirt with the Cable Car logo.

This year, we just order a couple of sandwiches at A.G. Ferrari across the street from the Castro and take them back to Jake's place. We eat in the living room, staring at the tree, which has lights but no ornaments.

'My heart just wasn't in it,' Jake says.

The only reason he even has a tree is that a couple of teachers at his school brought it over one evening and insisted that he accept it. They put the tree in the stand, set it up by the window, found the boxes of Christmas stuff in the garage, and helped him string the lights.

The floor beneath the tree is bare. 'We should at least put a couple of gifts under there,' I say.

'I learned my lesson on her birthday. It tears me apart to look at presents she's never going to open.'

I don't tell him about my own shopping spree, the dozens of presents wrapped and stuffed into my hall closet, each chosen just for her: a pair of ice skates, because I promised to take her to the outdoor rink at the Embarcadero this year; the pink knit scarf and matching hat; the porcelain doll with a little suitcase and parasol. Things purchased on credit, things I can't afford. I bought them all in a single day, rushing from one store to the next, grabbing anything I thought she would like. While I was shopping for her, I felt happy, maybe because the physical act of picking things up and carrying them to the checkout allowed me to harbor a ridiculous hope that Emma would be opening the packages on Christmas Day. When I got the presents home and saw them laid out on the floor, the happiness dissipated. I put everything in the closet, vowing to take it all back the next day. That was two weeks ago, and I haven't been able to force myself to open the closet since.

'Is it all right if I spend the night?' I ask.

'Sure,' Jake says, but he doesn't move toward me when he says it, and I can tell he'd rather be alone.

'Maybe tomorrow night,' I say. And then, unable to stop myself, I ask about Lisbeth. 'She's not — '

'No,' Jake says, 'she's not in town. She's spending Christmas on the East Coast with friends.'

'Oh,' I say, feeling stupid and relieved.

Jake takes my hand. 'You've got nothing to worry about on that front, okay?'

'Okay.' It's such a relief to hear him say it, to see in his eyes that he means it.

I call him late Christmas morning, but he's still in bed. 'I'd rather just be alone today,' he says. 'I've got some work to do.'

'But it's Christmas.'

'It's easier if I pretend it isn't.'

David from Parents of Missing Children invited me over to his house for a party, but I made up an excuse not to go. Most of the guests will be from the support group, and I can't bear the multiplied grief, the inevitable tears, the stories of holidays past. Instead, I spend the day with Nell. All day long, friends of her dead son Stephen stop by to say hello. She gives them eggnog and sugar cookies, and they bring her small gifts perfectly wrapped in expensive paper. By ten p.m., the last visitor has left. 'I can't go home,' I say. 'I don't think I can be alone tonight.'

'Of course not,' Nell says. 'Stay here. You wouldn't believe how comfortable this couch is.'

She fetches blankets and a pillow, and we stay up late into the night, playing gin rummy. I keep score on a legal pad, trying without success to

267

concentrate on the game. At one point, my pen runs out of ink and Nell retrieves a pencil from a mason jar on her kitchen counter. The pencil is wide and flat, and I'm nibbling on the yellow flesh when a memory from childhood comes to me.

'Where'd you get this?' I ask.

'I think I nabbed it from Home Depot.'

'Funny, the smell and taste totally take me back. When I was a kid, my dad was a building contractor, and sometimes I'd visit job sites with him. He had these big, flat pencils, just like this one, that he'd use to make markings on the lumber, and he'd let me entertain myself by drawing on plywood scraps.'

'There's a name for that, you know,' Nell says. 'It's a Proustian memory, so called because of the madeleine and lime-blossom tea in *Swann's Way*. Scientists think olfactory memories are some of our most emotionally powerful ones because smell is the only sense that's very closely associated with the limbic system, which is the part of the brain responsible for emotion. After Stephen died, I started taking my clothes to his dry cleaner and even having my blouses starched, which I've never done in my life, just because the starch they use reminds me of him. If I close my eyes when I'm wearing one of those blouses, I can almost pretend he's in the same room.' She smiles and plucks a card from the deck. 'Pretty nutty, huh?'

'Not really,' I say. 'I went shopping for Emma last week. I bought her this Tinkerbell nail polish that she used to wear all the time. When I got home, I put the stuff on. This really awful shade of pink. I put on two coats and drank three glasses of wine and then just let myself drift off, thinking about her, and you know what was really nice? I dreamt about her. I've dreamt of her dozens of times since she disappeared, but it's always a nightmare, where I'm looking for her and can't find her, or I'm trying to save her from something terrible. This dream was different. We were at the aquarium, the old one in the park before it closed down, and we were looking at the starfish, and we were both happy. It was the best dream, it was like she was right there with me. But then I woke up.'

'That's the unfortunate thing about dreams,' Nell says. 'There's always the part where you wake up.'

47

That day on Ocean Beach, Emma wore blue canvas shoes, size three, with a smiling monkey face decorating the sides, her name stitched across the tongue in red.

On Saturday, the third of January, Sherburne calls to tell us that a single shoe has been discovered by a tourist. It was wedged into a pile of rocks on Baker Beach in the Presidio, about three miles north of Ocean Beach.

'I was clothed, of course,' the man who found it told the police. 'Didn't even know it was a nude beach until I got there, and I figured, what the hell, may as well take a walk, you only live once.'

It's a short beach. There's not much walking to do there. You can take pictures of the Golden Gate Bridge, read a book, watch the nude men sunbathing in the cold. Thus starved for activity, one might take in every detail, such as a shoe wedged into a pile of rocks. I imagine the man bending down, tugging the shoe free just to give himself something to do, so as not to give the impression that he is looking at the nude men. He's about to raise his arm and sail the shoe out into the ocean when he notices the partially embroidered name.

He told the police that he had seen Jake on the *Today* show, had heard Jake's description of Emma's shoes, her clothes. He said he probably would never have remembered were it not for the fact that his granddaughter had a very similar pair of shoes.

What does he feel then? Pity for the father, that distraught and pleading man with the tousled hair and glasses? Or perhaps he experiences a quick lifting of spirit, an excitement at having been the one to find the shoe. All those police, all those volunteers, all that time spent searching, and it is he, a computer salesman from Dallas, who comes up with the clue. Perhaps he even envisions the television interview during which he describes the discovery, his own fifteen minutes of fame.

How easy it would have been for him to look in another direction, to rest his gaze on some distant surfer or seashell or sunbather, rather than on the pile of rocks. I will it to have been so, engaged always in this mental effort to turn back the clock, to rearrange the events of the past.

But the shoe has been found. The police now have a piece of evidence, however circumstantial, to back up their theory that Emma drowned. Worse, Jake has something to believe in, some small proof that it is true.

His first reaction, upon hearing the news from Sherburne, is fearful astonishment. 'Are you sure it's hers?'

I'm standing in the kitchen, stirring a big pot of soup on the stove, privy only to Jake's half of the conversation.

'What's hers?' I ask.

Jake covers the mouthpiece, turns to me. 'They found a shoe.' He punches the speaker

271

button on the phone, and Sherburne's voice fills the kitchen.

'We're pretty certain,' he says. 'Of course, you should see it to make sure. I'll bring it by this afternoon so you can have a look.'

'We'll come to you,' Jake says.

'It's all right, I'm in my car just across the park. I'll be there in ten.'

'Thank you,' Jake says. And then, oddly, 'Have you eaten? Abby's making potato and leek soup for lunch. You should join us.'

I find myself thinking how strange it is that one's manners remain intact even in the worst circumstances, that during this whole ordeal, as Jake's world has fallen apart, he has conducted himself with the utmost restraint and comportment. I've yet to see him lose his temper or his calm in public. Only in our most private moments has the depth of his fear shown through.

'Thank you,' Sherburne says.

Jake hangs up the phone, goes to the china cabinet, and takes out three of his best bowls. It's an endearing habit of his — he always uses the fine china for company, no matter how casual or spontaneous the occasion. One of the bowls crashes to the floor. He curses, drops to his knees, and begins picking up the broken pieces with his bare hands.

'You're bleeding,' I say, bending down to help.

He keeps picking up the shards, oblivious to the blood. 'It can't be hers, can it?'

'We'll see. Go rinse your hands. I'll clean this up.'

He makes no move to get up. He kneels there, his hands cupped around the bits of glass, looking at me incredulously. 'If it is her shoe,' he says, 'what does that mean?'

'It doesn't necessarily mean anything.' I'm trying to be calm, trying not to let him see my fear. Trying to be the levelheaded one in this moment, even though I feel panic rising in my gut.

I've just finished vacuuming up the last of the glass when the doorbell rings. 'I'll get that,' Jake says. His voice sounds off, the whole moment feels off. I think about Sherburne, on the other side of the door, holding in his hands the first actual piece of evidence to surface since this whole nightmare began.

From the kitchen I can hear Jake opening the front door. 'Come in,' he says.

And Sherburne, playing the polite guest. 'Smells delicious.'

I go into the living room, peck Sherburne on the cheek, hear myself chiming in, taking part in the strange game of avoidance. 'It's nothing fancy, just soup. The only thing I know how to make, save for biscuits and gravy.'

The top button on Sherburne's white oxford shirt is undone, and his tie is slightly askew. I recognize the tie — the same one he was wearing that night when he brought us into the station. He notices me looking at it. 'A gift,' he says, lifting the end and holding it up. 'From my daughter. She asked me to wear it this morning and I couldn't say no. She's got me wrapped around her finger, that one — you know how little girls are.'

This last sentence hangs in the air, and we're all looking at each other awkwardly, unsure how to proceed.

'I'm sorry,' Sherburne says, blushing. He clears his throat. 'We should sit down, I suppose.'

'Of course,' Jake says. Jake and I sit on the sofa, and Sherburne settles in the chair across from us. Jake reaches for my hand, holds it tightly.

Sherburne pulls a plastic bag out of his pocket. The bag is labeled with a white sticker bearing a series of numbers and letters and the word *Balfour*, handwritten in black ink. He opens the bag, pulls out a little shoe, and lays it on the coffee table in front of us.

The shoe is ragged and smells briny, ripe, like the angel wings Emma used to dig up at Ocean Beach. I came across a jar of them once, unwashed, stashed in a basket beneath her bed. The creatures had died inside their shells, and when I opened the jar her room was invaded by the dank, fishy smell.

I notice the toe of the shoe first, where Emma's name had been. The stitching is mostly gone, but bits of the *E*, one *m*, and the *a* remain. The red has faded to pink. On the side, there's a hole where the monkey's nose should be.

Jake stares at the shoe for several seconds, unmoving. Then he reaches out to touch it, run his fingers over the wrecked fabric. His fingers tremble. He begins, very quietly, to cry. He picks up the shoe and cradles it in both hands.

Sherburne sits silently. I find myself staring at the tie just to keep from looking at Emma's shoe, Jake's face.

I have a memory of childhood, a Sunday afternoon in Alabama. I remember the shoes I was wearing — a pair of white sandals with a tiny heel, the first heels I'd ever owned. I must have been about eleven years old. We had just finished lunch, and I was helping my mother with the dishes. I couldn't stop thinking about something the preacher had said that morning in church. He'd said that everyone has to make choices, and the choices we make determine whether we go to heaven or to hell when we die. My mother was handing me pieces of silverware, one by one. 'Wouldn't it be better not to be born?' I asked.

My mother stopped what she was doing and looked down at me. 'What?'

'If you're born, you might go to hell. Hell is the most terrible thing that could happen to anyone.'

'But you might go to heaven,' my mother said. 'And that's the most wonderful thing that could happen.'

'But if you were never born,' I reasoned, 'it wouldn't matter that you didn't go to heaven, because you wouldn't even know about it. I wish I'd never been born.'

Over time, I stopped worrying about hell. Now, for the first time in my adult life, the very basic question of existence presents itself again to me, and I find myself imagining with envy an alternate scenario, one in which I never took my place in the world.

★ ★ ★

We're on the sofa, and Jake is lying with his head in my lap. The lights in the living room are off, music softly playing on the stereo. The smell of the uneaten soup permeates the house. In the hours since Sherburne left, we've exhausted ourselves with crying and talking, analyzing the possibilities. Our conversation has gone round and round in endless circles. Hours ago, the light faded. Through the front windows we watched the fog rolling up the avenues. At one point, Jake suggested that maybe it was time to close the command post.

'At least now we know she's not suffering,' he says finally. It has taken him hours to come to this conclusion, to convince himself of its truth. Now that he's decided upon this version of the story, it is as if he'd been presented with incontrovertible evidence. 'At least she's not scared or in pain.'

In the months since Emma disappeared, there has been such gravity in Jake's expression, such tension, that he looked less and less like the man I once planned to marry. Today, as the hours wore on, something of his old expression began to emerge — a relaxing of the jaw, a smoothness of the brow. Now, the look in his eyes borders on peaceful.

I don't share his strange relief. I feel sick. I know that, for the sake of his own sanity, he has to believe she's dead; it's easier than accepting the possibility that she's alive,

276

suffering unspeakable things.

Around ten p.m. he gets up, goes into the kitchen, and puts the soup in the fridge. He goes upstairs and takes a shower, then comes back down in his bathrobe. He stands at the base of the stairs, looking at me. 'Spend the night,' he says.

It's the first time since his visit to the mortuary that he's issued such an invitation. We don't make love. We hardly even talk. But it's good to lie together in bed, our ankles touching. It's even good, after all this time, to hear him snoring.

I lie awake thinking of the shoe, unable to believe it is conclusive, unable to accept that it means anything at all. Surely any number of explanations could account for its presence on Baker Beach. Emma, for example, wanted to take off her shoes, but I would not allow it, as Ocean Beach is littered with broken glass. Maybe, after walking ahead of me, she simply disobeyed. Or maybe the kidnapper gained her trust by encouraging her to do so, after I had forbidden it. Perhaps the kidnapping was planned in detail and the perpetrator had a change of clothing so that Emma would not be spotted, in which case he would have disposed of the clothes she was wearing.

Why only one shoe, instead of two? And what of a body? Unless we see a body, we can never know for certain. Add to that the sightings — thousands of calls to the command post, hundreds of messages posted to the website. Just two days ago, a San

277

Francisco woman vacationing in Florida called to say she'd seen a girl who fit Emma's description in Fort Walton Beach. The lead went nowhere, but the fact is there are still leads. If even one is correct, then Emma might still be alive.

Sherburne has argued many times that Emma may have accidentally strayed too close to the water, but he says this because he doesn't know her. In my mind, I've gone over the possibilities countless times — could she have miscalculated the distance of the water because of the fog? Could she have seen one of those perfect sand dollars and, for a moment, forgotten her fear? I keep coming back to the same answer, which has more to do with conviction than with scientific probability: she could not have drowned, because that would mean she is dead. It would mean there's no reason to keep looking.

I once read an article about a wild elephant whose cub was stillborn. A photographer looked on in horror while the mother kicked the lifeless body, over and over, for three hours. Then something happened: the baby stirred. His mother had literally kicked him to life by stimulating his heart. Only instinct could drive her to do this.

While memory is the flimsy stuff of image, easily influenced by external suggestions, instinct is utterly internal. Memory may impose incorrect clues into my waking dream of that day at the beach with Emma, false images, dead ends. I'm willing to accept that memory fails me.

But instinct — that firmer, truer thing — tells me she is alive. Not possibly alive. Not hopefully alive. There are times when instinct speaks only in terms of absolutes. Emma is alive, and she is waiting for me.

48

The next morning I drive out to Baker Beach.
The twin arches of the Golden Gate Bridge peek
above the fog. There are no sunbathers out today
— too cold — just a teenage couple eating bagels
and sipping coffee on a picnic bench. He's facing
the table and she's facing him, legs wrapped
around his waist. Seeing them together like that,
so blissfully oblivious to the world, reminds me
of those early days with Ramon, how I'd suffer
through class waiting. When the lunch bell rang,
I'd sling my backpack over my shoulder and run
out to the curb, where he'd be waiting for me in
his beat-up Jeep Wrangler. Sometimes we'd drive
to the Dew Drop Inn for catfish fillets and
shakes; more often we'd just go to his place.
Then there would be the rush to get out of our
clothes and into bed, knowing I had to be back
to school in time for Mrs. Truly's French class.
The sex was so good I remember it still, but
sometimes I wonder if nostalgia paints those
days a different, better color. Maybe the reason
he seemed like such a phenomenal lover was
simply that I had no basis for comparison.

I wander north along the beach and pick my
way among the rocks, searching for something
the tourist might have missed, but find only the
usual trash — empty beer cans, a baseball cap, a
worn silver guilder that seems out of place and
out of time, like loot from some sunken ship. I

imagine Emma here, shoved up against these rocks, a stranger's hands on her. I can't shake the image. Maybe Jake's way is better, after all.

On the way home I stop by his house, but he's not there. The phone at the command post rings twelve times; not even an answering machine picks up. At my loft, I spend a couple of hours answering e-mail from findemma.com and making the usual phone calls. I have a list of every hospital in the country. Over the last few months I've called every facility at least once, and now I'm making my way through a second round of calls. It's always the same story — a bored switchboard operator who connects me to admissions, a series of hurried administrative personnel, my description of Emma, finally an impatiently uttered 'There's no one here by that name or description.'

It's almost noon when I leave my place on foot. It's sunny here, the main benefit of living in noisy Potrero Hill. When Jake and I first decided to get married, we briefly considered selling his two-bedroom house in the foggy Sunset and buying one out here, but by then the dot-com boom had already driven the prices prohibitively high. Before everything happened with Emma, I'd been thinking how much I was going to miss this neighborhood, its slightly dirty industrial charm, the crumbling Victorians with their tidy flower boxes and optimistic gardens, the ever-present hum of freeway traffic. I used to love walking in my neighborhood, could kill whole weekends drinking coffee at Farley's or browsing the shelves at Christopher's Books, eating barbecue at Bottom of the Hill. Now, all my old haunts have a picture of Emma in the window, and I can hardly remember a time before she was gone, before this horrific unknowing gnawed at my edges every minute of every day.

By the time I get to the Castro, my T-shirt and jeans are damp with sweat. I push through the omnipresent crowd, make my way to the command post. Looking through the window, I find myself face-to-face with Brian, who is peeling tape off the glass. The pictures of Emma are gone. The telephones, tables, chairs, and radio have disappeared. Inside, where a few days ago there were half a dozen volunteers, there is only Brian.

'What's this?' I say. 'Where is everyone?'

Brian steps down from his stool. 'Don't you know?'

'Know what?'

'Mr. Balfour called this morning and told me to close up shop.'

'What are you talking about?'

'The cops are officially closing the investigation.'

'That's not possible. Jake would have told me.'

Brian shrugs. 'I'm as shocked as you are.'

'They can't do this.' I grab one of the flyers he's just taken down and tape it to the window.

'Abby,' he says gently, 'they'll just get taken down again.'

One of Sam Bungo's slogans rattles through my mind. 'Every night, every day, strive to keep up your PMA!' PMA stood for positive mental

282

attitude. Sam believed that with a PMA, anything was possible.

'We could be *this* close,' I say. 'We could be hours away from finding her.'

'I know,' he says. 'I didn't think it would end this way. I met her once, you know. Mr. Balfour brought her by the school one Saturday. I was painting posters for our food drive, and I asked Emma if she wanted to help. Somehow she got her feet into the paint. She left little red footprints all down the hallway.' He wads up a ball of tape and tosses it into the trash can. 'It's crazy, that a sweet kid like that can go missing. Makes you think the world is just completely fucked up.'

A paralyzing despair sets in. How is it possible that I'm the only one who holds out any hope for her?

I step outside onto the crowded street. It's Sunday, and the Castro is teeming with tourists and teenagers, young men who've made the pilgrimage from the East Bay and Marin and Antioch to the lively gay mecca beneath the giant rainbow flag. A line of eager young guys has formed on Eighteenth Street, at the door to The Badlands. Outside Daddy's, graying men in black leather congregate. Each bar has its theme, its regular clientele. The mingled scent of smoke and something else — a cloyingly sweet, sexual smell — saturates the air. A crowd gathers outside the Castro Theatre. Today's film: a revival of *Barbarella*, and a Jane Fonda look-alike contest.

A hand brushes my leg, and I look down to see

a homeless teenager sitting on the sidewalk, gazing up through bloodshot eyes. He has a ring on every finger. 'Hey,' he says, 'I'll read you a poem for a quarter.'

I drop some change into his cup, push through the crowds, descend beneath Market Street, and step onto the outbound Muni platform just as the doors close on the K-Ingleside. In the second car there is a girl, nose pressed to the window, black hair spilling over her shoulders. As the train begins moving I rush forward and bang my fists on the glass. The girl jumps back, terrified. In a twitch of her face, a movement of her hand as she reaches for the woman beside her, I realize I don't know her. Something at the center of me deflates.

'You okay?' a man asks. On the crowded platform, everyone is staring. 'No,' I say. 'I'm sorry. I thought it was someone I knew.'

On the street again, in the too-brilliant sunlight, I begin walking. I don't know where I'm going. I walk through the afternoon and into evening — down Market Street, onto Montgomery, up Columbus, down Broadway. As the sun sets I find myself over in South Beach, standing beneath the Bay Bridge, looking up at the steel arcs. Cars rumble across. The cold gray waters of the bay lap against the edge of the city. The fog is rolling in, softening the angles of the buildings. The headlights of oncoming cars hover yellowish in the mist. The sheer number of cars is overwhelming. All those vehicles, by the millions, in which a kidnapper might make his escape. All those trunks in which a child might be hidden.

All the bridges a car might cross en route to somewhere else. There is a girl. Her name is Emma. She is walking on a beach. There is a girl. There is a girl. I feel the brittle threads of my sanity unraveling. The bay waters seem to be darkening, coming closer. It would be so easy to fall forward, so easy to simply forget. Up ahead, the stadium lights of PacBell Park glow bluish in the fog; a moment later I hear the roar of the crowd.

49

It's after nine in the evening when I get to Jake's house. He's in the kitchen filling the recycling bin with envelopes and flyers. When I walk in unannounced, he looks up and blinks slowly, as if emerging from a dark room. 'Hi,' he says, attempting a smile.

'Tell me you're not giving up.'

'Give me another option.'

'We keep looking.'

'I had a plan, Abby,' he says. 'The command post, television, radio. I kept giving myself benchmarks to go by. I thought we'd distribute ten thousand flyers, and we'd get a lead that would take us to her. When that didn't happen, I raised the bar: fifty thousand flyers, seventy-five thousand, a hundred. Every time I raised it, I thought this was what would do it, this time we'd get to her. And the reward money. I started at fifty thousand. Then a hundred fifty, then two hundred, four hundred, half a million. I've sold all my stocks, refinanced the house, and approached everyone I know and a hundred I don't in order to have the biggest cache of reward money possible. Nothing. And the volunteers. At the highest point, we had almost three hundred. Do you know I've done one hundred six radio interviews? Forty-two television spots? I've talked on the phone with hundreds of police officers all over the country.

I've done everything. I don't know what else to do.'

I go into the living room and switch on a lamp. The bulb sputters briefly, then dies out with a soft click. 'We could be so close.'

'You're ignoring the obvious,' he says. He sits on the sofa and picks a book up from the coffee table, sets it down again. Some philosophy textbook, with a ratty cover and Post-it tabs sticking out of the pages. 'Her shoe. Her little shoe. I could do a thousand more interviews, send out a million more flyers, and it wouldn't change the facts.'

I sit down beside him. 'You're making way too much of the shoe. It doesn't mean anything.'

He leans back and stares at the ceiling. His hand under mine is hot and damp. He smells different, not like himself, and I realize it's because his clothes have been washed with a different detergent. For as long as I've known him, he's carried with him the faint scent of Surf, but since Emma disappeared he's been having his clothes laundered at a place on the corner. He once told me that he couldn't bring himself to do the laundry anymore, because Emma used to help him. She loved separating the whites from the darks and measuring the detergent.

A bus passes on the street. A church bell chimes. The distance between us grows greater by the minute.

'I miss her so much,' he says, 'some days I don't want to get out of bed. A couple of weeks ago at Safeway, I picked up a pack of gummy worms, because she always expects them when I come home from the grocery store. I was at the checkout, and the girl slid the package across the scanner, and it hit me. I started bawling. I couldn't get myself together enough to take out my money, or even to get out of line. Several people were waiting behind me. The girl called her manager. He came over and asked if I needed help out to the car. I felt like a crazy person.' He squeezes my hand. 'There will be a lot of awful days, but we can't stop living.'

'I don't want to stop living. I just want to find her.'

'It's been almost six months,' he says. 'Six.'

His breath rattles softly. At this moment, I love him, but a startling possibility reveals itself to me: maybe I love *her* more. There's a longing so deep it feels as if my body has been emptied out, as if there is nothing at the center of me but cold blank air. During the past six months, Emma has been with me every day. She's the first thought on my mind when I wake up, the last image I see before I fall asleep. Her face, her name, are with me minute by minute. My life is guided by a single goal — to find her. Jake, meanwhile, has grown less distinct with each passing week, our conversations fewer and farther between, our moments of true connection dwindling to almost nothing.

To love a man is one thing, but to love a child is something else entirely; it is all-consuming. Before Emma, when people talked about the kind of love a child could provoke, I did not believe them. Then Emma came along, and now

I can't imagine living the rest of my life without her. Maybe love is a divining rod that seeks out the people who need you most. When I first began to fall for Jake, I saw Emma as part of the package. Now, she has moved from periphery to center.

The three of us made plans. Paris for her tenth birthday. Prague for her twelfth. At sixteen, when she gets her license, a driving tour of the States. I picture her at the Louvre, standing in front of the *Mona Lisa*, making funny faces. And then, a few years older, in blue jeans and pale pink lipstick, sitting behind the wheel, singing along to the radio, while Jake navigates from the backseat and I check off our list of roadside attractions. Her face is blurred, like a photo shot in low light with the subject moving too fast, but there is enough of her essential being in these images for me to believe in them.

Jake stands and paces. 'I want a service,' he says, biting his lip. He goes over to the window, pulls aside the curtain, and looks out at the street, his back to me. For a moment, the room is suffused with a soft yellow light.

'What kind of service?'

'A memorial.' He clears his throat and drops the curtain into place. The room goes dim again. 'To say goodbye.'

'Not yet. Just give me a little more time.'

'For what?'

'To look for her.'

'Stop. Please. You're only making it worse.'

He's still standing with his back to me when I go upstairs, into Emma's bedroom. I lie on top

289

of the covers and stare up at the ceiling. The room is beginning to lose Emma's distinct smell, and I wonder if Jake has noticed this. A year from now, will a visit to her room yield no particular smell at all?

I turn my head on the pillow and see something there, a strand of Emma's hair. I pick it up and hold it taut between my fingers, this object outside of time. I lay it across my forehead and wish for some jolt of electricity, some telepathic communication from Emma.

We used to sit on the bed together, legs crossed, and she'd lean back while I wove beads into her hair. For days after, she'd pull at the braids, leaving beads all over the house. The house was hers. Every inch of it bore some sign of her — the crayons on the kitchen table, her sandals by the back door, a shoe box of Barbie clothes under the coffee table in the living room. In the morning, she would often wake up before Jake and I did, and the sound of her feet padding down the stairs brought me into the day.

Downstairs, now, heavy footsteps. Down the long hallway, through the kitchen, the dining room, the den, stopping at the foyer. The front door opens. Perhaps he's thinking of going out. A minute or so later, the door shuts again, but I can still hear him down there. There's nowhere to go, nothing to do, no way to escape.

50

Brain injury patients often remember childhood in startling detail, but are unable to remember events from more recent years. They talk about friends they haven't seen in decades as if they'd just seen them hours ago. They may remember presents they received for their fifth birthday, but be unable to read even the simplest book.

Each day I sift through memories like a desperate miner panning for gold. Too many things turn up there — moments from childhood that are no use to me now, names and faces, places I haven't visited in years. The one thing I'm searching for, the clue that will lead me to Emma, remains buried, irretrievable. Each memory that surfaces distracts me from the task — just so much trash clogging up the brain waves. The memories come to me clearly, complete with sound and motion, even the suggestion of smell. I want nothing to do with this worthless information, but here it is, demanding to be noticed.

Gulf Shores, Alabama. I am nine, at the beach with my family. I remember a woman and a man, lying beside us on bright yellow towels. They were drinking iced tea from plastic cups and reading paperback books. Although they were probably the same age as my parents, they seemed to be blessed with some youthful spirit that my parents had never possessed. He was wearing surf shorts, and she was clad in a tiny black bikini. My own father wore khaki shorts and tennis shoes, my mother an ankle-length sarong and T-shirt. The couple was sitting with a boy my age who kept looking up at me and grinning. His hair was blond with a slight green chlorine tint, and he was very tan. On his nose was a spot of white sunscreen.

While my family sat under the shade of two umbrellas, a small cooler perched at each corner of a king-size sheet, that other, happier family lay glistening in the sun, their legs and arms dusted with sand. The woman had large breasts, dark brown cleavage plunging toward the gold clasp of her bikini. While my mother worked her crossword and my father listened to the Bama game on a transistor radio, and Annabel lay sleeping, I observed the family from behind my Mickey Mouse sunglasses, trying to devise schemes by which I might touch the woman's magnificent breasts.

The boy scooped sand with a plastic shovel and dumped it on his father's back.

'Son,' the man said, not glancing up from his book.

The boy tried the same thing with his mother. 'Why don't you go build a sandcastle?' she said. The boy pouted for a second, then picked up his bucket and shovel and went down to the water's edge. He worked halfheartedly at a sandcastle for a while, then tossed aside the bucket and shovel and stomped into the water. It was a hot, still day, the sun so bright the water was difficult to look at. From the beach the waves looked calm, but wooden signs posted at intervals along the beach said, *Strong Undertow. Swim at Your Own Risk.*

The boy ran in and out of the surf. I wanted to go join him, but my parents would not allow it. 'Swimming is for swimming pools,' my father was fond of saying. For a few minutes I watched the boy with envy. He kept looking back to see if anyone was paying attention. Once, I waved at him. He grinned, then flopped down on the sand and did a strange wiggling dance, his legs kicked up in the air, his mouth hanging open. After I while I grew bored and turned my attention back to his mother.

I don't know how many minutes passed before the woman sat up and looked out at the ocean. 'Tom,' she said.

The man turned a page of his book. 'Hmm.'

'I don't see Charles.'

She stood up and started walking toward the water. The man dropped his book and followed her. Then they weren't walking but running, both of them screaming, 'Charles!'

My father stood up and rushed down to the water's edge. Annabel woke, stretched. 'What's happening?'

Suddenly the atmosphere of the beach changed. The panic spread quickly in every direction, so that within minutes every adult on that beach was shouting Charles's name. The women held tightly to their own children, while the fathers shed shirts and sandals and leapt into the ocean. It was exciting and somewhat circuslike, as the torpor of the day exploded into chaos.

Lifeguards appeared. Fishing boats that had been anchored offshore began moving toward the beach. Before long, a patrol boat crept through the waves, sirens blaring. Charles's name was broadcast through megaphones. It felt as if time was speeding up.

When we gathered our towels and ice chests later that afternoon, the woman in the black bikini was sitting at the water's edge, screaming, her hair hanging in matted strings around her face. Her husband sat on his knees opposite her, silent and shaking. Between them, stretched out pale and bluish on the wet sand, was the boy. His eyes were open, his lips parted slightly. A piece of seaweed was tangled around his ankle. He looked beautiful and very clean lying there, perfectly still. I expected him, even then, to wake up — to kick his legs, wink at me, and laugh. A swell joke.

We drove home in silence. My mother wept as my father stared ahead at the road. A blast of thunder shook the car, and it began to rain. The windshield wipers ticked and squealed. At one point my mother turned around in her seat and clutched my and Annabel's hands. 'Girls.' That was all she said; she spoke the word so quietly, she might have been saying a prayer.

I wiped the fogged window and watched the miles of beach roll by, the sand dunes and towering sea grass, the little pink houses on stilts. Lightning flashed over the ocean. My shoulders stung from a slight burn. The car smelled warm and sweet. There was salt on my lips. I was thirsty, but didn't know how to ask, in that horrible silence, for something to drink. Annabel slept, her legs sprawled on the seat between us, her head tilted back at an impossible angle, mouth open wide. I kept glancing over to make sure she was breathing. I rested a hand on her warm foot, just to know she was alive. In those moments I loved her fiercely.

At some point I dozed off. The car hummed over the highway. In my restless sleep, I was vaguely aware of my mother staring at us, an odd light in her eyes, as if we were new and strange and special.

51

Day 184. After the support group, David invites me over to his place for coffee. I follow him to Cole Valley. His home is a restored Victorian on a quiet block. Inside, dark wood floors and utter silence.

He flips a switch in the foyer, and the house is flooded with light and music. 'Like it? I rigged it so that this switch controls all the lights in the house, plus the power to the stereo.'

'Impressive.'

'For a second, when I walk in, I can pretend I'm not coming home to an empty house.'

The focal point of the living room is a grand piano. On it rests the sheet music for 'Piano Concerto Number Five.' I strike a key, and it lets out a low groaning note. 'You play?'

He shakes his head. 'My wife does. Did. She was teaching Jonathan. He was pretty good. He had these ridiculously long fingers. I don't know if that really matters, but Jane thought it was a good sign.'

The mantel and end tables are crowded with framed family photographs — David and Jonathan at the entrance to Disneyland; Jane and Jonathan sitting at a picnic table, a bucket of Kentucky Fried Chicken on the table between them; the whole family waving from the bow of a ferry, the Statue of Liberty in the background. On one wall is a series of color photos shot inside a studio, against fake backgrounds. In a couple of the photos, Jonathan is playing with a cocker spaniel.

'You have a dog?'

'No.' He laughs. 'Never did. The dog's a prop. Jonathan wouldn't cooperate with the photographer, so she brought this puppy into the studio.'

'Cute.'

The photo reminds me of those awful Olan Mills sessions my mother used to drag us to. The studio was in a strip mall on Airport Boulevard, and it smelled of Lysol. The photographer always wore a T-shirt bearing the insignia of some fifth-rate college. He'd tell us we had good teeth, then make us lean against a fake wooden fence, smiling broadly and tucking our thumbs in our belt loops, as if life was some pastoral paradise, as if we didn't live in the suburbs.

'Decaf or regular?'

'Either.'

He leads me into the kitchen. More photos on the walls. When he opens the cabinet to get two mugs, I notice several kiddie-size glasses decorated with Disney characters.

David puts two frozen bear claws in the microwave, hits defrost, and starts a pot of coffee. 'I'll give you the grand tour while it's brewing. First stop, the guest room.' He leads me upstairs, into a wallpapered room that looks like it came out of one of those Southern home-décor magazines. 'I should probably turn it into a study. No one's slept in here in years. Jane used it for a while before she moved out.'

Above the wrought-iron bed hangs a framed

sketch of a boy. The hair is light brown, the chubby contours of the face filled in with peach-colored pencil. 'It's an age-progression sketch,' David explains. 'Jonathan at eleven.' There is such detail to the drawing, such expression in the eyes, it's difficult to believe I'm looking at a picture of a boy who never was. David reaches forward and adjusts the frame. Downstairs, the microwave shuts off and beeps three times.

Next, he leads me into a room with pale blue walls. Clouds have been stenciled onto the ceiling, and model airplanes hang from string all around the room. The twin-size bed is tidily made up with dinosaur sheets. There's a head-shaped dent in the pillow, as if someone were just sleeping there recently. David reaches up and touches a wing on one of the airplanes. 'Jonathan and I made a bunch of these together. He wanted to be a pilot.' He smiles. 'He also planned to train dinosaurs for the circus and work week-ends as a cowboy.' He tips the wing with his finger, and the plane begins to twirl. 'What did Emma want to be?'

I pretend not to notice his use of the past tense. 'She has her heart set on masonry. We tried to talk her into architecture instead, since the money's better, but she likes the actual construction. Last year Jake bought her a toy bricklaying kit. It comes with little plastic bricks, and this powder that you mix with water to make mortar. She started building a wall that she thought would reach all the way to the sky. Her plan was to climb the wall until she reached the moon, where she would build a new house for all of us to live in. She planned to throw lavish parties to which the presidents of all the countries of the world would be invited.'

'Sounds like she could have a future in politics.'

Future. The word sounds almost delusional, too much to hope for. Yet the only thing that keeps me going these days is exactly that — a wavering hope in the possibility of a future — Emma and Jake and me, doing all those things families do, despite the fact that, with each day, the hope decreases by a fraction.

'Great airplanes,' I say. As soon as the words are out of my mouth, they sound stupid, too casual. I wish I could think of something to say that would convey the sympathy I feel.

David surveys the dozen or so models soaring above his dead son's room. 'I have nearly a hundred more down in the basement — 747s, Cessnas, fighters, you name it.' His voice wavers. 'I just keep waiting for the grief to subside, but it never does. I keep waiting for the morning when I wake up and realize I don't want him back anymore. But every day, I want him just as badly as I did the day he disappeared.'

He moves closer, puts his hand under my chin, and lifts my face to meet his. I turn my mouth away, so that his kiss lands on my cheek — an old high school trick that feels awkward now, out of place in the adult world. David takes my hand and leads me across the hallway, to another bedroom. In this one there are no photographs, just a bed with white sheets, a wooden dresser, beige walls.

He goes in for the kiss again, and this time I let him. Even as I open my mouth, I know how wrong it is. Feeling David's tongue on my own, breathing the Ivory soap smell of his skin, I hear Sam Bungo's voice in my head: 'Situation, Participation, Extrication.'

David finds the buttons on the side of my skirt. The skirt falls, I hear the ping of buttons against the hardwood floor. Standing here in sweater, underwear, and shoes, what I feel is not lust, but pity. It occurs to me that perhaps David feels sorry for me as well. Maybe he sees my ongoing search as nothing more than a pathetic attempt to postpone the inevitable.

He kisses me again, slides his hand under my sweater, touches my breast. Then he takes off his clothes, item by item: his shoes, shirt, pants, socks — looking at me uncertainly while he undresses, as if he's waiting for me to call it off. And I'm telling myself, *Don't do this.*

David's chest is thin and hairless, his body pale, with blue veins snaking just beneath the skin. Maybe he deserves at least this small thing, this momentary comfort. He has lost so much, and I don't know how to say no. Standing there, he looks so insubstantial, more boy than man, except for the erection. My pity gives way to something else, and I can feel something moving through my body — a hot, insistent need. I can't deny that part of me wants to feel the pushing open, the good and painful pressure, the building toward release. Part of me wants to exit the world in this way. Part of me craves the act that

300

will help me forget for a moment.

He moves closer, his erection pressing against my leg.

'It's been six months,' I say. I'm not sure if he heard me, so I say it again. 'Six months to the day since she disappeared.'

He pushes me toward the bed, sits me down, and gently takes off my shoes. When he goes to turn off the light, I notice a birthmark on his right hip in the shape of an avocado. I think of Ramon, the first man I ever saw naked: his perfect arms, his muscular hips, his long legs and oddly small hands. I never really noticed his hands until I saw him naked, and when I looked at them for the first time, I felt a wave of tenderness for him.

The light goes off, and that's when I notice his digital clock, projecting the time onto the ceiling in huge red numbers: hour, minutes, seconds. It's the numbers that bring me back, the thought of Emma out there in the world somewhere, waiting.

'I should go,' I say, standing up.

He moves toward the bed. 'Don't.'

I maneuver into my skirt and slip on my shoes, already hating myself for what almost happened.

David stands inches away, naked, watching me. I'm angry with him for knowing, without asking, just which buttons to push.

'Goodbye,' I say.

'Please,' he says. 'Don't go. Spend the night. Nothing has to happen.'

I walk down the stairs and let myself out. Driving home through the nighttime chill, clouds of mist hovering in front of my headlights, I do not feel entirely solid, entirely alive in the world. I avoid the rearview mirror, the windows that reflect everything in the dark — afraid that, if I were to look closely, I would not recognize myself.

52

Photography is all about light. The word *photography* comes from the Greek words *photos*, meaning light, and *graphein*, meaning writing. Every time you take a picture, you are writing in light.

The function of a camera lens is to bend light. The function of film is to record the pattern of light transmitted through the lens. Film is just a piece of plastic containing light-sensitive grains, which undergo a chemical reaction when exposed to light. If you allow too much light through the lens, too many grains will react, and the picture will appear washed out. If you don't let enough light hit the film, too few grains will react, and the picture will be too dark.

Light is not only essential to the photographer's trade; it is also the photographer's greatest enemy. This is why a darkroom must be completely sealed off. Every darkroom has at least one safelight, usually a red or amber light that does not cause a visible change to light-sensitive materials. The safelight is used while transferring images from negatives to print paper and moving the prints through the chemicals.

There is a period, however, when every photographer is in total dark: when the unprocessed film is removed from the cassette and wound around the developing reel. This must be done precisely — making sure to get the film tight, and to touch only the edges. One slip of the fingers can ruin the entire roll.

The photographer relies completely on her eyes. She relates to the world through image, through the visual, what she can see. But for those few minutes, alone in the pitch-black darkroom, everything must be done by touch, by instinct, without sight.

What is a search if not an exercise in blindness?

In the hours after Emma's disappearance, I imagined the search area as a circle that expanded as the minutes and hours passed. Now, six months into the search, the area of possibility is nightmarishly large. The fact is, there is no limit to this particular search. Emma could be anywhere: in California, New York, London, Madrid. She could be in Alaska or Alabama.

From the beginning, I have been blindly groping in the dark.

The problem with a safelight is that it is never entirely sufficient for the task. You would always like to see more. You would like to be able to judge with absolute precision the density of the grain, the precision of focus. Yet, in the darkroom, you are immensely grateful for the safelight. Its vague illumination, after the experience of total dark, comes as a great relief. What I would give now for a safelight. Some small thing to guide me.

53

And we all go with them, into the silent funeral, Nobody's funeral, for there is no one to bury.

— T. S. Eliot, *Four Quartets*

Jake has been talking to a therapist. 'Closure,' the therapist says, 'requires a ritual acknowledgment of her death.'

Thus the casket. I went with Jake to pick it out. A funeral home on Geary, plush carpet and hushed rooms, next door to a burger joint. A man in a pin-striped suit led us down a long hallway to a set of double doors, beyond which an office was set up to look like someone's parlor. Grandmotherly, Victorian, with a curvy mauve sofa and three tall upholstered chairs. With one long, pale finger, the funeral director turned the pages of a leather-bound book containing photographs and ad copy. He tried to sell us something made especially for little girls, shiny white with hand-painted angels and flowers, satin lining in Pepto-Bismol pink.

'You can have something special inscribed on the casket,' he said, and proceeded to read us a rhyming poem written by Anonymous. The director gave a disapproving look when Jake went with the simple oak casket, no gaudy brass fittings or filigreed handles, no poem.

That was three days ago. The memorial service will be held today at eleven. 'I want you to be there,' Jake says now over the phone, his voice sounding extraordinarily tired. Coffee is percolating in the background.

It has been 198 days. This morning I did the math:

4,752 hours.

285,120 minutes.

17,107,200 seconds.

'Well?' He waits, breathing into the phone.

In truth, I don't have the right to deny him anything. Because I was not careful, because I looked away, because some maternal instinct in me faltered for a matter of seconds, because I chose the wrong direction in those crucial moments, Emma is gone. It is my guilt that has made this gathering necessary, my unspeakable failure that will bring these mourners together.

'Of course.'

I can hear Jake pouring a cup of coffee, a spoon clinking against the sides of the mug as he stirs the sugar in. 'You'll come over? We'll ride together?'

'Yes.'

I scan my closet for something black, put on tasteful makeup, and go over to Jake's house. We ride to the church together, not speaking, his eyes on the road, his face unreadable. I stand in front of the congregation at the big Catholic church, the church whose windows I've admired numerous times from the street. Most of the people we would have invited to our wedding are here, along with Emma's school friends and their

306

parents, the volunteers from the command post, Detective Sherburne, police officers who helped with the investigation. Someone, perhaps one of Jake's students, leaked the service to a reporter, and many strangers are in attendance as well. Even Leslie Gray is here, along with her cameraman.

Jake and I sit in the front row, holding hands. He is quiet, composed. Resigned.

Several people get up and talk about Emma — her first-grade teacher, her cello instructor, the mother of her best friend. We're fifteen minutes into the ceremony when Lisbeth arrives. She walks to the front of the church, presses past me in the pew, and plants herself on Jake's other side.

When it's my turn to speak, I look out at the crowd of somber faces and name all the things I love about Emma. I tell anecdotes in which Emma comes alive for the audience, repeating funny little things she said, making the mourners laugh at her dream of being a stonemason. I thank the good people of San Francisco for their support.

As I return to my seat, Lisbeth stands. It occurs to me that she's about to take the podium, as if she has some right to eulogize a child she doesn't even know. Jake grabs her firmly by the arm. 'No,' he says, in a voice loud enough for half the church to hear. Lisbeth clears her throat, attempts a smile, and sits back down.

When the service is over, I ride to the cemetery with Jake, behind the hearse that carries a small, empty coffin. The burial is a private ceremony, just me, Jake, the priest, a couple of teachers from Jake's school, and the family of Emma's best friend. Lisbeth is absent. As the coffin is lowered into the ground, Jake finally allows himself to cry in public.

I find myself crying, too. Yet, the whole time, I want to shout that this is a lie. There is no truth to this coffin, no truth to the small grave, the upturned earth, the smell of fresh-cut grass. Emma is alive.

'Maybe it's time,' Jake says as we're driving back to his house.

'Time for what?'

'Our wedding. It wouldn't have to be a big affair. We could just go to the justice of the peace.'

I briefly consider the possibility. Maybe it's not a terrible idea. Maybe we could forge a fragile peace in the early months of our marriage, learn to live together under these new terms, maybe even find a way to be happy.

'Well?' he says.

'You know I want to marry you, Jake. You know I love you — '

'I've been thinking about this a lot, Abby. Ever since her little shoe appeared, I've been thinking about trying to find a way to keep going. You see these parents on TV, parents who lose a child and turn their grief into something significant, something positive. And it occurred to me that I can't be like John Walsh. Maybe it's selfish, but I can't keep reliving this for the next thirty years. I want to get some kind of life back. Maybe one day you and I could start trying to have a baby. I know we can't replace Emma, I know another child won't eliminate the pain, but we have to find a way to move on.

'Do you remember a conversation we had a long time ago, when we first decided to get married? I told you that I loved you for a dozen reasons, and only one of them was that you would be a good mother to Emma. That hasn't changed.'

'I just don't think this is the right time, Jake.' I don't know what else to say, how to explain to him what I'm feeling. Part of me wants so badly to be with him, to get back to some sort of life together, that I wish I could take back my words as soon as I've said them. But the fact is I don't want a life based on a falsehood, on the illusion of Emma's death. My mother always accused me of desiring too much, of getting an idea in my head and being too stubborn to revise it to fit reality. But this is what I want, this is what, in clearer moments, I am still able to visualize: Jake and me and Emma, together as a family. Nothing less.

After a quiet reception at Jake's house, I go home, change clothes, and take the coast road south out of the city. It's four in the afternoon when I reach Half Moon Bay. I spend a couple of hours there, talking to surfers, showing the picture of Emma, the sketches of the couple from the van. On the way home I stop at the Taco Bell in Pacifica, which is perched on an absurdly beautiful piece of beach with panoramic views of the ocean. It's been a good surfing day, 'a fine west swell' according to the surf report being broadcast on someone's radio, and the surfers are giddy, spent, wolfing down tacos and bean burritos as if they hadn't eaten in days. I order a Coke, sit alone at a tiny two-top, and search the faces in the crowd.

The northbound lane of the coast road is crowded with day-trippers, and it takes over an hour to get back to the city. I take the Great Highway and veer right on Point Lobos Avenue, following Geary up through the Richmond, past the Alexandria and the Coronet. The latter has just closed down after eighty years in business, one more grand old movie house lost. It was Emma's favorite theater; now, the marquee reads: *Future Home of The Institute on Aging*.

I stop in front of the church and go inside. In front of the altar a few candles still burn. I sit in the second pew and stare up at the flickering candles, the Virgin Mary, the shiny figure of Christ spreading his arms wide on a gilded cross. The church is empty save for a homeless man sleeping in the back. I lower the bench, kneel, and make the sign of the cross. I wait for some electricity in my fingers, a voice whispering from the dark. *Jesus is calling*, the choir used to sing. If there is a voice, surely I will hear it now.

Kneeling, hands folded, forehead pressed to my thumbs, I pray and cry and beg, making promises to a God I've never met. I am emptied, as the preachers always said I should be, but no great spirit wafts out of the dark to fill the void. At some point I hear a shuffling of feet. The church is filling with parishioners for evening mass. As I walk down the aisle toward the door, eyes scan me briefly and look away. I must look like some lunatic in my wrinkled clothes, my sand-covered shoes, my matted hair.

In the car again I turn on the radio, just for something to fill the black space in my brain. On KALW, Roman Mars is leading a fund-raiser. On KQED, Michael Krasney is interviewing Craig Newmark and Jim Buckmaster. I turn the dial past commercials and talk shows, skipping several stations until I finally find music. It's that Wilco song, of course, and I know I'll spend the rest of the day trying to get it out of my head.

54

And thou, Mnemnosyne mine, who art hidden beneath the thirty seals and immured within the dark prison of the shadow of ideas, let me hear thy voice sounding in my ear.

— Giordano Bruno

The hypnosis appointment is on a Monday. Dr. Shannon has a posh office in Palo Alto, just off the square. The lobby is done in oak, and artwork in expensive frames adorns the walls. A single white sofa stretches around the entire room. An attractive young man sits at an antique desk, recording something in a big ledger. His eyes are a startling shade of green — colored contact lenses. He takes my name, gives me a clipboard and pen, asks me to fill out some forms.

At precisely one o'clock, the assistant ushers me into a large room that smells of leather, where a sturdy woman in an orange pantsuit and purple scarf is perched on a tall chair.

'Dr. Shannon,' she says, offering her hand. She has a big, toothy smile, and tiny freckles across the bridge of her nose that make her look like a wholesome country girl. She's nothing like I expected. When I talked to her on the phone and explained the reason for my visit, her calm, deep voice made me imagine a thin woman in a black sheath, someone aloof and sophisticated.

'Please have a seat, Abby.'

I sink into the recliner, feeling at an immediate disadvantage. Dr. Shannon is up high, in her hardback chair, while I'm down low with my knees in the air. 'Before we begin, you should know a couple of things,' she says, staring at me with a disturbing intensity. 'First, memory is a deep sea.'

I nod, mesmerized by her pantsuit, her whimsical ideas about color, wondering where she got the idea that orange is the new black.

'Second, one cannot conquer memory, just as one cannot conquer the sea. One may dive into it, explore, but one may not own it. Understand?'

I nod again.

'Third, one must always come up for air. That's why I'm here. I'm going to help you dive in, then I'm going to lead you up for air.'

'Okay.'

'Are you comfortable?'

'Yes.'

'Good.'

'Maybe I should tell you I tried this once before. I had a lot of hope for where it might lead, but it didn't work out.'

'Maybe you weren't ready yet,' she says. 'Are you ready now?'

'I think so.'

She glances down at my feet — knee-high black boots. 'You might want to take your shoes off and get more comfortable.'

I unzip my boots and place them by my chair,

embarrassed that I didn't take the time to match my socks this morning.

'Good. Now I'm going to lead you into a state of deep relaxation, and then I'll ask you to talk about that day on the beach. When you come out of hypnosis, you should be able to remember everything clearly. You may experience changes in your body, like a feeling of lightness or heaviness.' She glances down at her notes. 'On the telephone, you said you want to remember all the details of the day your little girl disappeared, correct?'

'Yes, my fiancé's little girl.'

'Is there anything in particular you're looking for?'

'I'm most interested in the minutes leading up to the disappearance, after we arrived at the beach. License plates would be good. Anything specific about the people in the parking lot. Especially this couple in a van. Any markings on their van would be helpful.'

'Let's begin by closing your eyes,' Dr. Shannon says. Then she begins to talk, her voice deep and smooth. She says that I am comfortable, that I am tired, that memory is a deep, warm sea. She says I should trust her. She tells me to dive in. For a while nothing happens. She keeps talking, a low monotone. At some point I feel my body becoming lighter, as if my arms are floating.

'Go back to that day at Ocean Beach. You're in the parking lot with Emma. Tell me what you see.'

'An orange Chevelle. There's a man inside,

reading the paper. Windows down. Hula girl on the dashboard.'

'Good. What else?'

'A line of ants struggling along the pavement. Emma stops to look. A dead sand crab. Emma's yellow bucket, her red plastic shovel, her blue shoes. She's stomping the ants and the crab.'

'Very good,' Dr. Shannon says. Her voice is quiet, steady. The scene becomes more vivid, and I feel the details of that day washing over me. The hum of cars on Ocean Boulevard. The fog like some pleasant dream. The foam crackling, a sandcastle that's been mostly washed away, with just one rounded turret remaining.

'Let's stay in the parking lot for a while,' Dr. Shannon says. 'Take your time.'

I see a rope stretched taut at the edge of the lot, where the asphalt is crumbling away. The rock wall is disintegrating. 'California is falling into the ocean,' I say, aware of my mother's words coming out of my mouth, her oft-repeated refrain. As a child, I used to look at the U.S. map on the wall of my father's study and imagine the country breaking apart neatly along the California border, the whole state simply dropping off and floating away.

'What do you see in the parking lot?'

'A yellow van, one of those hippie numbers. There's a woman looking out of the window, smiling, waving at Emma. The driver's side door is open, and there's a man standing there, barefoot, shirtless, waxing a surfboard.'

'What does he look like, this man?'

'Good-looking, unshaven, sandy blond hair,

315

muscular arms. He winks at Emma and says hello. She looks up at me, and I squeeze her hand. She squeezes back; she's small but so strong. She has little calluses at the base of her fingers from holding on to the handlebars of her bike. 'Hi,' she says. The man replies that it's a beautiful day. He has a lazy eye.'

'Which eye?'

'The left.'

'Tell me about the van. What does it look like?'

'Pale yellow. Rust around the tires.'

'You said there are curtains in the window. What color?'

'Blue, trimmed with little red beads. And there's a crack in the windshield covered with duct tape.'

'Very good. What else?'

'There's a bumper sticker just below the window where the woman is looking out. Big white letters on a blue background, but the only one I can see is a *T*. There's a small figure of a man riding a wave over the top of the *T*.'

'Good. Now, walk around to the back of the van. Can you see the license plate?'

I see the place where the license plate should be, a blank rectangle, but nothing more.

'What color is the license plate?'

I feel my palms sweating, and my arms feel light, weightless. I'm aware of the importance of the license plate, but unable to make anything of it. I feel a warm hand on my own.

'It's okay,' Dr. Shannon says. 'Look at the man. Describe him.'

'His fingernails are very short. He's wearing a

bracelet — a thin silver chain with something dangling from it. On his chest there's a tattoo, a wave breaking over his nipple. At the apex of the wave, an oval birthmark.'

'Does he have any other tattoos?'

'No, that's all.'

'Any scars?'

'I don't think so.'

'Okay, Abby, now I want you to concentrate on the surfboard.'

'It's a longboard, propped against the van. A reddish color.'

'Does it have any markings?'

'In the center, there's some sort of insect.'

'What kind?'

'No, not an insect, a frog, a golden frog.'

'Are there any words on the board?'

'Something etched into the wood on the tail. A brand, maybe.'

'What does it say?'

'I can't read it.'

'You're doing well,' Dr. Shannon says. 'Let's talk a little bit about the woman in the window. What does she look like?'

'Blonde. Older than the man, leathery skin, too tan. She looks kind of crazy, you know, like she's not quite right.'

'What makes you think she looks crazy?'

'I don't know, just a feeling.'

'Can you tell me anything more about the van, Abby?'

I search and search, but nothing more comes to mind.

'What about the other cars in the parking lot?'

'There's a postal truck, a motorcycle.'

'What kind of motorcycle?'

'Small, red, a Honda maybe.'

'Is there anyone on it?'

'No.'

She coaches me along for several more minutes, asking questions I can't find an answer for. I'm trying to get closer to the man and the yellow van, but each time I take a step, they seem to move away, becoming less distinct.

A hand on my arm. 'Time to come up for air, Abby. We're in my office. Now, slowly, I'd like for you to open your eyes.'

Dr. Shannon has moved her chair closer to mine. She smells faintly of cigarettes. Am I imagining it, or is there a thin trail of smoke in the air beside her? She lets go of my hand and begins jotting notes on her yellow pad. 'How do you feel?'

'Fine. Was I hypnotized?'

'Oh, yes.'

'I didn't feel hypnotized.'

'That's perfectly normal.'

'Did we get anywhere?'

'You tell me. Think back on the information you revealed. Is any of it new?'

I notice for the first time that Dr. Shannon's purple scarf is printed with white monkeys. Some of the monkeys are smiling, some frowning, and some are sitting with their hands in their laps, like obedient schoolchildren.

As I sift through the memories, I feel a sinking disappointment. I've been through all this stuff before — just the same tired details, the same meaningless clues. 'But the frog,' I say. 'That's new. I didn't remember the frog on the surfboard before. Or the bumper sticker.'

'Good,' she says. She seems pleased but not at all surprised. She stands up and does an odd little bow, an indication that we're finished.

'Thank you,' I say.

'Certainly. Give my regards to your brother-in-law.'

★   ★   ★

I meet Jake for lunch at La Cumbre. We sit at a table in the back, beneath a tiny square window. He slides a knife into his burrito. Beans and salsa bleed onto the plate. He looks at my untouched food. 'You're wasting away.'

I stab at the burrito with my fork, sip sugary orange soda from a bottle. Tinny Mexican music drifts from the speakers. It's 'Hotel California,' with the lyrics redone in Spanish. On the wall above Jake's head, there's a painting of a dancing woman in a ruffled red skirt and heels.

'I went to a therapist,' I blurt.

'That's good, Abby.' In his eyes I can see he is pleased with me. 'Did it help?'

'Not a therapist, really. More of a — '

'A what?'

'Well, she was kind of a hypnotist.'

He sets his fork down, rests his elbows on the table. 'Why?'

'I wanted to remember. And I did, I came up with something. Remember the guy in the van?

319

During hypnosis, I was able to see his surfboard clearly.'

'What are you saying?'

'It's new, something I hadn't remembered before. It means that there are buried memories. If I remembered that detail, maybe I'll be able to remember others.'

'Do you know what I keep hoping?' he says, jiggling the ice in his glass. 'I keep hoping that at some point we can talk about us, our future. Ever since the ceremony at the church, that's the one thing I've really wanted, but you keep avoiding the subject.'

How to tell him that, in my mind, there is no future for us without Emma? Until I find her it's impossible to proceed. 'I know this doesn't sound like much,' I say, 'but it could turn out to be a real clue.'

I think of something the girl at the surf shop, Goofy, told me about the lull — the gap in the waves that surfers use to paddle out to the lineup. 'Without that quiet period between sets,' Goofy said, 'it would be impossible to get to the waves. Thing is, sometimes the lull lasts too long. Sometimes you get where you need to go, and then you just have to wait, and wait some more, and you start to think the lull will never end.' I feel as though the last few months have been a maddeningly long lull, and now I finally have a chance to make progress.

We spend the rest of the meal in silence. When he gets up to empty our trays into the trash, I catch a glimpse of something on the bottom of his shoe — a price tag, still white. I know it's not

320

right to feel so angry, not right to feel this urge to scream. But what I'm thinking is that he has taken this small step: he has gone out and bought a pair of shoes. He is beginning to start his life over again.

55

According to Isaac Newton, time flows of its own accord, a uniform movement entirely independent of human minds and material objects. It is like a broad river with no beginning and no end, staying its course through eternity. Centuries before Newton was born, Aristotle conceived of time as a cyclical entity grounded in astronomy. When the heavenly bodies returned to the positions they held at the moment of the world's inception, time would begin again.

In the fourth century, Saint Augustine gave us the measurements of B.C. and *anno Domini*, ascribing to time a linear scale based upon Christianity. He also argued in favor of the subjectivity of time, postulating that time might not be tied to planetary movement. But it was Einstein who revolutionized our concept of time, claiming that each inertial system in the universe has its own time parameter; therefore, there is no such thing as absolute time.

I think of Mrs. Monk, my third-grade teacher, standing on top of a chair, tacking a homemade clock to our classroom wall. The felt hands were color-coded: red for the hour, blue for the minute, yellow for the quick, predictable seconds. There was no hint in this system of the true complexity of time, no accounting for the number that Nell has recently brought to my attention: 9,192,631,770.

It is a youthful number in the long, controversial history of time. 9,192,631,770: the number of oscillations of a cesium atom's resonant frequency that occurs within the unit of measure we know as a second. A single, tiny second. It was only in 1967 that the cesium atom's natural frequency was formally recognized as the new, international unit of time. Today, the Coordinated Universal Time is defined by a group of atomic clocks around the world, the most impressive of which, NIST-F1, is housed at the National Institute of Standards and Technology in Boulder, Colorado. The NIST-F1 is so accurate that it will neither gain nor lose a second in twenty million years. Imagine this: twenty million years of seconds, following one by one, in a precise, brilliant choreography of time.

Anyone can see that a second by these standards is, in and of itself, nothing at all. A second is an irrelevance, a trifle, a laughable and passing thing.

I keep coming back, hour after hour, day after day, to those few seconds on the beach. In the long, elegant march of time, they are nothing; but in a single life, those seconds — each one perfect in its synchronicity, each one lasting exactly as long as the one before and after it — are everything. I imagine that Newton was right, and time is a smooth-flowing river. I can see Emma, alone, standing on the bank, never changing. In my mind she is always exactly as she is in the final moment I saw her — a small girl with a black ponytail, a yellow bucket, her back to me. On the river there is a figure — me — floating by. The cesium atom swings back and forth with impossible speed, each minuscule oscillation, each second, taking me farther away from her.

56

Day 214. I park in front of Dean's Foggy Surf Shop. Goofy is inside, behind the counter. She gives me a little salute. 'You're back.'

'Any luck with those?' I ask, pointing to the two police sketches mounted on the wall behind the counter.

'Sorry. Nada.'

'I have a question for you.' I lay a piece of paper on the counter in front of her. It's a drawing of the frog from the surfer's board, re-created to the best of my limited artistic ability.

Goofy smoothes the paper with both hands. Her fingernails are short and trim, glossy. On her right hand she wears three silver rings — one with a topaz stone, one a miniature chain, one that looks like a wedding band.

'What's this?' she asks.

'I saw it on a surfboard. *His* surfboard.'

'Looks familiar.' She turns to a door leading into a back room. 'Hey, Luke?'

A guy comes out. Balding, early forties, all muscle except for the beer paunch straining his T-shirt. 'Yeah?' He looks as if he just woke up.

'My friend says she saw this symbol on a board out at the beach. You know it?'

'Sure,' he says, scratching his head. 'It's a Billy Rossbottom, you know, the Killer Longboard.'

'Oh, right,' Goofy says. 'I heard about that

325

board, but I never saw one myself.'

'Most people haven't.'

'Who's Billy Rossbottom?' I ask.

'Who *was* he, you mean,' Luke says. 'He used to have a great store in Pismo. Rossbottom was a real artist. Only used balsa from Ecuador, wouldn't touch polyurethane foam. There are hardly any of them around; they're worth a hell of a lot. Sad about Billy.'

'Sad?'

'He was killed in a plane crash last year, twin-engine Cessna taking him to Miami to meet with the bigwigs at Panama Jack. He was working some deal to license his name. Some think he was lucky to kick the bucket before he had a chance to sell out.'

'Doesn't sound so lucky,' I say.

'Depends on your perspective. A real tragedy about the boards, though. After he died, his sister closed the shop for a few weeks until she could figure out what to do with it, and one night it burned to the ground. Lost twenty boards.'

'Know anybody who has one?'

'Sure, a neurosurgeon who lives in Pacific Heights.'

I point toward the sketch posted behind the counter, the one of the man from the yellow van. 'He wouldn't happen to look anything like that guy, would he?'

'Sorry,' Luke says. 'It's not your man. The doctor's a bona fide senior citizen.'

'I'll ask around for you,' Goofy says. 'Hey, you got somewhere you have to be right now?'

'Not really.'

'What say we go over to the Bashful Bull 2 for that breakfast special I told you about?'

'That'd be nice.'

We walk up Taraval in the fog. The silence is broken by the L-Taraval rattling past, carrying a single passenger. I turn around and walk backward a few steps, so I can see the ocean down at the end of the avenues, the gray beach. 'This city just kills me,' I say. 'I've lived here most of my adult life, and it still gets to me.'

'I know what you mean,' Goofy says. She turns around, too, and we stand for a minute looking down. The fog is rolling in from the ocean, a white mass moving toward us. A stray seagull wheels overhead.

'You ever read any Armistead Maupin?' she asks.

'A little.'

'He has this quote from Oscar Wilde at the beginning of *28 Barbary Lane*. 'It's an odd thing, but everyone who disappears is said to be seen in San Francisco.' He left out the best part: 'It must be a delightful city, and possess all the attractions of the next world.' '

'Sounds like my town.'

'The problem with San Francisco is it's easy to get stuck,' Goofy says. 'You can't imagine living anywhere else, so you stay. And then one day you realize five years have passed, and you haven't done anything yet.'

'You're twenty-four,' I say. 'You've got time.'

'Not that much time. I turned twenty-five a couple of weeks ago.'

327

'Happy birthday. Twenty-five is a great age to be.'

I remember how, when I was her age, nothing seemed quite clear, and the lack of clarity was liberating. There were so many options, so many directions my life could take. I never would have imagined *this* direction, *this* life.

Inside the diner, Goofy heads straight for a booth in the back. 'You want to go for special number two,' she says. 'Two eggs, hash browns, bacon or sausage, toast, and coffee. Special number one, the French toast, is nothing to write home about.'

I'm mesmerized by the way she eats — completely absorbed in her food, as if breakfast is an event. She polishes off the hash browns, then folds two pieces of bacon into her toast. 'What about those surf lessons?' she asks, in between bites.

'I grew up on the Gulf Coast. I don't think I'm cut out for cold water.'

'You wear a wet suit. You get used to it.'

'What about college?' I ask, changing the subject. 'Are you still planning to go?'

'I looked into it. Turns out U. of Hawaii is too expensive.'

'San Francisco State is pretty good, and tuition is reasonable.'

'As much as I love this city,' she says, 'I need to see something different. Where did you go?'

'Tennessee.'

'The South could be interesting. I've never been down south.' She finishes off her scrambled eggs. 'Hey,' she says, 'you got family?'

'I have a sister in North Carolina. My mom died a little over five years ago, and I rarely talk to my dad. He lives in Germany.'

'My dad picked up and left when I was ten, and my mother died a couple of years later. I had a few foster families, but I kind of lost touch with them.'

'I'm sorry. I didn't know.'

'Sucks, but you just kind of make do. Having a lot of friends helps, but it's not the same. Must be cool to have a sister.'

'It is. It's nice to have somebody who remembers what things were like when I was growing up, a shared history.'

We're interrupted by the waitress bringing the check. 'Okay then,' Goofy says outside.

'Thanks for your help.'

At the same time, both of us lean in to say goodbye. Goofy goes for a hug, I go for a kiss on the cheek, and what we accomplish is an awkward cross between the two.

'Don't be a stranger,' she says.

57

For the next couple of weeks, I bury myself in work. A wedding at the Olympic Club, a CEO's fiftieth birthday party at the Top of the Mark, a restaurant opening in Redwood City. To look through the viewfinder and see someone else's life is a kind of relief, not unlike the feeling of stepping into a dark movie theater and getting caught up in someone else's story, someone else's problems, an alternate view of the world. When things were really bad between my parents, when the fighting reached a fever pitch, my mother would load a purse with soft drinks and candy bars, grab a wad of cash from my father's wallet, and tell me and Annabel to get in the car. Then we'd drive to the five-screen dollar theater on Airport Boulevard, splurge on jumbo bags of popcorn, and watch movie after movie. Annabel and I didn't care that the theater always smelled of urine, or that the movies were second-run, or that the popcorn was stale. If we concentrated hard enough, we could almost believe that the world onscreen was more real than our own, that our problems had vanished. This is what it's like to walk through the world with a camera: hiding behind the lens, I can almost forget what I've done and what it cost, if only for a minute or two at a time.

Several nights a week, Nell comes by with dinner, and we eat at my small kitchen table, talking. One night, while we're washing the dishes, she tells me about how she reconciled with her son in the months leading up to his death — sat by his bed, fed him tiny sips of water through plastic straws, changed his bedsheets and diapers, watched him die.

'But I can't forgive myself for all the years before,' she says, 'the years when I couldn't come to terms with having a gay son. One thing I know for certain is that nothing in your life can prepare you for being a mother.'

She hands me a coffee mug to rinse in the sink. It's green with red dots around the rim, a birthday present from Emma. I was there the day she painted it at a ceramics shop on Twenty-fourth Street.

'Maybe it's time,' Nell says, turning the water off and drying her hands.

'Time for what?'

'Time for you to make a life with Jake. You love each other. Before all this happened, you were so happy together. You told me once that you never thought you'd meet anyone who would be such a good match for you. Are you ready to just give all that up?'

'Of course not. But he's making me choose between him and Emma.'

Nell puts her hands on my shoulders. 'At some point you're going to have to start thinking about yourself, your life. I know you want to believe she's alive, but the fact is she probably isn't.'

I move out of Nell's grasp and rinse the last of the dishes. 'I thought you were with me on this.'

331

'I am with you, and so is Jake. He needs you, Abby.'

'*She* needs me.'

After she leaves, I bundle up in jacket and scarf, go outside, walk to the bus stop, and wait for the 15. I take a window seat.

The bus stops and starts, moving slowly through the city streets. All the while I'm searching.

Later, I call Jake. It's past midnight, and tomorrow's a school day. 'I know you're there,' I say into the machine. 'Please pick up the phone.' I imagine him sitting at the table with a cup of decaf, grading papers, trying to ignore the phone. 'Call me,' I say. 'I'll be up late.' I'm about to hang up, but then I bring the phone to my mouth again. 'I'm sorry,' I say. 'God, you have no idea how sorry I am.'

58

It's morning, day 221, and Nell has convinced me to accompany her to an art exhibit at SF MOMA.

'I can't,' I said last night. What I meant was I could not imagine doing such a thing. Going to an art show, as if everything was normal.

'The exhibit is called The Memory Artist,' she said. That caught my attention. 'The artist is Franco Magnani, who paints Pontito, the Italian village of his childhood, with amazing accuracy. The interesting thing is that he hasn't seen his village since 1958. He settled in San Francisco in the sixties, then succumbed to a mysterious illness that caused him to have incredibly vivid dreams of Pontito. Before the illness, he'd never painted, but his dreams were so detailed that they inspired him to try his hand at the canvas.'

'How does he do it?'

'While he paints, he pretends that he's back in the village. He turns his head at different angles, as though walking through the town. He sees everything before he paints it — his house, the church, the bakery. His memory is like a film reel.'

At this hour, the museum isn't yet crowded. Magnani's paintings of Pontito are displayed side by side with black-and-white photographs of the town taken in 1987. The similarities are striking, the paintings so precise as to have a photographic quality.

But there is also some distortion. Some scenes, for example, are composites of several different views. In others, the buildings appear magnified, the way they would if seen through the eyes of a small child. In the painting of the church where Magnani was an altar boy, the steps leading up to the church are wider than they are in the photograph, and the path behind the church leading to Magnani's childhood home is much more prominent than it actually was. A painting of his grandfather's house contains a flower bed that can't be seen in a photograph taken from the same perspective. The paintings present an idealized version of the place.

The literature accompanying the exhibit includes this quote by Magnani: 'Memory works as a constructive process that not only reproduces, but filters, changes, and interprets the past.'

The exhibit merely confirms what I already know: memory cannot be trusted. It is too much at the mercy of our desires and emotions. Does Emma, wherever she is, think of the way home? Does she remember her address, her phone number, the bottle-brush tree in front of the house? Does she carry in her mind a picture of the narrow sidewalk leading up to her front door? If I find her, when I find her, will she remember me?

59

Day 229. Goofy's voice on the phone, breathless. 'You should get down here.'

'What?'

'A guy says he saw the Rossbottom board at Ocean Beach.'

'Don't let him out of your sight.'

On the way to Dean's Foggy Surf Shop, I go twenty miles over the speed limit. When I get there, Goofy is standing outside with two guys who smile and say hello — not just polite, but friendly.

'This is Abby,' Goofy says. 'Abby, meet Darrin and Greg.'

Darrin wears a cast on his left arm. Fortyish and clean-cut, he looks like one of those doctor types who can afford to live in Pacific Heights but lives in the Sunset instead, just to be close to Ocean Beach. Greg is a short, muscular thirty-something with long side-burns and a crooked nose. He looks beat-up in that way I used to find attractive back in high school.

'Was it one of you who saw the Rossbottom board?' I ask.

Greg lifts his hand, and I notice he's wearing one of those WWJD bracelets. 'I did.'

'When?'

'Six or seven months back.'

'That's it,' I say, feeling a rush of nervous energy. 'That's when it happened — July. Are you sure it was a Rossbottom?'

'Positive. It was a cold day, and there was hardly anybody out. I was on the beach, waiting, hoping things would clear, and this guy comes up to me, wants to know about surf spots south of here. The first thing I notice is the size of his board — twelve feet — and then the frog. Couldn't believe I was seeing an honest-to-God Rossbottom. Pure balsa, it was beautiful.'

'What color was it?' I ask.

'Red.'

'You sure it wasn't a knockoff, dude?' Darrin asks.

'Well, that's what I thought at first.' Greg looks at me. 'There are only about thirty of these left in the world, so your chances of running into one on any given day are pretty slim. But it had the Rossbottom signature, you know, down on the tail, scratched into the wood. A little r, a big flourish on the m. Gorgeous craftsmanship.'

'What did he look like?'

'Blond, I guess, thirties, forties. I don't know.'

I turn to Goofy. 'Did you show him the sketches?'

She nods.

'It might have been him,' Greg says, 'but I really couldn't say. People come and go. I know the locals, but the rest all run together after a while.'

'Do you know where he was from?'

He pauses and thinks for a few seconds, twisting the bracelet around on his wrist. 'No, but he said he was planning to go see some Tico friends.'

336

'Pardon?'

'Ticos,' Goofy says. 'You know, Costa Ricans.'

'Yeah,' Greg says. 'He said something about testing out the Killer Longboard on the Gold Coast.'

'That's what they call Costa Rica,' Goofy explains, 'on account of the yellow sand.'

I think of the elusive bumper sticker from the yellow van, the uppercase T. At this moment, is it memory or imagination that fills out the word — Ticos?

'Did he say anything else?' I ask. 'Like about a family or anything?'

'That's all. He was just this guy, nothing special.'

'Did he say where he was headed in Costa Rica?'

'I told you all I know, sister.'

Darrin knocks his knuckles against his cast. 'I'm guessing he'd be on the Central Pacific coast. That's where you get the best beaches for longboarding. I was down there a couple of years ago, stayed in Playa Hermosa for a whole summer. You get a lot of American surfers in that area.'

'Sure,' says Greg. 'If the good Lord smiled on me and gave me a Rossbottom, I'd be itching to test it at Pavones or Boca Barranca. Maybe Tamarindo. Hermosa's nice because it's central to everything on the Central Pacific, in the middle of the action.' He crosses his arms over his chest and says, 'Good luck.'

'Thank you.'

'You're very welcome.' Greg catches me

337

looking at his WWJD bracelet. 'You know, Jesus was the über-surfer. All that stuff about him walking on water? He wasn't walking, dude, he was surfing.'

I laugh — a genuine laugh — feeling almost giddy with hope. This is the first real hope I've felt in a long time. Maybe it's nothing, but then again, maybe it's something.

'You got time for lunch?' Goofy asks.

'Sorry, rain check? I've got some packing to do.'

'I did pretty good, huh?' Goofy says.

'You did great. The next number two special is on me.'

Driving home, I find myself singing along with the radio. Finally, I have a next step: Costa Rica. That's something real. Movement. Not just sitting around and waiting. Not just searching the same old streets, finding nothing. Maybe it's a tangent, a step in the wrong direction. But there's the small possibility that it's none of those things.

I'm thinking about Costa Rica, how I used to want to go there. Ramon spent a month there when he was in college and always talked about how beautiful it was, how trekking through the rain forest was like being on another planet. 'Everything's on a different scale,' he said, 'the trees, the flowers, the insects. And the colors are really amazing.' Oddly, it's one item on a list of hundreds that I used to think I'd check off before my thirtieth birthday. I'd completely forgotten that list, all the things I never got around to. Looking back, it seems that it was somewhere around my twenty-eighth birthday that time suddenly sped up, and the months and years began to pass with frightening speed. My photographs are testament to this fast-forwarding of time — thousands of contact sheets stored in plastic sleeves in more than a dozen three-ring binders, miniature recordings of faces and places, images that, taken together and in their proper chronology, relate the narrative of my life. At the end of each year, taking stock, I'd realize how much I'd failed to accomplish.

Then came Jake, and Emma, and I began to feel that I was *doing* something again, going somewhere. Until that moment on Ocean Beach, when everything suddenly stopped. No more pictures, no more story. Just a terrible dead end.

★ ★ ★

I go over to Jake's without calling first. The house smells like eggs and bacon, his favorite evening meal. I find him in the kitchen grading papers.

'Hungry?' he asks, casual, as if the argument at La Cumbre never happened.

'No, thanks.'

I sit down across from him. He needs a haircut and a shave. Still, he looks good. I see what I saw in him that first day at the school, the deceptively disheveled look of a guy who, in truth, has it all together. But he's different now, too. Older. Less at home in the world. His confidence is gone. I can see it in the way he sits, shoulders slumped.

The way the pen rests in his hand — loose, without conviction.

'What's the topic?' I ask, nodding toward the stack of papers.

'Plato's dialogues — How can Socrates' disavowals of knowledge be reconciled with his confident action and bold moral assertions?'

'They get that stuff?'

'You'd be surprised.' He shuffles through the papers, then stops, as if forgetting what he was looking for. A plate of food sits by his elbow, untouched.

'I'm going to Costa Rica,' I say.

'What?'

'It's about the Billy Rossbottom board. There's a decent chance the couple from the yellow van is in Costa Rica, or at the very least have been there recently.'

Before he can say anything, I explain my encounter with Goofy and the guys outside the shop. He sits with his arms across his chest, listening silently. When I'm finished, he stands up and walks over to the sink, as if he has something he needs to do there. But he just stands with his back to me, looking down at the dirty dishes. 'Why are you doing this?'

'I have to. This is the last detail I can remember from that day, the last lead I haven't explored. I have to follow it through.'

'Some stoned surfer thinks he might have seen a guy with a frog on his surfboard, and that's enough for you to drop everything and head to Central America?'

'The guy wasn't stoned, and he didn't just

340

think he saw the board, he remembered it in detail.'

'Okay, let's say, just for argument's sake, that it's the same guy. That was a long time ago. If it really was him, and he really was going to Costa Rica, it's not likely he'd still be there now.'

'Maybe not. But if these people are kidnappers, they're not going to be itching to get back to the States. They'd probably want to lay low, just kind of disappear. And if he's serious enough to have this rare, expensive Rossbottom board, then it stands to reason he might want to surf these famous longboarding spots.'

'That's a lot of *if*s. You have to remember what Sherburne told us on the very first day. There are only 115 long-term kidnappings of children by strangers each year. That's out of almost 797,500 reports of missing children — .0014 percent.'

'This isn't about percentages,' I say. 'It's not like your Rubik's Cube. Numbers are irrelevant.'

'I wish that were true, but it's not. You want Emma to be alive, so you're taking every detail you can possibly fit into your belief system and using it to corroborate your theory.'

'Is that so different from what you're doing? You have to believe she's dead, so you ignore any evidence to the contrary.'

'You've got to let this go, Abby.'

'Why don't you come with me?'

'To Costa Rica,' he says, incredulous.

'Yes.'

He turns to face me. 'Every morning, I think I can't get up and face another twenty-four hours without Emma. But the memorial service did something, it helped somehow. And now I'm able to get through each day by reminding myself that Emma's not suffering. Do you know the things that went through my mind before that man found her shoe? Every day, every night. The horrible things I imagined?'

'I know. I imagined those things, too, and the problem is, I still do.'

Jake flinches as if he's been struck, but I can't back down. This is too important.

'If there's any possibility at all that she's still alive,' I say, 'how can we sit here and do nothing? I'm able to get through the days because I let myself imagine what it will be like when we have her back with us. I think about the first time we see her — what we'll say to her, where we'll take her. I think about how she might have changed.'

He bites his lip. His glasses have little spots on them, like they haven't been cleaned in a while. 'I love you, Abby. Through all of this, I never stopped. But I'm serious when I say you have a choice. Go on this crazy trip, or stay here and try to make a life with me.'

'Why does it have to be a choice?'

He turns away and starts unloading the dishwasher. One by one, he moves the glasses from the rack into the cabinet.

I go over to the dishwasher. 'Let me help.'

He doesn't look at me, just says, 'I've got a lot of work to do. You should go.'

'Please don't do this. I just need more time. I'm still the same woman you wanted to marry.'

'You're wrong. Neither one of us is the same.'

And he's right. I know he's right.

Driving home, the cool ocean air blowing in through the windows, I feel the full weight of my choice. I remember how, on the night of our first date, I called Annabel when I got home and gushed about Jake for over an hour. I was too excited to fall asleep. At dawn the next day I was still sitting on the sofa, staring out the window, fantasizing about a future with this man I'd just met. I knew he felt something, too, and I couldn't quite believe my luck. I still remember clearly how the phone rang at eight a.m. sharp, and even before I answered, I knew it would be him.

'Did I wake you up?' Jake asked.

'No. I never even fell asleep.'

'Neither did I,' he said. 'Can I see you this afternoon?'

'Of course.'

Everything, it seemed, was falling into place.

60

I spend the next day on the Internet, making
flight reservations, printing out bus schedules
and city maps, researching the most popular
surfing spots. The Frommers website says one
can get by in Costa Rica on thirty-five dollars a
day. Based on my current bank account, that
gives me three months. And then there are the
regular monthly bills. A cash advance on my Visa
will cover two months, but after that the credit
card will be useless. I still have some money due
from clients, but not much. When I'm forced to
actually sit down and do the math, the numbers
aren't encouraging, and I can't keep accepting
money from Annabel when she has a new baby
on the way. My only choice is to sell something.

Most of the art in my apartment is my own,
or work by friends for which I've made a trade
— nothing that I'd be able to sell for a significant
sum. But I do have one piece that my friend
Janet has been coveting for years. Janet collects
the work of Randolph Gates, an early-
twentieth-century photographer known for his
Southwestern landscapes. The photograph is
called 'Light in Arizona,' and it was a gift
from Ramon the day before I left for college
in Knoxville. Back then, I loved the way the
photograph captured the eerie quality of the
desert beneath a quarter moon, but I didn't
know anything about its worth. I had admired

it many times in Ramon's apartment, where it hung above the old brick fireplace. On our last night together, while I was lying in bed, Ramon got up, made some noise in the living room, and returned a few minutes later with a big, flat package wrapped in butcher paper.

'To remember me by,' he said, laying the package at the foot of the bed. Before I even opened it, I knew what it was.

'But you love this photograph,' I said.

'So do you, and I want you to have it.'

'We have forty-five minutes before my curfew,' I said. 'Come to bed.'

He set the package carefully against the wall, then told me all the things he was going to miss about me, promising to love me until I was in my grave. I tried to think of words that would hold some equal weight, but they came out sounding false. I drove to Knoxville the next day with the photograph in the backseat, swathed in bubble wrap. It has been with me ever since. I've never grown tired of it. It's not just the beauty of the photograph that makes me so attached to it. It was Ramon's final gift to me, and as such it has served, somehow, to freeze him in time. The photograph probably has less to do with the real Ramon — the man I did not love enough, the one I left — than with some idealized version of him. Like Magnani's paintings of Pontito, the image I've created of Ramon in my mind is not about the subject — Ramon — so much as it is about the person I was when I knew him.

The first time my friend Janet saw the photograph hanging in the entryway of my loft, she offered me six thousand dollars. 'Ask me again if I'm ever really desperate for money,' I said.

Janet did ask again, on two separate occasions. Each time, I said no without a second thought.

'It's a good offer,' she said. 'The most you'd get from a gallery would probably be five.'

'I'm beginning to think I could never sell it.'

'Let me know if you change your mind.'

I find her number in my address book and make the call. 'Wow,' Janet says. 'I haven't heard from you in a while. Not since — ' She clears her throat, embarrassed.

'I don't think I ever thanked you for attending the memorial service.'

There are voices and music in the background on her end of the line, and I realize she must be having one of her famous parties. I used to be invited to every one of them, but over the past few months most of my friends have gradually stopped calling. This is my fault: in order to receive phone calls, you have to make them.

'It was a beautiful service,' she says. 'How are you holding up?'

'Good days and bad days.'

'You know, if there's anything I can do . . . '

'Actually, that's why I'm calling. Remember the Randolph Gates photograph?'

'Of course.'

'Still interested?'

'Definitely.'

'This is kind of urgent. Can I bring it over tonight?'

'Sure.'

I hang up feeling a bit shaky. Cheap. As if I've just sold a part of my personal history for a song. The truth is, I'd sell far more than a photograph to find Emma. There's nothing I wouldn't do, no bargain I wouldn't make. Years ago, when my father divorced my mother for a younger woman he met on a business trip in Germany, I asked him how he could do it, how his conscience would allow him to simply abandon her. 'We all have a little Robert Johnson in us,' he said. 'We're all capable of bartering away our soul. The question is whether or not we chance upon the devil.' At the time, I thought he was just making excuses, but now I know he was right.

There's one thing I should do before I wrap the photo for Janet. I go upstairs and get my Leica. Then I adjust the lighting in the foyer, straighten the photo. I feel somewhat ridiculous, standing in my own apartment like some silly tourist, taking a picture of a picture. But if I develop the photo just right, striking the correct balance of light and shadow, I can maintain something of the original's character. It won't be the same, I'll always know it's a fraud, but it might at least be a comforting facsimile.

61

Day 231. Two-thirty in the morning, Valencia Street. Everything is dark except for the blue light of televisions flickering in a few apartments above the street, and the traffic signals blinking red. In my messenger bag, I have about a hundred flyers left. Yesterday afternoon I began one last marathon effort to flood San Francisco with flyers before leaving for Costa Rica. I left my car at home and tackled the city by foot and by bus to avoid the parking hassles. In the past sixteen hours I've hit every neighborhood — even the most dangerous parts of Hunters Point and the Sunnydale projects. My legs are ready to give out, my eyes are burning, my fingers are sticky from tape. If I get home by seven a.m., I'll still have time to pack my bags, leave a checkbook and set of instructions for Nell, and be at SFO in time for my two p.m. flight.

I tape a flyer to the window at La Rondalla. We used to come here so often the mariachi band knew Emma by name. She loved the sloppy burritos and bright crepe-paper decorations, the loud music, the rotund waitress who always brought her extra chips. I cross the street toward Dog-Eared Books, where Emma liked to sit reading with the resident tabby cat in her lap. The cat is in the window now, staring out, blinking slowly.

'You're up, too?' I say, tapping the glass. The cat yawns, curls into a furry C, and closes her eyes. I move on to the next storefront, the messenger bag bumping against my hip. Deep in the night is the best time to put up flyers. I can work much more quickly without the traffic, without people and strollers slowing me down. A couple of blocks up Valencia, as I'm taping a flyer outside Good Vibrations, a taxi speeds by. Seconds later it skids to a stop and makes a U-turn, Jim Rockford-style. I begin to walk quickly, realizing too late my own stupidity. Anybody knows this is no place for a woman alone at two-thirty a.m. The taxi pulls up beside me and I move toward the buildings, away from the car, picking up my pace.

Then a familiar voice calls out, 'You know, we really should stop meeting in the middle of the night.' I peer through the window into the cab's lit interior. It's Nick Eliot, grinning like a schoolboy.

'You scared the hell out of me.'

'Get in. I'll give you a lift.'

'I have a hundred more flyers to post.'

'Come on. You look like you're about to keel over. I'll take you back to my place and fix you something to eat.'

'I'm leaving the country tomorrow — today, I mean — and I wanted to get all these up.'

'Tell you what,' he says, opening the door. 'Leave them with me. I can do it tomorrow. I'll take you home after I feed you.'

'You sure?'

'Absolutely.'

Some people have a gift for making you feel okay, just by the fact of their presence; Nick is one of them. The coincidence of seeing him here is so strange, so oddly perfect, that I can almost believe for a moment in the existence of some cosmic designer peering down from above, pulling strings. If I were superstitious, I'd take this as a good sign about my trip to Costa Rica.

I slide into the warmth of the cab. There's a briefcase on the floor by his feet, a garment bag on the seat between us. 'What are you doing out this late? I thought I was the only one up.'

'Just coming home from the airport,' he says.

'Where were you?'

'Ljubljana. Have you been there?'

'No.'

'You should go. Great architecture, shopping, and museums. Something like what Prague was twenty years ago, before the backpacker invasion.' He puts his hand on my knee. 'You okay?'

'Yes, thanks for asking.'

His hand feels good, calming, and I realize that my happiness at seeing him is way out of proportion with anything I should feel for a casual friend. Jake used to be able to put me at ease this way, just by his touch, but that seems like such a long time ago. The blocks slide by, the night is quiet as a church. The electric bus cables overhead glint in the moonlight, forming a low, metallic canopy above the street. Nick looks straight ahead, slouching in his expensive suit.

'I'm really glad to see you,' I say.

He smiles. 'Likewise.'

We stop in front of a trashed-looking building at Harrison and Twenty-first. On the ground floor, there's a taqueria with a neon sign glowing in the window. Beside it, a lesbian bar, closed. Nick pays and thanks the driver. At the door to the building, he punches a code into the keypad, and the door opens onto a narrow flight of stairs. The stairwell, carpeted and dimly lit, reeks of stale cigarette smoke and discarded food from the taqueria.

'I know what you're thinking,' he says. 'Trust me. It's better inside.'

'I pictured you somewhere else, maybe Russian Hill.'

'I bought it the year I moved here, couldn't pass up the price. Besides, I travel about forty weeks a year, so it's not like I'm sitting around enjoying my place.'

On the third-floor landing Nick punches more numbers into yet another keypad and ushers me inside. The place is amazing, and not just in a Martha Stewart sort of way. It has an *Architectural-Digest*-meets-Industrial-Chic look. Clearly, nothing in the place came from IKEA, Home Depot, or Pottery Barn.

'How high are those ceilings?'

'Fourteen feet.'

'Just in case you have the Warriors over for dinner?'

'Exactly.'

The appliances are all brushed aluminum, the furniture sparse and angular: a tan sofa that covers the length of one wall, three chairs in soft metallic hues, a coffee table as big as my bed.

The dining area has a beige rug, on which stands a large oval table with steel legs and a concrete top that's been polished to a gray shine. The bedroom is set off with a mesh curtain. One entire wall is covered with built-in bookshelves made from art deco blocks. There must be two thousand books on the wall.

'How many of those have you read?'

'A few,' he says, looking slightly embarrassed.

The place reminds me of the cool spatula he bought me in Helsinki, only larger and more complex. 'This is amazing.'

'Can't take any credit for it. One of my brothers is an architect, and his wife's an interior designer. A couple of years ago, for my birthday, they redid the place. Knocked out the walls and got rid of my furniture. Problem is, I spend so little time here I still haven't entirely gotten used to the changes. It feels like someone else's flat.'

'I love it.'

'Thanks.' He walks over to the kitchen. 'Have a seat. I'm going to fix you something. You look hungry, very hungry. Do you like French toast?'

'Love it.'

'Good, it's the only thing I know how to make.'

While he cooks, I peruse the bookshelves. I can't detect any particular order in the arrangement or selection. He has a little bit of everything: Trotsky's *My Life* shelved beside *To the Finland Station*, Colette next to Jack London, *Lolita* and *Madame Bovary* bumping spines with several thick texts on the fall of communism in the Balkans. He has poetry by

352

Auden and Ashbery and Plath, essays by E. B. White, plays by Harold Pinter, a book of folk songs for the banjo by a Texan named Wade Williams. One whole shelf is dedicated to the Albanian writers Jiri Kajane and Ismail Kadare — in the original, as well as the French and English translations.

'I can honestly say you're the first guy I've ever met who has two Albanian writers on his bookshelf.'

'There's quite a bit you don't know about me.'

There are a number of books in French and German, a Neil Young biography, an encyclopedia of Chinese medicine, and a few dozen Southern novels, including Walker Percy's *The Moviegoer*.

Nick is cracking eggs into a bowl, mixing something with a whisk. 'You see anything you like,' he says, 'feel free to take it with you.'

'You've read this?' I ask, holding up the Percy book.

'Quite possibly the best book I ever read. Are you a Percy fan?'

'I tried once but couldn't get into it.'

'You should give it another shot,' he says, dropping a slab of bread into the batter. 'I insist you take it with you. It's actually quite apropos for you. There's this one great line I always come back to — 'To become aware of the possibility of a search is to be onto something. Not to be onto something is to be in despair.' '

'That's very nice. It's the truest thing I've heard in a while.'

He drops a chunk of bread in the skillet. The

bread sizzles, and the apartment fills with the fragrance of butter and cinnamon. 'You never mentioned where you're going.'

'Costa Rica.'

'Vacation?'

'No. It's about Emma. Long story.'

'What's your fiancé's take on all this?'

'He thinks I'm chasing a ghost. We fought about it. Unfortunately, *fiancé* probably isn't an accurate word at this point.'

Nick looks surprised. 'I'm sorry to hear that.'

'Are you?'

'I went through a bad breakup a couple of years ago, and I wouldn't wish that on anybody. Still, I'll confess I'd like for you to be single, for selfish reasons.'

He scoops the toast up with a space-age spatula, slides it onto a couple of red plates, pours two glasses of milk, and sits down beside me at the bar. 'Try it.'

I bite into the toast. The bread is thick and spongy. It tastes of butter, cinnamon, powdered sugar, and something else I can't quite identify. 'This is without a doubt the best French toast I've ever had.'

'Listen, do you have somewhere to stay when you get to Costa Rica?'

'I made a reservation online, someplace near the airport in San José.'

'Cancel it. The motels in the city are dodgy. I know a woman there who rents a room in her house. It's cheap and clean, she's friendly, and she speaks a little English. When do you arrive?'

'Around ten tomorrow night. According to

United Air, the shortest distance between San Francisco and Costa Rica involves Chicago and Miami.'

'I'll let her know you're coming.' He scribbles an address on the back of his business card. 'I'll write down a couple of restaurants, too. I know it's not a pleasure trip, but you have to eat, right?'

'Thanks.' I can't help smiling. 'I bet I could name anyplace — Budapest, Bucharest, Anchorage — and you'd be able to come up with several recommendations.'

He laughs, stabbing a piece of French toast with his fork. 'Not really — though, if you ever do go to Budapest, you should definitely stay at the Hotel Gellert — communist chic, great bargain. Last time I was there I had a piano in my sitting room.' He reaches into his pocket and pulls out a BlackBerry. 'Something else. There's this guy down there. Wiggins.' He punches some letters on the BlackBerry, then writes a phone number on another business card. 'You should call him when you get to San José.'

'Wiggins?'

'He's with the embassy. Might be able to help you. He's out of the country a lot, so if he's not around when you arrive, you should keep trying to make contact with him. Tell him you're a friend of mine.'

'How do you know him?'

'Long story.'

I'm wondering if this French toast is really some of the best food I've ever had, or if I'm just that hungry. I clean my plate and look up to see him staring at me, grinning. 'Sorry,' I say, wiping my chin. 'I was famished.' I realize that I'm actually taking pleasure in this food. Maybe it's true what everyone has been telling me, the thing I refused to believe: life does go on.

'No apology necessary. I love a woman with an appetite. Now, keep this number handy. Don't forget.'

'I won't.' I take a sip of the milk, and it tastes so good I chug down the whole glass. 'What's in this French toast, anyway?'

'Nestlé Nesquik and vanilla extract are among the secret ingredients.' He wipes a spot of syrup off my chin. 'Tell me something.'

'What's that?'

'If we'd met under different circumstances — you know, if you hadn't been engaged, if things had been more normal in your life — do you think we might have had a chance?'

It's not a question I have to think about. 'I do.'

'It's all about timing, isn't it?' He circles the rim of his glass with one finger. 'Listen, international phone calls are a pain down there, but there are plenty of Internet cafés in the tourist areas. Promise you'll drop me a note every now and then.'

'I will.'

'And call me when you come home, so I can badger you into having dinner with me. No pressure, not a date, just dinner.'

'Of course.'

'One more thing. Do you speak Spanish?'

'*Un poco.*'

He goes over to the bookshelves and comes

back with a pocket-size Spanish phrase book and a copy of *The Rough Guide to Costa Rica*. 'Just to help you get by.'

I slip the books into my bag. 'Why are you so nice to me?'

He shrugs. 'I like you. But you know that already.'

'Funny, single women always say it's impossible to meet a good straight guy in San Francisco. But I'm not looking, and here you are. Half the single women I know would kill to date someone like you.'

He grins. 'Maybe they already did and they weren't too impressed.'

'Thanks,' I say. 'For these, for everything. I better go. Long day tomorrow.'

'Let me drive you home,' he says. 'I'll just get my keys.'

Then the drifting, the forgetting, and a hand shaking my shoulder.

'Abby?'

'Hmmm?'

'You fell asleep.'

I'm still sitting at the bar, my head resting in my arms. 'What time is it?'

'Four-fifteen. I was only gone for a couple of minutes. You conked out.'

Then his arms are under my legs, my back, and he's carrying me, and it's a sensation I remember from childhood, the way my father would rock me to sleep, then carry me to bed; half awake, cradled in his arms, it felt as if I was flying. Nick lays me on the couch, disappears for a moment, and returns with a blanket.

'I can't stay here,' I say, sitting up. But the couch is soft, and I'm so tired I can barely keep my eyes open.

'Just for a little while.' He slides a pillow under my head and pulls the blanket up to my chin. 'I'll wake you up early.' The last thing I remember before falling asleep is the sound of Nick brushing his teeth.

At 5:35 I wake to a quiet apartment. I tiptoe over to his bed and find him sleeping in a blue T-shirt and boxers, one foot dangling off the edge. Uncovered like this, unaware, he looks less like a mysterious jet-setter, and I fight an urge to crawl in beside him. I imagine how warm his skin would be, the pleasant pressure of his legs against mine. I imagine how, in another life, another time, I might be lying beside Nick right now, with nothing bigger to worry about than our weekend plans. I've thought of it more and more lately — how much better it would have been simply to never have met Jake, or Emma. If I'd never met them, I couldn't have hurt them, and I couldn't know what I was missing by not having Emma in my life.

I look at Nick one last time, scribble a thank-you note, grab my messenger bag, and slip out as quietly as possible.

Leaving like this, so early in the morning — while the city is deserted and the shops are closed and a pinkish light is settling over the streets — reminds me of family vacations when I was a child. My mother would come into our rooms before dawn, usher us outside in our pajamas, and settle us into the back of the

358

station wagon. Annabel and I would lie side by side, a single blanket spread over us, and drift in and out of sleep as the car wound through the quiet neighborhood.

The smell of my mother's coffee would fill the car, and we would hear the rustling of the maps, my parents' quiet whispers. It was on those morning escapes from our ordinary house and our ordinary lives that my parents seemed to belong together; the front seat seemed to be a very long distance away, and with their maps and coffee, their whispered plans, they appeared to live a secret life. Annabel and I would wake up in some unfamiliar town as the car rolled to a stop outside a McDonald's or Stuckey's. We'd change clothes in the back of the station wagon, then go inside for breakfast and a bathroom break. At some point inside the restaurant, with the sun streaming through the windows and the business of the day settling in, our regular lives would resume, our parents would begin to bicker, and the ride through the dark streets in our pajamas would feel a dream, like a false but pleasant memory of a thing that never happened.

When I told Annabel about my trip, she was less than enthusiastic. 'Are you sure you've thought this through?' she said.

'I have.'

She was quiet for a minute. 'I still believe what I told you in the beginning — you have to follow the search to its logical end. I just worry about you, Abby.'

'You're my sister,' I said. 'It's your job to worry. But I'm not crazy, if that's what you're getting at. It feels really good to have a plan. It may not be a perfect plan, but it's something.'

I hurry to the bus stop at Folsom and Twentieth. A couple of early risers are already waiting — a woman in hospital scrubs, a nervous teenager who looks like he's been out all night. No one speaks. No one meets the eyes. Somewhere, a motorcycle revs to life, one long, angry roar. Five minutes later, a bus appears down Folsom, a moving beam of light in the near-dark of an urban morning, its fluorescent interior impossibly bright.

Just before the bus reaches us, sparks fly in the air, and the pole connecting the bus to the matrix of wires above swings free. The teenager beside me curses softly, shoves his hands into his pockets. What he does next is so startling that for a moment, I believe I'm imagining it: he begins to cry.

The bus comes to a stop, and the driver slowly gets out. With the bored patience of someone who's done this hundreds of times, he uses a long stick to guide the pole back into place. More sparks, and then he's on the bus again, and in a few seconds he pulls up beside us. The woman in hospital scrubs steps back to let the teenager get in first. Head down, he moves to the back of the bus, and I'm thinking it must be some girl, some tragedy that for the moment seems impossible to survive. And I want to tell him that you find a way, somehow, to get through the most horrible things, things you think would kill you. You find a way, and you move through the days, one by one — in shock, in despair, but you move. The days pass, one after the other, and you go along with them — occasionally stunned, and not entirely relieved, to find that you are still alive.

62

We begin again, we never give up.

— Lars Gustafsson, *The Death of a Beekeeper*

On the afternoon of day 232, I wake to rain, a thunderous racket on the tin roof. Outside, something creaks and moans. It takes a minute to remember where I am — the long flight, the missed connection, the late arrival in San José, the disorienting taxi ride through unfamiliar streets.

Through the window, I can see a stand of bamboo trees, tall and golden, swaying in the wind. Everything here is captured in a state of rampant growth; everything is alive. The rain comes down in torrents, and minutes later subsides to a trickle. Raindrops slap the banana leaves just outside the window. Roosters crow in the distance, dogs bark. A church bell tolls — one, two, three, four, five.

A few hours ago when I arrived, a middle-aged woman greeted me at the door. Two small children clung to her legs.

'*Buenos días*,' I said. 'I'm Nick Eliot's friend.'

'*Bueno*,' she said. 'I am Soledad. I expecting you.' She smiled and stepped back, motioning for me to come inside.

She showed me to my room and I thanked her, explaining in broken Spanish that I was very sleepy.

'*Bueno*,' she said. 'First you sleep, then you eat.'

After she closed the door, I collapsed on the small bed and drifted off to the comforting din of children and television, dishes clattering, a dog barking.

Now, the house is filled with the good smell of something cooking. When I open the door, the children rush to greet me.

'Roberto,' the boy says, tapping his chest proudly. He points to his sister. 'Maria.'

They follow me down the hall to the bathroom and giggle when I try to shut the door, which won't close all the way. When I come out, Maria grabs my hand and leads me to the kitchen, where Soledad is frying plantains and beans.

'Food?' Soledad asks.

'*Sí*.'

She gestures for me to sit down. The children join me at the kitchen table, chattering in English. 'Where are you from?' Roberto asks.

'California.'

'Hollywood!' he says, getting so excited he leaps out of his chair. 'Do you know Arnold Schwarzenegger?'

'No, I live in a different part of California. San Francisco.'

Maria puts her hand on my arm. 'Do you know Mickey Mouse?'

'Yes,' I say. 'Mickey Mouse said to tell you hello.'

'Really?'

'Yes. You speak very good English. Where did you learn?'

'TV,' says Roberto.

'Smurfs,' Maria adds.

Minutes later the table is piled high with food. Soledad pours warm orange Fanta into four small glasses. Except for a soggy muffin on the flight from Miami, I haven't eaten since I left San Francisco. I eat ravenously, and Soledad piles a second helping onto my plate. Her English isn't much better than my Spanish, but we're able to communicate by having the children translate. Roberto and Maria are her grandchildren, I learn, and their mother works as a housekeeper at a hotel in the city.

I ask how she knows Nick Eliot. Apparently, he rented a room from her five years ago, and he's kept in touch ever since.

She says something in Spanish to Roberto, who swallows a bit of rice before turning to me and translating.

'Is Mr. Eliot your boyfriend?' he asks.

'No,' I say.

'Yes he is!' Roberto insists, giggling.

After dinner, I ask if I can take a bath, and Soledad gives me a towel and a small bar of soap. Through the crack in the door, I can see Roberto and Maria, knees tucked under their chins in front of the TV, Soledad's feet tapping the floor as she rocks back and forth in her chair. The old tub is deep and immaculate, and it feels good to soak away the grime of travel.

After my bath, I ask Soledad if I can use her phone. I dial the number for Nick's friend Wiggins, and on the third ring a woman answers. 'U.S. Embassy,' she says. She sounds as if she's

364

got a million other things she'd rather be doing.

'I'm looking for Wiggins.' Saying it, I feel a bit ridiculous. That's all I have to go on. No title. No first name. Just Wiggins.

There's a pause, a shuffling of papers. Then, 'Just a moment, I'll connect you.'

A man's voice comes on the line. 'Yes?'

'I'm looking for Wiggins,' I repeat.

'He's out of the country.'

'When will he return?'

'A couple of months. Who wants to know?'

I tell him the whole story. It comes out in a rush, a jumble of breathless sentences: the disappearance, the search, the clues that led me here.

'Does the FBI have a case open on this?' he asks.

'They were working with the SFPD, but the police closed the investigation.' I can hear my own case falling apart as I talk.

'I'm sorry, but this sort of thing isn't really our jurisdiction. If someone from the Bureau sets a lead, we'll get involved.'

'But Nick Eliot told me to call Wiggins.'

'Nick Eliot. The name doesn't ring a bell. Listen, if you find your little girl, call us, and we can help with the locals.'

'Please,' I say, 'there must be something you can do.'

'Why don't you call again in a couple of months, when Wiggins is back. Good luck.'

The line goes dead. When he hangs up, I feel more alone than ever in the search, yet somehow more resolved. Maybe it's a long shot, maybe

Jake was right. Perhaps I'm putting too much faith in the minor details, clinging to every bit of circumstantial evidence that will fit into my belief system. But I feel certain that finding the couple from the yellow van is my best hope of finding Emma. This is my final option, my last unexplored set of clues — the woman at the Beach Chalet staring so obviously at Emma, the timing of the van's departure from Ocean Beach that day, the Ticos bumper sticker, the longboard — and in my mind the pieces fit together. They simply have to.

In bed, I consult my guidebook. Buses depart the main terminal in San José for Playa Hermosa at nine o'clock weekday mornings. I try to sleep, but my mind won't rest. For the first time since Emma's disappearance, I'm truly angry with Jake. He should be here; we could accomplish more together. He shouldn't have given up.

I don't think Jake would understand it if I told him that being in this foreign place feels like a new beginning. I'm finally free of the endless repetitions that characterized my search in San Francisco: the daily trips to Ocean Beach, the countless returns to the same streets, the same dead-end clues. Memory researchers have a theory to explain a common experience: the feeling that we know a word but it is just out of reach. The theory is called blocking, and it holds that the tip-of-the-tongue sensation occurs when our effort to remember leads us away from the word we want to retrieve, diverting us instead to some other word. The desired word is there, but we can't access it because we've become

366

sidetracked; we're following the wrong route. The words that get in the way are called interlopers.

Is it wrong to imagine that Costa Rica might clear my mind, that here, in this unfamiliar place, the interlopers might be banished?

When I wake at seven the next morning, the smell of coffee fills the house. The children are in front of the fuzzy television watching American cartoons and drinking chocolate milk. Soledad is already in the kitchen, the flesh of her arms jiggling as she works the spatula over the grill. The scene seems so ordinary, so fundamentally human, I find myself not just hoping, but truly believing, that Emma could be here in this country.

'*Bueno*,' Soledad says, looking over her shoulder. 'You have good sleep?'

'*Sí. Muy bien.*'

She puts a plate in front of me — a big serving of rice and beans topped with two fried eggs. She stands by the table while I eat, hands on her hips, watching. 'You like?' she says, wiping her hands on her apron.

'I like.'

'Good! In California you no get good breakfast!'

'Not like this,' I agree.

I help her clear the dishes, then pay the bill — just twenty American dollars. I thank Soledad, say goodbye to the children, and wait outside for the taxi. The driver gets out and loads my pack into the trunk. '*La estación de autobúses?*' he says.

'*Sí, por favor.*'

'Where you going?'

'Playa Hermosa.'

'Is very beautiful. You will like.'

At the bus station, a man at a card table is selling tickets to Hermosa. By nine-fifteen I'm on my way, a warm wind roaring through the windows. I keep thinking about what Nick said: *To become aware of the possibility of a search is to be onto something. Not to be onto something is to be in despair.* I have to believe I'm onto something; it's the only thing that keeps me going.

63

Playa Hermosa. A cabin on the beach. A single naked bulb, two dirty beds, a wall so thin I can hear the people in the next cabin snoring. A long, narrow mirror, unframed, hanging on the wall beside the door. In the mirror: a startling find, a ghost. Jutting hip bones, dark circles beneath the eyes.

Rain pelts the tin roof of the cabin. It begins as a single tap, then another, and another, gaining speed, until it's a steady thrumming, a hard racket in the brain. Soon it's a full-fledged storm, growing heavier by the minute. There is the smell of rain, and of the sea, and some sickly sweet smell that saturates the unwashed sheets. I switch off the light and lie fully clothed on the bed, listening to the howl of the storm. Through the tiny screened window, I can see occasional flashes of light.

Something about the rain, the saltwater smell, reminds me of Alabama. A couple of months before Emma disappeared, the three of us took a trip to Gulf Shores. Jake had never been down south, and he wanted to see what it was like, get a feel for where I came from. We checked into one of the nicer hotels in Orange Beach, and on our first evening we sat on the sand and watched the sun set over the Gulf. After that, it rained the entire week.

We spent mornings by the covered pool at our

hotel, afternoons at the Pink Pony Pub. Emma drank Shirley Temples while Jake and I downed sweet iced tea and Bud Light. We'd sit in the smoke-filled restaurant and watch lightning split the sky in two. The lightning fascinated Emma, who was used to San Francisco's calmer rains. It was what I missed most about the Gulf Coast, the drenching rainfall and booming thunder. San Francisco storms are so subtle, they can hardly be called storms at all.

'It smells weird,' Emma said, 'like the sky's on fire.'

'That's ozone, nitrogen, and ammonia acids you're smelling,' Jake said, always ready to turn anything into a lesson. It was fun seeing the world through his eyes, like a trip back to grammar school, when everything had a simple scientific explanation, every question had an answer.

It felt good to be back home, even if it wasn't under the best of circumstances. One afternoon I took Emma to the souvenir shop with the giant shark at the entrance, the shop I'd visited dozens of times as a kid, and let her choose a basket full of T-shirts and knickknacks for her friends. The best memento we have from the vacation is a photograph of the three of us standing in front of Moe's Christmas and Gun Store on the beach road. I still remember the guy who took it, an elderly gentleman with a lifetime tan and a shirt that said *Bama Forever*.

By the end of the week, Emma was teary-eyed and tired, and we were just as pale as when we'd arrived. 'Alabama wasn't exactly as I pictured it,'

Jake said on the flight back. We agreed that our next beach vacation would be somewhere more exotic — Tahiti or Costa Rica. I never imagined that I would be coming here alone, that future snapshots of my life would contain a singular subject.

There is a girl, her name is Emma, she is walking on the beach. I look away. Seconds pass. I look back, and she is gone. I keep thinking about the seconds, the ever-expanding circle. How I set this chain of events in motion. How I must find some way to make amends.

* * *

The next day, I wander up and down the beach, which is crowded with American surfers and backpackers. I search for the Rossbottom board, the blond couple, the yellow van. Driving to Costa Rica wouldn't be easy, but it can be done. Back home I read a blogger's account of driving through the Sonora Desert, then through the highlands of Oaxaca, on into Guatemala, Honduras, and Nicaragua. The border at Penas Blancas is notoriously lax, so someone with a good poker face could probably hide a child in the back of a van and bring her through with no documents. Like Jake said, it's a big *if*, a whole lot of *probably*, but it's the best thing I've got to go on.

Late in the afternoon, I find a cabin for rent for three hundred dollars a month — better and cheaper than the one I stayed in last night. It's simple, tiny, and clean, with a tin roof and a small window with a view of the sea. I decide it will be my base of operations, my temporary home.

It doesn't take long to settle into the rhythm of beach life. There's no reason to get up early, because everything is closed. My only hope is to meet people — surfers, mainly — and the easiest way to meet them is in the bars and restaurants at night. Many of the town's inhabitants are seasonal, coming here for three months or so until their money runs out, then heading back to the States. On my second evening in Hermosa, I discover a little bar just a few steps from my cabin. The staff is made up of North Americans and young Ticos. Over the next week, I get to know all of them by name. Each day I pick up a little more Spanish and, hopefully, earn a little more trust from the surfers, but it still feels like I'm no closer to finding Emma.

'You should try it,' says a forty-something computer programmer from Atlanta. Meaning surfing. Meaning loosen up. It's my third day in Hermosa, and we're sitting side by side at the bar. Beautiful South is playing on the speakers, and the TV is tuned to a football game between the Delaware Blue Hens and the Citadel. The computer programmer's name is Deke. He reminds me of a guy in a soap opera, with his perfect hair and his overconfident way of staring into my eyes for long moments. He keeps glancing up at the TV, yelling, 'Go, Hens!' Rumor has it Deke has been to bed with half the North American girls in this town, and a few of the Ticos, too.

'Surfing's not for me,' I say. 'I'm afraid of deep water and speed. Plus, I couldn't handle the lack of control.'

'That's the best part,' Deke says, putting his hand in the small of my back, slipping it under my tank top.

'Watch it.'

He makes a joke and raises both hands in the air, a gesture of surrender, but I can tell he's startled by the rejection.

A few hours later I meet Sami from Galveston, who supports her sun-worshipping habit by bartending and cleaning rooms at a local motel. She's thirty-six and has a boyfriend back home who builds limousines. He's waiting for her to get Costa Rica out of her blood so they can get married and have babies.

'We came here together seven years ago. He eventually got tired of it, but I never did. Thing is, the longer I'm here, the more I think about *pura vida*, and the less I think about babies,' Sami says, polishing the bar with a damp rag.

When she asks me what I'm doing in Costa Rica, I tell her I'm taking photographs for a Lonely Planet guidebook. It's my cover, the only way I know to explain my presence here. The Leica I carry everywhere I go, slung over my shoulder, seems to be enough to verify my story. Over the next few days, Sami and I become friends. Sometimes in the late afternoon, when business is slow, Sami will ask one of the cooks to watch the bar and she'll walk out to the beach with me, and we'll sit on the sand and watch the surfers catching the last waves before turning in for the evening. Their bodies are sleek and lovely in the fading light, and the blue of the Costa Rican sky is a blue I've never seen before. The wet bodies emerging from the surf, boards propped on their shoulders, look like the bodies of dancers, and it's hard to believe they're just ordinary boys and girls from dull Midwestern towns.

On my fifth day in Hermosa, I'm sitting on the beach with Sami, a couple of beers between us on the sand. I take a piece of paper from my pocket, unfold it, and hand it to her. 'Does this look familiar?'

'Should it?'

'It's a symbol on a board.'

She looks more closely at the image of the golden frog, which I downloaded from the Internet. 'Oh, sure. The Killer Longboard. The guy who made them kicked the bucket not long ago. Billy Rossbottom.'

'You know of him?'

'Who doesn't? Rossbottom came into the bar a couple of years ago. He was a big flirt, buying drinks for all the ladies. Nice guy, left a tip bigger than his bill. The day after he died, we had a big party on the beach in his honor.'

'I'd like to get my hands on one of those boards,' I say. 'You see any around here?'

'Just once. They're really rare, you know.'

'The one you saw, when was that?'

'I don't know, several months ago.'

'Do you know who the guy was?'

'Girl, actually.' She gives me a look like she's trying to figure me out. 'Why are you so interested, anyway? You don't even surf.'

'I'm looking to buy one, a gift for a friend,' I say, feeling guilty for the lie. But I don't want to show my hand yet, don't want my business spread all over the coast. I'm afraid that if the couple from the yellow van is here, and if they catch wind of me, they'll move on. For that reason, I've yet to show anyone the forensic sketches; they're tucked away in my backpack in the cabin, waiting for the right moment.

Sami finishes off her beer in one long gulp. 'I'll keep an eye out for the board.'

'Thanks.'

'Abby,' she says, popping the cap off another beer.

'Yeah?'

'I've got a good sense for people, and there's something you're not telling me.'

'What makes you think that?'

'A single professional woman, alone in a little surfing town in Costa Rica. You don't surf. You're older than most of the people here.' She winks. 'Present company excepted.'

'I told you, I'm working on a guidebook.'

'Doesn't make sense,' she says, leaning back on her elbows and tilting her face up to the sun. 'If that was the case, you'd be long gone from Playa Hermosa by now. So are you going to tell me what the deal is, or do you want me to guess?'

At that moment, I make a conscious decision to trust her. My mother always said my biggest flaw was that I tried to do everything on my own, but my biggest strength was a kind of obsessive determination. She had this story she loved to tell about how when I was fourteen months old, I once spent the better part of an hour trying to get a sock on my foot, and I refused to let her help me. She had evidence of the event, fifteen minutes of scratchy black-and-white film in which a baby who looks nothing like me struggles with a lacy white sock and a chubby foot. I never did get the sock on.

'Come by my place tonight after you get off,' I say.

She hums a few bars from the *Twilight Zone* theme song and says, 'I'll be there. Shall I come in disguise? Maybe a black cape and mask?'

She shows up at my door after midnight, reeking of pot. 'Want some?' she asks, pulling a joint out of her pocket.

'Thanks, I'll pass.'

'Suit yourself.' She plops down on the unused bed. 'So what's the big secret?'

'I lost my little girl.'

'What?'

'Actually, my fiancé's little girl, Emma. On the beach in San Francisco. I'm down here because I think she was kidnapped, and I believe the people who did it may be in Costa Rica.' I don't tell her what a long shot it is, don't let onto the fact that I'm chasing my last lead. Maybe what I need more than anything right now is simply for someone to believe in my plan.

'Not funny,' Sami says. 'Stop fucking with my head.'

'It's true.' I lay the police sketches on the mattress next to her.

'Shit, you're not kidding, are you?'

'Have you seen them?'

'They don't look familiar.'

'You sure? The guy, he has a tattoo of a wave on his chest. He's medium height, muscular, has a lazy eye. She's thin, bleached blonde, a little crazy-looking.'

'What's the Killer Longboard got to do with all this?'

'This couple was at Ocean Beach the day Emma disappeared. The guy had a Rossbottom board.'

Sami's eyes get wide. 'I can't believe it,' she says. 'A kidnapping. That's movie shit.' She's quiet for a moment. 'Surfers are a tight-knit group, you know. Best keep your eyes open and your mouth shut for a little while. Let me help. I'll ask around about the board.'

'Thanks. Another thing. I don't really know where to look. I've been over my map of Costa Rica a hundred times, and I'm lost.'

'You should meet Dwight. He's a bartender at the Pink Pelican. He's not all there, but he's been here for twenty years. Knows the whole country by heart. I'll hook you up.'

'I owe you.'

'Hey,' Sami says, 'I'm starved. Got anything to eat?'

'Bananas, Oreos, peanut butter, white bread, and chips.'

'You're a veritable health food store,' she says. 'I could sure go for a peanut butter and banana sandwich.'

I go over to the little table underneath the

window, which I've transformed into a makeshift kitchenette with a coffeepot, Bunsen burner, paper plates, and silverware. I make two sandwiches, with a side of Pringles.

Sami takes the top piece of bread off her sandwich, lays a few Pringles on top of the bananas, and puts the top back on. 'Hey, you ever been to Graceland?'

'No.'

'I went a couple of years ago. Funny thing is, the Graceland Mansion isn't a mansion. It's just like a regular house, only bigger, with uglier furniture. But there's this restaurant across the street where you can get fried peanut butter and banana sandwiches. They're so fucking good, I had two and bought a third one to go. It'd be worth going back to Graceland just to get that sandwich.'

The peanut butter tastes good, even feels good against the roof of my mouth, and I realize that I've been eating regularly for the past week. I stick my finger in the waistband of my shorts and notice that, even though I'm still much too thin, the fit is getting slightly more snug. Everyone's been telling me I had to get on with my life, and I've been thinking, all along, that they're wrong. I've been thinking that there's no getting on with anything as long is Emma is missing. But my body, it seems, has made its own decision.

I think of Emma, wherever she is, and I wonder if she's healthy. Is she growing, gaining weight? Is her face changing? Among my meager luggage, I brought a small album containing a

378

couple dozen photos of her. In some she's with Jake, in some she is alone, and in one the two of us stand together on the grounds of the Legion of Honor, with the fountain in the background. The first photo in the book was taken at Crissy Field a couple of weeks after I met her, and the last one was taken the day before she disappeared. Even in that short span of time, a single year, her features underwent a gentle metamorphosis — her face thinning, her widow's peak becoming more pronounced. An adult can look pretty much the same for a decade or more, but in childhood the alterations occur so rapidly that photographs taken just months apart can be startlingly different.

The album has room for five more photographs. I don't remember now whether or not it was a conscious act to leave those final sleeves empty as I was packing for this trip. I tell myself that there will be more pictures to fill out the book, that the narrative which began with the very first photo at Crissy Field has not come to an end. I tell myself there is a future, and it is not a terrible, unbearable one. Surely there will be more pictures, a complete and happy story. In waking dreams, despite everything, I picture this: Emma and Jake and me, together, getting on with our lives.

64

The next day, as promised, Sami introduces me to Dwight, who's six foot two and can't weigh more than a buck fifty. He's balding on top, very tan, and it's impossible to guess his age. When we get to the Pink Pelican at ten o'clock in the morning, Dwight's the only one there. He's doing some sort of sidestep behind the bar, lifting and lowering his arms like a bird in flight. He reminds me of somebody, but I can't place the resemblance.

'Hello, ladies.'

'My new friend Abby needs your help,' Sami says.

He stops sidestepping and reaches over the bar to shake my hand. 'Hello, new friend Abigail. How can I help you?' That's when I realize who he reminds me of: Sam Bungo. Something about the male-pattern baldness combined with exuberant youthfulness, and the way he says my full name. Sam Bungo used to do that, refused to call me by the abbreviation because he thought Abigail sounded British, and he had a thing for the Brits.

'I was hoping you could tell me the best longboarding spots,' I say.

He grabs a rag to polish the already immaculate counter and gives me a questioning look. 'You surf?'

'No. I'm doing research.'

'Lonely Planet,' Sami chimes in, pointing to my camera. 'She's a photographer.'

'Right, dude. Here, I'll draw you a map. But you've got to promise to put me in your guidebook.'

'It's a deal.'

'Not just my name. I want a photograph.'

'No problem.'

Dwight takes a pencil from behind his ear and begins to draw a map on the back of a paper menu. He starts with the Caribbean coast. 'You've got Playa Bonita, north of Limón, and to the south there's Cahuita, nice beaches. Best bet on that side for surfing is Salsa Brava, the hollowest wave in Costa Rica. You know what 'Salsa Brava' means?'

I shake my head.

'Angry sauce, roughly translated. Fucking poetry, man. Only way to know what I mean is to surf the sauce. Pound for pound, it's as intense as any coral reef double-up right tube in the world. You like poetry? You look like a woman who can appreciate a good metaphor.'

'Sure, I like poetry.'

'I thought you would,' he says, leaning closer. 'I can really get into a chick who can get into poetry. Listen, how old are you?'

'Easy,' Sami says. 'She's married.'

'No shit,' he says, looking at my left hand. 'If you're so married, where's your wedding ring?'

'Left it at home. My fingers swell in the heat.'

'Right.' It's hard to tell if he believes me, but he looks back at his map and begins scribbling again. 'Truth is you won't find much action out that way now. Best time to go to the Caribbean coast is between February and April. During the summer, anybody who knows his ass from his tail fin is on the west coast.'

He keeps drawing and talking, marking the prime spots with a green star.

'Up top is Ollie's Point, named after Oliver North. Once upon a time there was a secret airstrip there. They used it to run guns and shit to the Contras, but you can't get there by road, you have to hike in. Way down south on the Pacific side, toward Panama, you've got Matapalo, killer right point break with house-size waves, west swell. Then Playa Pavones, some of the most perfect waves on the planet. Going on up the coast you get Dominical. Real quiet. Pretty consistent beach breaks year-round. Then there's Playa Espadilla at the entrance to Manuel Antonio National Park, real touristy, so you get your trolls and waxboys, of course, but when the big swells come into the bay, it's awesome. Some good action at the north end of the beach, too.' He moves his pen up the map, marking Quepos, Roca Loca, Puerto Caldera.

'And you and I, Mrs. Abigail, are here.' He winks like we're in on some big secret, and draws a big heart to mark the spot for Hermosa, midway between Quepos and Puntarenas. 'Then there's Boca Barranca, no place for random standers.'

'Who?'

'You know, weekend surfers, folks who aren't serious about the sport. Boca Barranca is a river mouth about a hundred kilometers northwest of

San José. Real popular with longboarders because it doesn't get hollow, and on a really good day you can catch a half-mile ride. It's also home to the granddaddy of all longboarding contests, Toes on the Nose.'

'When's that?'

'Early June. Every longboarder who's worth his weight in sex wax will be there.'

'Thanks,' I say. 'You've been really helpful.'

'Hey, that's not all. You don't want to miss Tamarindo, way up on the north Pacific coast. Just your speed. There's a big expat surf community there, but it's a little more upscale than most of these other places. Tamarindo's got spas, bakeries, museums, you name it. A bookstore even.' He scribbles a number on the top of the paper. 'And in case you need a personal tour of Hermosa, you know who to call,' he says, handing me the map.

'I'll keep that in mind.'

'Hey, let me know when you're divorced, sweetheart.'

'Will do,' I say, standing to leave.

'Hold on. Aren't you going to take my picture?'

'Of course. Just stand there and look natural.'

Dwight picks up a cocktail shaker and gives me a toothy smile. 'Gorgeous,' I say, pressing the shutter release three times for authenticity's sake.

65

Day 237. I stop at the Internet café near my cabin and spend a few minutes answering e-mail. Nell's latest message says all the bills are paid and it's quiet in the neighborhood; when am I coming home? Nick is in Helsinki again. 'I saw a girl in a watch shop who reminded me of you,' he writes. 'I left Wiggins a message telling him all about you.' A second e-mail, sent just a few minutes later, says, 'Would you find me strange if I admitted that I miss you?'

There are two e-mails from Annabel. 'I'm plumping up,' she writes in the first message, dated three days ago. 'See attached photo.' In the picture she's standing in profile, her belly just beginning to show. Her auburn hair is cut shorter than I've ever seen it, her face is a bit heavier. She's one of those women who actually look better pregnant, all radiant and round.

The second e-mail from Annabel is only two words. 'Any luck?'

'Too early to tell,' I reply.

No e-mail from Jake, even though I've sent him three since I arrived.

The next morning, I take thirty thousand colónes out of the ATM and catch the ten o'clock bus for the three-hour ride to Boca Barranca. An American surfer I've seen hanging around Hermosa takes the same bus. Doug is a grad student in American History, on break from

Ole Miss. He's meeting friends in Jaco this weekend. He's carrying nothing but a small duffel bag.

'Where's your board?' I ask.

'You can't bring them on the buses, so I just rent one in each town. What's your story?'

'I'm writing a guidebook. I'm also looking for a Killer Longboard.'

'A Rossbottom?' he says, surprised. 'For what?'

'A gift for my brother. Cost no object. Have you seen any?'

'I wish.'

'If you do, would you mind e-mailing me?' I hand him one of the handwritten cards I made up last week, featuring my e-mail address and the message *Looking for a Killer Longboard. Will pay top dollar.*

At Jaco, Doug shakes my hand and wishes me luck. I'm left alone on the bus with a family of Costa Rican tourists, a couple of German-speaking surfers, and a boy with a paper sack full of Wrigley's gum who looks too young to be traveling alone.

About a half hour north of Jaco, we cross a bridge over a wide brown river. The driver pulls over on the other side of the bridge. 'Photo!' he says, opening the doors. 'Very good photos!' I follow the family off the bus. The kid with the gum sleeps through the commotion. Standing on the bridge, I look down into the grimy water fifty feet below. Six enormous alligators are moving slowly upstream, and another four are lying in the sun on the riverbank.

The tourist family takes some photos, and so do I. As I press the shutter release, I realize these are the first photos I've taken since Emma disappeared that have nothing to do with the search or with work. I'm taking them because the scene before me is interesting, and I'm thinking, as I shoot them, about how they will look when developed. I'm thinking about the way the dull green alligators will almost disappear against the brown water, and the way the ripples fan out from their rugged bodies. I'm thinking about the sun, which is too bright; it would be better to capture this shot at dawn, soft light falling over the muddy river.

A couple of hours later, we approach Puntarenas. Shacks everywhere, snuggled up beside roadside food stalls. A slimy-looking river pours into the ocean. We grind to a stop beside a sprawling stucco motel that looks as though it hasn't been used in years. I check in with no problem, nineteen dollars for the night. 'It's low tide,' says the guy at the desk, a Tico who speaks near-perfect English. 'Best time to get a look at the beach. I'd get on out there if I were you.'

The room itself is so dirty and dark that even ten bucks a night would feel like a rip-off. I change into a clean pair of shorts and tank top, then walk along a dirt path to the beach, stopping along the way to buy a *refresco* at a run-down cantina. The drink is ice cold, its shocking sweetness balanced by the tartness of *tamarindo* fruit.

A finger of land juts out into the murky water. The peninsula is hemmed in on one side by the river mouth and on the other by a brown curve of bay. The ground is covered with sharp, slippery barnacles, and there's an unpleasant smell in the air. The beach is deserted except for a kid, eighteen or nineteen years old, who's sitting alone with his board, staring out at the water. There are four or five guys out there surfing, all of them bunched up in the same spot.

I go over to the kid. 'I'm Abby,' I say, holding the camera aloft. 'With Lonely Planet.'

He pushes a lock of bleached hair away from his eyes. 'Jason. With Jason and Company.' He laughs at his own joke.

'Mind if I sit down?'

'Suit yourself.'

'What can you tell me about this place?'

'One of the longest left breaks in the world.' He grins. 'If you're willing to risk your health for a good ride.'

'Why's that?'

'See how dirty the water is? It's sewage. I've heard rumors of surfers contracting hep A and meningitis here. This one guy I know saw a dead horse float right into the lineup. And you've got the crocs to consider.'

'Seriously?'

'It's documented. You get these badass saltwater crocodiles that come out into the estuary to feed on the carcasses. Not a pretty sight.'

'Ever seen one yourself?'

'No, but I've seen pictures.'

Jason pulls out a pack of cigarettes, offers me one.

'No thanks,' I say. 'I'm not much of a smoker.'

'Me neither.' He produces a plastic lighter, cups his hand over the tip of the cigarette, and lights up. 'Waterproof lighter,' he says. 'Best invention ever.'

'Ever go to Toes on the Nose?' I ask.

He squints into the sun. 'I don't compete, but I come down from Miami every year to watch.'

'Were you here this year?'

He nods. 'Last four in a row.'

'Did you by chance see anybody with a Killer Longboard last year?'

He turns to look at me, suddenly interested. 'Sure did. Gorgeous board, dude. I'd seen one a couple of years back in Maui. What I'd give.'

'Do you remember the guy who owned it?'

'There were two. One was Australian, the other was some American dude.'

'What did they look like?'

Jason shrugs. 'Like surfers.'

'The American, was he alone?'

'You sure got a lot of questions.'

'I'm trying to buy a Killer Longboard.' I thrust my card at him, but he doesn't take it.

A guy in a big leopard-print hat comes walking down the beach in our direction, and Jason raises an arm to greet him. 'Yo, pimp! You got worked!'

'Too crowded out there,' the guy says. 'Conan and Slime Dog were in the impact zone. Thought I could thread the needle between them, so I caught the wave and made the drop, then the fat lady sang.'

'It's all good,' Jason says. 'Meet my friend Lonely Planet.'

The friend tips his hat and does a little bow.

'Later,' Jason says, standing up and dusting sand off his rear end. It's an amazingly flat rear end, completely devoid of contour. He grabs his board, and he and the friend jog down toward the ocean. Moments later they're in the water, paddling.

I spend a week and a half in Barranca, talking to everyone who will listen. One other person, the hotel clerk, remembers seeing a couple of Killer Longboards here during the last Toes on the Nose contest, but, like Jason, he doesn't remember much about the owners. 'They haven't been back since then,' he says. 'You should come back in June for this year's contest. Pretty quiet around here most of the year, but during contest week this place is elbow-to-elbow.'

I thank him for the information and make a reservation for the week of the competition. 'Meanwhile, if you see anybody with a Rossbottom board, call me,' I say, handing him my card.

'Is there a commission in it for me?'

'Of course.'

'Cool.' He turns back to the television, *The Love Squad* dubbed in Spanish. From the words I can make out, it seems two brothers are fighting over the same woman. 'You ever catch this show?' he says as I'm walking out the door. 'It's goddamn great TV.'

I'm trying not to feel disheartened that the

competition is more than three months away. In three months a child could starve or suffer terrible abuse. In three months a child could die. In three months, anything could happen.

66

I catch an afternoon bus back to Hermosa. Watching the hills roll by — the coffee plantations and cinder-block homes, an occasional horse, scattered shacks — I feel a gnawing sense of defeat. Back in Hermosa, I drop my stuff off at the cabin and head over to Sami's bar.

'No luck, huh?' she says.

'How can you tell?'

'You don't exactly have a poker face. What next?'

'I'll spend a couple of nights here, then hit those other towns Dwight told me about. If all else fails, I'll head back to Boca Barranca in June for the contest.'

'You'll find her,' Sami says, but there's no conviction in her voice. She can't meet my eyes when she says it, can't back up her reassuring remarks with any kind of reason. I know she's the kind of person who just tells you what you want to hear. I can imagine her on the phone with her boyfriend in Texas, year after year, telling him she'll be back to the States in a jiffy. Telling him she loves him, she misses him, it's no fun here without him.

I pay another month in advance for the cabin in Hermosa, and from there I take day and weekend trips all along the Pacific coast, with its long, brilliant beaches and occasional upscale hotels, hidden coves and sleepy surfing villages, palm groves and paddy fields. I ask questions, thrust my card into the hand of anyone who will take it. Sometimes I ask about the board, and sometimes I describe the man from Ocean Beach. 'Medium height,' I say. 'He's got this tattoo of a wave on his chest. Drives a yellow van. Possibly traveling with a blonde woman a few years his senior.'

My story shifts to suit the person I'm talking to. Sometimes the guy's my long-lost brother who has fallen out of touch with the family. Sometimes he's my ex, and I broke his heart, and I've realized I can't live without him. The stories get more outlandish depending on how much I've had to drink, or how little I've been able to sleep. There's the story about how my mother needs a kidney transplant, and he's the only match. And the story about how I owe him money, and I just came into an inheritance, and I want to get my accounts in order. The one about how I found the Lord, I'm apologizing to everyone I ever wronged in a serious way, and he's number five on my list. There are stories about the board, too: it's my sick brother's dying wish to have one. I work for a big movie production company in L.A. and we're doing a ground-breaking documentary, a sort of *Endless Summer* for the new millennium.

I'm getting good at lying. I can look anyone in the eyes and tell them any story. Yet, my lies amount to nothing. Occasionally, someone will say they've seen a Rossbottom board, but the details never add up with the couple I'm looking for. It was always a long time ago, or in some other country, or the board was seen by a friend of a friend. Among the rumors, I find no real leads, and I push the thought out of my mind that this trip was a stupid move, just a lengthy diversion leading nowhere. I can't allow myself to believe this, can't accept that I will go home without Emma. Everything depends on my finding her.

Once, near the town of Puerto Coyote, stopping to pee along an empty trail, I'm startled by a loud rustling in the trees. I look up to see a pair of toucans, their comical yellow beaks streaked with brilliant orange, the tips stained blood red. These magnificent rare birds, which once would have sent me into photographic ecstasy, mean little to me now. Just birds in a tree on a trail leading into the woods.

In Tortuguero, I rise early with the roosters. They're ubiquitous in this country, a nationwide alarm clock. I make my way along the rocky beach and watch the giant sea turtles, like large brown remnants of shipwrecks, moving slowly just below the ocean's surface. In the forest behind the beach, the trees drip with snakes and howler monkeys. There is an unsettling, dangerous beauty in this part of the country, the kind of place where a person might simply disappear. Here, I am struck by the impossibility of my mission. Even as my body regains strength, I worry that my mind may be slipping further away.

I think of Jake back in San Francisco, teaching his classes and eating dinner alone, keeping the door to Emma's bedroom shut. I wonder if he ever thinks of me, or if the effort not to think of Emma takes every bit of his energy, every ounce of his fight. I wonder if, every now and then, he remembers what it was like to love me, to be on the verge of marriage. Does he ever roll over in bed, expecting to find me there, and wake with a start when he realizes that I'm gone?

One thing I've always admired about Jake is his resolve; after making a decision, he rarely wavers. Now, though, his resolve works against me. Here is what I know: at this point, there is not a thing in the world I could do to make him want me back. We crossed that line when I left San Francisco.

No, I tell myself. Maybe there is one thing, one impossible thing: I could bring Emma back to him.

I keep coming back to that moment on the beach. I keep coming back to the panic, the slow unfolding of fear. One moment she is there. The next, she is not. In between these two realities — her presence and her absence — there is a thing, a dead seal pup on the beach. Its still, spotted body, its blank, staring eyes.

I have a dream, some nights, in which I lay my hands on the seal pup and will it to come to life. Seconds pass in which nothing happens, and then a shudder runs through its cold body. The seal begins to breathe; its eyes open and focus on me. In this dream I turn from the blinking seal to see Emma, just a few yards down the beach, walking toward me, holding a bucket of sand dollars. In this dream, she never left. I turn away from the living seal and see her there, and I think, *What a terrible night it's been.* In the dream, I am so relieved I voice my elation aloud: *Oh, it never even happened.* Emma sets the pail on the sand before me, and we begin to examine the sand dollars, one by one.

67

From Tortuguero, I return to Hermosa. Sami has no news for me. She's been asking about the board, to no avail. 'Your best bet is still probably Toes on the Nose,' she says. 'In the meantime, you should check out the Caribbean side.'

'Dwight says there's not much surfing there this time of year.'

'True, but most tourists go to Limón at some point or another. It's really popular with Americans. Couldn't hurt to check it out.'

The next day, I leave town again. The trip to Limón takes seven hours. The bus, which reeks of sweat and onions, comes to an abrupt halt every ten minutes or so. The driver has the radio turned up high, and passengers have to shout to be heard. I think of California and wish I was there. I imagine clean white sheets and my own car, hushed cafés, my chilled darkroom with its familiar chemical smell. The bus trip gives me way too much time to think — about Emma, about Jake, about the absurdity of my being here. How can I hope to find one couple in an entire country? And what if this one couple — like the man in the orange Chevelle, the postal worker, Lisbeth — is just some false lead, just another one in a long line of interlopers distracting me from the true path? When I'm alone, it's too easy to doubt what I'm doing, too easy to believe that Jake is right, that my endless search is hopeless.

On the bus I read *The Moviegoer*. I can understand why Nick loves this book. It's about a melancholy man who searches and searches but never really finds what he's looking for. He goes to movies. He dates his secretaries and marries his cousin. He speaks at great length about what he calls 'the malaise,' and I know just what he's talking about.

In Limón, I rent a dirt-cheap room in the center of town for a week and wander the musk-scented bars. The people of Limón speak a richly accented English that I can barely understand. The rhythm of the language is punctuated by calypso music spilling into the street, and the city is crowded with beautiful Jamaican men courting young women from the States. I start showing the sketches of the couple around, asking if anyone has seen them. Limón feels very different from the surfing towns on the Pacific coast; no tight-knit community this, it's more of an urban jungle. People glance at the sketches and shrug their shoulders, sometimes looking at me as if I've lost my mind.

Dozens of times a day I am offered pot, cocaine, heroin. In the street I ignore hisses and groans, dodging local men who offer to sleep with me under the palms for twenty dollars a go. Before, I would have been terrified by such a place, put off by the warnings of guidebooks and other expats, but now it seems I have very little to lose.

Then, one night, as I'm waiting to hail a cab to

my motel, a strange man approaches me. He glances around to make sure we're alone, then holds a knife to my neck and forces me into an alley. 'No scream,' he says, pressing the blade against my skin. He whispers obscenities into my ear while groping wildly at my hips. I can smell tequila on his breath, sweat on his filthy shirt. My heart races. The blade is warm against my neck, not cold as I've always imagined a knife would be. He tears one strap of my dress with the knife, nicking my skin. Drunk, he struggles to unzip his pants. It occurs to me that this man is going to rape me. I'm surprised to realize that I don't feel panic. Part of me wants to fight or run, and part of me wants to simply give up. Part of me thinks it is somehow just that things have come to this.

But then I feel something hot and wet on my face, and realize the man is kissing me. His breath is rank, and his thick tongue pressing against my own makes me gag. He responds by shoving his tongue farther into my mouth. If I die here, I think, no one will ever find Emma. If I die here, I will never see Annabel's new baby.

'AIDS,' I say, hoping the word translates. Then more loudly, pushing him away, '*Yo tengo* AIDS!'

He throws his head back and laughs, trails the blade of the knife along my throat, down across my breasts, then lets me go. He grabs my purse and staggers away. 'You very lucky today, gringa,' he says over his shoulder, laughing. 'Next time not so lucky.'

I run into a crowded street. I can feel my

money pouch against my skin, strapped around my waist. Somehow, in his drunkenness, the mugger didn't notice it. Everything is in it: all my cash, my passport. Fortunately, I left my camera in my room. Shaking, I manage to hail a cab back to my motel.

I stand for a long time in the tiny shower, still feeling the place where his blunt fingers kneaded my skin. It's anger I feel more than fear. I am, after all, an adult, and I was capable of escape. What about a child? What does a child do?

I gather my few belongings and lie on top of the sheets, waiting for dawn. The children in the next room are crying, a woman's voice attempting to console them with soft words. A man is yelling. The diatribe is followed by a smacking sound, the mother's cries, another smack, then silence.

I imagine someone hitting Emma, and worse.

I sit on the edge of the bed, my heart beating wildly. The scene of the attack plays over and over in my head. I'm tempted to go home, just catch the next flight to San Francisco, arrive sometime tomorrow in that familiar city with its familiar fog. I could take a taxi to my apartment, sit for a long time in my tub, soaking away the grime of travel. I could fall asleep in my own bed, wake to the familiar sounds of traffic. I could browse through my orderly closet for a clean shirt, clean pants, get dressed to a favorite CD — maybe Al Green's *14 Greatest Hits*. Then I could knock on Nell's door, and share a cup of strong, good coffee.

I have to keep reminding myself that there's a

reason I'm in this country. There's a reason I can't go home.

Finally, a rooster crows, the darkness dissipates, and the smell of frying bacon rises from the street. I leave the key at the desk, take a taxi to the bus station, and board the first bus to San José. Late in the afternoon, following a connecting bus and a long, bumpy ride over ruined dirt roads, I arrive again at Playa Hermosa. Sami is just getting off work. We open a couple of cold beers, sit on the darkening beach, and watch the last surfers coming in from the water. Their slender bodies drip and glow in the leaving sunlight. Each surfer is attached to his board by a leash encircling his ankle, like some seafaring umbilical cord. Even in groups like this, each surfer looks entirely alone, his board held at his side like an extension of his own body; I can't help but envy the peace they seem to find in solitude.

'What the hell am I doing here?' I say. 'This is crazy. This can't go on forever.'

'That's what I told myself seven years ago when I moved here.'

'Do you think I'm fooling myself?'

Sami stretches her brown legs out on the sand. 'I don't know.'

The truth is, neither do I. Nonetheless, I look at every surfboard, examine every face. Always, from one coast to the next, in highland and lowland, rain forest and cloud forest, by night and by day, I keep in mind a set of images, the layered mental photographs that drive my endless search: a yellow van; a longboard with a golden frog at its center; a good-looking man with a tattoo of a wave curling over his left nipple; a blonde woman with a wrecked smoker's face, prematurely aged. I carry the police sketches in my daypack. At night I study them, memorizing every feature.

And Emma. Always Emma. In my mind I make up endless variations of the face I know by heart. Like a forensic artist whose job is to add years to the face of a missing child, I add elements that might alter the image from the photographs: a tan, a pageboy haircut, long braids, a baseball cap. I add and subtract weight, imagine the contours that might be etched into her smooth face by months of worry and fear. I give her scars — a tiny white line on her cheek, a raised gash along her arm, a badly scraped chin.

I return to the same towns again and again, ask the same questions, see the same faces. Everywhere, I look for her. I wake each day with the fragile hope that I may find her. It is this hope that propels me through the day, that gets me out of bed and into the sunlight. It is with this possibility in mind that I am able to eat and sleep and bathe.

Each day is a microcosm, a snapshot of the search in miniature. Each day begins with conviction and confidence: conviction that I'm pursuing the correct path, confidence that I will soon find her through a combination of logic and perseverance. As the day wanes, my confidence fades. By nightfall, I am plagued by insecurity, and I go to bed wondering if Costa Rica has less to do with the search for Emma than it does with my own desire for escape.

Every night, as I crawl beneath the scratchy sheets in some unfamiliar bed, my hope subsides by a fraction. Every moment's a little bit later. Every day, her face becomes less clear.

At night, in the darkness, the sea is reduced to black and white. All that is visible from my window is the white of the breaking waves, long lines spreading out from their centers. The whiteness rises out of the dark sea. There is no color, no light, no way for the eye to judge what is there and what is not.

68

Day 278. Poas Volcano. On the precipice of the crater, I find myself staring into a cloud. Inside the crater there is nothing but white, a white with depth and presence. A white so intense it feels as if I have reached the end of the world, or possibly the beginning. A white not unlike the fog in San Francisco — opaque, impenetrable.

The air smells dense and egglike. Below the cloud, I am told, lies a small turquoise lake of steaming water. In 1989, the crater lake gradually drained away, and researchers later found a pool of liquid sulfur about six feet in diameter, the first of its kind ever observed on earth. Volcanoes of this type are common on Io, Jupiter's glowing moon.

I can't resist the temptation to bend over the railing and lean into the abyss. I feel a stirring, something internal, impossible to name. A sense of the world opening up, of time unfolding. A dangerous disarming.

I remember Jake, kneeling by the bed, head bowed, lips moving silently, fingers working over the beads of the rosary. Is this it, then? Is this what he experiences in those long, soundless moments of prayer? This surrender, this forgetfulness?

But the forgetting only lasts for a moment. Walking down the ash-strewn path, past bromeliads four times the size of my hands, past twisting trees and red-throated hummingbirds, past chattering schoolchildren and big, rowdy families, I am thinking, again, of the search. How it has led to nothing. No child, no answers. Nothing.

In the 1870s, the German philosopher and scientist Hermann Ebbinghaus became the first scientist to take an experimental approach to the study of memory. Shunned by the scientific establishment, he worked alone, with himself as his only subject, eventually producing the classic text *Memory: A Contribution to Experimental Psychology*. The research culminated with his famous curve of forgetting, which showed how rapidly memory evaporates: 56 percent of learned information is forgotten within an hour of being encoded. By the time one day has passed, another 10 percent is gone. A month after the information is learned, 80 percent of it has vanished.

How long will it take for me to forget that day at Ocean Beach? How many years must pass before the sound of waves no longer reminds me of the terrible thing I've done? I've tried so hard to remember every detail of that morning, yet I'd like to believe that a day will come when I'm not haunted by the image of Emma holding her yellow bucket, walking away from me.

69

Two months in Costa Rica, and I have settled in. Sometimes San Francisco seems like the distant past, part of some other life. Jake and I have spoken only once since I arrived. I've called more than a dozen times, but I always get his answering machine. Each time, I imagine him sitting in the kitchen, grading papers, listening to my voice, not answering. I try not to imagine Lisbeth sitting there with him.

A few days ago, I called in the middle of the night. I must have caught him off guard, because he picked up the phone. 'Hello?' he said, a note of panic in his voice. I could not help but wonder if, in his half-asleep state, he was reverting to the past. Perhaps, in that moment of partial awareness, he believed it might be the call about Emma.

'It's me.'

'Pardon?'

'It's Abby.'

Long pause. 'Hi.'

'Sorry to call in the middle of the night. You're not easy to get in touch with.'

'I've been busy,' he said.

There was no static on the line, just his voice, deep and smooth, exactly as I remembered it. 'You sound as clear as if you were in the next room,' I said.

'You too.'

'I wish you were,' I said. 'In the next room, I mean.'

'Abby . . . '

'I just wanted you to know I miss you.'

He sighed. 'Where are you?'

'In Tamarindo. It's pretty here.'

'Are you okay?'

'I'm fine. You?'

'Passing the days.'

All those times I tried to reach him, I knew exactly what I would say to him. I would tell him I still loved him, still wanted to make a life together. I would tell him I was very, very close to coming home. But once I had him on the phone, my mind went blank. I could hear him getting out of bed, walking across the floor, opening the lid of the toilet. I could picture the bathroom, his shaving cream and razor placed neatly on the shelf above the sink, the blue towels hanging over the shower rod. I could hear him peeing, and the intimacy of that sound made me lose it completely.

'You've got to talk to me,' I said. Even as I said it, I knew I had no right to ask this of him, that what we had together ceased to exist that moment on Ocean Beach when I looked away. I knew that his attempt at reconciliation the day before I left for Costa Rica showed far more generosity than most men would be capable of.

'I'm sorry,' he said. 'I really do have to get some sleep.'

The line went dead. I called back, but he didn't answer.

70

Day 304. Playa Hermosa. The long gray beach, surrounded by volcanic rock and tropical forests, is as familiar to me now as Ocean Beach. Annabel's voice on the other end of the line. 'When are you coming home?'

'Soon.'

'How soon?'

A tiny sand crab scuttles across the tile floor of the phone booth. 'I have a pet,' I say. The sand crab finds my foot and begins climbing up by way of my big toe. 'Remember when we used to collect sand crabs at the beach? Remember how we'd trap them in mason jars? We never could keep them alive for more than a few days, no matter how well we took care of them.'

'I'm worried about you,' Annabel says. 'What about your work? What about everybody here who loves you? Your new niece is due in eight weeks.'

'You know I wouldn't miss that.'

'I *don't* know,' she says. 'I feel like I'm losing hold of you. We hardly ever talk.'

'I was looking at the calendar today,' I say.

'I know. Impossible to believe it's been close to a year.'

A year of her alone, or dead, God knows what. 'I've made a decision,' I say. 'I already hate myself for it, but I've made it. I don't know what else to do.'

Annabel lets out a little yelp. 'She kicked. She's getting restless in there. You should see me. I look like the Goodyear blimp.'

'I'm coming home after Toes on the Nose,' I say.

I can almost hear Annabel smiling. 'Thank God.'

Even as I make this promise to Annabel, I'm thinking, *What next?* The search itself is so much a part of my life now, I cannot imagine going through a day without pursuing it in some way. Work only takes up so many hours. Eating and sleeping only take up so many more. I cannot imagine having a free hour and spending it in some frivolous way — shopping or seeing a movie, meeting friends for drinks. I cannot imagine an hour that does not include the idea of saving Emma, this ultimate, impossible goal. An hour in which I am simply alive and content, going about the mundane business of living.

71

Day 329. Crossing over the alligator bridge north of Jaco once again, I feel less hope than dread. After this, there is nowhere left to go. If I don't find what I'm looking for here, I have to accept that I won't find it anywhere.

At the entrance to Boca Barranca, there's a huge banner that says *Welcome to Toes on the Nose*. It's true what the guy at the hotel desk said: the place is so crowded it's unrecognizable. Cars, people, buses, bicycles. There's a carnival atmosphere in the air, radios playing loudly, vendors selling trinkets, local girls plaiting hair in the shade for three American dollars.

At three o'clock in the afternoon, the bus drops me and more than a dozen others at the hotel. I wait in line for nearly an hour. 'You're back,' the clerk says, sliding my key across the desk. 'I didn't think you'd show. I was tempted to give away your room.'

'I never heard from you,' I say.

'I kept my eyes open, but those two guys with the Rossbottom never came around. You might get lucky this week, though. We have a record number of entries.'

I find my room, change into a tank top and sarong, grab my camera, and head out to the beach. The contest doesn't start until tomorrow, but a huge party is already under way. A couple of DJs are set up under tents, speakers blasting.

There are guys hawking raffle tickets, girls in hot-pink bikinis handing out free CDs, Ticos grilling chicken to sell to the surfers, makeshift bars offering beer and tropical cocktails. There are a couple of camera crews here from American and Costa Rican television stations, as well as a few lone photographers.

I wander through the crowd, camera in hand. As always, I am watching, hoping, every nerve in my body attuned to the remote possibility of Emma's presence. I search the entire crowd, stopping here and there to snap a photo. People are friendly, drunk, and approachable.

'I'm looking for a Killer Longboard,' I say to a young woman who's here to compete in the Women's Longboarding Classic. 'Have you seen one?'

'No, but I've had my mind on the heat.'

Another photographer approaches me. He's wearing a Hawaiian shirt unbuttoned to the waist and a pair of ill-fitting shorts. 'Louis,' he says, shaking my hand.

'Abby.'

'I'm on assignment for *Surfing Magazine*.' He holds up his laminated ID tag. 'No tag,' he says, glancing at my chest. 'You independent?'

'Lonely Planet. We're doing an international surf guide.'

'No kidding. I've got some great shots from the Siargo Cup. Think they'd be interested?'

'Maybe, you should call them.'

For the rest of the afternoon and evening, I alternate between sitting on the beach and wandering among the crowd. The sun goes down, the surfers come in, the beach party continues. The music gets louder, the crowd gets rowdier. People are drunk and familiar, ridiculously young, offering me beers, which I accept. I take advantage of their friendliness, asking if they've seen a guy with a tattoo of a breaking wave on his chest. Asking if they've seen a little girl, about this tall, who answers to the name of Emma.

Around ten p.m., a guy who can't be older than twenty-two sits on the sand beside me, pops the top on an Imperial, and presses the cold bottle into my hands.

'Where you from, sister?' he says, slurring his words.

'San Francisco. You?'

'Idaho.'

'You're a long way from home.'

'So are you,' he says. 'Want to spend the night with me? I got this great cabin just down the beach a ways. Good weed. And I've been told I'm a sensitive lover. Name's Thor. Like the Vikings.'

'Thanks for the offer, but no thanks.'

'I urge you to reconsider.' He's closer now, his cool breath on my face. Good-looking, tan, and lean. Beautiful lips.

I'm a little dizzy from the beer, but not dizzy enough to do something that stupid. 'How old are you?'

He grins. 'Old enough.'

'I'm sure you'll make someone very happy tonight, but I'm afraid it's past my bedtime. Yours too, if you're competing tomorrow.'

'Surfing is like driving,' he says. 'I do it better drunk.'

I stand to go, and he grabs my ankles. 'You don't know what you're missing.'

Back in my room, I lie down on the hard bed, beneath sheets that don't feel quite clean, and fall into a fitful sleep. Tomorrow. Yes, tomorrow.

72

By the time I get outside at eight o'clock the next morning, the beach is already busy. Groups of surfers have set up camp with bright umbrellas, ice chests, and banners announcing the names of their surf clubs. Several surfers are already out in the water, warming up. I lay my towel down by the guard tower and settle in. My supplies include three bottles of water, a cheese sandwich, my camera, and a pair of binoculars I picked up a couple of weeks ago in Playa Hermosa. I point the binoculars out to the lineup, but even with the magnification, the guys are moving too fast for me to get a good look at their boards.

'Look at that,' the lifeguard says. 'Shoulder-high peelers breaking on two different peaks. This should be a good one.'

'You bet,' I say. 'What time is the first heat?'

'Half an hour. The judges are setting up.' He nods toward a long table set up in the sand a couple hundred yards away. There are three judges, all bare-chested. One of them is wearing a cowboy hat.

I sit, wait, and watch. The morning haze lifts, and the sun comes down bright and hot. By ten o'clock the beach is hopping. Surfers jockey for a place in the lineup. Guys high-five each other as the scores are announced. During the second heat, one of the guys moons the crowd just before the wave closes around him.

It's like an enormous frat party, everybody hungover from last night's binge, but surfing their hearts out anyway. If I were in Boca Barranca for any other reason, I could really enjoy this. I think of all those mornings my senior year of high school, when Ramon would pick me up at the 7-Eleven across the street from school and we'd drive out to Gulf Shores. We'd spend the day on the beach, and I'd come home late in the afternoon, sunburned and tipsy, sneaking to my bedroom before my parents could get a look at me. Even then, I understood those were perfect days, something to treasure. My parents' marriage had taught me that grown-up love was different; there was something angry and hard about the kind of love my parents shared. Then Ramon was gone, and there were years of dead-end relationships, where things just didn't click. Then there was Jake. Before I met him, I'd forgotten that sex could be so good, that conversation could feel so easy.

'You're a good talker,' I once told him, after listening to him riff for half an hour on quantum mechanics.

'You're a good listener,' he replied.

At noon, I leave my towel by the lifeguard stand and wander up and down the beach. Thor from last night is standing at one of the makeshift bars, drinking tequila. 'Hair of the dog?' I ask.

'You got it,' he says, but I can tell he doesn't recognize me.

I order a Bloody Mary and wander among the tents, searching the faces, the chests, the boards. After four months of studying surfboards every day, I've come to recognize some of the brands and models: the Hobie Vintage 9′6″ with its rolled V bottom; the pretty blue and yellow Robert August 9′6″ What I Ride, equipped with a signature fiberglass fin; the 10′6″ Freeth Model by Malibu Longboards, named after the first known surfer in California. But no Rossbottom.

I go back to my towel and sit down to watch the next heat. There's a lot of commotion on the beach, everyone crowding close to the water. 'What's all the fuss?' I ask the lifeguard.

'That's Rabbit Kekai,' he says, pointing to a lone surfer paddling out.

A few minutes ago there were a couple dozen surfers in the water. Now, it's only him. 'Where's everybody else?'

'Giving him room. Out of respect. Rabbit's the most famous living longboarder in the world. Hell, the most famous living surfer. He started surfing in Waikiki when he was five. Learned from the greats — Duke Kahanamoku, Tom Blake. Eighty-four years old, and he can still put any guy out here to shame.'

Even I can see why Rabbit Kekai causes such a stir. He looks like he belongs in the water, at one with it. He doesn't fight the surf, like some of the younger guys do. He flows with it. It's a beautiful thing to watch, even for a layperson like me.

Half an hour later, the next heat is announced, and the ocean fills with bodies. Once again, I walk up and down the beach, searching. It's under a big blue umbrella that I finally see it. Towering twelve feet tall, with the sun glinting off the deck. Red, with a golden frog at the center. The rider is standing behind it, supporting it with one hand, his face and body hidden, one leg jutting forward, foot digging in the sand. I walk slowly, eyes focused on the frog, afraid to believe what I'm seeing. My heart races. I can actually feel it swelling and pumping, a hard, fast rhythm inside my chest.

Then I'm within five feet of the board, and there's no question it's a Billy Rossbottom. There's the signature down on the tail, scratched into the wood. A small r, a big flourish on the m. Several guys and a couple of girls are gathered around, talking to the owner, whose face is still obscured. My legs feel weak.

The surf thunders, the sun beats down. I look around, trying to concentrate. A few children are standing nearby. I search their faces, look into their eyes; each one is too young or too old. Not one of them is Emma.

I take another step. The hand moves, and the board turns so that it is in profile, exposing the man behind it. He runs his hands over the deck, talking to the onlookers. Then I'm standing in front of him, holding my breath, looking into his face.

Hair: brown.

Eyes: brown.

Height: tall.

Tattoo: none.

Accent: Australian.

Just one glance into his face, one look at his bare chest, and I know it isn't him. Not my man from Ocean Beach. Just some guy with a Killer Longboard.

The beach spins, the breath goes out of me, the camera slips off my shoulder, and suddenly I'm sitting on the ground, sobbing like a child, like a crazy person. Staring at this man who isn't the one. And those children behind him, who are not Emma.

A hand reaches down. A big hand, a kind face. 'You all right, love?'

I accept his hand. He pulls me up. 'Sorry,' I say. 'It's just the sun. I'll be fine.'

73

Casey Lopez. Corona, California. June 5, 1971. Twelve years old.

Benjamin Jent. Lexington, South Carolina. June 6, 1986. Four years old.

Miles Sevreva. Las Vegas, Nevada. February 16, 1992. Three years old.

Joseph Moore. Welch, Oklahoma. December 30, 1999. Sixteen years old.

Tyrone Johnson. Chicago, Illinois. July 6, 2001. Ten years old.

Jimmy Schadler. Chicago, Illinois. July 6, 2001. Three years old.

Ashley Rubin. Bridgeport, Connecticut. November 7, 2001. Eleven years old.

Grace Costa. San Diego, California. April 25, 2002. Two years old.

Twyla Chandler. Richwoods, Missouri. October 6, 2002. Eleven years old.

Melissa Berquist. Saint Louis, Missouri. June 11, 2003. Nine years old.

Angela Simpson. Houston, Texas. November 16, 2004. Eight months old.

Lily Taylor. Reno, Nevada. April 21, 2005. Four years old.

That night, in my dingy motel room in Boca Barranca, I can't stop thinking about where the girls go, and the boys, the teenagers, that endless procession of vanishing children. One moment they are here beside you — in the grocery store, the mall, the park, at the gas station, on the beach — and the next minute they are not. It is easy enough to find the names and dates, the place from which they were abducted, their age at the time of kidnapping. But the essential information, their current location, whether they are alive or dead, is missing.

Months of searching turn up nothing, not even the faintest clue. It seems as if they are nowhere, as if the cells and skin of which they are made have simply evaporated. But the laws of physics demand that they must be somewhere, alive or dead. Some remnant must linger in the world. The vanished are not truly gone — they are only gone from you.

And Jake. I can't stop thinking about Jake. His hands, with their chalk and eraser smell. His long pale feet in sandals, the leather stiff with salt water. His chest, the coarse, dark hairs I used to feel against my cheek at night. His breath in the afternoon when I met him after work, the sweet mint of his gum layered over the taste of peanut butter from the sandwich he'd had for lunch. I think of Jake in fits, in photographic swatches, never in the whole. I think of the parts, not the sum, and I know I will never find that same beautiful amalgamation in another man.

It's so hot I've stripped the top sheet off the bed. The mosquitoes are at their business. I'm wearing nothing but underwear; there's a wet cloth pressed to my forehead, another on my stomach. I can hear the guard making his rounds in the hall, boots thudding against cement.

People are partying in nearby rooms. Next door, a couple is having sex. It's eight p.m. in San Francisco. I imagine Jake sitting in his big leather chair in front of the television, the evening's darkness closing in, the television muted so that he has to make up the words. It's a game we used to play, ascribing pithy remarks and intellectual dialogue to the voluptuous blondes on *Frat House Diaries* and the pumped-up gym rats on *Iron*. There would be a couple in a hot tub, a bikini-clad twenty-something talking a mile a minute, ensconced in steam, and Jake would have her quoting Hegel. He'd do the voice for the women and I'd do the guys; bouncers would recite Muriel Rukeyser, cops would hold forth on Diebenkorn.

I miss that game, those long nights of talking. I miss everything about Jake, more than I ever thought possible. In my weaker moments I wonder if I have only wronged him once again by coming to Costa Rica instead of settling down with him. When this happens, I take out my photos of Emma. I look at her face, and I attempt to recall her voice, and I read the names of the missing children recorded in my notebook. More horrifying than the names themselves are the dates, stretching back decades. Where are their parents now, their aunts and uncles and grandparents, the friends who loved these children? Each unsolved case must represent a vast network of despair, numerous lives that stopped dead in their tracks on the day the child disappeared. Each missing child is someone's most painful memory, someone's most significant point of reference. For every name there is someone else, unnamed, who waits for a child to come home.

74

Well?' Annabel says.

'She wasn't there. Of course she wasn't there. Everyone was right. I was wrong. It's over.'

'I'm so sorry.'

'You know, I really believed I could find her. Remember my senior year of college, when you came to see my photography show in the student union?'

'Of course,' Annabel says.

'There's something I never told you. I was the last person in my class to get a show. The very last. Everyone else did one during the fall semester, but my professor thought I wasn't ready. In the end, the only reason I got to do the show was that I spent every night for three months in the darkroom, long after everyone else was in bed, working my ass off. Then, over time, I built my own business and made it work out of sheer stubbornness. I know I wasn't blessed with obvious talent. My art has always been something else: hardheaded determination. It always worked for me before. I thought it would work this time, that if I was determined enough, for long enough, I'd find her.'

'You did everything you could,' Annabel says.

'It wasn't enough.'

'Where are you calling from?'

'Playa Hermosa. I'm packing up.'

No tears now, I can't find them. Even the

422

anger is gone. All that's left is a dry, empty space. This longing that will never be satisfied. This guilt.

'Come home,' Annabel says.

'Next week.'

'Do you mean it?'

'Definitely. I'm just going to go down to Manuel Antonio for a couple of days.'

'You shouldn't be alone. Come on home.'

'It's supposed to be beautiful. I'd be crazy to come all this way and not even see the country's major attraction.'

'You can see it some other time.'

'I need to do this. I need to clear my head.'

'We decided on a name,' Annabel says. 'Margaret.'

'That's pretty.'

'And with your blessing, we'd like for her middle name to be Emma.'

How to tell her that I can't give my blessing for that? All these months of trying to remember, and now there's only one thing I want: to forget.

★ ★ ★

I have a recurring dream in which I am standing on a hillside, watching a train pass. The train, moving silently over the tracks, seems to have no beginning and no end. Every now and then, I'll glimpse the interior of the train through a window. Each time I get a glimpse into one of these windows, the person inside is doing some specific thing, in a specific place I have known: my mother, washing dishes at the big double sink

423

in the house where I grew up; Annabel, diving off the bow of the boat into the warm waters off Petit Bois Island.

I haven't had the dream since Emma's disappearance. I kept waiting for it, kept hoping to wake with it still vivid in my mind. Through the window I hoped to see a moment on Ocean Beach, some buried memory that would solve the mystery. But I dream instead the most mundane things.

On my last night in Playa Hermosa, the dream returns. I am deep into sleep, the rain battering the tin roof of my cabin. I see the train, the window, and within the frame of the window, a girl. A dead girl, lying on a bed, her body partially covered by a sheet. White ankles, white feet, stiff white fingers. Eyes closed. I wake with the sheets soaked, a metallic taste in my mouth. I tell myself it means nothing. It is, after all, just a dream. I go out onto the covered balcony and watch the storm moving over the ocean.

75

The New England patient H.M. was the man for whom time stood still.

When H.M. was twenty-seven, Dr. William Scoville decided that the best way to cure his patient's epilepsy would be to remove portions of his brain, including most of the hippocampus and the amygdala, the small, almond-shaped bit of tissue where emotional memories are stored. The procedure was a terrible failure. Not only did H.M. continue to suffer epileptic seizures; he also lost the ability to form new memories.

For nearly three decades, Dr. Brenda Milner visited H.M. on a monthly basis. Over the thirty years of Milner's work, not once did H.M. recognize her if she had been out of his sight for more than a few minutes. 'He lives today chained to the past,' Milner said. 'You can say his personal history stopped with the operation.'

Many of H.M.'s earliest memories remained intact. He remembered taking swimming lessons at an indoor pool as a child, and spending nights in a big house in the country. He remembered the layout of the country house, the chickens on the wallpaper in the kitchen. He even remembered what type of perfume his mother wore. But he never knew, from one minute to the next, where he was or whom he was speaking to.

H.M. once tried to explain to his doctors what it meant to be deprived of memory: 'Every day is alone in itself, whatever enjoyment I've had, whatever sorrow I've had.'

What a horror, and yet what a gift. To relegate sorrow to the past, a past that is truly behind you. To endure a terrible guilt, and then forget it. To wake each day with a clean emotional slate, and no knowledge of your own mistakes.

76

Day 332. Early in the morning I meet Sami at the bar. She makes some mimosas, which we carry out to the beach. We watch the sun come up, a bright white light spreading over the soft blue water. Afterward, she walks me to the bus stop.

'That's all you have?' she asks, glancing at my backpack and shoulder bag.

'I travel light. I threw some stuff away.'

She digs her heel into the sand, squints against the sun. 'I'll see you around?'

'Sure. Call me if you're ever in San Francisco.'

'I will.'

'When do you plan to head back to Texas?'

'Texas?' she says, grinning. 'What's that?'

When the bus arrives at eight a.m., the town is just beginning to wake up, the surfers heading out to the water one by one. I envy the simplicity of their lives, how their routines are governed by the rhythms of the tide. I envy their perpetual state of forgetting, the way their minds are occupied so fully by the surf that everything else recedes.

If it weren't for Annabel and the baby, I might stay here. Just go back to my cabin, unpack my things, settle in for the long haul, and learn to surf. It's an easy place to live, an easy place to leave the rest of the world behind. And isn't that, in part, what I've been doing here? Escaping

427

Jake, his pain, the city that holds so many memories.

An hour into our journey, the bus breaks down. The driver spends half an hour cursing and banging around under the hood, then orders everyone off the bus. We sit on the side of the road for two hours, baking in the heat. By the time another bus arrives, my T-shirt and sarong are soaked through. I probably should have just gone home. If I had gone straight to San José, I could be in my own bed late tonight. I try to imagine walking into my apartment, putting down my things. Showering in my bathroom, eating food in my kitchen. Walking into my darkroom. Beginning life again. I try to imagine it, but the fantasy doesn't ring true. How will I go back and simply be myself again?

I spend the night in Quepos. The next morning, I take another bus the short distance along the winding road toward Manuel Antonio National Park. I get off at Playa Espadilla, a long, gray-sand beach crowded with sunbathers. I walk west, away from the restaurants and hotels, toward the less populated end of the beach, which backs up to evergreen forest. There is something startling in the juxtaposition of bright blue sea and deep green forest, so close to one another, almost touching. The vast space of the ocean is set against the tangled, dark mass of mangroves and palms.

I picked up a new Holga a few weeks ago at a thrift shop in Tamarindo. Now, I take the camera out of my bag. Pairing a Holga with these colors and this brilliant light is likely to yield something that looks more like a painting than a photograph. Blurred edges, bright colors overlapping. I came to this country to find Emma, but what I will take home is nothing more than this: a photograph of a beautiful Central American beach in summer. Two or three photos of alligators lounging in a murky river. A volcano crater buried in fog.

The beach is teeming with girls of all ages — toddlers and ten-year-olds, teenagers and grown women; brown, dark-haired local girls, and blonde North American girls in various stages of sunburn. Short girls, tall girls, fat girls, thin girls. Laughing girls and quiet girls.

Ticos wander down the beach, selling soft drinks and bottled water from Styrofoam chests. Boys with boogie boards run in and out of the surf. Middle-aged men tote longboards down to the water and dive in, paddling toward the lineup. I mentally note the locals, the waxboys and random standers. I can pick any surfer out of a crowd and know instinctively whether he or she belongs here. My brain is so crowded now with surfing's strange terminology, I wonder what I've forgotten to make way for this new esoterica. A useless knowledge, just so many words that will remind me, always, of my failed search.

I take it all in with my eyes, with my little plastic Holga. The sun is too bright, blinding. Everything is whitewashed by the brilliant sun. I'm parched and walking, clicking the shutter release, advancing the film. Again and again and again. The sound of it soothes me. Click. The sound of my old life. To think it takes so little to transform a passing moment into something resembling permanence. A click — light entering a lens. Later, the chemicals and drying trays. The fixer and stop bath. The glossy paper that reveals a thing we saw once and then forgot entirely.

We take pictures because we can't accept that everything passes, we can't accept that the repetition of a moment is an impossibility. We wage a monotonous war against our own impending deaths, against time that turns children into that other, lesser species: adults. We take pictures because we know we will forget. We will forget the week, the day, the hour. We will forget when we were happiest. We take pictures out of pride, a desire to have the best of ourselves preserved. We fear that we will die and others will not know that we lived.

Click. Click. Click.

Just photographs of strangers. A postcard kind of scene. Serene. The beauty of a tropical beach. The smooth brown bodies. The happy children. This is what I will carry home with me: this nothing that is a photograph, this falsity that conveys the simple happiness of a beach scene in summer. A stranger looking at these photographs would see nothing of my guilt, would not begin to guess at the emptiness inside me.

And then. A shape in the sand about fifty feet away. A bright green towel, and on the towel a girl. A movement. A twisting of the hands as the girl leans back on her elbows and raises her face to the sun. A profile.

My heart like a malfunctioning machine, going

430

too fast. A dry, cardboard taste in my mouth.

Yellow sundress, a long ponytail.

The girl's hand comes up to swat an insect from her face — that motion, the way the fingers are held tightly together when she does this.

Not possible, of course. My sweet dream of some happy ending. *She was on her way home, she was giving up, and then, suddenly, at the last minute . . .*

I come closer, telling myself it can't be true.

When I'm about fifteen feet away, she glances in my direction. Does she see me? This girl who cannot possibly be Emma? Is she looking at me or just looking past me?

A family of five passes between us, carrying ice chests and boogie boards. For a moment, I can't see her. Then the family is gone, and she's still there. Yes, looking at me.

Sun in my eyes. There are a hundred girls. A thousand, a million girls. The world is full of girls who could look like Emma. Girls of her approximate age and weight. Girls who could look like the girl you lost. I vowed I would never forget her face, and yet now, I'm not sure.

A cloud intersects the sun, and in the softer light she is looking at me still. Hand lifted to her eyes. Not looking beyond me but at me, right at me. As if she's seen me before. As if she knows me.

The mind plays tricks. The mind wants to believe that you cannot do this thing to your life and to the life of the man you love, the life of a child in your care. The mind wants to believe that you cannot lose her, and never, ever find her.

The corner of her mouth tips up — not a smile, exactly, just something she does when caught off guard, a facial tic she experiences in moments of confusion. A mirror of her father. I allow myself to think this for a moment, allow myself to believe that the face of the girl is the face of Emma, and that Jake's genetic code is somehow imprinted there.

But no, of course not. The mind plays tricks. For how many years will I do this — pass through the world with a vague belief simmering somewhere in my subconscious? How many thousands of times will I see a face and think, for a moment, that it is Emma's?

The girl raises her hand again, swatting at flies, then shields her eyes. She's looking at me, straight at me; she doesn't look away.

So close now, just ten feet. Eight. Six. A bright green towel, a girl alone on the beach. Too young to be alone on the beach.

Just four feet between me and this girl. This dream of Emma.

The sun again. A momentary blindness. The mind plays tricks, I know this. I know the mind cannot be trusted.

And then I'm standing beside her, looking down. Her green eyes gazing up at me, and I tell myself: this is Emma. No one else. Not a look-alike, not a mirage, not my imagination. My knees go weak, my heart jumps, my breath leaves me. Emma.

The sun bright and sharp, blinding.

'Emma?'

My voice comes out wrong, not a whisper

432

exactly, but something weak, high-pitched.

She doesn't respond. She pulls her knees to her chest and hugs them, staring up at me.

I glance around, looking for adults who might be with her, but there are none. Just Emma sitting on a big green towel, alone.

And it *is* Emma. Isn't it?

Not a dream of her. *Her.*

There are two other towels laid out beside her, an empty beer bottle, a plastic bucket and shovel set, a red Igloo ice chest. On top of the chest, a British rock magazine.

I kneel on the sand beside her. 'Emma?'

No response.

'Emma?'

Again, nothing.

'Do you remember me?' I say.

For a few seconds she doesn't move. Then she nods, slowly, her eyebrows forming into a frown.

Relief, confusion, a surge of overwhelming joy. The ground, unsteady beneath my knees. More than anything, I want to touch her, to put my hands on her face and know she's really here. I reach out carefully and touch her cheek. She flinches.

My heart giving out. No words to say what I'm thinking. No way to believe what I'm seeing.

She's too thin, her cheekbones too well defined, but her skin is brown and healthy. She has taken on the golden glow of summer children. There is something unfamiliar about her, something in her features that is not as I remember it. I try to place the difference, to name it — is it her eyes, the set of the mouth, a squaring of the jaw? Her hair is long, trailing down her back, almost to the ground. It's lighter than it used to be, with streaks of auburn. She's wearing a yellow dress printed with white flowers, too short, not entirely clean.

'We've been looking for you,' I say.

I'm trying to control my voice, trying to be calm, trying not to frighten her, but the tears are coming, I can feel them on my face, fast and hot. The tears mingle with my suntan lotion, and my eyes burn.

She presses her lips together. Surprise, confusion, tears welling up in her eyes, too. 'I've been waiting.'

'What?'

I'm imagining it, I tell myself. I'm imagining that this girl is Emma. And I'm imagining her words. 'What did you say?'

'I've been waiting, Abby. Where were you? Where's Daddy?'

Shock. Disbelief. This is Emma, sitting on the sand beside me. I wrap my arms around her, holding on. Sobbing, looking down at her face, Emma's face, not believing. This little girl limp in my arms. On a beach, thousands of miles from home. I cannot trust in the reality of this moment, because it is too unbelievable to be true. Missing children do not come home. Detective Sherburne told me this. Jake told me this. Everyone told me, but I refused to believe. What comes home when a child goes missing are the remains, found many months or years or decades later. The child does not come home — not alive, not still a child, not with long

434

beautiful hair and a tan. Not staring into your face, saying your name.

There are not so many real surprises in life. There are sudden deaths, of course, and the occasional twist of good fortune. But good surprises of the monumental sort — my mother always told me these things did not happen. And yet, here, now, is the proof: there are surprises, miracles. Emma on a beach in Costa Rica. Emma alive.

I lean back and stare into her face again. To be sure. Am I seeing clearly? Hearing clearly? But it's her, I'm certain. Not a single doubt now, this is Emma. Impossibly, it is Emma.

I try to regain my composure and devise a plan. Among the nearby faces, no one looks familiar. Would I recognize the couple from the yellow van if I saw them now? Is that even who I should be looking for?

'Who's been taking care of you, honey?'

'Teddy and Jane.'

'Where are they?'

She points to the ocean, to a group of surfers in the distance.

'Have they been nice to you? Did they hurt you?' I ask the questions before thinking. I'm not sure I want to hear the answers, not yet. And besides, there's no time.

She shrugs, stretches her skinny brown legs out in front of her, and digs her toes into the sand. 'We went to the butterfly farm,' she says. She raises one hand in the air, spreads the fingers wide. 'I saw butterflies this big.' She drops her hands to her sides, sifts sand through her fingers, doesn't look at me.

There's so much I want to know, so many questions. Where has she been living? Has she been hurt? What have they told her about us? And how did they take her? What did they say that day on Ocean Beach, how did they convince her to go with them? But these are questions for later. I must get her away from here.

She brushes a strand of hair out of her face. 'Where's Daddy?'

'He's waiting for you. It's time to go.'

She is silent, gazing out at the water. 'Okay,' she says, and then the tears come, soundlessly.

I stroke her hair. 'It's okay, sweetheart. I'm here. I'm finally here.'

She stretches her hand out to touch my arm. Her fingernails are bitten to the quick. She is wearing light blue nail polish that's chipped around the edges. These long months, I've envisioned our reunion. I've rehearsed the things I would say to her. Now all the rehearsed things fall away, and it is just the two of us, looking out at the blue ocean where it meets the blue sky, the bright sun beating down. A drop of sweat trickles from the nape of her neck, down her spine, disappearing beneath her dress.

The tiny hairs on her arms have turned blonde. I wrap my arms around her again, feeling the warmth of her skin. This time she hugs back — just the tiniest pressure, but I'm sure she's hugging back. I can feel her small hands, pressing lightly.

I am aware of the importance of time, aware that I must get her away from here. Along with

436

the elation, there is a sense of panic, a knowledge that I must choose the proper course of action. I hold her face in my hands and look into her eyes. 'Ready?'

She wipes her nose on her arm. Something about that gesture — so childish, so unaware — sends a stab to the center of my heart, and I can't see for the tears. I stand, reaching out to take her hand, and she allows me to pull her up. In one startling moment I realize she has grown by a good three inches. Her shoulders and legs have a muscular quality that wasn't there before.

'This way,' I say, pointing into the trees. She hesitates, standing still, our arms stretched taut between us.

'What about Teddy and Jane?' she asks.

I kneel down in front of her. 'Your daddy and I have missed you so much.'

'They told me to stay here. I'll get in trouble.'

'You won't get in trouble,' I say. 'I promise.'

Kneeling before her, trying to convince her to sneak away with me, I feel almost criminal, and I think of the kidnappers, wondering if they felt the same way I'm feeling now — this sickening sense of urgency and impatience, the fear that something will go wrong, someone will thwart our escape. Latin music wafts from a restaurant down the beach, mingling with the happy shrieks of children. The sun is high and huge. My sunglasses are no match for the Costa Rican sun at noon, which bleaches everything to a whitish pastel and makes the air into a dizzying display of heat waves.

I tug gently at Emma's hand. She takes a step,

then another, slowly. In front of us there is the line of trees, and escape. Behind us there is the ocean, and the danger of detection. What will I do if Teddy and Jane come up to me, screaming that I'm taking their child? Who will be believed?

Walking past the crowds of sunbathers, my feet plowing into the sand, holding tightly to Emma's damp hand, it feels as though everything has slipped into slow motion.

And then, this is what we do: we simply disappear. The jungle takes us in. One moment we're out in the open, on the beach, where anyone can see us. The next moment we're standing on a narrow path scattered with pebbles and broken shells. Only then do I notice that Emma is barefoot, and her feet are scarred and blistered. For a moment I try to carry her, but she's too big now, and I can't move fast enough. 'I'm sorry, baby,' I say, setting her down. 'You'll have to walk. We need to move quickly.' I give her my flip-flops, which are too big, but she doesn't complain.

We pass over a little creek, then begin the steep descent toward the road. I never let go of her hand. At one point, I feel her fingers wiggling in mine, and I loosen my grip a little. I can't stop looking at her, can't stop marveling at the miracle of her presence. To have Emma here, with me, hand in hand. To see her face and hear her voice. Only now do I admit to myself that there were times when I believed I would never see her again, times when I believed, like Jake did, that she was dead. To think that I was going home. That I might have stepped onto a plane two days ago and never found her.

There's a rustling in the leaves above us. Emma stops, becomes very still, squeezes my fingers. 'Look,' she whispers, pointing to a movement in the trees. 'Spider monkeys.'

There are about a dozen of them, swinging fast, moving through the canopy of trees. Their tiny bodies are gray and wiry. I look at Emma, her face turned up to the green growth, her eyes wide and bright. It's not just her height, her hair, her weight. She has changed. And I'm struck, at last, by the full force of what has happened. She is here with me. We're making our escape. Could I be dreaming? Have I entered some hallucinatory state? But the smell of the ocean, the sound of birds, the feel of her hand in mine — all of these things serve as proof that the moment is not merely my imagination. This is not a fairy tale, not a dream; this forest is real, this child is real.

Minutes ago, she was lost. Now, she is found.

My heart is beating painfully fast, and I'm out of breath, more from elation and fear than from physical exertion. I kneel down and look into her face, still trying to believe. 'Emma?'

'Hmm?'

'Is it really you?'

'Yes. It's *me*.' Something in the way she says 'me,' something impetuous in the emphasis. Verging on sassiness — just as Emma always did. She looks over her shoulder, as if she, too, is now afraid of getting caught. 'Let's *go*,' she says, tugging at my hand.

Five minutes later we emerge from the jungle

439

onto a narrow, paved road lined with palatial houses. It's another half mile to the main road. There, we stop and wait for a taxi or bus. I buy a big straw hat and dark sunglasses from a roadside stand. 'Put these on,' I say. She doesn't question me; it is as if she understands the necessity for disguise. The only time I let go of her hand is to take the money from my purse to pay the vendor.

I peer down the road — just cars and motorcycles rounding the bend. Why is there no bus, no taxi? What's taking so long?

'Baby,' I say while we're waiting, 'how did you get from San Francisco to Costa Rica?'

'We drove.' She frowns. 'It took forever, and they don't have air conditioning.'

'What kind of car do Teddy and Jane drive?'

'A van.'

'What color?'

'Yellow. It's always breaking down. They made me hide under blankets in the back every time we saw the police. It was scary.'

'You don't have to be scared anymore, okay? We're going home.'

I think of that first day, the first clue, how the van seemed less like evidence, more like a misleading distraction, a question. I look for it now, as I did those months at Ocean Beach. I imagine the moment when Teddy and Jane return to the towels and find her absent. Will they feel that same sense of confusion that I felt eleven long months ago, and then the rising panic, the awareness that she is gone? Will they curse those minutes in the ocean when they had their eyes turned toward the coming waves, those minutes when they forgot one crucial fact: Emma on the beach, alone?

Surely they've noticed her missing by now. I imagine them running up and down the beach, shouting her name. Approaching strangers with the news, 'We've lost our little girl.'

No taxis come. It seems like forever before the bus to Quepos arrives, but when I look at my watch I realize that only nine minutes have passed. The glass doors open, and Emma steps on, pulling me behind her. '*Buenos días*,' she says to the bus driver.

'*Bueno*,' he says.

'Quepos?' I ask.

'*Sí*.'

I drop the coins into the box. We could be any mother and daughter, going home from a day at the beach. Emma takes the first open seat, halfway back, and I sit down beside her, my heart beating wildly as I try to solidify my plan. In Quepos we'll catch a bus to San José. In San José we'll get a hotel room, then call Jake. He won't believe me, I'm sure. He'll think it's someone else calling, not me; he'll think it's some cruel prank.

A few more passengers climb on board, the door shuts, and then the bus is moving. The smell of the beach, of mangroves. And the smell of Emma, coconut lotion and childish sweat, salt in her hair, maybe a couple of days without bathing. She lets go of my hand, and I realize I've been holding on so hard my knuckles hurt. She stretches her fingers and stares out the window for a few seconds, then takes off the sunglasses and looks up at me.

'Abby?'

'Yes?'

She bites her lower lip, thinking. It's a gesture straight from her father, an exact imitation. I don't remember her ever doing this before. And then she says, 'Where *were* you?'

Not an accusation, exactly, just a question, a thing she can't understand. I try to come up with the answer. I want to tell her how desperately we wanted her back, how every minute was filled with the thought of her, but there are no words to explain.

'I was looking for you everywhere,' I say, pulling her close. 'You know that, don't you?'

'I thought you and Daddy forgot me.'

'Oh, baby, we never forgot. We were looking for you every minute.'

We arrive at the bus station in Quepos just in time to buy our tickets for San José. No time to call Jake. All I can think about is getting her out of town. With each step we take, the search area widens for Teddy and Jane. With each passing minute, their chance of finding us decreases.

We're the last passengers to board, and the doors close loudly behind us. The bus is crowded, but fortunately two vacant seats remain in the back, across the aisle from one another. Even this small distance seems too great. I sit sideways, my legs in the aisle, my hands on Emma. Afraid she'll get away somehow. Afraid that if I let go, even for a moment, she will disappear like the fog of a dream.

'When can I talk to Daddy?' Emma says.

'As soon as we get to San José.'

'Where's San José?'

'Just a couple of hours from here.'

'Will Daddy be in San José?'

'No, he's in San Francisco. We have to call him to come meet us.'

She glances over to the seat beside her, where a teenage boy is snoring, then turns back to me.

'What about Mommy?' she asks.

'What?'

'Mommy. Will she be there?'

'Sweetheart,' I say, 'do you mean Jane?'

'No,' she says impatiently. 'Mommy.'

'Have you seen your mommy?' I ask.

She nods. 'We went to see her at a motel.' Emma holds up her left hand and wiggles her index finger, showing off a glittery ring, the kind you can get for five dollars at Claire's Boutique in the mall. 'She gave me this.'

I swallow hard, unable to believe what I'm hearing. 'How do you know it was your mommy?'

She reaches into her dress pocket and pulls out a faded Polaroid. 'It was her,' she says, pointing to a slightly younger, slightly slimmer Lisbeth. In the photo, Lisbeth is standing in Golden Gate Park, Jake by her side. Jake holds a tiny baby in his arms. He's smiling, Lisbeth isn't. Both of them are squinting into the sun.

I feel as though all the air has suddenly been let out of my lungs.

'Where did you get this?'

'Mommy gave it to me.' She takes the photo

443

from me and puts it back in her pocket.

'When?'

She shrugs, already growing bored of the conversation. 'I don't remember.'

I'm trying to process the information, trying to make sense of this impossible new fact. I remember what Jake told me that night at his house, after Lisbeth made her dramatic appearance at the press conference and showed up at his door: *She wanted to know what would happen if Emma was found — could we give it another go, try to make a family.*

'Did you see her more than once?' I ask.

'Yes, but I haven't seen her for a long time.' Emma bites her lip, as if she's trying to decide whether or not to tell me something. 'She said Daddy was going to come get me and we were all going to live together, but he never did.'

So many questions: Was Lisbeth there the day of the kidnapping? How do Teddy and Jane fit into the picture? What were their plans? How did they treat her?

'Do you remember the last time we were together?' I ask. 'Do you remember looking for sand dollars on the beach?'

'Sort of,' she says. She turns away from me and presses her forehead against the window.

'Can you tell me what happened that day?'

'Can I have a *hamburguesa* for lunch?' she says.

'Of course you can.'

There are so many things I want to know, so many connections I'm trying to piece together. But Emma has had enough of this conversation.

Something about the casual way she disregards my questions actually gives me hope. Research has shown how well children adapt, their amazing ability to recover from trauma. Despite her long absence, she seems so much like herself, the stubborn girl who was never shy about saying what she wanted. She swings her legs back and forth, tapping her feet against the floor. Her hands are in her lap and now she's looking straight ahead, a slightly stunned expression on her face. The bus rumbles to a start and lurches forward. There is the rattle of glass as passengers begin lowering the windows, trying to get some relief from the heat.

'I'm thirsty,' Emma says after a few minutes.

I give her a bottle of water from my purse. The water is warm, but she downs the whole bottle in less than a minute.

'I have to go,' she says a few minutes later.

The bathroom is only a couple of feet away, but I get up with her and stand outside until she's finished. She comes out grimacing, holding her fingers to her nose. It's a nothing gesture, universal among children, and yet I'm strangled with emotion just to see her doing this thing, this normal thing. Alive.

77

We arrive in San José at four in the afternoon. I find a taxi just outside the station and ask the driver to take us to the nicest hotel. He must have his own version of 'nice,' because he drops us off at a less-than-impressive motel ten minutes from the bus station. The guy behind the desk, a teenager in a black button-down, chats with Emma in Spanish while I fill out the registration form. I have one hand on the pen, one hand on her shoulder. As I'm paying for the room, I realize that I left my bag and my Leica at the hotel in Quepos. In the urgency of the moment, I completely forgot they were there. No matter — I have my money and passport. I'll have the other things sent to me.

Outside our room, I fumble with the big wooden key chain. Inside, I draw the curtains. The room smells like cigarette smoke. There's a tiny TV, tile floors, a chair, a couple of lamps. A cheap painting of the Wild West hanging above the full-size bed. Emma sits in the chair by the window and plays with the controls on the air conditioner. It's an effort to keep my distance, an effort not to take her in my arms and hold on to her with all my strength.

'Where's Daddy?'

'I'm about to call him.'

My hands are shaking so much I can barely hold on to the phone. I remember that afternoon at the Beach Chalet so many months ago, when the Russian woman pressed the phone into my hand. I hesitated for a moment before dialing Jake's number. I knew I had to call him; I knew he had to be told. And yet I understood that, once I made the phone call, there would be no way to turn back the clock.

Now, the situation is reversed. And still I have this hesitation, this desire to hold on to the moment. I lost her, I found her, she is in this room with me. It is a moment of near-perfect happiness, and part of me doesn't want to disturb it. In a single moment on the beach, I destroyed Jake's life; in the months that followed, I watched it fall apart. Minutes from now, possibly seconds, I will begin to put it back together.

I dial his home number. No answer. Then I try his cell phone. Again, nothing. 'Call me,' I say each time. 'It's urgent.'

I'm ashamed of the relief I feel when he doesn't answer, ashamed to be grateful for the time this gives me. A few more minutes alone with Emma. She sits quietly in the chair, staring at her feet. There's a ketchup stain on her dress.

It occurs to me that I haven't fed her. How could I have overlooked this simple, basic need? 'You must be hungry,' I say.

She nods vehemently.

In my purse I find cheese crackers, a Snickers bar, and a banana. I arrange these things on the little table in front of her, then pour bottled water into a plastic cup. 'We'll get you some real food soon. Cross my heart.'

I dump the contents of my wallet onto the bed, rifle through colorful paper money, receipts, and business cards, and find the phone number Nick Eliot gave me.

'U.S. Embassy,' a genderless voice says.

'I'm looking for Wiggins.'

'One moment.'

When the line clicks over, I get voice mail. 'Wiggins here,' the voice says. 'Leave a message, and I'll get back to you.'

'My name is Abby Mason,' I say. 'I'm a friend of Nick Eliot. He said he was going to explain my situation to you. Please call as soon as you can. It's urgent. It's about Emma Balfour. I found her. She's right here with me. We're staying at Villa Grande in San José, room 212.' I read off the number taped to the phone, then add once again, 'It's extremely urgent.'

Emma has finished the crackers and is working on the candy bar. She eats fast, without looking up, hardly pausing to chew. She has a spot of chocolate on her chin. I stare at her, the facts slowly sinking in: she's here, she's alive, she's safe. Her hair is lighter now, her skin is browner, she is taller and too thin. But she is Emma. I go over to the chair. When I put my hand on her face, she doesn't flinch, doesn't move toward me, just stops mid-chew.

'Honey, are you okay?'

'Yes.' She lifts a hand to her face, and her dress rises higher on her legs. She's so thin.

I hug her carefully, and she leans into me. 'You're safe now. We're taking you home.'

For a moment, it seems as if she's going to cry

448

again. But then she wriggles out of my arms and says, 'Can I watch TV?'

'Of course.'

I turn on the TV and hand her the remote. She flips past *The Road Runner, Sesame Street* dubbed in Spanish, and finally settles on a Spanish-language soap opera. She watches it for fifteen minutes, mesmerized. I sit on the bed with the phone in my lap, waiting. Every now and then Emma mumbles something to the TV. She knows all the characters by name.

When the phone rings, both of us jump. I'm not sure I'm ready for everything that will happen now.

'Abby?'

It's Jake. After all this time, he still has the ability to calm me with his voice, simply by saying my name. 'Your message said it was urgent.'

I am aware of the fact that I'm about to step over a line, aware that my words will set a whole new chain of events in motion. 'I have news, Jake.'

I can tell by the dead quiet on the other end of the line that Jake doesn't believe me. He's waiting to hear about some flimsy new clue, some unconvincing piece of evidence.

'She's here,' I say.

Silence.

'What?'

'I'm sitting in a hotel room in Costa Rica. Emma's *here*. In the room with me.' There's a pause, a long moment of disbelief. 'It's true,' I say. 'Emma really is here.'

449

A shriek and a sob, and, 'Oh my God. Are you sure?'

'I'm sure.'

'Is she okay?'

'Yes.'

'It's not possible,' he says. 'Let me talk to her.' Even as he says it, I can tell he doesn't believe that Emma will actually come on the line, doesn't believe this phone call is real.

Emma's still staring at the television, chewing her fingernails.

'Sweetheart?' I say.

She mutes the TV and looks at me. 'Is it Daddy?'

'Yes. He wants to talk to you.'

We're sitting knee to knee — her in the chair, me on the bed. I hand her the phone. 'Hello,' she says quietly.

I'm leaning in close, and I can hear Jake on the other end. 'Emma? Baby, is it you?'

'Yes. Where are you?'

'I can't believe it's you.'

'Daddy?' she says again. 'Why aren't you here?'

'I'm coming to get you, baby. I missed you so much.'

'Hurry.'

She holds the phone out to me, as if it's some alien object that might bite or blow up. She has that same stunned expression she had on the bus.

'Tell me she's okay,' Jake says. He's sobbing so loudly the words come out garbled.

'She is.'

'Oh God.' He's laughing, crying, trying to catch his breath. 'Where *was* she? How did you find her?'

'On a beach. I was just walking down the beach, and she was there.'

'I don't believe it. It's not possible. I won't believe it until I see her.'

'You need to get on a plane,' I say. 'Call back as soon as you have your ticket.'

He's crying and laughing, breathing fast. 'I don't want to break the connection. I'm afraid I'll wake up. This is a dream, right?'

'It's not a dream. She's really here.'

'Tell me what she looks like. Is she okay? Has she changed?'

Emma is sitting with her legs up in the chair, her arms around her knees, staring at me with those green eyes, her hair long and wild. Her shoulders are slightly pink, and she's wearing an ankle bracelet — a thin silver chain with a tiny heart charm. I've never seen the bracelet before. Was it a gift from Lisbeth? I wonder. How many trips did she make to Costa Rica, bearing cheap gifts and complicated lies?

'She's beautiful,' I say. 'Totally beautiful.'

'Let me talk to her again. I can't believe this is happening.'

I hand Emma the phone. She turns away from me and stares out the window, phone to her ear. She sits there, listening and nodding, occasionally saying yes or no. Once, she even utters something that comes close to a laugh. 'I miss you,' she says at one point. 'They said you were going to move here and we could live together. I kept waiting.'

This time, I can't hear what Jake is saying on the other end. After about ten minutes, she hands the phone to me again.

'Abby?' Jake says.

'Yes.'

'I'm so sorry I didn't believe you.' He pauses to catch his breath. 'Where has she *been*? Who was she with?'

'She was with the couple from the van, that's all I know.'

'You were right,' he says. 'It's incredible. All along, you were right. You're sure she's okay? No one hurt her?'

'Yes,' I say. 'She's really okay.'

The truth is, I don't know for sure. Emma seems fine, but there's no telling what happened to her in the past year. No telling what kind of life she had with Teddy and Jane, no calculating the long-term effects.

'Just let me say goodbye to her. I can't believe this.'

I hand Emma the phone one more time. 'Bye, Daddy,' she says then. And for a moment, just an instant, it is as if she was never gone. The way she says goodbye to him, as if we're just away on vacation. As if this is an ordinary phone call on some ordinary day.

'There's one thing,' I say, before hanging up.

'What?'

'Lisbeth. Don't say anything to Lisbeth.'

'Why? What do you mean?'

'She's been here, Jake. I don't have any details, but I know she's been here.'

452

'God,' he says. 'I should have known.' I hear a thud on the other end of the line, like a fist hitting a wall. 'I can't believe she sat here in my goddamn house and I didn't figure it out. I can't believe I trusted her.'

'She put on a good act.'

'I'll call Sherburne on my way to the airport,' he says.

There's noise on his end of the line — a zipper, keys. I imagine him in his bedroom, packing his messenger bag for the trip — wallet, passport, cell phone charger.

'Thank you,' he says. 'Thank you so much. Tell Emma I love her. Tell her I'll be there very soon.'

Putting the phone down, I feel an overwhelming sense of relief. As if every moment for the past year has been leading up to this one, singular event: the phone call to Jake, when I tell him everything's okay.

'I'm still hungry,' Emma says.

'Then let's eat.' I dial the front desk and order room service. Two *hamburguesas* with extra cheese, *papas fritos*, chocolate milk, and two Cokes.

Half an hour later the food arrives, and Emma tears into it as if she hasn't eaten in days. She eats her entire hamburger and half of mine, plus most of the french fries. She eats for twenty minutes, not talking, then puts the meager leftovers in the trash and says, 'May I have my bath now?'

'Of course.'

I go into the small bathroom and run the water for her. When I come out into the room, she's already completely undressed, standing in front of the television with her hands on her hips, waiting.

'Your water's ready,' I say, feeling strangely formal, as if Emma is a guest I don't quite know how to please.

'Thank you.'

As she brushes past me into the bathroom, I notice a purple bruise in the small of her back. My breath catches. Is this just an ordinary bruise, the kind children get every day, or did someone do this to her? She climbs into the tub and concentrates on tearing the paper off the tiny bar of soap. I sit on the edge of the tub and hand her a washcloth, searching her body for more bruises. Thank God, I don't see any.

'Honey, how often do you take a bath?'

She dunks the washcloth in the water and begins to soap her arms. The dirt comes off in streaks. 'Teddy says we don't need to because we swim in the ocean every day.'

'You swim? You're not afraid?'

'I was at first, but I'm not anymore. Teddy bought me a boogie board so I could learn how to surf. It was fun.'

'Do you like Teddy, sweetheart?'

'He's okay. Jane is mean, though.'

'Mean how?'

She shrugs her shoulders. 'Just mean. She always fussed at me about every little thing. Sometimes she spanked me.'

The anger fills me up, and I try not to think about the thousands of ways they might have

454

mistreated her. I try instead to concentrate on her beautiful face, the little soap bubbles gathering on her shoulders, her arms.

'Would you like for me to wash your hair?' I ask.

'Yes.'

She slides her feet down to the end of the tub, lies down, closes her eyes, and dunks her head underwater. She stays under for a few seconds too long — and I remember how she used to hate to put her face underwater, how she couldn't stand to hold her breath. Just as I'm about to reach down and bring her up, she lifts her head, gasping. Water streams down her shoulders, and her hair is plastered to her back. I squirt shampoo into my palms, then place my hands on her head, so carefully. At the moment of contact she jerks her head away — an instinct, an unconscious response — then, just as quickly, she relaxes.

As Emma leans her head back into my hands, I'm struck by a memory from childhood: Annabel is an infant, and my mother is bathing her in a blue plastic tub. My mother takes my hand in her own and places it on Annabel's soapy head. Annabel's hair is fine beneath my fingers, her skin as soft as felt. I couldn't have been more than three years old, and yet the memory is as clear as if it had happened yesterday.

The phone rings. It's Jake, elated, calling with details of his flight. He makes me take the phone into the bathroom so he can talk to Emma again.

This is it. The end of the search. The end of

the nightmare. I want to believe that it will also be a kind of beginning — for me and Jake, for Emma, for the family we once planned to be.

In the tub, Emma has her head underwater, blowing bubbles. I realize, watching her, that there are so many ways we'll have to get to know her again.

'You're turning into a prune,' I say. 'Ready to get out?'

She stands and holds her arms up. I wrap the towel around her. 'Are you sleepy?' I ask.

'Yes.'

'We don't have a nightgown, so we'll have to make do.'

I fashion my sarong into a dress for myself and give Emma my T-shirt to sleep in. It's not exactly clean, but it will do. She holds her arms up in the air so I can slip the shirt over her head, then she climbs into the bed. I tuck her in and lie on top of the covers beside her, watching her sleep. Touching her hair, her shoulders, her beautiful face. Still not believing. Still trying to take it in. I'm so tired, but I don't close my eyes; I can't stop looking at her.

At two a.m., the phone rings. 'Abby Mason?' an unfamiliar voice says.

'Yes.'

'Wiggins here. Just got your message. Sorry to call so late.'

'You don't know how happy I am to hear from you.' I go over to the chair by the window and speak as quietly as possible.

'Don't get too excited yet. I'm actually in

Honduras right now, but I've made arrangements to come back to Costa Rica tomorrow morning. Nick told me the story a while back. To be honest, I didn't think you'd find her. Weird things happen, huh? I just contacted our people in San Francisco and had them fax the forensic sketches to me. They've talked to Emma's father and are bringing the ex-wife in now. What I need you to do is tell me how you found her. Did you see her kidnappers?'

'No, but I got their first names, Teddy and Jane.'

I tell him the whole story. It comes out in a rush, a jumble of breathless sentences. 'They're driving a yellow van,' I say.

'Where do you think I might find it?'

'They were at Playa Espadilla earlier today, but that was hours ago.'

'I'll send some people out to Manuel Antonio right away. Can you be reached at this number tomorrow?'

'I'm taking Emma to the airport at seven a.m. to meet her father. I haven't thought beyond that.'

'I'll send somebody over to escort you to the airport in the morning. He'll deal with any issues you run into there. Emma can go home, but you're going to need to stay in the country for a few days, maybe longer. When we find these two, you'll have to make an ID.'

Not *if*, but *when*. His confidence is reassuring. 'Thank you,' I say. 'Thank you so much.'

78

An inhuman shriek awakes me, followed by other shrieks, a cacophony of them, just outside our window.

'The howler monkeys,' Emma says, opening her eyes and stretching. Her brown skin is damp from sweat. Despite the noisy air conditioner, the heat is stifling. Last night, I lay awake for hours, staring at the miracle of her. At some point I fell asleep. Now, once again, I am struck by the beautiful impossibility of her presence.

The clock says 6:15. 'Time to get up,' I say. 'We're going to the airport.'

'Now?' she asks.

'Very soon.'

'And Daddy will be there?'

'Yes.'

She looks at me warily, as if she isn't sure she can believe me.

Twenty minutes later, there's a knock at the door. I peek out the curtain to see a young guy, striking Italian features, no more than twenty-seven.

'Who is it?' I ask through the door.

'Wiggins sent me.'

I open the door.

'Name's Panico,' the guy says, reaching out to shake my hand. 'Mike Panico.' He looks over my shoulder into the room, where Emma stands barefoot, wearing the same dirty yellow dress she had on yesterday. 'You must be Emma.'

She nods.

He smiles at her. 'I understand a lot of people have been looking for you.'

At the airport, I buy Emma a new dress and sandals. The dress is slightly too big, the sandals slightly too small, but Emma does a little twirl, modeling the ensemble as if it's the most beautiful thing she's ever worn.

Afterward, Panico takes us to a small room on the second floor. The room contains only a table and four chairs, all of which are bolted to the floor. Two of the chairs have circular metal bands on the sides, with keyholes for locks, and I realize that the bands are for locking down criminals. Beige paint is peeling from the walls.

Panico shuts the door and kneels down so that he's eye level with Emma. 'Looks like you're going home. What's the first thing you're going to do when you get there?'

'I want a hamburger and chocolate shake from Cable Car Joe's.'

'I don't blame you,' he says. 'It's impossible to get a good burger in this country.'

Emma smiles, and I feel myself relaxing. Panico reaches into his jacket and pulls out a coloring book and crayons, which he sets on the table. 'Do you like to color?'

She nods shyly.

'I used to love to color when I was a kid,' he says. 'But I never had much talent for it.'

Emma sits down and begins flipping through the coloring book. I sit across from her. '*El gato*,' she says, pointing to a drawing of a cat. She selects a yellow crayon from the pack and begins to color. 'Do you know Spanish?' she asks me.

'A little.'

She turns to Panico. 'Do you?'

'*Sí, señorita.*' They exchange a few sentences in rapid Spanish, and he says something that makes her laugh. I can only make out the word *pie*, but even that may be a faulty translation.

Emma inserts Indigo into the sharpener on the back of the box and turns the crayon. Then she blows on the pointed tip, bows her head over her book, and sets to work on *el gato*'s water bowl. The waxy scent of crayons mixes with something else. The odor is coming from Emma; even though she bathed last night, she has taken on the slightly feral, salty-sweet smell of kids who aren't properly cared for.

Panico moves his chair closer to her. 'Can I ask you some questions, Emma?'

'I guess.'

'Where have you been staying?'

'Sometimes on the beach, sometimes in the van. Sometimes we go stay with Teddy and Jane's friends.'

'Do you know where their friends live?'

'Different places.'

'Did they tell you how they know your mom?'

'Teddy is Mommy's cousin,' Emma says. 'Can I color now?'

Emma tugs at her ear, and I feel grateful for this small, recognizable gesture, this nervous habit she's had as long as I've known her. She looks up at me, then Panico, and says, 'Are Teddy and Jane in trouble?'

'We just need to find them to ask them some questions,' Panico says.

Emma returns to her coloring. Sitting here with her, I feel both elated and nervous. Gone is the easy camaraderie that had developed between us in the weeks before she went missing, and I'm still trying to discover what essential thing in her nature has changed. How much of this new Emma is simply the natural process of growing up, and how much of it is the result of spending so many months with her kidnappers?

A voice booms over the intercom, announcing arrivals and departures. Each time the speaker in the corner crackles to life, I hold my breath. Let the flight be late. Let Jake be delayed in customs. Just a little more time with her, a couple more hours, a few more minutes. Of course, I want Emma to see Jake. Of course, I'm excited about the reunion. But I'm dreading that moment when they step onto the plane, beginning the trip away from me.

Finally there's a knock at the door, three taps.

Emma jumps a little, and so do I. Her back is to the door. Her head remains bowed, but her hand goes suddenly still. She stares at the coloring book and squeezes the crayon so tightly her fingers turn white. Panico opens the door, and there's Jake standing on the other side. He's got no luggage except a messenger bag slung over his shoulder. In one hand he's holding an enormous, auburnhaired American Girl doll, decked out in an embroidered dress and black shoes with fancy laces. He stands there for a moment, staring at the back of Emma's head, as if he's afraid to believe it's her. He has gained weight, and his hair is longer.

I reach over and touch Emma's hand. 'Look who's here.'

She glances up at me, still holding on to the crayon, but she doesn't move. Jake comes to the table and kneels down beside her. When she sees him, something changes in her, something lets go, her face softens and her lips turn up in a tiny smile. Jake drops the doll and takes her in his arms. For a long time he sobs into her hair. Finally, he holds her away from him at shoulder's length and says, 'It's you. I can't believe it's really you.'

'Of course it's me, Daddy.'

Panico glances away. Like me, he must feel like an intruder on this intimate scene.

Jake looks up at me. 'I can't believe it.'

'I know.'

He picks Emma up, takes a step in my direction, and hugs me tightly. He smells so good, looks so good, feels so good. 'You were right all along,' he says. 'I'm so sorry I doubted you.'

Emma looks at the doll on the floor, and a grin spreads across her face. She wriggles out of his arms.

'Meet Felicity,' Jake says. He kneels and sets Emma down.

Emma touches the doll's hair, runs her fingers over the white lace at the hem of the dress. 'She's pretty.'

Jake is staring at Emma as if he doesn't quite

believe she's really here, as if he expects to wake up at any moment from this incredible dream.

'Our flight out isn't for another two hours,' he says to me. 'Do you have time for coffee?'

I can't help laughing. 'Are you kidding?'

Panico steps forward. 'I'm with the embassy,' he says to Jake. 'I'll meet you at the gate and make sure you have no problems boarding the flight. Do you have her passport?'

'Yes,' Jake says, tapping his coat pocket. 'Thanks for your help.'

'Don't thank me,' Panico says. 'Abby's the one who pulled this off.'

'What do you know so far?' Jake asks.

Emma is busy tying and untying the laces on the doll's shoes. 'The man from the yellow van is Lisbeth's cousin,' I say quietly. 'At least that's what they told Emma.'

Jake shakes his head, incredulous.

I carry the doll, Jake carries Emma, and we walk down to the café, Panico trailing after us. Emma keeps staring at Jake, and he keeps staring at her, and I keep staring at the two of them. It feels so strange, so impossible, the three of us together like this, walking through the airport like a normal family.

'You need a haircut,' Emma says, running her fingers through her father's long bangs.

'Then I suppose you'll have to give me one as soon as we get home,' he says, his voice choked with emotion.

At the café, we order coffee, a fruit shake for Emma, and some pastries.

The three of us take the most private table, one over by the window. Jake pulls Emma's chair close to his own. He starts to cut her pastry into tiny bites, the way he used to do, but Emma pulls the plate toward her and says, 'I can do that.'

'Sorry,' he says, smiling. 'I guess you've grown, haven't you? God, look how much you've grown. You're taller.'

She grins, looks like she's about to say something, but then shoves a bite of pastry into her mouth.

'What?' he says.

'I'm taller, but you're fatter.'

We all laugh at that, even Emma.

'I missed you so much,' he says. 'So much. You have no idea.'

Emma wipes her mouth with the back of her hand and stares down at her plate, chewing.

I know he's trying hard not to ask questions yet — all the obvious, terrifying questions. He's staring at her, mesmerized.

'Your bedroom is just like you left it,' he says. 'You even have some Christmas presents.'

Emma's eyes go wide. 'When can I open them?'

'As soon as we get home.'

'And birthday presents,' I say.

She looks confused. 'My birthday?'

'It's in November, remember?' Jake says. 'You're seven now.'

Her eyes light up. 'I'm seven?'

A voice comes on the intercom, announcing the departing flight for San Francisco.

464

'That's us,' Jake says. 'Baby, are you ready to go home?'

'Yes.'

He reaches across the table and takes my hand. 'When can you leave?'

'I don't know. Hopefully soon. There's still a lot to do here.'

My conversation with Jake feels like some awkwardly staged play. The choreography's off, the lines fall flat, both of us are speaking a little more loudly than necessary. I find myself wondering what the possibilities are for us now. When I left for Costa Rica, he made it clear it was over between us. But doesn't this change things? Haven't I done the one essential thing I had to do to win him back, to make our lives normal again?

There is no way to ask these questions of him. This is nothing like the scene I imagined, nothing like the reunion I've been picturing in my mind ever since I arrived in Costa Rica. I pictured the three of us going home together, a family. But the truth is Emma and Jake are the family, the two of them alone.

I go over to Emma, lean down, and hug her. I don't want to let go. 'Bye, sweetheart.'

'You're not coming with us?'

'I need to stay here for a little while, but I'll be home soon.'

'Okay.'

'Bye, Jake.'

'Thank you so much,' he says. 'It's a miracle.' He takes my hair in his hand and flips it over my shoulder, the way he did on our first date. This

465

simple gesture is enough to spark my hope, enough to make me think we may find a way to make it work.

Jake picks Emma up, and as they walk away, she glances back and gives a little wave. 'Adios,' she says.

'Adios.'

I watch them walk toward the departure gate — Jake moving quickly, as if he can't wait to get out of here. They could be any father, any daughter, on their way home from vacation. I could be any girlfriend, the unnecessary part of the equation that, once subtracted, leaves the proper sum.

79

Afternoon. A hotel room in San José, waiting. Day 335. As I mentally note the number, I realize that the calendar I've been obsessed with for the past year is now irrelevant. I get to start over from scratch. Yes, it is 335 days since I lost her. But it is also two days since I found her.

I'm sitting on the balcony. Spanish music is playing loudly next door, but not loudly enough to drown out the noise of a couple having sex. I saw them earlier, checking in. He was thin, she was fat, and they had no luggage. I should be doing something — writing thank-you letters, sending e-mails, calling everyone I know. But to whom would I write? I've been on the phone all morning. I've already told Annabel, Nell, and Nick. Like Franco Magnani, the memory artist who was obsessed with his childhood village, my tunnel vision over the past year has caused my circle of friends to dwindle; there's no one else to call.

Jake and Emma arrived home last night to a few dozen well-wishers, crowding the airport with welcome-home signs and stuffed animals. Jake called from the house to let me know they'd arrived. 'Can I talk to Emma?' I asked as he was hanging up.

'She's already asleep.'

'Tomorrow?'

'Of course.' There was a long pause. Then he

said, 'Thank you. I can't believe this is happening.'

For so long, every waking minute has been devoted to finding Emma. Now, I'm not sure what to do with myself. I turn on the television — *Indiana Jones and the Temple of Doom*. I struggle to keep my eyes open. I think of Emma, at home in her very own bed. I imagine Jake sitting at her bedside until she falls asleep. At some point, growing tired, he decides to go to his own room. But at the doorway he stops, unable to leave her. He stands there all night, watching his daughter breathe, that beautiful child. Maybe at some point she wakes up, cries out, and he rushes to her. But for a moment, in her confusion, she does not recognize him. She doesn't recognize the bed, the room, the stuffed animals lining the walls. 'Where's Teddy?' she says. 'Where's Jane?' And how, I wonder, will he answer that?

On the television there are explosions, snakes, Kate Capshaw in a thong swimsuit, bathing in a muddy river. The couple in the next room grows quiet; laughter wafts down the hall. Sleep comes.

A jolt. A knock at the door. A rhythmic, bouncy knock, sort of like the way Annabel used to knock on my bedroom door when we were kids, our own special code. For a moment, waking, I think the knock is inside the dream, but there it is again. I straighten my dress — one of several items I bought this morning at an open-air mall near the hotel — and answer the door. It's a guy of medium height, wiry build, wearing a Cuban shirt, a straw hat, and loose khaki pants. He's very tan. He's clearly American, but there's something different about him. He's nothing like the tourists who wander the markets of San José, looking over their shoulders and clutching their wallets.

'Wiggins,' he says, stepping into the room. 'Nice place you got here.'

'Thanks.'

'I didn't mean it,' he says.

'Pardon?'

'About the room. It was a joke.'

'Oh. Right.'

I'm not prepared for Wiggins's sunny disposition. I guess I pictured a guy in a flak jacket and combat boots, shouting into a walkie-talkie. The couple next door starts up again.

'Sorry about the sound effects,' I say.

'No need to apologize. It's not like you planned it.' He jingles something in his pocket and pulls out a massive key ring. 'Ready?'

'Where are we going?'

'Police station. There's the matter of identification.'

'Pardon?'

'We need you to pick these folks out of a crowd,' he says.

'Are you telling me you got them?' It seems impossible, too much to ask for.

'Yes, I'm pretty sure we did.'

Last night, over the phone, I explained to Wiggins the details of my search. I imagined that his own hunt for Teddy and Jane would take weeks, months even. Now, something feels off. I'm wondering if this is all there is to it. He

469

captures the bad guys, and I make the identification. It seems too easy, after all these months of searching. I guess some part of me wanted to be there when they made the arrest, to see Emma's captors cowering before a group of armed police officers. Maybe I wanted a SWAT team, camera crews, shots fired. I wanted them to feel, for a moment at least, the fear Emma must have felt when they took her. I wanted them to know what it's like to experience overwhelming dread.

In front of the hotel, there's a tanklike Jeep with several antennas. It's high off the ground, spattered with mud. Wiggins opens the passenger-side door and I climb in. Inside, there are all sorts of gadgets. He gets behind the wheel and turns the engine. It doesn't rumble the way I expected, but instead lets out a soft purr, like a humble Toyota.

'What's all this?' I say. 'Is there a satellite somewhere in space transmitting our conversation to Washington?'

'Something like that.' He leans down and speaks into the stick shift. 'The white snow gathers by the red door.' He straightens up, pulls out of the impossibly narrow parking space in a single swift motion.

I like this guy. I can imagine being friends with him in some other life, how I'd invite him to my dinner party and he'd tell riveting stories of international intrigue, filled with shady characters and complicated, implausible plots.

'Where were they?' I ask. 'How did it happen?'

'The Costa Ricans picked them up a few

470

hours ago. They were sleeping in a van like the one you described, and they matched the sketches. They were parked on a dirt road by the beach just a couple of miles from Manuel Antonio.'

'You're kidding.'

'Nope. Your average criminal isn't very smart.'

'Have you talked to them yet?'

'Well, *talk* might not be the right word. But the answer is yes. They confessed. This ID is a technicality.'

'What about Lisbeth? Did they say anything about her?'

'She paid them ten thousand dollars.'

'I don't understand. What were their plans? Were they just going to live down here with Emma indefinitely?'

'Seems they didn't think very far ahead. Lisbeth told the SFPD that she just wanted to spend a little time with Emma, claims Jake wouldn't let her see her and she didn't know what else to do. Her story is that things just got out of hand.'

'None of it makes any sense.'

'These things rarely do. That's what I mean when I say criminals generally aren't very smart. Most of them lack the ability to think through to the end of the plan. They get one idea in their head, one story — the perfect scenario, in which everything goes smoothly and the outcome is ideal. But when one little thing goes wrong, when the pieces stop fitting together, they can't figure out how to revise the plan and come up with a workable solution.'

We drive the winding roads through Quepos — past a schoolyard where children are playing soccer, past the bus station and a grocery store, white churches and decrepit offices and a smattering of tourist hotels. Soon, the city gives way to jungle, and we're bumping along a pitted dirt road, tree limbs slapping the Jeep.

'So,' I say, catching my breath. 'How long have you been doing this?'

'This isn't my usual job. I'm more of a — what's the word — peacekeeper.' Something about the way he says peacekeeper doesn't sound the least bit pacifist.

Then just as suddenly, the jungle gives way to a small clearing, and we take a sharp turn onto a newly paved road. The smell of tar rises in the heat. A large, hand-painted sign proclaims *Bienvenida* in bright red letters. It seems a grand affair for the town itself, which is just a cluster of wooden houses, a fruit stand, a chapel, and a single-story brick building, arranged on either side of the new road. Wiggins parks the Jeep in the dirt in front of the chapel, where an elderly woman is selling things from a card table: three plastic combs, a couple of warm orange sodas in bottles, and Costa Rican scenes painted on blocks of wood.

'This way,' he says, nodding down the street. 'I never asked how you know Nick.'

'I'm a photographer. He was a client. What about you?'

'We once worked together at the UN, or something like that.'

'He never told me he worked at the UN.'

472

'I bet there's a lot he never told you.'

We stop in front of the brick building. It's nothing special, just a one-story affair with an unpainted wooden door and a few dingy windows. But in front of the building is a garden with bougainvillea growing wild.

'You ready to do this?' Wiggins says.

'Not really.'

I look at the ground and take a deep breath, steeling myself. My feet have tan lines in the shape of the plastic thongs I've been wearing since I arrived in Costa Rica. Now, in the new leather sandals I bought this morning, I feel somehow out of place.

Wiggins opens the door and ushers me through. Inside, the air conditioner is on, and the room smells like newspaper and cheap cologne. Three men in uniform are playing checkers and drinking beer at a table in the corner. '*Hola!*' they say. They all seem to know Wiggins. A hulk of a man rises to greet us. He smiles, revealing a shining row of silver braces. Wiggins exchanges some rapid-fire Spanish with the men for a couple of minutes before the man in braces leads us out of the room.

We pass through a metal door, down a corridor lined with empty cells, three on each side. The hallway reeks of burnt coffee and body odor, along with a faint scent of urine. My stomach turns: fear, anger, nervousness, all roiling around together. The officer inserts a big skeleton key and pushes the door open. My mouth tastes sour, and I have my hands in my pockets to hide the fact that they're shaking.

These last eleven months, every time I've prepared myself for something, imagining possible outcomes and steeling myself to face them, the event itself has been a surprise, something I could not have predicted; all my preparations have amounted to nothing.

Then we're in a tiny room. The door clicks shut behind us. Bars span the entire length, and behind them are a dozen men and women dressed in street clothes, looking bored and sweaty. There's no air conditioner in here, just a couple of electric fans stationed on this side of the bars, blowing into the cell.

The man with the braces jiggles his keys. The fans emit a weak clickety-clack.

'Well?' Wiggins says.

I don't have to study the faces, don't have to deliberate. There they are, sitting on a bench in the back. Her hair is pulled back tight in a ponytail, just as I remembered it. He has gained weight, gone pudgy around the face, but it's him. I'm surprised to find they don't look frightening, they don't even look criminal. I search for some family resemblance that Teddy might share with Lisbeth, but find nothing. Teddy and Jane are sitting close together, almost huddling, holding hands, like those couples I'd occasionally see in church when I was a kid, couples who clearly didn't belong, couples who had been goaded into attending a service in exchange for a Thanksgiving turkey or a bag of secondhand clothes.

Both of them are looking at the floor. Teddy is bouncing his foot up and down, biting his fingernails. His manner is nothing like it was that day at Ocean Beach — the laid-back confidence of a man who was completely aware of his own appeal. A couple of days ago, seeing how thin Emma had become, I wanted to kill him. Now, the anger is still there, but instead of red-hot rage it's just a sick feeling in the gut.

'It's them,' I say, nodding toward the back of the cell.

'Which ones?'

'On the bench,' I say. 'The blond ones.'

The woman looks up, as if her name has been called. I catch her eye, try to gauge her expression. Is there remorse in her face? Fear? Anger? I see none of that. Her face is blank, the eyes dull. I hold the woman's gaze, determined to confront her, if only in this small way, but she quickly looks away.

'Certain?' Wiggins says.

'One hundred percent.'

I've gone over this moment in my mind hundreds of times. I imagined coming up with just the right phrase, just the right tone, that would force Emma's kidnappers to understand the cruelty of what they had done. In my fantasies I always found some way to take my revenge with the most harsh and honest words. Now, my throat is tight, my mouth dry, and the words won't come.

We step back through the door, down the corridor, and into the air-conditioned room, where an ancient fridge hums loudly.

'What now?' I ask.

'I'll take you to your hotel,' Wiggins says. 'I'm

guessing you're ready to get back to California.'

'And them? Teddy and Jane?'

'Charges have to be filed, then there will be an extradition. I'll call you with the details.'

Outside, a light rain has begun to fall. I can hear it slapping the trees, the cement paving stones, the street. We're in the middle of nowhere, a few cleared acres buried within a wild jungle that seems to be closing in. Far off in the distance there are mountains, pale brown against the white sky.

He opens the door of the Jeep for me, then goes over to the driver's side and climbs in. 'Delta 687,' he says, sliding the key in the ignition.

It sounds like some secret code, and I imagine a half dozen agents in some faraway government room, leaning in and listening, making important decisions based on this tiny piece of information. This world of international influence that Wiggins — and, apparently, Nick — inhabits seems so far removed from my life, much like the surf culture did a few months ago, and I'm reminded yet again how much that single moment on Ocean Beach changed everything, rearranged the context of my life in ways that cannot be undone.

'Pardon?' I say.

'Delta 687. That's your best flight out. It leaves at nine o'clock tomorrow morning.'

'Of course. I thought you were — '

Wiggins starts the engine and glances over at me. 'Yes?'

'Nothing.'

I watch the scenery roll by — the mountains, the enormous green plants growing wild, the tiny houses with their brown dirt yards. It occurs to me that I'm going to miss them. I'm going to miss a lot of things about this country.

Tomorrow is the twenty-second of June. Tomorrow, I'm going home.

80

A cool Gulf Coast afternoon, waiting for the storm. Three p.m. and the sky was dark as evening. Hurricane Bertha was on her way, and my mother had sent me and Annabel to the grocery store for supplies. Our cart was filled with gallons of distilled water, cans of Campbell's soup and Starkist tuna, bottles of Gatorade, two new flashlights, and a dozen batteries. The shelves had been ravaged, and the aisles were bustling with customers in that giddy pre-hurricane state. The checkout line stretched all the way to the meat counter in the back of the store. The guy in front of us, whose cart was filled with ramen noodles, Heineken, several rolls of silver duct tape, and a box of tapered white candles, turned and smiled at me. He had black hair, cut very short, and was wearing a University of Arizona T-shirt.

'Excited?' he said.

'About what?'

'The hurricane.'

Annabel rolled her eyes and pinched me on the elbow. I shrugged my shoulders. 'Not so much.'

'My first,' he said. 'Just moved here from the desert.' He kept glancing down at my legs, and I knew he was old enough that he shouldn't be looking at me that way. 'Got any advice?'

'Boards,' I said, 'not duct tape.'

He looked confused.

'For the windows,' Annabel chimed in, in a tone that was clearly meant to indicate that he was the dumbest guy in the world.

'You put plywood on all the windows,' I explained. 'Duct tape's just a shortcut.'

He shifted his weight to one foot, and as he did so his T-shirt raised slightly, revealing a patch of hair sliding in a straight line down his belly, into the waistband of his jeans. He caught me looking, grinned. 'Anything else?'

My face felt hot, but I didn't care; I was enjoying the game. I plucked the box of candles from his basket. 'What's this for, a romantic dinner?'

He winked. 'You fishing for an invitation?'

'You offering?'

Annabel crossed her arms over her chest. 'Please,' she said, snapping her gum.

'Seriously,' he said, leaning in close to me. 'What's wrong with the candles?'

'It's no picnic when the lights go out. You want hurricane lamps and flashlights.' I dropped the candles back into his cart and picked up his only jug of water. 'And you'll need more than this unless you're planning on drinking out of the neighbor's pool. Last time, we had no water for nine days.'

The line moved. He bumped his cart forward with his hip. 'I'm clearly unprepared,' he said. 'What I need is a personal hurricane coach.'

'How much does it pay?'

'That's negotiable,' he said, laying his warm hand on my shoulder, allowing one finger to slip

479

beneath the skinny strap of my tank top.

'God,' Annabel said. 'She's not even fucking legal.'

'Don't pay attention to my sister,' I said. 'She worships Satan.'

A few minutes later he was standing by the station wagon, helping me load bags into the back. Annabel stood off to the side, arms crossed, glaring at both of us. Above the parking lot, birds careened in confused circles, while the traffic lights on Hillcrest Road snapped back and forth in the wind. When all the bags were in the car, he shut the door and held out his hand. 'Ramon.'

'Abigail.' His hand was hot, and he held on tight for a couple of seconds before letting go.

'So,' he said, 'can I go to jail for asking for your phone number?'

Annabel held her stomach, bent over in mock agony, and pretended to vomit.

'Why don't you give me yours instead?' I knew that if he called my house, my parents would have questions I wouldn't be able to answer.

He reached into the back pocket of his jeans and pulled out a leather wallet, from which he extracted a business card. *Ramon Gutierrez*, the card said. *Portrait and art photography*. I slid the card into my pocket and opened the driver's-side door.

'Get in the car,' I said to Annabel, who looked like she was about to haul off and punch him.

She flipped him off one last time and said, 'I've got two words for you, mister. Jailbait.'

Ramon ignored her. He waited until Annabel

was in the car before he rubbed a spot of oil on the ground with the toe of his boot and said, quietly, 'You'll call?'

'Yes.'

I did not understand then that I was at the beginning of something, that each choice leads to some other choice, and another, and another, so that a single, seemingly meaningless decision reverberates through an entire life. I did not know it was a moment in time that would help to shape the course of my life, that I would spend the decade and a half after Ramon's death searching for someone who could love me as completely as he did. Only now do I understand that it was this search that led me to Jake, and therefore to Emma.

'You cannot step in the same river twice,' Heraclitus said. Since the composition of the river changes from one moment to the next, it is never the same river. Everything in the universe is in a constant state of flux. Everything changes. Nothing stays the same.

Once a moment has passed, it is gone. Any choice you could have made has already been made. I want to step again into the river. I want it back — the time, the choice, the tiny, irretrievable seconds.

81

A playdate. That's what Jake calls it. He's on the other end of the line, and there's a lot of noise at his place: television, dishes clattering, Emma's voice in the background.

'I thought maybe I could take her somewhere,' I say. 'Like shopping, or the zoo.'

I've tried to see them every day since returning from Costa Rica two weeks ago. Twice, I went over to his place for dinner. Emma ate silently, while Jake and I made awkward conversation about work. It struck me as the kind of conversation my parents had after everything went sour, when they were no longer connecting, merely pretending. The last time I was there, Jake walked outside with me at the end of the evening. The front door was slightly ajar, and he kept looking back at the house, as if Emma might slip out at any moment.

We were standing by the car, and loud music was playing at a house down the block — a high school party, probably, with the parents out of town. I pulled my jacket tight around my shoulders. The lights of the avenues were reflected in the fog. I took a step toward him and leaned into his chest. 'I miss you.'

He didn't say anything.

I put my arms around him. 'Maybe we could try again.'

There was a long pause. His body relaxed a

little. For a moment I felt hope, a sense of possibility. 'Abby,' he said. My name. That was all. There was a heaviness in the way he said it, a resignation. I got in my car and drove away.

That was five days ago. Now, I'm trying to sound cheerful, like the happy platonic friend, calling for a casual outing with the daughter. 'I'd love to take Emma somewhere fun. I've seen so little of her since she . . . came back.'

There's a pause. I imagine him moving out of Emma's earshot. 'For a playdate?' he says quietly.

'You're invited, too,' I add. Something smells off, and I realize the eggs are burning on the stove. I rush into the kitchen, turn off the burner, dump the blackened eggs into the sink, and open the window.

'Everything okay over there?' he asks.

'Fine. Just a little accident in the kitchen.' Then I wish I hadn't confessed. Each small mishap is further proof of my incompetence, my irresponsibility, every mistake added up and jotted down in his mental ledger, one long list of evidence that I have no business spending time with Emma.

I can hear him pacing. 'When were you thinking?'

'This weekend, maybe? Whenever it's convenient.'

'Okay.'

On the appointed day, I spend two hours getting ready. I change my outfit four times. I keep putting my hair up, then down, then up again. I call Annabel, whose due date is just over

483

a week away. I'm flying out to see her on Wednesday, and will stay until the baby is born.

'Help,' I say. 'I'm losing my mind. I've tried three different shades of lipstick.'

'Take a deep breath,' she says. 'This isn't the Miss America pageant. It's the zoo.'

The zoo. I'm not thinking about tigers and giraffes, reptiles and penguins. I'm thinking, instead, about how many square acres the zoo inhabits. How many nooks and crannies, how many bathrooms, how many dangerous places.

'I'm terrified.'

'You'll do fine.'

I want to believe her. I remind myself that I was the one who found Emma. My instincts were right, my determination paid off. Surely this means something to Jake.

At his place, I ring the doorbell. For about a minute, nothing happens, so I ring it again. I can hear movement inside, footsteps on the stairs. The door opens.

'Hi,' Jake says.

I look past him into the living room. 'Is she ready?' The television is tuned to TV Land. It's *Bewitched*, one of the old black-and-white episodes.

'Listen, Abby.' He doesn't have to say it. I already know what's coming. I can feel my heart deflating. He shifts his weight from one foot to the other. One hand is on the doorknob, and he makes no move to let me in. 'Emma's not, she's not feeling so good.'

I glance up the stairwell and see her, standing half out of her bedroom door. From here, she looks fine. 'Hi, sweetheart,' I call up to her. She smiles and gives me a little wave. Jake comes outside, closing the door behind him.

'What does she have?' I ask, trying to control the emotion in my voice.

'Pardon?'

'What is it? The flu? A fever?'

'Her stomach's been hurting. Probably just something she ate.'

'I could stay here and help out.'

He bends down to pick up a pizza delivery flyer someone left on the doorstep. 'Look, it's just not a good time.'

'Tomorrow. I'll stop by tomorrow?'

He shoves his hands in his pockets. He won't meet my eyes. 'I don't know.'

'Please don't do this.'

'I'm sorry,' he says. 'I need some time. We need some time, just Emma and me.'

'How much time?'

'I don't know. She's so confused — about Lisbeth, about Teddy and Jane, everything.'

He pats me on the shoulder once, awkwardly, then goes back inside, shutting the door behind him.

I can hear his footsteps inside, moving up the stairs. I turn to walk away, but then can't. I head back up the walkway and ring the bell. No answer. Then I'm banging on the door, like some lunatic version of myself. I know, even as I'm calling his name, that he's not going to open the door.

I'm aware how absurd I must look, how desperate. Leaning against the door, I feel an old familiar panic. But for this panic there is no plan of attack, no systematic method by which I might go about setting things right. Jake has made his decision; this time, it's out of my hands.

I would like to think that, months from now, he will think of me as the one who didn't give up, the one who persevered after the search grew stale, after the command post shut down and the police gave up and an empty coffin was lowered into the ground. I would like to think that, eventually, he will find a place for me in his life. But in truth, I know that's only a false hope. The moment of elation when I called and told him that Emma was safe will always be overshadowed by the months of anguish and fear. To him, I will always be this: not the one who found Emma, but the one who lost her. The one who looked away.

I don't know how long I stand on the tiny square of front lawn, staring up at Emma's window. The ground feels unsteady, as if at any moment the grass beneath my feet might shift. And then, just briefly, it does. Nothing more than a shudder, a whisper inside the earth. So soft, so subtle, they won't even mention it on the news or in the paper. But somewhere, in a bright building filled with equipment, a needle bounces, recording the arrival. Perhaps the seismologist, alone in his humming room, has drifted off to sleep. Perhaps the machine beeps, waking him. He gets up from his chair and goes over to the seismograph. Maybe he makes notations, celebrating in his scientific heart the complexities of plate tectonics.

After a while I get in my car and drive out Lincoln toward the ocean. I turn right on the Great Highway and go past the Beach Chalet, up the hill, past the Cliff House, and into the parking lot at Land's End. In the fog, I walk the rocky path down to the old Sutro Baths. The tide is out, and inside the old holding tank is a pool of murky water in which things float — beer cans, a Nerf ball, a wrecked buoy strangled by seaweed. Wandering among the ruins, I'm thinking about the drowning I witnessed at Gulf Shores when I was nine. I remember how, driving home, my mother cried softly in the front seat, turning around every few seconds to look at us. Annabel was sleeping, her sunburned legs stretched over my lap. I remember feeling very exposed, as if my parents were seeing us, really noticing us, for the first time. I became aware of some uncomfortable shift in our relationship. I felt in that moment as if our parents loved us too much, and that love seemed too heavy for me to bear.

Of course, I was only nine. How much of this did I perceive at that moment, and how much do I supply now, from a distance of twenty-four years? Twenty-four years, and I cannot shake the memory. Not just the images — the dead boy laid out on the sand, his weeping mother with her enormous breasts, the bit of bright white suntan lotion on the dead boy's nose, the crowd of women standing around the destroyed family on the beach — but the emotions as well. All of it is perfectly clear to me, as if I had experienced it only moments ago.

And I wonder what memories will stay with Emma two decades from now, what moments will stand out in her eleven months of absence. Will she remember the fear, or merely the confusion? When she is older, will she look at the bare chest of her lover and think of Teddy, the tattoo that curls delicately, like a wave? Will she remember the interior of the van, the smell of the cheese the kidnappers always kept in Saran wrap in an Igloo ice chest? Will the ocean be for her a treacherous place where unpredictable things happen? Or will she someday take a trip to Costa Rica with her own children, and feel a sense of peace, of belonging? Maybe she'll look for the little restaurant where she used to sit with Teddy and Jane, drinking mango shakes.

Of course, there are other things she might remember. Things that are emerging slowly, things the therapist tells Jake about. Sometimes, Teddy and Jane would get in terrible fights, screaming matches that ended with punches and, once, a trip to the hospital, where Jane had to have a broken arm set in a cast. This must have been terrifying for Emma, who was accustomed to Jake's calm, mild-tempered ways. Once, to punish Emma for some small disobedience, they left her alone in a friend's cabin for an entire night and day, with nothing to eat but a box of macaroni and cheese. Emma told the therapist that she mixed the pasta and cheese with hot water from the tap, because she knew she wasn't supposed to use the stove. That was one of Jake's rules that stuck with her: never use a stove without adult supervision.

On a few occasions, Lisbeth showed up and told Emma her own warped version of the story — that she never wanted to leave Emma in the first place, that Jake had sent her away when he met me. Over time, Emma must have begun to believe the lies.

Here is what I know: these memories that Emma must endure are of my making. We were walking on the beach. It was a summer morning, foggy and very cold. I looked away, at a dead seal. In that moment, the clock was set in motion, and Emma's mental map was permanently altered. This is the truth. There is no getting away from it. I think of S., the man who could not forget. In some way, we all share his burden. Memory is the price we pay for our individual personalities, for the privilege of knowing our own intimate selves; it is the price we pay for both our victories and defeats.

I imagine my own memory of this past year as a tumor, lodged deep in the hippocampus. A tiny black thing that will neither grow nor go away, a hard knot inside the graceful maze of the brain. Tiny as an almond, but exerting a constant pressure.

A few days ago, I went to the public library and returned the books on memory that Nell had checked out for me. They were several months overdue. It would have been cheaper to replace them instead of paying the fine, but I did not want to keep them. I would prefer to simply forget everything I've learned about memory, for none of it is knowledge that I can possess in the impersonal way one knows the names of foreign capitals, the number of rings circling Saturn, the date man touched down on the moon. No, it is a body of information that will always be associated in my mind with those long months of Emma's absence; it is tainted knowledge.

If possible, I would cleanse my mind of Aristotle and Simonides, Sherevsky and the anonymous N., and all the events that have transpired since that day on Ocean Beach. During the last few years, scientists have discovered that memory is linked to certain genes; the manipulation of these genes may hold the key to controlling what we remember and what we forget. In the future, it may be possible to take a drug immediately following a traumatic event — something like a morning-after pill — that will eliminate the memory of the event altogether. There will be no need to remember rape or robbery, car accidents or kidnappings. A child's mind could be pharmaceutically conditioned to forget the day she was snatched away from her parents, or the moment she broke her arm, or the day she saw her dog run over by a car. And why stop there? Perhaps entire units of memory could be extricated — a painful divorce, a humiliating job, a lengthy academic failure. This voluntary amnesia wouldn't have to be limited to individual grief. I imagine thousands of victims of natural or national disasters — earthquakes or terrorism, tornadoes or the assassination of a president — lining up at clinics the day after a terrible event to take their forgetting pill. We could become, then, a nation of forgetters, a culture without memory, without grief, without regret.

To the right of the baths, a dirt path leads to a viewing platform that leans precariously over the ocean. At the turn of the century, you could stand here and gaze out at the Pacific, or watch the swimmers diving off wooden platforms into one of seven sea-fed swimming pools. The entire structure was encased in a dome of glazed glass. Today, the view of the Pacific is shrouded in fog. On the eastern edge of the viewing platform is a narrow brick staircase, bordered by a rusted side-rail, large sections of which are missing. The stairs plunge steeply to the bottom, where two large rectangular holes are cut into the cement. From the top of the stairs, I can see the drop through the holes, down to dark water and sharp rocks. The last time I was here, I took these stairs to the bottom and gazed down into the pits, looking for Emma.

S. had no choice but to remember everything. The rest of us remember the highs and lows — moments of great happiness, as well as the things that pained us most. While the day-to-day falls away, while faces blur and rooms where we once lived lose their shape and color, we cannot escape our worst memories. This city will always be full of trap-doors that remind me of the search. Metal Dumpsters and dark alleys, shops and bars and libraries. There is no way to revisit these places without remembering the most terrible things. In every neighborhood, on every street, I have looked for Emma. I would like to think that these memories might someday fade. But even now, on a moment's notice — in the darkroom, in a store, on a bus — my mind will return of its own accord to that day. Invariably, the feeling of panic returns, my mind begins to spin, and my stomach churns. The mind plays tricks.

From the baths, I take the dirt path up to Louis's, where the sidewalk begins. I wander down past the Cliff House, past the Camera Obscura. The fog is so dense Seal Rocks are barely visible, just vague outlines jutting up from the gray water. A family of tourists, shivering in their shorts and sandals, are gathered at the pay telescope. I'm not sure what they hope to see. I remember the first time I came to San Francisco as a teenager with my parents. The trip was one of my mother's ongoing attempts to 'save the family,' a vague phrase she'd toss out every few months, when the anger between her and my father had reached a fever pitch and divorce seemed imminent. Year after year we made these dismal trips — to San Francisco, Chicago, New York, Montreal.

On that trip to San Francisco, we took a ferry to Alcatraz. We have photographs from the journey; I was wearing a denim miniskirt that was obscenely short, and Annabel looked funereal in her goth garb and black eyeliner. There is a photograph of the two of us together in one of the tiny cells that was used for solitary confinement. We're standing with our hands on our hips, elbows touching, no smiles. A stranger looking at the photo might surmise that we were two sisters forced to stand side by side, that we were angry with each other, posing for the picture in the aftermath of some terrible fight. But I remember differently. I remember, on the ferry to the island, my parents sat inside while Annabel and I stood on deck. We huddled together for warmth as the boat slipped through the fog.

'I wish they'd go ahead and get it over with,' Annabel said.

She was talking about my parents' life together, their hopeless marriage. 'Me too.'

It was the first time in months that we had talked about anything of substance. That long, melancholy summer was marked by a silence that seemed absolute. My parents rarely spoke to one another, and Annabel and I had sunk into an adolescent quietude, speaking only to communicate the most mundane sorts of things: *please pass the salt, when does the plane leave, we'll meet you by Coit Tower at 4:35.* We felt like no sort of family. Like four strangers randomly seated in the same compartment on a train, waiting to be relieved of one another's company. In that darkened cell on Alcatraz Island, it wasn't anger that radiated from our unsmiling faces; it was boredom, a sense of being in the wrong place at the wrong time, with the wrong people for company.

During the ferry ride from Alcatraz to the pier, Annabel stayed inside, sharing a hot dog and stringy french fries with a college boy she'd met in the gift shop. I stood alone at the rail, watching the city approach. Fogbound, San

Francisco looked like a place in a dream, not quite real. It was a beautiful city, unlike any place I had been. I thought of my parents down below, sitting as far apart as the bench would allow, each simmering in their separate unhappiness, all the ugliness of their past fights piled between them, an invisible yet insurmountable wall.

Years later, when my parents were in the midst of their bitter divorce, my mother would tell me, 'There's a line you cross in a relationship that you can't go back from. It's different for every relationship. Your father and I crossed that line twenty years ago.'

I vowed that, if I ever had a family, I would handle things differently. I imagined a man, a child, a harmonious home. Three people with ties so strong, nothing could sever them. I did not imagine, in those days, my own vast capacity for failure. I did not understand that a single moment, a choice poorly made, an eye turned in the wrong direction, could cause a crack in a relationship that would grow wider, day by day, until the gap was too wide to cross.

I take the steps down to the beach. A faint fishy odor permeates the air. The brownish sand is littered with tiny blue jellyfish, slippery underfoot. The water is strangely flat. Across the Great Highway, the broken windmill rises over Golden Gate Park like some prehistoric beast. The crisp scent of eucalyptus blends with the ocean air. I kick off my shoes and feel the cold sand. Fog settles over the western edge of the continent. There is no horizon visible, only white blending into gray. I am struck again by the lonely magnificence of this city, its impossible and dangerous beauty.

A shape moves toward me down the beach. A surfer, board held at her side, the diving suit shimmering with water. A blue stripe stretches from shoulder to ankle. The surfer lifts her arm and waves. I glance behind me to see who she might be waving at, but there's no one behind me. As the distance closes, I can make out the long dark hair, the smallish figure. Goofy.

'You're back.' She smiles, exposing that odd, lovely tooth.

'Good to see you.'

'You too.' Goofy goes in for a hug. 'Sorry, now you're all wet. Hey, congratulations. I saw the story on the news. You found her.'

I nod.

'That's amazing.' She moves her weight from one foot to the other. There's a long pause. 'Really. I was telling all my friends about it. Totally amazing. Like a miracle or something. I think about it all the time. It's so cool.' She reaches out and squeezes my arm. 'Looks like you put on a little weight.'

'I tried.'

'So, you ready for that surfing lesson I promised?'

'Sure. When?'

'How about now?'

Goofy puts her hand on my shoulder and leans toward me. I can smell the wax from her board, a sweet grapefruit scent. She's gotten a haircut, or, more likely, given herself one; now she has bangs, very short, slightly uneven. 'Last chance. I'm leaving day after tomorrow. Going to college, just like I said.'

'Where?'

'Fayetteville, Arkansas. Can you believe it? I have a friend there who can get me in-state tuition. It's dirt cheap. No beaches, no surfing, no temptation.'

'That's great. Congratulations.'

'So? What about the lesson?'

The truth is I've got nowhere to go. No one to see. No reason to refuse. I've spent the last few months in the company of surfers, yet I've never once surfed. I've walked miles and miles of coastline, yet I cannot recall the last time I stepped foot in the water. 'Why not?'

'Excellent. Let's go to my place. I'll fix you up with a suit and board.'

I slip on my shoes and follow her up the beach to the parking lot. I climb into her car, an old Volvo station wagon with the backseat removed. She slides her board in, and we ease onto the Great Highway. The windows are down and the radio is playing — *every song is a comeback, every moment's a little bit later.*

'God,' Goofy says, turning the dial. 'I'm so sick of that song.' She dials past static and live talk radio and eighties revival, finally stopping at Chris Isaak, 'San Francisco Days.'

Her place is on Forty-sixth Avenue. It's a little pink bungalow, situated just a few yards from the street. 'My roommates are in Vegas,' she says, unlocking the door. 'I've had the run of the place for a week. It's great.'

496

Her bedroom is just off the foyer. A closet of a room, with dark blue walls and lots of plants, all thriving. On the floor beneath the window, there's a twin-size mattress. Several boxes sit on the floor, taped and ready to go, labeled neatly: *records, clothes, kitchen*. There's one box that hasn't been sealed yet, a jumble of disparate things arranged on the floor beside it.

'Where's the rest of your stuff?'

'This is it. I'm just taking the essentials.' She points to the open box. 'I've been keeping this memory box all my life. You know, photos, old letters, my first video game, all sorts of junk. I hardly ever open it. But now, looking through it, I'm wondering if I shouldn't just get rid of it all.' She kicks at the pile on the floor. 'Really, what use is this stuff to me now?'

I pick up a trophy that's lying on its side. It's one of those generic trophies, a plastic base with a figurine on top — also plastic, but painted gold. The figurine is a girl with pigtails, standing with her arms at her sides, with blank eyes and an open mouth. The little inscription plate has fallen off, leaving just a faded rectangle beneath it. 'What's this for?'

'Fifth-grade spelling bee. Third place.' She reaches over and takes it out of my hand, examining it closely. 'I don't even know why I kept this thing, maybe because it's the only thing I ever won.'

'What was your word?'

'Acquiesce. A-C-Q-U-I-E-S-C-E. And this,' she says, holding up a red, white, and blue potholder. 'Foster Mom Judy was really into arts and crafts. We spent Fourth of July that year making patriotic kitchen accessories.'

She tosses the potholder into the trash, then picks up the box and holds it over the garbage can, dumping everything in — photos, papers, a little red diary with a broken lock. I'm impressed by the alacrity and speed with which Goofy is leaving everything behind, going on to something new.

'Aren't you sad to be moving?'

She stands there for a minute, hands on her hips, thinking. 'Sure, but it's time for a change.'

She pulls a wet suit out of the closet. 'Here, put this on,' she says, looking me up and down. 'It should fit.' She keeps talking, and I realize she's not going to leave the room. At first, I try to be modest. I pull the suit on under my skirt. But it's difficult to squeeze into the tight, stretchy fabric, and before long Goofy is standing in front of me, pulling the wet suit over my hips, saying, 'Here, let me help.' Then she's rearranging my breasts to get them into the big neoprene suit, and I'm reminded of a Saturday at Gayfer's Department Store when I was twelve, when a woman in a red pantsuit fitted me for my first bra. I can't say why, but I start crying.

'Hey,' Goofy says, cupping my face in both hands and wiping away the tears with her thumbs. 'What's up? You want to talk about it?'

'I don't think so.'

'The water will make you feel better,' she says, turning me around. 'I know it always works for me.' Her finger traces an irregular circle on my back. 'Birthmark?'

'No. I got a bad sunburn when I was thirteen. My whole back peeled, except that one spot. It gets darker every year.'

'Like a skin memory,' she says. The zipper snaking up my spine is cold, and a shiver goes all through me. 'Your body's way of reminding you how stupid you were. I have one, too.'

She pulls up the right leg of her wet suit, revealing a deep purple scar around her calf. 'First time I surfed, I went under hard and got tangled up in the leash. There was this weird moment underwater, when I couldn't tell which direction was up or down, and I was swirling around inside the wave, and I could feel the leash cutting into my skin, and I saw my own blood — and I swear, it was the most peaceful moment of my life. I had no control at all over the situation — I was completely at the mercy of the wave, and it felt fucking great.'

We walk back to the beach in silence. Then we're standing on the sand just below the parking lot, stretching, and the ocean looks vast and impossible, and I realize there's no way I'm prepared for this, and I'm trying to come up with a way to tell Goofy I'm just too scared to do it. But there's no time, because all of a sudden she finishes her stretches and begins to trot, shouting, 'Follow me.' It's that slow, excited jog all surfers seem to share, as if every muscle in her body is anticipating the ocean. I jog along behind her, until the sand gives way to rushing foam, and we're wading against the current. The water is like ice, a quick shock that sends an electric jolt to my brain.

'Just do what I do,' she says, and then we're on our stomachs, arms paddling, moving away from shore. My arms ache, my fingers are numb, my mouth fills with seawater — but something about this feels right. We paddle hard for ten minutes, then Goofy gets into a sitting position on her board. After a few tries, with Goofy shouting encouragement, I'm sitting, straddling the board, out of breath.

'What now?' I say.

'We wait.'

'How long?'

'Maybe a minute, maybe an hour. Just relax.'

'I'm scared to death.'

'Don't be. When I give the word, start paddling fast. Then just lean into it. Let it take you in.'

'You make it sound easy.'

Gradually, my body adjusts to the temperature. Goofy stays close by, but she doesn't talk. The clouds shift briefly, revealing an orange slip of sun; moments later it disappears. I can hear the surf crashing on shore. The sea moves gently beneath us, lifting and lowering, lifting and lowering. I feel sleepy, but aware.

'You could go with me,' Goofy says after a while. She's sitting up on her board, feet dangling in the water, hands poised in front of her as gracefully as a girl at finishing school. She looks good here, at home, as if this is where she's meant to be. I have a hard time imagining her landlocked, stuck in a desk in some airless college classroom.

'What?'

'Take a road trip. I rented a Ryder truck. I've got room.'

'That's a tempting offer, but I don't think I'm cut out for Arkansas.' The waves move up and down, up and down.

'What's keeping you here?'

'Lots of things,' I say, but I can't think of anything specific to tell her. 'Want to know how wacky my family was?'

Goofy smiles. 'How wacky?'

'When I was a kid, my mom bought me and my sister these notebooks that we were required to write in once a year. On the morning of December 31, after breakfast, she'd send each of us to our separate rooms, my father to his study, and she'd go into the kitchen. We had to spend the morning evaluating our lives, what significant things we had done or failed to do during the past 364 days. At noon, she would call a family meeting around the dining room table, and we each had to read off our list.'

'Heavy.'

'Then she made us say what we would have done differently, if we could go back and do it again. We were kids, you know, so it wasn't all that interesting. Like, 'I wouldn't have stolen Cindy Novak's Hello Kitty pencil case,' or 'I would have taken better care of the sea monkeys.' By the time my sister and I were in high school, we started making things up just to get under our mom's skin, like 'I wouldn't have slept with the football team.' '

Goofy is quiet, looking out at the horizon.

501

'Sounds nice,' she says. 'I could get into that, family meetings.'

'The weird thing is, I can't break the habit. Once a year, I take stock. I was thinking about it last night. I feel like a year of my life has been sucked into a void, some bottomless black hole. A nightmare year that hardly seems real. I lost Emma, I found Emma, end of story. And now I'm stuck. I don't know where to go from here. I can't figure out what happens next.'

Goofy doesn't say anything for a few minutes, just dips her hand in the water and swishes it back and forth, disturbing a school of tiny fish. They dart away, lightning fast, a flicker of silver bodies.

'I wish I could be like you,' I say, 'wish I had the guts to just pick up and go, start fresh.'

The truth is, I don't know how to start again, and yet I have to. For so long there was only one thing that mattered: finding Emma. Now that I've found her, I feel, for the first time in my life, completely directionless. Lately, I've been making lists, trying to figure out what to do next. At my place, I have all these undeveloped rolls of film in the fridge, pictures I took years ago, that I just never got around to developing. Maybe I could start there, with work. And there's my new niece, Margaret, due in just one week. I can't wait to meet her, hold her, watch her grow.

And there's Nick, still a mystery to me, a possibility I don't quite know how to define. I can see myself in his kitchen. He could make French toast, and I could make bacon. We could sit at opposite ends of his long sofa, face-to-face, reading silently. That would be nice.

He's been calling me since I came back, but I've yet to see him. The first call came a couple of days after I got home. It was the middle of the night when the phone rang, and I was sitting on my couch watching a movie, unable to sleep. Between the first ring and the time it took me to get to the phone, I created an entire story in which Jake was on the other end of the line. He was calling to tell me he'd been thinking it over, and he realized he couldn't live without me. He'd tell me that he needed me, that Emma needed me, how quickly could I get there?

But it wasn't Jake, it was Nick. 'I figured you'd be awake,' he said.

'I am.'

'Can I come over?'

'I'm sorry,' I said. 'I don't think it's a good idea.'

Part of me wanted to see him, to go to bed with him, to give in to the temptation that had nagged at me since the moment I met him. But a bigger part of me wanted to stay true to the conviction, which sustained me over so many desperate months, that I could be Jake's wife and Emma's mother, that if I just looked hard enough and long enough, everything would fall into place.

'Have you heard of the *confabulatores nocturni*?' Nick asked.

'Who?'

'The *confabulatores nocturni*, men who tell stories in the night. Alexander of Macedon used to gather these men to tell him stories in order to ease his insomnia. If I can't see you, at least let me tell you stories. You can listen to me until you fall asleep.'

'Okay,' I said. I carried the phone to bed, crawled under the covers, and listened. His story that night was about a remote village in Denmark — Freetown Christiania — and an enormous, red-bearded Icelander who lured him into a strange bar, where he was forced to trade his wallet for a Peruvian panpipe.

'You're making this up,' I said.

'No,' Nick insisted, 'it's true.'

The story went on for a long time. At the end of it he asked, 'Can you sleep now?'

'I think so.'

And I did. I hung up the phone and slept very well. Twice more since then, Nick has called me in the middle of the night to tell me a story. It strikes me as one of the most generous gifts I've ever received. Maybe he was right when he said that relationships — the big ones that change our lives — in so many ways come down to timing. If I had met Nick before I met Jake, it's possible none of the events of the past two years would have happened. I might be living in Nick's loft on Harrison, reading his books, listening to his stories — never knowing what it's like to love a child, and to lose her.

'I've been having this crazy idea,' Goofy says.

'What is it?'

'Never mind. I shouldn't — '

'No, tell me.'

'I've been thinking maybe we could be like family — you know, you could kind of be the

504

sister I never had.' She squints her eyes, embarrassed. 'Nothing too intense. Maybe we could talk on the phone once a month, you know. And send each other birthday cards, that sort of thing.'

This totally takes me by surprise. The way she says it, I can tell she's been thinking about it for a while. 'Sure. I'd like that.'

'Cool.'

The ocean moves beneath us, a slow, hypnotic motion. In my legs, a weightless sensation. Dr. Swayze, ninth grade, on the anatomy of a wave: *A wave is not water in motion; it is simply stationary water with energy passing through it.*

It seems like a long time has passed when Goofy nods toward the horizon, says, 'This is it,' and begins paddling in the direction of the oncoming swell.

The wave gains momentum. My heart skips a beat, maybe two. My arms tense, my eyes focus. Every nerve in my body is awake. I think of Emma, the first time I saw her — the small yellow purse she carried, the way she stood in line for tickets at the Four Star, one hand on her hip, like a miniature adult. I think of the first time Jake made love to me, his soap and eraser smell. I think of Ramon, and realize I'm older than he was when he died; he always seemed so grown-up, so at ease in the world, and yet I have outlived him by five years. I think of Gulf Shores, my mother on the beach, waving to me from her red towel, while I stood knee-deep in the current, the sand shifting beneath my feet. I remember her years later, looking nothing like the woman I knew, gazing up at me from a face wrecked by disease. 'Promise me one thing,' she said. 'Promise me you'll find someone and settle down, have a family.' And when I said, 'Yes, I promise,' I really almost meant it; I believed it might be a thing I could do.

None of these memories seem quite true — in a way they all feel like someone else's life, snapshots from a stranger's photo album. I think of Annabel, my one constant, the one relationship I've really done right. Annabel in the backseat of the car, lying with her feet across my lap, the steady *shush-shush* of her breath. Annabel now, in the Polaroid she just sent — belly round, hair cut short, just days from delivery.

Yesterday I found a roll of film, unprocessed, marked 'Crescent City, California.' In the darkroom, I took the film from its cassette, wound it around the metal reel, dropped the reel into the developing canister. After processing the film, I allowed it to dry, cut the negatives in strips, laid the strips across a piece of photo paper, and made a contact sheet. From the sheet I selected several negatives to print. It felt good to be in the darkroom again, going through the slow, even rhythms: enlarger, developer, fixer, stop bath, water bath.

When the photographs were dry, I took them downstairs and placed them side by side on the floor — a scene in sequential still life, a story laid out, plain as fact. Jake and Emma and me, together, in a small coastal town near the Oregon border.

The camera caught our arrival at a beachside motel. Emma stands beneath the hotel's sign at night, pointing up at the neon dolphin. In the next photograph, she's sitting beside a big rock on the beach, her legs buried in the sand, face tilted toward the sun. In the next, she and Jake are riding the water slide at Tsunami Town, a decrepit theme park that pays homage to the tidal wave of 1964. The slide rises twenty feet in the air and swoops down over a miniature replica of the twenty-nine city blocks that were destroyed. Here is Emma, in bathing suit and pigtails, sitting in Jake's lap on a plastic mat. In one photo they're tiny, just dots at the top of the slide, and in the next they're coming straight toward the camera, feet slicing through the water.

A few times during that weekend, I let Emma try her hand at the camera. It's easy to tell which pictures are hers; they're close-up, often shot from below, a child's strange perspective. There's the pint of Häagen-Dazs Vanilla Swiss Almond ice cream we bought in some all-night grocery. There's a picture of the bathroom sink, Jake's wet razor lying beside a tiny bar of motel soap. There's the dim interior of the sad aquarium: a shark's slick belly, the beautiful underside of a jellyfish, several photos of a sea horse — its curlicue tail, the multicolored creature suspended as if by magic in a murky tank, alone.

The final photograph is my own. I took it in the motel parking lot as we were leaving. Jake is helping Emma into the car. Her shoulders are dark, her feet bare, her profile to the camera. She's smiling at Jake, who has one hand on her back but is not looking at her. He's looking at a car that's pulling into the next space. I remember the car — a beat-up Chevy, going too fast. In the photograph, if one is inclined to look for such things, one can see a father in action, a father in control. He is aware, at once, of exactly where his daughter is, exactly where the car is. He does not take his hand off the child, nor does he take his eye off the car; in every moment, he is alert to potential dangers. And there, in Emma's profile, is another piece of the story: she is aware of one thing only — her father, whom she trusts completely.

Last night I sat on the floor for hours, staring at those pictures. I could not bring myself to look away. Here is the truth, this is what I know: it was June, summer in Crescent City. Emma was six, Jake and I were in love, and we were beginning to be a family.

We forget, we remember, the mind has its own stubborn will.

Now, as the wave comes toward us, I make a note to remember this particular moment, I vow to write it down when I get home: the strange orange tint of the fog, backlit by the sun; the arch of Goofy's back as she paddles; the jagged lines of Seal Rocks, closer than I've ever seen them; the Pacific's cold, sweet smell.

I think of Crescent City, the tsunami that buried a town. I think of those twenty-nine city blocks where the activity of the day was proceeding — the bank tellers counting money, the postal workers sorting mail, the schoolchildren marching single-file to lunch. Thousands of miles away, in remote Alaska, an earth-quake shook the mountains and caused the plates beneath the earth to move. Deep down, the ocean rumbled. The people of Crescent City, lost in the dull business of living, did not feel the shift. They did not sense the energy that created a wave so enormous it would raze their quiet town.

Even if our scientists were to solve the problem of memory, we would still be at a loss. Memory, by its nature, is merely retroactive, nothing more than a way of acknowledging how we got to where we are. We will never be able to hear the cesium atom, its furious oscillations, each millionth of a second bringing us closer to some monumental change. Even if we can figure out some perfect equation by which to assess the past, we will never be able to devise a like-minded equation to solve the future.

Goofy motions to me. The wave is closer now, like a gray wall, rising. I can feel my body lifting, little more than a cork on the tide. I can feel the wave gathering force behind me.

'This is it!' Goofy shouts. In one swift motion she is standing, knees bent, arms spread, like a seabird poised for flight.

I take a deep breath, paddle furiously, and wait for the wave to carry me back to solid land. Water gushes around me, the board shakes, I cannot see, but somehow I know I am moving forward.

Acknowledgments

The following books were instrumental in my research: *The Art of Memory*, by Frances A. Yates; *Memories Are Made of This*, by Rusiko Bourtchouladze; *Searching for Memory: The Brain, the Mind, and the Past*, by Daniel L. Schacter; *The Girl's Guide to Surfing*, by Andrea McCloud; the indispensable website Surfline; and *San Francisco's Richmond District*, by Lorri Ungaretti. I came across the *confabulatores nocturni* in Jorge Luis Borges's essay 'The Thousand and One Nights.'

Thanks to my fabulous agent, Valerie Borchardt, for her belief in this book; my wonderful editor, Caitlin Alexander, for her patience and diligence; Anne Borchardt and Bill U'Ren for their insightful commentary on early drafts; Misty Richmond for her photography expertise; Erin Enderlin and Jay Phelan for early readings; and Jiri Kajane for the excellent souvlaki. I also wish to thank Bay Area Word of Mouth and the folks at Simple Pleasures in San Francisco for support of the moral and caffeinated varieties.

My gratitude to the late Bill White, who gave me a beautiful place to write in Costa Rica. Thanks also to Lawrence Coates, Wendell Mayo, and Bowling Green State University for giving me time and space to complete the book while I was a visiting writer there.

This book would not have made it to publication without the help of Kathie Phelan and Purevsuren Sukhbaatar, who gave me precious hours to work by caring for my young son. Above all, thanks to Kevin.

We do hope that you have enjoyed reading
this large print book.

Did you know that all of our titles
are available for purchase?

We publish a wide range of high quality
large print books including:
Romances, Mysteries, Classics
General Fiction
Non Fiction and Westerns

Special interest titles available in
large print are:
The Little Oxford Dictionary
Music Book
Song Book
Hymn Book
Service Book

Also available from us courtesy of Oxford
University Press:
Young Readers' Dictionary
(large print edition)
Young Readers' Thesaurus
(large print edition)

For further information or a free
brochure, please contact us at:
Ulverscroft Large Print Books Ltd.,
The Green, Bradgate Road, Anstey,
Leicester, LE7 7FU, England.
Tel: (00 44) 0116 236 4325
Fax: (00 44) 0116 234 0205

Other titles published by
The House of Ulverscroft:

THE SONGWRITER

Beatrice Colin

New York, 1916. While war rages in Europe, vaudeville performers sing the newest songs by night and young women march for the vote during the day. Monroe Simonov, a song-plugger, is in love with a Ziegfeld Follies dancer who's left him for California. Inez Kennedy, a department store fashion model, needs to find a wealthy husband before she must return to the Midwest. Anna Denisova, a political exile, waits for the overthrow of the Tsar. Then America joins the war, jazz sweeps the city's dance floors, the old order is swept away by newly minted millionaires and the nation is gripped by the Red Scare. The world is rapidly changing, but Monroe, Inez and Anna are still subject to the tyranny of the heart . . .

NOT MY DAUGHTER

Barbara Delinsky

A pregnancy pact between three teenage girls stuns their parents, shocks the town and electrifies the media. Susan Tate, one of these mothers, has struggled to do everything right. A single mother herself, she is the headmistress of the girls' high school. Soon fingers start pointing, criticising her as a role model. She is seen as unworthy of the responsibility of young students, and as a lax mother. Battling with the implications of her daughter's pregnancy, Susan knows that her job, her reputation and her dreams are all at risk. The emotional ties between mothers and daughters are stretched to breaking point. Can they all fight back against the rising tide of scandal and find their own way?

ROOM

Emma Donoghue

Jack is five and excited about his birthday. He lives with his Ma in Room, which has a locked door and a skylight, and measures eleven feet by eleven feet. He loves watching TV, and the cartoon characters he calls friends, but he knows that nothing he sees on screen is truly real — only him, Ma and the things in Room. Until the day Ma admits that there's a world outside . . . Told in Jack's voice, *Room* is the unsentimental and sometimes funny story of a mother and son whose love lets them survive the impossible.

THE DOCTOR AND THE DIVA

Adrienne McDonnell

It is 1903. Dr Ravell is a young obstetrician, already highly regarded; his patients include women from all walks of Boston society. But he's flattered when a family of illustrious physicians asks him to treat one of its own members. Erika von Kessler is a beautiful opera singer who has struggled for years to become pregnant. As the young doctor's attraction to her increases, and his treatments prove ineffectual, Erika's despair worsens. Meanwhile Erika's husband Peter, a man of zest and daring, is willing to embark on adventures and personal gambles. But when Dr Ravell takes a great risk that may imperil his promising career — a secret he can share with no one — it is a decision that will change all their dreams and destinies.

THE MISSING BOY

Rachel Billington

Thirteen-year-old Dan hasn't returned home; his parents don't know whether he's run away, been kidnapped — or something worse. For one family, the world is about to fall apart. At first Dan is sleeping rough, revelling in his independence. But with every passing day, his world is becoming darker and more frightening. A hundred thousand children run away each year. Most come back. But will Dan? Dan's mother, Eve, a drama teacher, can't focus; his father, Max, only knows how to flee his own demons; and his aunt, Martha, while trained to control difficult situations as a prison officer, struggles to hold it all together. Gradually, all three begin to recognise just how badly they have failed the missing boy.

MEN & DOGS

Katie Crouch

Hannah Legare's life in San Francisco is unravelling. Her marriage is on the rocks, her business is bankrupt, and she can't shake her conviction that her father — missing after a fishing trip twenty years ago — might still be alive. On a trip to her hometown of Charleston, she begins to tug once again at the loose threads of her father's disappearance. Her uproarious and sometimes downright dangerous quest unsettles her uptight brother and unflappable mother, and brings her into worryingly close contact with Warren, the childhood love she thought she'd left behind. But has Hannah been looking for answers in all the wrong places?